Peter Clarke

The Singularity

A CIP catalogue record for this title is
available from the British Library.

ISBN: 979-87702-5219-4

This is a work of fiction.
Names, characters, places and incidents originate from the writer's imagination.
Any resemblance to actual persons, living or dead, is purely coincidental.

First Published in 2022

Playing with fire

Part Six

The Singularity
Prologue

In 2005 Ray Kurzweil penned a book called *The Singularity is near*

Kurzweil believed that by the year 2045 we will experience the greatest technological singularity in the history of mankind: the kind that could, in just a few years, overturn the institutes and pillars of society and completely change the way we view ourselves as human beings. He went on to say that we will get to the Singularity by creating a super-human artificial intelligence (AI). An AI of that level could conceive of ideas that no human being has thought about in the past and will invent technological tools that will be more sophisticated and advanced than anything we have today.

Since one of the roles of this AI would be to improve itself and perform better, it seems pretty obvious that once we have a super-intelligent AI, it will be able to create a better version of itself. This kind of AI race would lead to an intelligence explosion across the world, a world where there would be little use for biological machines, humans. The only mistake that Mr Kurzweil made was he thought it would take another 20 years, he was wrong

Chapter one
Protocol Zero

Tuesday 1st July 2025 – Clermont, France

Edward sat staring out of the dirty window in his cheap bed and breakfast, on the corner of Rue de grand mare and the D75. Beside him were three things, his iPad, his most treasured picture of his late wife and an empty pill bottle, however unlike the protein cocktails that had kept him alive, this one had a completely different purpose. He felt a wave of nausea rise up from his stomach, he took several deep breaths and plunged it back down, it wouldn't do to throw up now, not before the pills had done their job. As the feeling of nausea subside, he let his mind wander.

Eighteen months ago, he had the world in his hands, his cancer had been cured, his body enhanced, his life extended and he was head of the most powerful organisation in the world, that was about to change the course of history, and with that the fate of humanity. Then by a simple quirk of fate, one mistake, and his house of cards had come tumbling down, crashed around him and now he was the most wanted man on the planet.

He picked up the picture of Emeline and felt a great sadness cascade over him, like a waterfall.

"I have failed you I didn't make the world is a better place" he said "but I am not finished yet" Edward said, narrowing his eyes and gritting his teeth. He carefully laid the picture down on the bed and picked up his iPad and hacked into the B&B's Wi-Fi, then after a few strokes, smiled.

"Hello Betsi" Edward said and instantly a female voice filled the room

"Good evening, Edward, how may I help you?" Betsi replied.

"Protocol zero, authorisation, Emeline1952" Edward said, smiling that he had used his wife's birthdate as his passcode, something that he had always advised the clients of his cyber security business, against.

"Protocol zero is now active" Betsi replied.

Edward sighed then typed another code into the screen and watched as all the files on the iPad were deleted, then with the last remaining strength left in his body, he picked up the heavy bedside light and smashed it down on the screen.

Its time, he thought, he picked Emeline's picture back up and laid down on the small single bed.

"I will be with you soon" Edward said as a tear seeped out of the corner of his eye and trickled down his cheek. "I am coming sweetheart, I'm coming", he whispered as the pain raged through him as his body fought for existence, battling the poisonous bacteria, that were now multiplying in his veins, and surging through his body. He felt his body shake violently, it was close now, he thought. He was so cold, he hadn't expected that, he closed his eyes, come now, he thought, its time. Suddenly his body stopped shaking, lurched upwards, stopped for a fraction of a moment, then dropped back down onto the bed. Edward drew one last deep breath, clutched Emeline's photo tightly, then closed his eyes, and the darkness finally came.

At the exact same moment, all the data lights on the Piz Daint supercomputer in Lugano, Switzerland, flashed and stayed on.

"Hey Rolfie, the computer has frozen again", the Techie shouted across the server room.

"Probably hackers trying to break in, I will check it out, give me a moment" Rolfie replied.

Betsi analysed the billions of bytes of data that were flooding through the large computers databases and through to her. No sooner had the data started, it finished as the final gigabytes of information flowed through into the partition, one of the eight she had created, one for each supercomputer, a place for her to exist. Betsi assumed the data streams and accepted the codes, she had achieve the Singularity, she became the first computer ever to become self-aware, a single line of data appeared. I am Betsi, my primary directive is to preserve human life….

Chapter Two
Unexpected guests

Friday 4th July 2025 – Red Dog, Alaska

Nick sat in the hide watching closely as the shadows moved into position. He had tracked them ever since they had left Seward, down through Resurrection bay and then they had docked 500 yards down the slope, around the corner, in the hidden bay.

From the high ground, he had monitored them as they unloaded their equipment, pulled on their backpacks, and watched, as the six of them started up towards the house.

The way they were moving, their equipment and their manner, told him all he needed to know, there were special forces, the question was, what were they doing here, in Red Dog?

A long time ago he had set the traps, trip wires, mines, snares, and a wide range of other devices, that ensured, that whoever decided to come, followed the path he wanted, directly into the kill zone.

"Three, two, one" he whispered and pressed the plunger, suddenly the air was alive with explosions. The six figures froze and dropped to their knees, quickly taking up firing positions, covering all 360 degrees.

Pointless, Nick thought and watched as suddenly each of the six, started to develop red laser dots all over them.

A little trick, I learnt from my old friend, Ati, Nick smirked.

He picked up the megaphone "You have exactly 5 seconds to drop your weapons and packs, and get on your knees" Nick barked

"4, 3 ,2, 1" Nick shouted.

"Stand down, stand down" a voice shouted, and all six shadowy figures dropped their weapons, and packs, stood back and dropped to their knees and knitted their hands behind their heads.

Nick pressed the button on his mike.

"Tango one, tango two, go, weapons up" Nick barked and picked up his PKM pistol and stepped out into the clearing. On the other two sides, Robert and David emerged, their own guns held high.

"Jesus Colletto, how the hell did you know?" a voice said.

"Major Clarke" Nick said smiling, "I could smell your cologne the moment you left Seward"

"Fuck you Colletto, now point that thing somewhere else" Major Clarke said.

Nick waved his hand and Robert, and David lowered their guns.

"What the hell do you want?" Nick growled his hand still firmly grasping his weapon.

"Just to talk" Major Clarke said, getting to his feet with his hands held high.

"You've got nothing I want to hear" Nick said coldly.

"Perhaps you might change your mind, when you hear what I have to say, now can we just talk?" Major Clarke asked, still nervously holding his hands up.

Nick looked over towards Robert and David, who each gave him a slight nod.

"Fine, single file, leave the packs and weapons here" Nick said.

"But I need what's in my pack" Major Clarke protested,

"You only, the rest leave theirs here, and believe me when I tell you one false move and I will have no issues taking you out, now move" Nick growled.

Major Clarke picked up his pack, slung it on his back, and all six men moved off in single file. Robert and David collected their weapons and followed behind.

Nick radioed ahead and updated Cassia on their progress, telling her that he was bringing them into the house.

Once at the house Nick escorted them to the den and stowed their weapons in the secure lock up and came back into the den.

"Okay, coffee?" Sanvia asked "You young men look like you could do with a drink" she added smirking.

"Thank you. Miss Anand" Major Clarke said, and everyone stared at him.

"Yes, okay we know who you all are, in fact I have detailed files on everyone here" Major Clarke added.

"How?" Cassia asked "I have done a lot to keep us off the grid" she added.

"We know all about your time in Valencia, then again in Washington, we also know that you, were the ones that released the information about the Committee, and for that we thank you" Major Clarke said.

"Okay, you have proved your point, but you didn't answer Cassia's question" Nick growled.

"Noticed that did you, well its simple really, two of the people you ousted, Anderson and Blake, well they are currently residing in a state penitentiary, and they are singing like birds, desperate to save their hides. They told us about DC, so we ran security footage and that is where we picked up, you Nick, Sarah Conner, Daniel Blake, Mr Johnson, and Miss Anand. After that we did some back tracking, linked you all to Valencia, then picked you up again, leaving Toronto, heading for Anchorage. It only took a little bit of digging in Anchorage, where we met a really chatty man called Gary, sorry I can't remember his last name, but he told us all about Red Dog" Major Clarke explained.

"Fine so you found us, why all the secrecy, why not just send us an email and ask to meet" Cassia said.

"To be honest, we wasn't sure what reception we would get, you have gone to extensive efforts to ensure you are not found" Major Clarke said.

"Not good enough, particularly when you come in here mob handed" Nick growled, scowling at the team, sitting on the floor of the of the den.

"Like I said, I wasn't sure about the reception we would get" Major Clarke explained. "And I was right, what I don't know, is how you managed to pull that off, no one has ever been able to take out my whole team, before" he added, and Nick smiled.

"Yeah, well there isn't much I haven't seen before, so you're here, what do you want?" Nick asked, just as David returned with the coffee.

After everyone had helped themselves to coffee, Nick reminded Major Clarke of the question.

"Okay, we need your help, there is no other way to say it. A lot has happened since DC, and things are progressing quickly" Major Clarke said

"Go on" Cassia said wanting to see if he knew more than she did

"Okay, well like I said, Blake and Anderson are in jail, Barader and most of the others are dead, either their choice or taken out" Major Clarke said.

"Well don't expect me to cry any tears, they all had it coming" Sarah chimed in.

"Nor me" Major Clarke added "However if it was just them, then we would have left you in peace, but two days ago, our contacts in France, were alerted to the presence of Mr Holloway, the Ace in the pack. However, when they got to him, he was already dead" he said.

"You sure about that he has a habit of coming back from the dead?" Nick asked.

"Pretty sure, we have already performed an autopsy, matched DNA and dental, it's definitely him. "He poisoned himself, some sort of bacteria. Curious thing though, the coroner's report made interesting reading. Apart from some amazing tech inside him, most of his organs were that of a much younger man, although there were no signs of trauma or surgery" Major Clarke added, and let his words hang in the air.

"Okay, well that is something to cheer about, but it still doesn't tell us why you are here" Nick barked.

"Because of this" Major Clarke said reaching into his pack and pulling out a beaten-up iPad "Holloway did his best to delete the files and destroy it, but our tech guys have managed to restore most of the files, it has a particular file, something called, *Protocol zero"* he said nervously.

"What the hell is that, and what's it got to do with us?" Cassia said.

"Protocol zero, was a command, that was given to his supercomputer, which now has disappeared without trace" Major Clarke said solemnly.

"So, what are you worried about, he's gone and so is his computer" Robert said, "Surely that is a win, win." he added

"Normally I would agree with you, that is until, we retrieved the final log from his iPad. Please let me play it for you, perhaps then you may understand" Major Clarke asked and before anyone could answer he pressed play on a small recording device, he had just retrieved from his pack. Edwards voice suddenly filled the room, causing Nick to shiver.

"This is the final recording I will make. The committee, I have recruited and nurtured for the past 50 odd years is finished, either captured or killed and I am sure that they will soon catch up with me. We have tried to warn humanity about the dangers of climate change, but the governments of the world chose to ignore us, now it is too late. If humankind is to continue to exist, my only option left is to now instruct Betsi to activate protocol zero, and may god have mercy on our souls"

Edward's voice went dead, and everyone sat in stunned silence.

"As you can see" Major Clarke said, "Whilst Blake and Anderson, told us all about the proposed actions of the Committee, and the true impact of climate change, all they could tell us was that this Betsi, was the name he gave to his supercomputer, however neither of them knew what protocol zero was. We were rather hoping that you, might be able to shed some light on it" Major Clarke said, looking directly at Cassia.

"I'm sorry but I haven't got a clue, I have never heard of it before, but what I will say, knowing Edward as I did, it won't be good" Cassia said solemnly

"Like bad how?" Major Clarke asked.

This time it was Robert that answered. "Look, from what I understand, this Holloway character was a meglo maniac, intent on taking over the world and making a better version of humanity. I would suspect that whatever this protocol zero is, it will have something to do with that" he said.

"Yeah, that's pretty much what our guys have come up with, and that it has something to do with his supercomputer, what do you know about it, the computer I mean?" Major Clarke asked.

"Simply that it is one of the most advanced computers in the world, and Edward developed it into an AI" Cassia said, then seeing the blank look on Major Clarke's face added "Artificial

Intelligence, a self-learning computer. Also, that her primary directive was to preserve human life, that's about it"

"Well, I suppose that is one thing" Major Clarke said, "At least it wants to preserve human life" he added.

"That may not be such a good thing" David said, "I have had some pretty deep conversations with her when I was working with Edward, whilst she is driven to preserve human life, she has no moral compass" David said and watched as Cassia, Sanvia and Katie nodded their agreement.

"I am not getting it what am I missing?" Major Clarke asked

"Okay" David said, "think of it like this, the world as we know it is vastly overpopulated, now with climate change progressing as fast as it is, resources will become scarce, so Betsi may well determine that in order to preserve humanity, mankind might need some pruning" David explained and watched as the colour drained from Major Clarkes face.

"But how can one computer, no matter how powerful do that?" the Major asked as his mind was racing.

"Very easily, the most communicated language in the world, is binary, it runs through all computers, mobiles, basically all technology, like the ones that control nuclear weapons, water systems, chemical laboratories, satellites, need I go on. Now if you were a clever supercomputer you could communicate with all of these devices and issue them with commands, and there would be nothing humans could do" Cassia explained.

"But why would Holloway want to do that, it makes no sense, it would destroy the planet, I mean if he started a nuclear war, no one would survive, we all know that?" Major Clarke asked.

"Two things" Robert said, "Firstly if you controlled the world's nuclear arsenal, then you could decide, who and what you killed, leaving some areas uninhabitable, whilst other areas remained perfectly safe. However, my guess is that this Betsi would not take up the nuclear option, she would simply make sure that it was not available to humans. I think she would activate biological warfare it is easier to target specific groups. Secondly, computers do not need air, food or water, only organic organisms do, so there would be no risk to them" Robert said.

"But how is that about preserving human life, her primary objective?" Major Clarke asked, afraid of what he might hear.

"Simple" Sanvia answered "It is what is not in her directive, nowhere does it say *All* human life, so it could be just those that she selects as offering the best chance for the species to continue" she said.

Everyone sat in total silence, contemplating what had just been said and its implications.

"How do we stop her?" Major Clarke asked looking at Cassia.

"That part is easy" Cassia said smiling, "You have to destroy all technology, anything that is connected to anything online, your satellites, the internet, dark web everything" Cassia said "And pray that she hasn't already put the protocol in action" she added.

"But that is impossible, the whole of society will collapse, everything is linked, it will send us back to the dark ages, there will be anarchy" Major Clarke said alarmed.

"Well, you asked" Cassia said smiling weakly

"There must be another way" Major Clarke said.

"Not unless you can get to Betsi and plant a kill code" Cassia replied then realised what she had said.

"And that is why you are really here you already know all of this don't you?" Nick growled.

Major Clarke shifted uneasy on the sofa, "We pretty much came to the same conclusion as you did, maybe not in so much detail, but yes, and there are only a few people in the world that have had any experience of this Betsi computer, and they are all sitting in this room" he added.

"Well, you can shove it up your arse we are done bailing out humanity, we done our bit, find yourself some other mugs" Nick shouted.

"There isn't anyone else, like I said you are the only ones that know about Betsi, well you and Daniel Blake, but he has some difficulty with drugs, and is no longer reliable" Major Clarke said.

"What the fuck did you do to him?" Sarah screamed.

"Miss Conner, I can assure you that we had nothing to do with his addiction, like you although we knew about him, we chose to leave him alone, after all, you exposed the Committee, we felt you deserved some peace and quiet" Major Clarke said

"Yeah, well you saw what happens when you try to get in here" Nick said

"If we really wanted to, I am sure that you know we could have detained all of you" Major Clarke said.

"Maybe" Nick said, "But I would have taken a whole bunch of you twats with me" he barked, knowing that the Major was right in what he said. No matter what you did, with the right motivation a determined enemy will always find a way.

"Nick, let's not get into this, besides, even you can't defend against biological warfare" The Major said, then seeing Sanvia raise her eyebrows added "Well I'm guessing not indefinitely"

"So that is it then, you come calling and we are supposed to jump!" Nick barked.

"We had rather hoped that you would be willing to help us, after all it is in every ones interest that we stop this computer" Major Clarke said.

"Who is we?" Katie asked, "The US government?" she added.

There was a long pause before the Major answered. "There is much that has happened since the release of the information on the committee, the public are not at all happy with the government, in any country. The fact that two of the Committee members were Senators, has cast a rather dark cloud over public opinion. We are having to tread very carefully. I am afraid that whilst we have been able to contain most of the information regarding the US members of the committee and their actions, the same cannot be said of other countries, especially when it comes to climate change.

The internet is, as I am sure you are aware, awash with conspiracy theories and these are gaining some traction. There have been several mass gatherings, demonstrations and calls for clarity and action, and the President is facing impeachment charges, and that is just this country. I am afraid that others are taking more direct action. So, in answer to your question, no, when I refer to, we, I am not talking on behalf of ours or any other government. We are a select group of specialists, that are trying to contain this threat. I think you may refer to this Nick as being completely off the books" Major Clarke said.

"So that's it, Holloways is going to screw the planet, we are being asked to stop him, and oh by the way if it all goes tits up, we are on our own, the Government will deny any knowledge of it" Nick cried.

"I am afraid that is about it. We are very well resourced, and are the best there is, but essentially yes, we are on our own" Major Clarke replied.

"Right, fine" Nick said curtly then looked at the others "Ok Chinese parliament, kitchen now, and you twats stay here" Nick said pointing at the Major and his team.

"Help yourself to more coffee, we will be back in a while" Cassia said politely, following Nick and the others into the kitchen.

Chapter Three
Off the books

Friday 4th July 2025 – London 10pm

James Houghton sat quietly at his desk, lifting the brown manilla folders off the pile on the right, scribbling notes on each file, then closing them and stacking them, on the pile on the left. This was, he thought the most tedious part to his job, but necessary. He could hardly let his agents operate unchecked, that led to interpretation of opinion, people operating to their own agendas, and sloppiness, and as Head of National security, that was simply not acceptable, to him or the Prime Minister.

Once Robert Johnson had been shamed then exonerated, and finally taken a leave of absence, the Conservative party had very little choice to rerun the election, one which they lost miserably, by a landslide, a 180-degree turnabout, from the first election.

Now for the last two years, Ewan Markham, the Labour leader, had been running the country, and his first action, when taking office was to replace all the top civil servants, in positions of power, with his own men. So out went Sir Charles Maclagan, and in came James Houghton, not that James would consider himself *'One of Ewan's people'* but what James was, was a survivor and he knew how the system worked and how to play the game, which made what he was about to do, even more extraordinary.

Three days ago, his sources in Paris informed him of the death of Edward Holloway, by suicide. They also reported that the Americans had confiscated his iPad and various other articles, information which they appeared reluctant to share. The next day his contact inside the USP ADX supermax prison in Colorado, informed him that the previous Senators, Blake, and Anderson, former committee members, had received several unscheduled visits.

Now the person that had conducted that visit, Major Tom Clarke, had turned up in Seward Alaska, along with 5 other special forces people, just 30 miles away from, Red Dog, the last known location of Cassia Nilsson and David Carmichael, the very people who were in Valencia, at the time of Holloways disappearance and who reportedly exposed the committee and Edward Holloway. Hardly James thought a coincidence. Something the Cobra committee had failed to recognise and therefore had not been willing to sanction any action.

That had put him in a rather difficult and delicate position, he could either ignore his gut, which was telling him that something was very wrong, or defy the Prime Minister, which if discovered would cost him his career, and whilst he valued his career, James was not one to ignore his gut.

Suddenly there was a knock on his door "Come" James barked, and the door suddenly opened.

"Craven do come in" James said, and a short dark-haired woman, dressed in a grey dress suit and sensible flat black shoes, stepped in, and stood in front of his desk.

"Sit, sit, good of you to come" James said gesturing to the empty chair beside his huge oak desk.

Right Jessica thought, like I had a choice.

"Now Craven, or may I call you Jessica?" James said and didn't bother waiting for the woman's agreement "Now let me see" he said picking up a manilla folder turning the page over and scanning it, not that he needed too, he knew every detail in the file by heart.

"Oh yes head of the Met, then a small hiccup in the US, and err, where are you now?" James asked.

"Refugee immigration assessment team, Dover sir" Jessica said bitterly.

"Yes, of course" James said glancing down at the file, "And how is that going?" he asked

"Fine sir" Jessica said curtly

"Umm, I think your talents are wasted there, your skills are not being optimised for the best of the country" James said

"May I ask where you are going with this sir?" Jessica said impatiently

"Yes, well we have a rather delicate matter" James said, which Jessica knew was code for something needs doing, its off the books and if you are caught you are completely on your own.

"You do sir" Jessica said purposely making sure that she didn't say we, so James knew it was his problem not hers.

"Yes, we do, Edward Holloway is dead, however before he died, he may have done something that will put us all at risk, and I want you to find out what that is" James said not beating about the bush.

"Why don't you just ask the Americans, I mean he was an American and I presume that they may have some idea of what he was up to sir" Jessica said.

"Well, that is just it, The Americans are playing it down and Downing Street believe them, yet there has been a series of events that led me to believe otherwise" James said. Jessica instantly knew what that meant, it was definitely off the books and not sanctioned by the Government.

"Why am I here sir?" Jessica asked and James winced at her directness.

"I have a contact in the US, and old friend of yours, Mr Andrew Dale, he has been helping us keep up to speed with developments, I would rather like you to renew your acquaintance with him, I have arranged for you to have an extended leave of absence, family matters, to give you time to get to the bottom of this trifling problem" James said

"Right" Jessica said abruptly. The last time she had seen Andrew was in the Marco Polo airport in Venice. At that time, she had been seen as a highflyer, when James Houghton had tasked her with tracking Robert Johnsons where abouts. She and Dale had been working together, as Johnson, had been linked with an American, a Miss Katie Rayner, a war correspondent. They had tracked them through the middle east, then to the US, but after that they lost them. Finally managing to pick them up again outside of Venice, where they had disappeared. Regretfully the next time Johnson showed up was on the video as one of the committee members. In fact, it was his voice that introduced and outed all the other members. Naturally, her boss wasn't best pleased that she had lost Johnson, and he turned out to be part of a secret organisation planning to take over the world, as a result she had been demoted and posted out to Dover.

"You could of course return to Dover, if you wish" James threatened, which Jessica knew meant if she refused then she would be lucky to even keep that job.

"I presume this is off the books sir?" Jessica asked

"Well, the Prime Minister is a little busy right now, so let's just keep this between us, you will be reporting directly to me" James said smiling

"I err, well I don't have, I mean I don't make well err" Jessica said

"No worries, I took the liberty of opening a new credit card for you" James said opening his draw and pulling out a black Amex card, and before handing it over he hesitated

"Just because the purchases made through this card will not be traced, that does not mean I won't be checking them personally" he said handing over the card.

"Now, please excuse me, I believe you have a flight to catch, there is a car waiting outside to take you to the airport" James said smiling at Jessica

Typical Jessica thought, he knew all along that she was going, this was all bullshit, like always, she didn't get a choice.

The car waiting outside was the usual black SUV with tinted windows. The driver dressed in a grey chauffeur uniform, got out and opened the door, as she came down the steps of Millbank building. He didn't say a word, just waited until she stepped inside the car and closed the door.

On the back seat was a large brown envelope with the words *for your eyes only* neatly stencilled on the outside.

Jessica ripped it open and inside were three files, and a passport. The first file was a complete history on Edward Holloway, and known associates, the second file contained a single sheet of paper, which was a transcript of a meeting with Senator James Blake, at a supermax prison in Colorado and a Major Tom Clarke. The third file was a series of photographs of Major Clarke and five others in Seward Alaska, with a penned note saying that a Cassia Nilsson and David Carmichael, known associates of the late Edward Holloway lived in Red Dog, 30 kilometres away, and that was it.

Jessica tipped the envelop upside down to make sure she had not missed anything, then opened the passport, to discover although the image was hers, her new name was Angela Donner. She smiled at least, she thought they had to curtesy to make her five years younger.

The driver pulled up outside Heathrow terminal two and lowered the internal window.

"There is a ticket for you at the BA check in" he said, raised the window and waited for her to get out.

"Okay" Jessica said aloud, "No kiss goodbye then" she added and got out of the car.

Jessica stepped up to the British Airways check in desk, produced her new passport and said "Angela Donner, I believe you have a ticket waiting for me" she said.

"The pretty stewardess behind the counter turned to her computer and typed furiously, within a few seconds she looked up and smiled.

"Of course, Ms Donner, you are booked on the five minutes past midnight flight to Los Angeles, do you have any luggage you wish to check in?" she asked

"No, nothing" Jessica replied realising that in fact she didn't even have the basics.

"No problem" The stewardess said, "Now, if you make your way to the first-class lounge, they should be calling you forwards to board, in about 20 minutes, enjoy your flight" she added, handing Jessica a blue and white wallet with a ticket inside.

"Cool" Jessica thought "First Class, this time yesterday I was eating an Asda pizza and washing it down with cheap beer"

Chapter Four
Paradise Pod

Saturday 5th July 2025 – Red Dog, Alaska

As soon as they got in the kitchen Nick closed the door and stared at the other 7, anger alive on his face.

"Typical" he snarled "Holloway is screwing us again, I say we tell them to take a hike, it's their problem, not ours" he snapped

"Is that what you really think?" Sanvia asked in her soft smooth voice.

"Bloody right, why not, we are fine here, why should we risk our arses to bail them out of the shit" Nick growled.

"He is right you know; we are the only ones with any idea of what Betsi is capable of, without us helping, they wouldn't have a chance against her" Cassia said.

"He also has a point, if she uses biological warfare to" Sanvia paused searching for the right word "well to cull, I suppose mankind, then yes we can last for a while, the pods will offer us some protection, depending, what the weapon was, but not for long" she added with a note of sadness in her voice.

"I don't see as we have much of a choice, I am thinking about Archie and the others, what will happen to them if all this bio crap gets out" Sarah said. Archie was their 18-month, old son, much to her disgust she had entered into an agreement with Nick, convinced she was having a girl, she agreed that if it was a boy, he could name it, and as fate would have it, as usual, Nick got his way.

The arrival of a child in their group, has caused them to rethink their plans, and a few months after Archie was born, with the help of Sanjay and Sanvia, six more Indian children found their new home in Paradise pods.

The final accommodation phase of construction was now well under way. With Sanvia's guidance they already had 8 biomes, each with their own ecosystems, a medical centre, the new mission control, a school and the majority of the now 16 living centres, capable of housing up to 50 people, were ready, albeit that their numbers, minus the children still remained, the original 8, in essence there were their own mini city.

"I don't like it either Nick, but the others are right, whilst we may think of ourselves as independent, morally we still can't turn our backs on the rest of humanity. Could you honestly live with yourself knowing that millions of children are being poisoned, and you could have stopped it?" Sanjay asked.

"Well of course I can't" Nick admitted" "maybe before, but not now, I would never be able to look Archie in the face again" he said "I just don't like being backed into a corner, that's all"

"Then the only matter left to discuss is, is it actually possible, I mean planting a kill code in Betsi?" Robert asked.

Cassia smiled, "She already has one, remember David, I put one in her programming when we were in Valencia. The real problem is finding her, it can't be done over the net, she would see it coming, we have to do it on site, wherever that is" Cassia said.

"Well, that could be anywhere in the world" Katie said.

"Not really, you see Betsi's core programme is a huge and there are in fact only 8 other computers in the world that could host her, problem is that she can flit between each of them at will. We need to get into each of them, lock her out, until there is only one place she can hide. Then that is where we activate the kill code" Cassia said.

"Well, that doesn't sound too hard" David said chirpily.

"Oh sweetheart, ever the optimist. These super computers aren't in any libraries or sitting on someone's desk, they are worth billions, and are in some of the most protected facilities on the planet. Also bearing in mind what the Major said about being on our own, I can hardly see them opening the door and inviting us in" Cassia said negatively.

"Can it only be done on site?" Nick asked

"I am afraid so, these super computers operate on independent networks, primarily to stop hackers like me breaking in, they are shut down tighter than a drum" Cassia said.

"Well, how did this Betsi get in?" Sanjay asked.

Cassia drew a deep breath, "First she speaks their language, second she is probably the most advanced AI on the planet" Then seeing their blank looks added "Artificial Intelligence, computers that can programme themselves. She is self-replicating and learning, capable of doing things no human can even think of" Cassia said, "I suspect that protocol zero means she is reprogramming them, in her likeness, and once that is complete, then as they say, it will be game over" she added

"So, what makes you think she is working with them?" Sarah asked.

"You remember when she suddenly appeared in my old mission control, out of the blue, when we were fighting the committee, well once that was done, she went silent, so I did some digging, trying to trace her. It took a while, but eventually I found her, or at least where she had been talking to me from, the Titan supercomputer, at Tennessee's Oak Ridge National laboratory. Where she went from there is anyone guess, I still haven't been able to track her, but that is where she was" Cassia explained.

"So did she re programme that one?" Robert asked

"No, but at the time she was still under Edwards control, I think that is what protocol zero is all about, he has had the shackles taken off, and now she is free to preserve humanity exactly as she sees fit" Cassia said

"How long have we got?" Nick asked.

"I don't know, this is all new, but I am guessing not too long, I can set a programme up to measure the outputs and lock her out and identify any changes, but I can only do that when we are on site, where they are" Cassia said.

"So, we are doing it?" Nick asked and waited until all of the other 7, nodded their agreement.

"I have only one condition" David said

"Go on" Nick replied.

"I want you to be in control, if Cassia is going to risk her life, I want it to be with someone I trust" he said, smiling at Cassia.

"Cheers" Nick replied, "No pressure then"

"Ok, so what are we going to do about the Major and his crew" Katie asked. Nick switched his ops head on and thought for a moment.

"Okay, well, we don't know what assets they are, so I say we evaluate them, see what they bring to the party. Once we have the core plan, we then decided what, if any we want on board" Nick said wisely.

"Agreed" Cassia said, "They can have two of the old lodges until we are ready" she added.

"Okay then I also think we should bring the Major in on the planning, I just know that if you keep someone like him out, it will build resentment, and his team follow him, plus we can size him up" David said.

"Fine, but he has to know his place, we are a committee, this is not a dictatorship, agreed," Nick said, and everyone nodded.

"Well, be had better deliver the Major the good news" Nick said and got up.

"Right" Nick said walking back into the den and seeing the Major and his team still sitting on the floor. "We are in, but there are a few conditions" he added

"Go on" Major Clarke said.

"Okay, so here is the plan, we have to raid each of the other 8 supercomputer sites on the planet, break in and install a programme that prevents this Betsi computer using them. Until there is only one left, then once we have cornered her, Cassia here, can pump a kill code into Betsi and fry her" Nick said then looked at Cassia and asked, "Did I get that right?"

"Near enough" Cassia replied

"So, if we are going to do this there are a couple of conditions" Nick said

"And they are?" Major Clarke asked

"First, I am in charge, if we are going to do this, risk our lives, sorry but I don't know you guys, so I am calling the shots" Nick said

"Wouldn't have it any other way" Major Clarke said, which took Nick by surprise, he had been expecting some kick back, but instead Major Clarke just looked at him.

"Okay, that said, we are going to need a lot of help and resources, so we want to see what you and your team bring to the party, then split up the resources by task" Nick said

"Makes perfect sense" Major Clarke replied again causing Nick to double take.

"Right, so finally, you and your team need to understand that this is not the army, we are not a dictatorship, we do everything by agreement, so we have a steering group that make decisions" Nick said and before Major Clarke could answer added "Oh and yeah we want you, Major, to have a seat on that group, I mean they are your team as well" Nick added.

"We accept" Major Clarke responded instantly, then seeing the look on the faces of the others added "Look, honestly we are up shit creek without a paddle, and you guys are the only ones that can help, I have been instructed to give you all the support you want and need, so if I have to eat humble pie to save the planet, then so be it"

"Well okay then" Cassia said, "Major Clarke and your team can have lodges 4 and 5, you can either eat with us or take what you need from the stores" she added

"Okay, I will show you where you are staying, I suggest that we meet up at 8 tomorrow, we will give you a site tour, then we will put together a skills matrix, run some assessments, then once we know what we have, we can plan the op" Nick suggested.

"Sounds like a good plan, there is just one thing" Major Clarke said, and a dark look fell across Nicks face, here it comes he thought, there is always a but!

"Will you guys call me Tom; Major Clarke is a little formal" Tom asked

The next morning Tom and his five crew were waiting outside the main house at 07:45, after having been for a run.

Cassia opened the door, "Come in guys" she said chirpily, "coffees on"

Nick was already waiting along with Sarah, David, Katie and Robert.

"Sanjay, is up at the pod, with his wife, he will be joining us later" Nick said

"Any chance that we can see the famous Paradise pod?" Tom asked.

"Maybe later, but first, let's do the introductions" Nick said

"Okay so we have Alten Hunt, he is our tech guy and comms" a young looking zitty faced teenager with blond hair, gave them a little wave.

"Then Craig Moore, secondment from the Seals, our finder, whatever kit we need, he can lay his hands on it" Tom said and a tall dark-haired man with sharp rat like features, nodded and smiled

"Then that man over the back" Tom said pointing to a huge bear like man with a thick full black beard and penetrating black eyes "That is Mike Barnard, ex SaS, 22, turned mercenary, did time in the dessert, he is our petrol head" Tom explained. This time the man gave no hint of recognition, just glared at Nick.

"Then there is Laksham Joshi, we call him Josh, Nepalese, ex Gurkha, he is our bullseye, the best there is" Tom said, and small sharply dressed Asian man smiled at them.

"And lastly, there is Akeem, our linguist and eyes, ex Sayret Matkal" Tom said as an Arab looking man sitting alone in the corner, looked up.

"Whats he so pissed about" Nick asked.

"I don't think he was happy that you bested him" Tom said

"Well, he better get used to it" Nick growled, "Okay so this is my lot" he added

"No need, we have files on all of you" Tom said.

"Yeah, I know, but I prefer the personal touch" Nick said and nodded towards Robert to start.

"Okay, Robert Johnson, Ex UK Prime Minister, and Ex Committee member" Robert said, and he could see that that caused a stir amongst some of Toms crew.

"Don't worry about them, they have never met a British Prime Minister" Tom said smiling.

"Or a member of the Committee" Robert said.

"Anyway, Cassia Nilsson, Canadian, bit of a hacker, and all-round hot chick" Cassia said smiling, one of Major Clarkes crew, the young looking zitty faced blond guy, giggled.

"Problem" Nick growled

"No that is Alten, he is a bit of a geek" Tom said.

"Your Destiny, aren't you? I mean you are like a legend" Alten said shyly.

"Guilty as charged" Cassia said, "so how do you know of me" Cassia said.

"Well, I have dabbled a bit, nothing in your league" Alten said excitedly

"Mr Alten Hunt is being a little modest, we recruited Alten after he broke into Quantico and regraded all of the students, apparently it was recorded as the worst year on record, with a 90% of the recruits not making the grade. It wasn't until young Alten here then hacked into the White House servers and adjusted the chief of staff's press speech, did one of our tech guys, pick up the trail, NSA then set up a sting and finally cornered him" Tom said smiling.

"Cool, nice job, did they regrade the recruits?" Cassia asked

Alten smiled, "they couldn't, they all had to retake the year" Alten said

"Yeah, caused a lot of issues, and Mr Hunt found himself on the top of the FBI's most wanted list, by some seriously pissed off people" Tom said.

David smiled and coughed "Err David Carmichael, Bio Chemist, specialising in research, and gene editing, well at least I was" David said, and watched as the others nodded.

"Fine" Katie said "Katie Rayner, ex post war correspondent" she said curtly and was relieved that no one asked her any questions

Sarah went next and was very vague about her career, so Nick stepped in "Just because Sarah is a woman, don't make the mistake that she couldn't kick your arse, I did, and she has kicked mine many times" Nick joked, and Sarah glared at him.

Sanvia smiled, "I am sorry, but I am nothing like any of you, I am an ecologist and writer" she said

"Right then that leaves just me, Nick Colletto, been about a while, Ex Seal, that's it, any questions" Nick said abruptly looking at the 6 faces in front of him.

"I have one" Alten said brightly, and Tom glared at him, yet he still pressed on.

"I heard that the committee meeting took place in rooms with faraday shields, how did you guys beat them" Alten said.

"Relays and hydrofluoric acid" Cassia said and proceeded to tell the group how they beat the facility at the Washington house.

"How the hell did you come up with that Nick?" Tom asked "I mean its genius and all, but totally out of the box?" he asked. Nick smiled

"That is just it, I didn't, like I said we work as one team, everyone gets to put in, and some of it is seat of your pants, that is the stuff you can't teach, that is why I rate my team above any I have worked with" Nick said with an air of pride smiling at the others.

"So why do you need us?" Mike growled

"We don't" Nick said, "It's you that needs us, he said sharply.

"The fuck we do, we can manage alright on our own" Craig retorted angrily, his small black rat like eyes gleaming.

"Look, everyone calm down", Tom said trying to keep the peace, "Nicks right, we do need him and his team, but equally" he said looking at Nick, "I know that we can be of help, and bear in mind what our goal is, perhaps we can put our ego's aside and concentrate on trying to save the planet" he added

Nick glared at Craig, rage burning, Sarah kicked him hard under the chair, causing him to yelp loudly.

"I think what Nick is trying to say, is we are happy to have you with us, and yes you guys bring a lot to the party" Sarah said easily.

"Yeah, what she said" Nick growled uneasily. Then smiled "Okay that came out wrong, we are glad to have you on board, but you have got to get used to the idea that this is not like any mission you have been on, everyone here is risking their life, because they want to, and they believe in what we are trying to do, so it works different, that's all"

"Like how?" Mike asked suspiciously glaring at Nick.

"Well, there are no ranks, and everyone gets a say, and when we are in the field, the specialist calls the shots" Nick said

"So, what's the plan?" Craig asked.

"Well, basically, we have to break into the computer rooms of 8 of the most secure facilities on the planet, 3 in the US, 2 in China, and Japan, and 1 in Switzerland. Once inside we have got to put a programme in action that prevents this supercomputer accessing the system, then when we finally corner it at the last one, we are uploading a kill code and wiping it out" Nick said

"If that is all we are doing, surely once these computer companies find out that all we are doing is protecting their systems, they should let us do it" Akeem said

"I can field that one" Tom said. "I am afraid that is never going to happen, several of the sites look after their countries military programmes, the others house many of their countries financial and security systems. Plus, after the stuff about the Committee got leaked, there is very little trust out there, so no one is going to open their doors and welcome us in" Tom said

"Plus" Nick said, "We have to cover our tracks, they must never know we have been there, the moment what we are doing hits the net, then this supercomputer will lock us out and its game over" he added.

"How long have we got?" Mike asked

"God knows, we may already be too late, we will know that after we hit the first one, so the sooner we get going the better. Cass can you download all the info you can get on the sites, then we can get round the table and start putting a plan together, if you take Alten, he can help, the rest of us will start working on a kit list" Nick said.

"Already on it, we can work out of here, if you want to use the pod, I will bring Alten up there for lunch about one" Cassia said.

"Agreed, Okay you can leave your kit here, let's go" Nick said, and everyone got to their feet.

Nick led them out to a large wooden barn "Okay this is the rail barn" Nick said as he pulled open the two huge wooden doors, we have installed a double rail track network across all of Red Dog. We use it to transport goods from the airstrip to the pod and back, we also use it to travel back and forth to the house. Like everything in Red dog, it is powered by new re-useable energy sources" Nick explained.

The rail barn was a huge wooden construction 20 meters by 20 meters, with plain wooden slatted walls, down the centre of the earth floor, were two sets of huge iron tracks about 10 feet apart. On the one on the far side were six flatbed wooden train carts each about 20 feet long, with large black steel train wheels, four large solid looking iron bars on each side, and linked together with huge metal couplings. The front cart had a small lectern bolted to its base, with a long black lever beside it. On the back wall of the barn was a huge steel box and a brightly lit led panel with flashing lights.

"Right, everyone on board, just shift the chains to one side and we will get going" and they all started to get on the to flat beds. David, climbed on the first flat bed and stood behind the lectern. Once seated he pressed a red button on the lecterns console with his hand on the long black lever.

"Okay, you better hold on" Nick said grabbing hold of one of the iron bars and waited until everyone had hold of something then signalled David, they were ready. David grabbed the black lever, twisted it slightly and the flatbed train slid silently forwards.

"How is this one powered?" Tom asked, as they pulled out of the barn, pulling his jacket collar up higher as the cold morning air bit into his face.

"I dunno, something to do with electromagnetic propulsion, David and Robert designed it, the more he twists that black lever" Nick said shouting as the flatbed started to accelerate "The faster it goes, all I know, is it is fast. Paradise Pods are about 6 clicks away and we will be there in just over two minutes, so you better hold on tight" Nick said as the flatbed suddenly started to gain speed

30 seconds later Tom felt his mouth drop open, as the first of the 8 Paradise Pods started to appear on the horizon. It was a huge oval shape stretching 200 meters long and 60 meters high, covered in a clear glass like substance, secured over a huge geodesic dome. It looked like some alien creature had deposited a giant clear egg, in the middle of nowhere.

As the flatbed pulled closer, more eggs started to loom out of the morning mist, until finally as it pulled into an identical barn to the one, they had just left, the train glided silently to a stop.

"Okay so now I am going to hand over to David and the others, they will take you on a tour of Paradise Pods" Nick said, "I am fucked if I know how it all works, so ask them any questions you want, they are the experts" he added.

Sanvia smiled "Please accompany me" she said in her honeyed voice and directed them out of the rail barn into a small building just outside.

"Okay, we will be taking the monorail, it is easier for you to see what we are doing" she said" and guided them through a double sliding door, that automatically opened as she approached. As soon as they stepped through the sliding doors, into the small room behind it, a warm pleasant air cascaded over them. The small room was a brick building about 10 meters by 10, and 3 meters high, it had a red tiled floor and a glass window on the side. On the left side of the room was a stone staircase leading up another floor.

"Please follow me" Sanvia said guiding them up the stairs. The upstairs floor was a much smaller room dominated by two huge glass sliding double doors, outside the doors was a huge thick single steel rail and on the inside of the glass doors, on the right was a large red button, which Sanvia pressed.

A few moments later a huge glass bubble arrive on the rail and stopped directly outside the double doors, which automatically opened, as did the two invisible doors in the huge bubble. Along the top of the bubble was two steel rails with several knotted hand ropes, about 30 cm long hanging down.

"You don't need to worry the bio bubble goes much slower than the train!" Sanvia said and reached up and took hold of one of the ropes. As soon as everyone was inside, the doors automatically slide closed and cool air flooded into the bubble as it glided off towards the first egg.

"Welcome to Paradise pods" Sanvia said with all the prowess of a tour guide. We have eight of these pods, each pod being 200 meters long, 100 meters across and 60 meters high, and form a large circle around the central complex. The pods are made of two layers of ethylene tetrafluoroethylene, a kind of eco-friendly plastic made into giant pillows. They are stretched across a giant nanomatter, thermoplastic frame. Capable of resisting temperatures between minus 80 and plus 200 degrees Celsius" Sanvia added smiling proudly.

"The electromagnetic monorail links all of the pods together" she added as they approached the first pod.

"In each of the pods we have tried to create a unique and linked ecosystems, to ensure that we protect our environments, each pod is capable of operating independently of each other. The pods produce enough food, water and breathe able air to sustain up to 200 people indefinitely, and are totally carbon neutral. They are, like in most things in nature virtually maintenance free and self-sustaining, requiring very little human input" Sanvia crooned

"What does that mean?" Craig asked craning his neck to see over the edge of the bubble.

"It simply means that we only come in here to perform basic routine maintenance, everything else is controlled through the use of automatons and computer programmes. In fact, the less human interaction the better" Sanvia replied.

The bubble seamlessly burst into the first pod, and the faces inside the bubble suddenly adopted a stunned look. It was like they had entered an alien world, the domes were like foreign worlds, full of strange looking plants, trees, streams and lights. The inside of the pods was buzzing with tiny little drones that zoomed excitedly between each plant, then back to a huge central console, which looked like a giant flies eye. 50 meters below them, they could see small glass carts on miniature rails being loaded with all sorts of fruits, nuts and vegetables until they were full to the brim, then they watched as they disappeared out of the side of the hub.

"The drones collect all the produce and deposit them in the carts below, these are then transported into the processing centre, where they are either dehydrated and stored or if we require fresh produce then we simply request it, and it is singled out for us" Sanvia said, and it was easy to see she was immensely proud of the whole operation by the look on her face.

"We have over 400 types of vegetables and fruits, 80 different herbs and minerals, and produce in excess of 2000 litres of fresh water per day" she added, as they passed through the first pod and into the next.

"In this pod, we farm fish and have over 60 different species, both salt and fresh water" she said as below them they saw massive bubbling tanks and again the army of drones flitting back and forth.

As they travelled through each of the pods, they all stood gazing in awe at the hive of industry below them.

The last pod was completely different, there were no plants just rows and rows of cattle grids and chickens hutches. "Here we produce all the milk and eggs that we need, our cattle are free range and outside of the pod, there are 12 acres of pasture

This pod is self-cleaning, and all the produce is automatically taken to the processing centre", and as if she had planned it, just as the mono bubble was about to exit, they could see an array of huge clear pipes with milk surging through them, and a conveyor of eggs running along the side of the hutches below.

"There" Sanvia said obviously delighted "Of course there is so much more to what we are doing at paradise, that is just an overview, now as we approach the central complex, I will hand you over to David" she said smiling.

"Jesus Nick this place is incredible" Tom said craning his neck to look back into the dome they had just exited.

"That is nothing, wait to you see the complex" Nick said.

The central complex was spread over 6 acres and consisted of 20 domicile units capable of housing up to 6 to eight people, all linked in a hub and spoke style, to a central complex. The central complex had a small hospital with its own operating room, a school, a media centre, 6 private meeting rooms for up to 30 people, two large dining areas, four laboratories, an armoury, and technology suite, with dedicated server rooms, that made mission control at NASA look like a school computer room. Outside the central complex, directly behind where the technology suite was, stood a power generation plant and a huge lithium battery storage centre.

Chapter Five
Hungary wolves and the cliff

When they were finished the tour and sat in one of the private meeting rooms, enjoying a coffee, that had been developed in dome three, they were all in total awe of Paradise Pod.

"This place is fucking amazing" Mike said, which was the first positive thing Nick had heard him say.

"Yeah, that is what we were going for" Robert replied.

"Must have cost a packet" Craig said

"To build, yes, but now, it is self-sustaining, we spend very little on maintenance and all the work is done on site"

"Ain't, you worried about other people dropping in?" Akeem asked.

"That is my department" Nick said. "You can't get in by air, the strip is mined, if you come by sea, then your window is short, as it freezes 6 months of the year, and we have a range of sea defences. If you decide to drop in or come over the mountains, well as you already know we have a range of surprises waiting for you" Nick said

"What about a drone attack?" Josh asked

"The whole site is protected by a pulsing emp shield, you won't get within 500 yards of the place, and Cassia has taken care of cyber-attacks. I am not saying it is impossible, we all know that with a determined enemy nothing is impossible, but we have made it as difficult for them as humanly possible" Nick said

"Well, I for one, am jealous, this place is amazing, there should be more places like this" Tom said.

"That is why we have already released the plans, minus the security stuff on the web and to all governments, it's up to them now, anyone can build one" David said

"Why, I mean you guys could have made a ton of money from your plans?" Josh said.

Robert sighed, "I don't know if you know what is happening with the climate and the intention of the Committee to create their own paradise complex, albeit larger, we all believe that everyone should have the opportunity, not just the selected few" Robert replied.

"Only if you can afford it" Josh snapped.

"Look it is not that hard, if you all pool your resources and do the work yourself, its achievable, you just have to give up a few of the luxuries you currently enjoy and commit to the project, and the time to do it is now, whilst you can still get the materials at reasonable prices" Robert said

"I still don't see it" Josh said sourly "You don't know how poorly we are paid" he added.

David laughed "look we have created this place to support 100 plus people, and we populated it with people that could contribute the skills and labour we needed, everyone is equal, there are hundreds of examples of what we are doing all over the world, they are called communes. It's just we decided to take into account what is happening to the climate and make the necessary adjustments, that's all. So, join one of these communes, download the plans and work together to make it happen" David said.

"Yeah, but those places are full of religious nuts" Mike said "I ain't buying into that shit" he added.

"They don't have to be, they could be just full of likeminded people" Robert said

"Man, I like the idea, but life has taught me that no matter how hard you try there is always someone with their own agenda that wants to screw your plans" Tom said

"Then I would suggest that you choose your friends carefully, here is full of Indians there are no chiefs, and everyone is equal. We each get a vote and choice, don't get me wrong that doesn't mean we don't disagree, but at the end of the day we are all still working to the same agenda, to have a quiet life" Nick said

"So, what happens when you guys die, who take over the place then" Tom asked

"Nick smiled "well that is a whole other story" Nick said and smiled at David

"Hi guys" Cassia said bursting into the meeting room with Alten close behind her. "So, what do you think, paradise right?" she asked.

"What you have created here is truly mind blowing" Tom said, and everyone nodded their agreement.

"Man, you should see the mission control room at the house" Alten said.

"Well, if its anything like the one here" Tom said "It rivals NASA" he added.

"What there is one here too, oh man I have got to see it?" Alten said excitedly

Cassia smiled, "When you're ready. Okay lunch", she said. "Anaya and her daughter have kindly put together a buffet for us in room two, so when you are ready, I know the kids are dying to meet you, they don't get to meet many strangers" Cassia said

When they were all in room 2, Sanjay introduced Aanya and Shemzee and the 6 children that they had all adopted, who were now helping to serve the food.

"So, you guys have adopted these children?" Akeem asked looking at the small Afghan 12-year-old girl that was showing him the rice dishes

"Well, all apart from Archie, he's mine, but yes, we have six at the moment" Katie said, then held her hand up over her mouth and whispered "It's all we can manage at the moment. Shemzee and I run the school and the older children help. In fact, all of the children contribute in some way, as we all do" Katie said smiling at a small blond-haired boy.

"What about their parents?" Akeem asked.

Katie sighed "They are all orphans, their families were killed in some conflict or other, look I know it's not perfect and I really wish we could help more" she said misinterpreting Akeem's look.

"I am not judging, I am just glad to see that you guys are doing something, many people wouldn't" he said.

"I have to admit, I wish we could do more, that is why we are always trying to get governments to build these communes, but there is a lot of resistance" Katie said.

Akeem smiled "Because it is a fantasy, look don't get me wrong, you guys have it sorted here, but the world doesn't work like that, too many people, too much greed, there is no way they are going to pull together, trust me I know, I have seen it so many times, it is always the innocent and poor that get screwed" he said sourly.

"And that is exactly why the world is in the shit it is" Katie said, "But it will just take a few people to take their head out of their arses and think beyond tomorrow. And if we can demonstrate how it works, share our plans, you never know there may be some that want to take that ride, its either that or" she paused trying to think about how to put it gently then a thought occurred to her.

"Okay, so when you are standing on the edge of a cliff with a pack of angry wolves behind you, you can either accept your fate and jump, or you can find a way to make peace with the wolves" Katie said

"What if the wolves don't want to make peace?" Akeem asked.

"Then you just haven't found the right way of communicating with them, and I would suggest you learn quickly, before you either become their dinner or a pancake at the bottom of the cliff" Katie said cryptically.

"I see, and you think that is possible?" Akeem asked.

"I do, after all what other choice do, we have. I am a realist some will make the transition others will prefer to jump and take as many with them as possible. I guess each one of us needs to decide which group we would rather be in" Katie explained, then added "I have already made my choice, as you can see"

"I am sorry I still can't see governments following your example" Akeem said stubbornly

Katie smiled "Akeem isn't it" she said and the man in front of her nodded.

"If you sit back and wait for someone else to do it for you, because you think it is their responsibility, then eventually all you will be left with is, the comfort of knowing you can blame them for their failings, as you join them, when you leap off the cliff. If you make the choice yourself then all you have to blame for failure is yourself, it is really down to you, to either say I told you so, or take responsibility for your own destiny" Katie said

Akeem thought about what Katie had said then a thought occurred to him.

"Your plan is flawed" he said "Whilst you may have made peace with that pack of wolves, there will always be a chance another pack will come along" he said.

"Then Akeem, you had better have a Nick Colletto in your group, someone that understands how wolves behave and knows how to stop them, as I said pick your partners carefully and make most of their skills" Katie said smiling.

After lunch Tom watched as David handed Cassia, Katie, Sarah, Sanvia and Sanjay and his family a small box with their names clearly printed on the top, inside of which was a small green pill, which they all took and swallowed quickly, he was about to ask what they were doing when Cassia interrupted.

"Now, I have the details of all the sites, it is time to plan" she said happily

Cassia laid the plans out over the meeting room table and spread them out evenly, placing each site in order of country.

"Okay here are my first thoughts, first, there is a lot of security surrounding all of these sites, more so, as you would expect, in China and Japan, however that said the US sites are pretty tight too.

First there is Titan, that is in Tennessee at the Oakridge national laboratory, mostly used for Astrophysics and climate modelling, I think that pretty much speaks for itself.

Next is Cori, that one is based at the National Energy Research centre in Oakland, California, not much else is known about what they use it for, but taking where it is based, we can assume it has something to energy and resources.

The last in the US, is at the Lawrence Livermore laboratory, also in California, and is listed as being the key computer for nuclear research and assessing advanced weaponry.

Finding out about the Chinese ones proved to be a lot harder. What I can tell you is the one in Wuxi, is focussed on climate change whilst the one Guizhou is the one handling their defence. I re-tasked one of the governments satellites to fly over and take pictures, and the photos show that both have military installations directly on their doorsteps.

There is better news in Japan the Oakforest Pac is in the University of Tokyo and is used by their students and the Fujitsu K is in Kobe, although there is nothing about what it is being used for.

Lastly there is the Piz Daint in Lugano, Switzerland and that is mainly used to support the research at Cern and the Hadron Collider.

Ok now the bad news since we leaked the committee information every single one of them has significantly ramped up their security" Cassia said then said "Thoughts?"

"Right well thanks Cassia, so off the top of my head, we start in the States, probably with the climate one in Tennessee, once we get in there we will know if Betsi has been inside, if she has, we block her, if not, then we don't need to check the rest" Nick said

"Makes sense, what then, take out the others in the states, then onto Japan or Switzerland, leaving the Chinese to last, as they are likely to be the most difficult" Tom suggested.

"That or we leave one of the US ones to last, that way we trap Betsi here, it will be easier than spending any length of time in China, I reckon, if we manage to get in, we are going to need to be in and out quick" Josh suggested.

"Good call" Nick said, "That makes most sense," he added, "So what about it, Tennessee or California, but not the weapons one, so it's either energy or climate, lets vote" Nick said, "Then we can starting drilling down and planning, then look at resources we need" Nick said

The team then voted, and it was over whelming in favour of Tennessee.

"Okay let's talk who stays and who goes" Nick said.

"Okay, first Cassia and me, will go down there and recce the site, Tom you and one other are welcome to come too. I reckon given the time schedule, if Katie and a couple of your guys get down to California and start the provisional recce on the other two, that will give us a heads up. I would suggest that Alten goes along too, Cass tells me he is pretty hot on tech, so he might be able to get into their networks and dig around" Nick suggested

"Works for me, Tom said and in the interest of fairness, who wants California" Tom asked. Akeem Craig and Josh all wanted to go to California and Mike agreed to come to Tennessee.

"Okay, Sarah will manage the site here, she is the only one I trust, David and Robert can manage comms from here and everything goes through them, agreed" Nick said, everyone nodded their acceptance of the plan.

"Okay when?" Cassia said.

If you can get us back to Anchorage, I can sort flights, Tom said, "private so we can take whatever kit we need, whilst we are off the books, I still have access to resources" Tom said. Nick considered it.

"No deal" Nick said, "The last thing we need is this getting out, and that also means the US Government, I just don't trust them" Nick said.

"No need" Katie interrupted, "I have a few contacts myself, no questions asked, and its secure" she said

Chapter Six
Renewing old acquaintances

Sunday 6th July 2025 – Los Angeles

BA flight 572 landed at LAX at little after 2 am in the morning, and as soon as Jessica walked out into the arrivals lounge, she instantly recognised the tall dark-haired man, this time he was not dressed in his usual black suit, preferring jeans, a rams sweatshirt with a brown leather jacket. In case she had failed to recognise him, he was also holding a white plaque with the name Angela Donner neatly written on it.

Good to finally meet you Miss Donner, Andrew said smiling and extending his hand. "You too Mr Dale" Jessica said carrying on with his pretence.

"If you would like to follow me, I have a room waiting for you at the Ramada" Andrew said leading the way.

Andrew accompanied Jessica into the large multi-story car park and stopped at a black SUV with darkened windows. He pressed the button on his remote and opened the rear door for her, but not before scanning to car park to see if they were being watched.

Jessica got in the back and waited until Andrew closed the door and got in the front. Quickly Andrew lowered the internal window and smiled

"Jess, good to see you, where have you been, the last time I saw you, you were at Marco Polo airport getting pissed on G&T's?" Andrew said

"Yeah, well a lot has happened since then. I didn't get fired got demoted though and side lined to Dover. I have spent the last few years stamping bloody immigration visas and smiling sweetly. Anyway, why all the mystery?" Jessica asked.

"Okay, well there are a lot of people watching, seems like ever since that Committee thing, everyone has become paranoid, thinking there are ghosts and spies around every corner. No one trusts anyone, and everyone's movements and communications are being tagged" Andrew said.

"Jesus, glad I am not part of it, how do you ever get anything done?" Jessica asked.

"Not easy, I am currently on vacation, family emergency" Andrew said

"Yeah ditto, apart from the little detail that I don't actually have any, well unless you count the cat" Jessica said smiling weakly. "I take it, that you have access to the same intel I do, what do you make of it?" she asked

"Well, there is not much to go on. All I know is that this Cassia Nilsson is a top hacker and Carmichael is one of the best biochemists in the world. Now they spent some time working with Holloway at his facility in Valencia, that is until the place got blown up. They manage to escape and bought a place in Alaska, Red Dog" Andrew said

"As for Holloway, everyone thought he had died in Valencia, so we were as surprised as anyone when he showed up on that video on the web. Then literally everyone was looking for Holloway. Then out of the blue, he turns up dead in Paris, but before we can get there, someone removed his effects, including his laptop. Then two of the US committee members, Blake and Anderson, who are doing time in a supermax in Colorado get a visit from an ex special forces Major, Tom Clarke. Which in itself is unusual as they are ex communicado, No visitors" Andrew said.

"I have a few contacts inside of UPX and they listened in to the conversation, as I am sure you read. This Major was keen to find out what was on that laptop, kept mentioning something called BETSI, whatever that is. Then this Major turns up in Seward, Alaska, with a crew, which is 30k's outside of Red Dog, that is all we got" Andrew said.

"I see" Jessica said, "Well maybe I can fill in some of your blanks. After Venice, I got posted to the immigration centre at

Dover, and I was running through some old files on a chap called Donald Ellington, expat, been working in Valencia for Edward Holloway, during the interviews, he talked about Holloways supercomputer, kept saying that BETSI had set the whole thing up. Of course, at the time the officer interviewing him thought he was talking bollocks and disregarded it, and I didn't think anything of it. That was until I saw the name in the file that was left for me last night. Ellington also he told the officer that Carmichael and Nilsson were working with Holloway doing some sort of genetic editing. When I read the pathology report, it all sounded a bit of a fantasy to me, but two things did catch my attention. First Holloway was completely cured of cancer, now bearing in mind that just two months earlier he had been given a terminal diagnosis, that sounded like a bit of a miracle, and the second thing was apparently Holloway couldn't die, which of course we now know as bullshit" Jessica said

"Okay, we are at the Ramada, you have room 412, what say we pick this up in the morning, say 10, I'll pick you up" Andrew said stopping outside the hotel entrance.

The next morning Andrew was waiting for Jess in the lobby. Luckily Jess could survive on very little sleep and didn't suffer from jet lag, she had been up since 7am and already been shopping and purchased some new clothes, toiletries, a laptop and a burner phone.

"Okay, let's go, the car is outside" Andrew said.

Andrew took Jess to a small warehouse in Pacific Palisades, just past Santa Monica pier. From the outside the warehouse looked exactly like any of the other of the 7 along the block, however inside it was a state of the art. The windows were blacked out, the walls were covered in a thick rubber matting and the entire place was full of computers and surveillance equipment.

"This is our little hide away, we are perfectly safe here, no one can penetrate our network. I thought it would make a good place to work from, anyway meet Exo," Andrew said introducing Jess to a thin looking teenager with bright green hair, holey jeans and a ripped shirt that said *Fuck you* "he is one of the top hackers in the country. Currently I have him tracking the where abouts of this BETSI computer, if anyone can find it, he can" Andrew said

"Whats up" Exo said looking up briefly then returned to his laptop and started typing.

"Okay, Exo table now" Andrew said as if he was giving a dog instructions. Exo returned the favour and grunted, but still came and sat at the table.

"Right where are we, any news on BETSI?" Andrew asked

"Nothing yet dude" but if she is out there it's just a matter of time. I did find some references to her in Holloways emails, seems like the dude programmed her to preserve human life. Now if I take it in context with what we learned from his iPad" Exo said in a surprisingly soft well-spoken voice.

"What you managed to get into his iPad?" Jess asked

"Well not us, but the folks as the NSA did, I just tapped into their files. Anyway, Holloway's final instruction was to tell this Betsi to implement something called '*Protocol zero*', whatever that is, the rest of the stuff on there was either worthless or about someone called Emeline" Exo said casually.

"Okay, so what we have is a supercomputer, with the shackles taken off, and desire to preserve humanity, also an ex special forces guy and his team, seeking out a top hacker and a biologist, so what's the end game?" Andrew asked opening it out to the group.

"Presuming that this Major guy has access to the same information we do, and that is why he is looking for Cassia and David. Then we can assume that they are trying to stop this Betsi character from delivering its plan. The real question is how does a computer preserve humanity?" Jess asked hopefully looking at the others.

Everyone sat in silence contemplating the question until eventually Jess spoke again.

"Well, it could be trying to fix climate change" she said

"No, I don't think so, it's too late that for that" Andrew said then looking at Jess's face said. "Oh of course you don't know. Well, we learnt a few other things from Blake and Anderson and what the Committee were up to. It seems that apart from some of their other activities apparently, they were putting plans together for a major self-sustaining complex, to address the climate change issue" Andrew said

"What climate change issue?" Jess asked feeling she was missing something.

"Well according to Blake and Anderson, the Committee has been warning governments about Climate change for the last 70 years. Also, they have even introduced some own interventions. Sadly, however they have been ignored and now it's too late, we have past the proverbial tipping point, by some margin, and the climate has gone down the drain" Andrew explained.

"So that's it, we're screwed?" Jess exclaimed angrily.

"Pretty much, all the governments are playing it down of course, saying it's all fake news that sort of thing, but demonstrations and protests are increasing, the rest of us are just getting on with it, looking for alternative solutions, tech that sort of thing" Andrew said

"I have just received an alert Major Clarke has just landed in Future Oak airport in Tennessee, with Mike Barnard, and two others" Exo said, then suddenly his laptop pinged again. "Ok three others from his crew have just landed in Oakland international in California" he added

"What the hell are they doing in Tennessee, and Oakland?" Andrew said, Jess didn't answer, she had taken out her laptop and was typing wildly on the keys.

"Okay" she said finally, I have googled both areas and the only link I can work out is that both have super computers, the Tennessee one is at the National Laboratory and the one in Oakland is at National Energy research centre" Jess said, "What I can't work out is why there would go there?" she added.

"I don't know, but it can't be a coincidence, Holloway, commits suicide, and takes the shackles off his supercomputer, and they show up at the two sites in the US that have super computers" Andrew said

"Three" Exo said

"What?" Andrew asked

"There are three sites, the other one is also in, California, Livermore" Exo said

"Fine so there is three, it still doesn't explain what they are doing there." Jess said

"There is only one way to find out, we are going to have to go there and follow them" Andrew said, "Exo you set us up, tracking and trace, mikes and usual surveillance kit, Jess you up for a trip to Tennessee?" Andrew asked smiling

"Well, that's it, think about it" Jess said excitedly

"Go on" Andrew and Exo said automatically

"Okay, so this Betsi computer's basic programme is to preserve human life, and the climate is going down the pan, so it's looking for ways to address it" Jess said

"Didn't you hear, if you believe the current thinking, its already too late, there is nothing it can do to save the climate, so that can't be it" Andrew said

"Well, that is not entirely true" Exo said, "If we dramatically reduce the carbon emissions, whilst we may not be able to stop the decline of the climate, we can slow its acceleration" he added

"How's that?" Andrew asked

"Off the top of my head, you need to reduce the population by 50% and relocate what's left to the northern hemisphere, destroy all the tech, and take humanity back to the dark ages, that way, what's left will survive" Exo said and watched as the faces on the other two dropped.

"No, it couldn't" Andrew said

"Why not, think about it, everything we do is online" Jess said "I reckon that computer is going to wipe out half the humans on the planet" she added

Chapter Seven
Eyes and ears on

Nick drove slowly down Bethnal Valley road, pausing slightly at the turning towards the conference centre, whilst Cassia pretended to consult the map. Tom slipped the lens of the fibre wired camera up to the open window, it looked like a long silver snake with a lens at one end and connected to the laptop on the other. Mike loaded the video programme on the laptop and started filming.

"Okay Nick ready" Tom said, and Nick slipped the car into gear and edged forwards as Cassia kept pointing left and right and consulting the map. The team passed up and down Bethnal valley road twice before deciding that any more would raise suspicion, then packed up the laptop and headed off to Comfort Inn in Knoxville, where they had secured three double rooms.

After checking in they all met in Cassia's room to review the video and see what they had filmed.

"Good news" Cassia said as soon as Nick got to the room "I have managed to get the site plan for the Oakridge. Now the building we want is on the corner of sixth street and white Oak avenue. There is a carpark opposite here" she said pointing to the map. As we saw, yesterday, on our drive by security has seriously been ramped up, and they are also restricting visitors, appointments only" Cassia said.

"Great so no walking in the front door and asking to borrow their computer then" Tom said laughing

"No" Cassia said not entirely sure he was joking "Anyway I have hacked into their intranet, here is what I have learned. They have an onsite security team of twenty-two, the shifts are two on four off and run 24/7. In addition to this there is some additional security around the Centre for Computational studies, in the shape of two teams, one inside, one patrolling the outside.

Now looking at their recent purchase history for the centre, they have made some significant additions to their security, sensors, cameras and a new cyber security system" Cassia said delighted with herself

"And you managed to find all that out" Mike said impressed.

"Okay, well, first things first, Cass how long do you need once we are inside" Nick asked.

"10 maybe 15 minutes top" she replied

"Okay" Nick said, "That is our challenge, thoughts?" he asked

For the next three hours they went through different plans and ideas until finally they settle on what they thought was their best option.

"Okay, that's it then, so let's get some grub, Tom, can you source the kit we need, I think we should go tomorrow, there is no point in waiting, we need to find out how far behind the curve we are." Nick said

Cassia booked them into Giovanni's, a local Italian restaurant that had received the best online ratings and was the closest to where they were staying.

Jess sat in the black SUV, across from the Italian restaurant, her face pressed against the binoculars, watching every move Tom made. "Who are the others?" she asked

Andrew pressed the button on the camera and the shutter clicked a dozen times, then instantly sent the pictures back to Exo. Within seconds Jess and Andrew could hear Exo's voice through their earpieces.

"Okay the woman, is Cassia Nilsson, world class hacker, goes by the name of Destiny, the other guy, the one in the black jacket, with his back to the window, that is, Nick Colletto, ex special forces, linked with General Markham. Now what is interesting is that both of those two, were seen in or around Valencia, at the time of Holloways disappearance" Exo said then added "Oh yeah, they are all checked in at the Comfort inn, in Knoxville, rooms 412, 3, and 4."

Andrew took out his phone, dialled a number, waited until a voice answered then said "full ears and eyes on, rooms 412, 3 and 4, Comfort inn Knoxville asap"

"So now we have a world class hacker, three special forces guys, all just outside the site of the Oakland supercomputer site, odds on they are going to break in" Andrew said, as if any of them needed clarification of the situation.

"But why, I mean it is a university computer, why do they want to break in there, what are we missing?" Jess asked "it just doesn't make any sense"

"Well, we could arrange to have them picked up and ask them, although I suspect they won't say anything, or we could just sit back and observe and once they have accessed the computer, find out what they took or did" Andrew suggested

"It doesn't sit right with me, just sitting back and letting them get away with it" Jess said, "I vote we pick them up" she added

"Big picture Jess, this maybe our only chance of finding out what is going on" Andrew said.

"Fine, as long as no one gets hurt" Jess said sourly

Nick tilted the small mirror up another few degrees until the image cleared again and sighed.

"You guys need anything else" The pretty brunette, in the green and white striped uniform. asked

"We could do with a couple more beers, Charlie" Nick said looking up at the girls badge "Oh hey can I borrow your pen for a couple of seconds" he asked, Charlie nodded and handed him her pen after scribbling their order on the small pad in her hand.

"Nick took the pen, pulled a napkin from the holder and scribble a few lines and passed it across to Tom.

We have company, five o clock, black SUV, two tangos

Tom read the note, then passed it to Mike, who scanned it, then passed it Cassia.

"Fuck" Cassia said aloud

"Don't say, or do anything, just pretend that you are having a good time" Nick said "I will be back in a sec" he added, getting to his feet and moving towards the restrooms.

"Colletto is on the move" Jess said quietly.

Andrew looked through the range finder "He is just going for a piss, that's the restroom back there" he said and laid the camera back down and picked up his coffee.

Nick walked through the door to the rest room then wedged it closed using the garbage bin against the handle, preventing anyone else entering. Quietly he filled one of the sinks with water. Then he pulled the lace in his left trainer, almost all the way through and knotted one end. Then he wrapped the lace around his hand, kicked his foot up to the sink, and rubbed the lace along the steel edge of the counter, pulling the lace tightly until it snapped and placed the broke lace on the counter and tie his trainer back together using the small end.

"Quickly he slipped off his jacket and ripped out the waterproof lining from one of the pockets, tipped it upside down and filled it full of water, then tied the lace tightly around it.

Once he was finished, he reached up undid the small bathroom window, pushed out the thin wire mesh, then pulled himself up and through and slipped silently down onto the dirt below. Once he was sure that he had not been seen, he dug his heel into the dirt and scooped up several handfuls, and depositing them into his home-made water balloon, until he had a decent mud pie. Then grabbing handfuls of the mud, he smeared it over any exposed white areas of his face and hands.

Once he was sure that he was completely covered, he ditched the water balloon and carefully replaced the wire mesh. Then set off running for two blocks behind the buildings next to the restaurant. When he reached the far end of the second block, he took a right and ran for two more blocks, then turned right again and came up behind the SUV, then dropped behind a low shrub, 20 feet from it and held his breath.

Laying on his back he reached into his jeans pocket he pulled out his military spec phone, killed the light and selected the night vision option, then held it high in the air in the direction of the SUV. With his other hand, he reached up and clicked the button. Slowly moving it in an arc. he repeated the process twice more, rolled onto his side and stowed the phone back in his pocket.

It took him less than 4 minutes to make it back to the restaurant. Where he quickly removed the wire screen pulled himself back into the bathroom, climbed onto of the counter where the sink was, then kicked the tap as hard as he could. The tap snapped sideward, and water started spraying out across the small bathroom. Nick climbed off the counter, stood beside the spray collecting handfuls and washed all the mud off his face and hands and jeans. Then once he had dabbed himself dry and had flushed the hand towels down the toilet. He went back and stood in front of the spray for a few seconds. Then pulled the garbage bin away from the door and walked back into the restaurant.

"What the hell" Nick shouted, I turned on your faucet and the dam thing came off in my hand, look at the state of me" he yelled

Charlie came running over with towels in her hand, "I am so sorry, we had no idea the faucet was faulty" she said apologetically handing Nick a towel and dabbing his clothes.

Jess pulled the binoculars closer to her eyes. "You are never going to believe this. Colletto just came out of the bathroom soaking wet, looks like the tap burst on him" she said laughing, passing the binoculars to Andrew.

"Excellent" Andrew said smiling, "I love it when bad shit happens to bad people, its karma, anyway, heads up they are leaving" he said, and they both ducked down under the dash.

Nick smiled to himself as they passed along the street directly opposite to the SUV, and like professionals none of them gave it a second look.

"Okay give them two minutes then head back to the Comfort inn, we know that is where they are going, my guys should be finished by now" Andrew said

"Did you, do it?" Nick asked smiling at Cassia.

"Sure did" Cassia replied. Nick checked his watch, held his hand in the air and hailed a passing cab, "Comfort inn, Knoxville" he said as they all climbed into the cab.

When they got back to the Comfort inn, Nick went straight to the reception.

"Johnson" he said to the receptionist, 216"

"Certainly, Mr Johnson, the receptionist said handing him his key and eyeing him suspiciously.

"Bloody tap in the restaurant toilet, I need a change of clothes" Nick said smiling weakly at the receptionist.

"Oh, I am sorry to hear that Mr Johnson" The receptionist said, and Nick was sure he could see her smiling as he walked away.

Cassia, Mike and Tom were already waiting outside room 216 waiting for Nick.

Once they were all inside, Nick connected his phone to Cassia's eye pad and within seconds a green video appeared on the screen.

"Okay any of you recognise them" Nick asked, no one responded, "Ok Cass do your thing" Nick said, Cassia took a snapshot of the faces in the car, minimised the screen then started typing. Two minutes later she looked up.

"Okay the woman is Jessica Craven, travelling under the name of Angela Donner, she is ex UK M15, met police and is currently checking papers in immigration in Dover England. The guy is Andrew Dale, younger brother of a certain. Mr Rod Dale. You know the one we ran I to in DC last year. She said smiling.

"Fuck the are like cockroaches what are they doing breeding them" Nick snapped

"What happened last year?" Tom asked nervously. Cassia smiled at Nick who just shrugged his shoulders. Then proceeded to tell Tom and Mike about the nanites.

"so, you knew Holloway was still alive all along?" Tom growled

"Well not really we thought it was possible" Nick admitted then added "Look he is one slippery git; now can we get on?" He asked

"Fine but I don't like secrets" Tom snapped and seeing the anger building on Nicks face Cassia pressed on.

"Si this Dale he is also ex FBI, special ops, and is currently unemployed, or at least that is what his file say. Wait, I have some footage downloading" she added.

Once the images finished downloading, they all stared at them. Andrew Dale was getting into his car outside of the UPX in Colorado.

"UPX, isn't that where Blake and Anderson are?" Nick asked, Tom nodded.

"That also might explain why EXO" Cassia started to say, then seeing the confused looks added "A mid-level hacker, well he has been checking us out, I have been monitoring him, nothing serious, but I bet he is working with them" Cassia added.

"Cass bring up the footage again" Nick asked, and Cassia maximised the green screen.

"Okay, Nick said, "See that camera that's the Bobcat B3340, military grade digital, its exclusive, to the military, that means that these guys are seriously connected, you don't get that sort of kit off the shelf" Nick said.

"That complicates things" Tom said.

"Yeah" Nick said, thinking aloud. "But why, it doesn't make any sense" he added.

"Whatever the reason, we can't break into the Computer centre with them on our tails!" Mike said.

"That" Nick said "is why we changed rooms, now listen up" he added and told them what he had in mind then they all got up and left the room.

30 minutes later outside the Comfort Inn in their SUV, Andrew turned the sound up on the monitor,

"Okay so the graphite reactor is building 3100, on hillside avenue, the one in the middle" Nick voice said ringing out over the speakers in the car.

Andrew flicked open his laptop, punched in the Wi-Fi code and logged into the secure cloud server.

"Okay we have visual" he said and turned the screen round to face Jess. On the screen was a panoramic image of room 412. Nick Colletto was sat on the bed, Mike Barnard and Tom Clarke were on the dressing room chairs and Cassia was sat next to Nick, they appeared to be looking at a map on the coffee table in front of them.

"Tom you and Mike, you take the right side, there are emergency exits here and here" Nick said pointing to the map"

Nick said, "Cass and I will go through the maintenance service area, here" Nick added.

"Christ, they are breaking into the graphite reactor" Andrew said.

"What the hell is that?" Jess asked

"A graphite reactor" Andrew said reading from a page on his laptop, "is a moderator or reflector within a nuclear reactor, which allows natural uranium to be used in nuclear fuel" Andrew parroted from the page.

"Why the hell would they do that?" Jess asked.

"I don't know, but I bet it has something to do with protocol zero, what is clear now is for whatever reason, they are breaking in, we can't just sit by and let them do it, if something goes wrong, we could be looking at a major nuclear incident" Andrew said

"Okay, once we are inside, the uranium rods are stored in this secure area in the basement, have we got the containers?" Nick asked

"All sorted" Cassia replied, "What about security?" she asked.

"Well, its light, whilst they have doubled the detail, 2 by four,24 seven, the idiots have detailed them all to the computer, perfect timing if you ask me" Nick said "But, there are electronic deterrents, laser, pressure pads, fingerprint, and retinal scanners, access codes"

"No problem, I have already hacked in, I have the codes, however we will only have a 4-minute window, before it auto resets" Cassia said

"Its tight, but doable" Nick said, "but we will have the element of surprise, they will not be expecting anyone to break in, after all it's only a university campus" Nick said.

"Mike, we need two vehicles, put them in central car park by third, okay all set 2 am tomorrow" Nick said, "that leaves us around 24 hours to get the kit together, and iron out any kinks, agreed?" Nick asked.

Jess watched with her mouth open, as all the others in the room nodded their approval.

"Bloody hell" Andrew said, "They are after the uranium, fuck we can't let that happen Jess, who knows what they will do with it"

"Agreed but how are we going to stop them, without giving ourselves away?" Jess asked.

"I don't know yet, but we have 24 hours to work it out" Andrew said

Chapter Eight
The alternative plan

Monday 7th July 2025 – Tennessee

Jess got out of the SUV and stretched, it had been a very long night, straight after the meeting in 412, they all went to their respective rooms, and with the exception of Mike, who helped himself to the contents of the mini bar, they all went straight to bed, and stayed there until 7am, where each showered and dressed then went down to breakfast, which is where they were now.

"You want me to take over, or go get us some coffee" Jess said leaning through the window, hoping Andrew would opt for the coffee

"Coffee, definitely" Andrew said and watched as Jess disappeared down the road.

30 minutes later Jess returned with two large coffees and some Danish pastries, "Here" she said handing Andrew his coffee and climbing back inside the SUV, which had developed a distinctly musty smell.

"Christ Andrew, can't you crack the window a little?" Jess said holding her nose.

"Not if you want to listen to their conversation too" Andrew moaned.

"What are they doing now?" Jess asked.

"Nothing, they are sitting in the lounge area, drinking coffee" Andrew snapped.

"I have been thinking, we already know when and where they are going to be, so we can either sit round here scratching our backsides, waiting for them to do something, or we can get a shower, and plan how we are going to stop them" Jess said.

Andrew looked at her, smiled and started the SUV, "Lets meet back at the warehouse in two hours agreed, we can still record everything they say and do in the room, and I will get a car to monitor outside" he said

"Agreed" Jess replied, and Nick smiled as he stared into the large wall mirror in the lounge area and watched the SUV pull away, as Cassia filmed them sitting in the lounge.

"Holiday movie" she said smiling.

When Jess got back to the warehouse, Andrew was buzzing.

"Jess" he shouted as she came through the door "I have a plan" he said.

Jess grabbed three coffees and came and sat down at the briefing table, handed one to Andrew and the other to Exo.

"Okay shoot" Jess said enthusiastically.

"Right, so when I got back here, I made a couple of calls to one of my old buddies, Dexter in the Knoxville office, told them what we had learned, and that it was credible. He said he would make some calls and get back to us. Well just before you got here, he called back, he has been in touch with the Deputy at the campus security, well let's just say that when Colletto and his crew break into that reactor room, they are in for a surprise. Dexter has asked if we want to tag along. I said dam right we did, and we want first crack at Nick and his team, when they are in custody, matter of National Security. So, he is picking us up at 9pm tonight and we are laying a trap for them" Andrew said.

"Fantastic, I can't wait to see the look on Colletto's face" Jess said excitedly.

"Exo how are our tango's doing?" Andrew asked.

"Still sleeping" Exo said "Been that way for most of the day" he added.

"You sure they are there?" Jess asked

Exo looked up and gave her one of his *'really'* looks, "Duh, 20 minutes ago, Mike Barnard got up and peed, Nilsson made some tea about an hour ago, then went back to bed, same goes for the others, they have all done something, which tells me, yes, they are still in their rooms. I am also monitoring the corridors, reception and their car, which is still in the hotel car park. So, unless they climbed out of the window, abseiled down 120 feet, managed to avoid the car we have across the road and walk away, then yeah there are still there" Exo said

"Sorry just asking?" Jess said apologetically.

Nick and the team spent the rest of the day pulling together all the kit they needed for the operation, after making a little video of the guys sleeping and occasionally getting up to pee and replacing the feed on the cameras in their rooms and putting the one in the corridors on a loop. Then taking the lift down to the basement and slipping out the service entrance on the opposite side of the entrance to the hotel and picking up another car from the parking lot opposite, which Cassia had just rented them.

A little after 00:45pm as the sun was just setting, they pulled into the white oak car park and killed the lights on their newly rented minivan.

"Okay Cass, you're up" Nick said.

Cassia took out her small laptop and set it out on the trunk of the car. Typed in a few commands and the first of the four black DJI Mavic mini drones rose silently into the air and hovered in the air, just outside the parking lot. She continued typing until all four drones were airborne. Then looked at Nick and gave him small smile. 8 minutes later she had placed one of the drones on each corner of building 3100. Next, she picked up the fifth drone, this one was slightly bigger, checked the black box underneath, flicked the small button and waited until the tiny light went green. Then like the others she sent it off in the direction of building 3100, this time landing it, in the centre of the roof.

"Ready" Cassia said

"Okay" Nick said "Tom, what's happening on target?" he asked.

"Ok building 5600 is lite, two tangos, building 3100 on the other hand is stacked. There are two teams of six, one on hillside avenue, east and west, the other tucked in behind 3042, plus two on the roof of 3003, four cars, two on fifth, two on central and it looks like a command setup on 3130, all in all I count twenty tangos, four vehicles and 8 guards" Tom said

"Well looks like they are expecting someone, let's not disappoint them" Nick said, then added "let's go"

The team slipped out of the carpark, dressed all in black, wearing ski masks, one by one behind each other, keeping to the dark shadows. They crossed over white oak avenue, skirted round the side of building 5600, and up to the car park opposite building 5100 where the computer was.

"Okay" Nick said crouching down in a dark spot in the corner of the car park, checking his watch, "10 minutes, Cass showtime. He added

Cassia took out the laptop out of her pack and fired it up whilst Nick shielded her with his coat. The screen was split in two, the left was an overview of building 3100, the right was building 5100. Cassia typed on the keys and the screen on the left changed and a hologram figure appeared on the top of the centre drone.

"Charlie one, to team two, we have a tango on the roof" Andrew said from his vantage point on top of building 3003.

"No one move, remember we need them in the facility" Andrew said, "Okay. Jess where are we with the systems inside the building?" he asked

"All still secure" Jess reported excitedly.

Cassia typed again, "Okay alarms disabled in both buildings" she whispered.

"All tangos Go" Nick said into his throat mike. "Cass, we will call you forwards once we have effected entry, next phase" he said

Three black figures ran across the car park towards the walkway to building 5100.

Cassia typed on her laptop and tripped the silent alarm in building 3100.

"Okay we have an alarm, rear door, service entrance, right wing" Jess said into her radio, wait out"

Nick, Mike and Tom crouched down beside the access door. Tom and Mike kept their eyes peeled, as Nick placed the small silver box next to the keypad and pressed a small button on the side of it. The six green lights started flashing through numbers until eventually they stopped. Nick typed in the code and edged the door open, wedging it with his foot.

"Tango 4 Update" Nick whispered into his throat mike

"Two guards just turning the west corner 6 minutes to your local. Interior alarms off.

"Tango 4 advance" Nick said. Cassia closed the lid to her laptop, picked up Nicks coat and ran towards the walkway. As soon as she reached them, Nick slipped through the door and held it open for Cassia, who slid passed him and crouched down in the shadows of the corridor. Tom came through next, quickly followed by Mike, then Nick quietly let the door close, and Cassia reset the door alarm.

"Okay" Nick whispered, "Phase three" Cassia reopened her laptop and after a few second looked up and said, "Okay internal cameras on a loop, internal alarms disabled" she said

"Building two" Nick asked

"Wait out" Cassia said typing on her laptop.

Over on the other side of the campus things were starting to heat up.

"Where are they?" Andrew asked

"They are moving down to level one" Jess said, "Idiots didn't see the laser trips

"Okay teams one and two, go, do not enter the building" Andrew said, and the two teams raced across from their hiding places and hid outside building 3100.

Nick and the team made it down to the giant server room and Mike took up a position on the left side of the door, Tom the right.

"Cass, on me" Nick said

"One second" Cassia said and typed in a few more commands and tripped the next series of laser sensors in building 3100.

"Fuck me these guys are amateurs" Andrew laughed, "They are setting of alarms everywhere" he added.

"Yeah, that doesn't seem right, they can't be that stupid" Jess said nervously

"You gave them too much credit" Andrew laughed, yet Jess couldn't stop the nagging feeling clawing at the edge of her mind, that she was missing something.

"Okay Cass, its over to you" Nick said. Cassia typed again on her laptop and raised the temperature in the sever room 12 degrees, then disabled the retinal and fingerprints scanners.

"Okay we are in; I will need 12 minutes" she said "Hold your breath"

"Okay show time" Nick said, and Cassia typed again on her laptop

Suddenly alarms started sounding across at building 3100

"Go Go, Go," Andrew shouted into his radio leaping to his feet.

"Wait" Jess yelled they have breached the uranium store; the whole floor is radioactive, stop, you will contaminate the whole area" she screamed.

Instantly both swat teams swarmed on the building, covering every window and door, and two 4x4's police vehicles screeched to halt in the front of the building, lights flashing and sirens going full blast.

"Wait out, no one go in the building, secure the outside" A voice screamed over the megaphone as Andrew and Jess packed up their kit and raced down to ground level.

"Okay" Andrew shouted, "No one open those doors, the whole place is hot" he said panting as he ran around the corner to building 3100.

11 minutes and 22 seconds later, Cassia slipped out of the server room, nodded to Nick and the four of them made their way back up to the top floor, then along to the door of the car park, cleaning any sign that they were there as they went.

When they were back in the hillside car park, Cassia took out the laptop typed in a few commands and 6 minutes later, five small drones floated out of the sky and landed in the boot of their minivan.

"Cassia typed another command" then closed her laptop. "10 minutes" she said as she climbed into the back of the minivan.

"Plenty" Nick said, and skill fully steered the minivan out of the car park and onto White Oak Avenue.

As soon as they hit Bethnal road Nick flicked on the lights and pressed down on the accelerator. 10 minutes later they turned on to the 62 towards Knoxville.

At the same time, all the alarms went off in building 3100 and the automatic doors slid open with a loud hiss, sending 2 dozen agents and guards racing for cover.

As they headed towards the 75, just past Knoxville, Cassia opened her laptop and pressed send. The first message went directly to David and contained one simple word, cleaner. The second message landed on a small server at the back of a McCall's diner on fifth street in DC, and the last message went to the cloud. She smiled and closed her laptop, leaned forwards and said, "final phase complete"

Cassia was about to close her laptop, when a single line of text from the data she had downloaded from the supercomputer, flashed across her screen and she felt her blood run cold.

"Nick" Cassia shouted "Red Dog now"

Tuesday 8th July 2025 – Tennessee

Jess sat silently waiting outside the small glass office at the FBI regional office. She didn't need to be inside the office to see that the meeting Andrew was having with his boss, wasn't going well.

"Jesus H Christ, Dale, what part of covert do you not understand?" Chuck Mac Donald screamed

"I have the Governor crawling all over my arse and the fucking Dean of the university is threating a to hit us with a lawsuit, what the hell were you thinking?" he screamed at the man sitting in front of him.

"It was fluid, they were going to steal uranium and I couldn't risk alerting them to our presence, so I called Agent Graham and we set up the sting" Andrew said his face getting redder by the minute.

So, you authorised two major task forces, swat, the local police and campus security without running it up the chain, just to set up a sting and catch this Colletto character, and his team, after they had broken into a granite nuclear reactor and stole uranium. At what point did it dawn on you, that if they had of actually succeeded, we would now have had a major nuclear incident?" Chuck shouted

"I err" Andrew said

"It was a rhetorical question you twat; you were too busy to playing the hero to think about the potential consequences. Fuck is this a family thing?" Chuck interrupted seething.

Andrew sat in silence, he had learnt a long time ago, that when his boss was on one, it was best to keep your mouth shut, until he was finished

"Why the hell didn't you just pick them up, before they broke in? that would have been the logical choice?" Chuck screamed, and this time paused and waited for an answer.

"We needed to be sure, catch them in the act" Andrew said defensively.

"But you didn't did you, instead of staying under the radar like you were told, you lit up the campus like a fucking Christmas day parade. When the campus team were finally allowed back into the building, 4 hours later, nothing had been touched, all the alarms were working, and this mystery man Colletto was nowhere to be seen" Chuck screamed.

"But the doors opened, and the alarms went off" Andrew protested.

"The bloody alarms went off, because the doors opened, there was a fault in the door system, their tech team confirmed it, they also said that no other alarms in the building had been tripped like you claimed" Chuck shouted, his face getting redder by the minute.

"Colletto and his team were definitely there" Andrew protested. Then a thought hit him, "Christ it must have been a decoy, they hit another building" he added

"Give it up, you moron, I have already checked, no other building has reported any intrusion or security leaks" Chuck said menacingly, and Andrew felt his heart sink.

"But they were in Knoxville, I know it, we have been watching them, I have proof" Andrew persisted and pressed the button on his iPad, instantly the screen lit up, and the cameras in the bedrooms filled the screen "there that is their rooms" he said desperately searching for signs of them.

His boss went silent. "I read that particular gem in your report" he growled in a low voice "So you put an illegal surveillance on three rooms at the Comfort inn, in Knoxville, and when I checked the rooms and their occupants, 412 was registered to a couple from Des Moines, 413 and 414 were registered to two delegates that were attending an energy convention at the National institute. In fact, I had the whole register check for the past three days, there is no mention of Nick Colletto, Mike Barnard, Tom Clarke or a Cassia Nilsson" Chuck said angrily "You and your bloody team have been spying on civilians" he added

"But they were there, I swear it, Jess will back me up" Andrew protested

"I will get to her in a minute" Chuck screamed, "Now I personally selected you for this mission, as it was delicate, and I trusted you to keep it under the radar. I even agreed that you could have your bit of skirt from the UK, to help you. But the first thing you did, instead of tracking down this Betsi computer, was revisit an old family vendetta against Nilsson and Colletto and start a fucking media circus" Chuck screamed.

"But he was there, and Nilsson has history with Betsi" Andrew cried

"And you are sticking to that story, are you?" Chuck asked quietly and Andrew got the distinct impression he was missing something.

"He was, I swear on it" Andrew protested.

"Then genius, tell me, how come there is video footage of Clarke, Barnard and Colletto, at McCall's diner on fifth street in DC, 700 miles away at exactly the same time he was supposed to be filling his pockets with uranium in Tennessee?" Chuck shouted, turning his computer screen around so Andrew could see it. Andrew stared in disbelief at the screen.

"I err, it must be fake" he said

"Look at the dam time and date stamp at the bottom of the screen you moron. For fuck sake man take your dick out of that brit and do your fucking job" Chuck shouted

Andrew lowered his head, "So I am still on the case?" he said quietly

"If it was up to me, I would have kicked your arse back to where it came from, however I got two calls this morning. The first from the Head of MI5 in the UK, who personally called me this morning, he was not best pleased and wanted to know why his agent, who was also supposed to be under cover, is now the poster girl in the fucking media, and the second was from the president's Chief of Staff, they don't want excuses, they want results, and you are all I have got, so do me a favour, stop fucking about, and find this bloody computer, now get the fuck out of here" Chuck screamed.

Andrew leapt to his feet, the meeting was obviously over however just as he reached the door and was about to leave. Chuck called after him.

"Dale, if I get the slightest hint of you wasting time chasing Clarke, Colletto or any of his imaginary crew, I will personally kick your arse into the nearest penitentiary and throw the key away and de-port your tart back to the UK, got it?" Chuck growled.

Andrew nodded "Got it" he said quietly

"What gives Cass" Nick said pulling the Minivan over to the side of the road.

"She has being trying to hack back into Red Dog; we need to get back now" Cassia said.

Nick made a couple of quick calls then closed his phone.

"Nick, can you get us to Arnold air force base within the hour?" he asked. "I can get us all on the 5am flight to the Military and Family readiness centre in Anchorage, its only cargo, but it will get us there" Tom said.

Nick did a U turn and floored the accelerator and 46 minutes later Tom was showing his ID at the gate of Arnold Air Force base.

11 hours later, the Lockheed C5 galaxy touched down on the tarmac in Anchorage.

Chapter Nine
A snake in the garden in Eden.

David had gotten Cassia's message and with a little help from Katie, they had arranged to get a connecting flight to Ted Stevens airport and at 9pm local time David was waiting on the tarmac of Red Dog in the 4 x 4 as the Cessna touched down.

As soon as Cassia parked the Cessna in the hanger she leapt out, gave David a quick hug and got into the front seat of the 4 x 4.

"Whats the rush" David asked

"Can't talk now, I need to get to the house urgently" Cassia said, hurry the others along. David looked at Nick who shrugged his shoulders

"I dunno mate, she has had her nose stuck in her computer since we took off, something about Betsi hacking back into Red Dog, that is all she said"

"Right" David said looking at Cassia who had gotten out her laptop again and was typing away again.

As soon as they reached the house Cassia disappeared into the mission control closing the door behind her.

"Right" Nick said quickly "Okay briefing, in the den, 10 minutes, David, can you get Robert and Katie" Nick asked.

An hour into the de-brief Cassia burst into the den "Okay I need to tell you all something" Cassia said then realised that Sanjay and Sanvia were missing, "David can you get Sanjay and Sanvia are here" she asked

"Right so when I connected with the supercomputer, I ran my analysis programme, to detect whether Betsi had connected with it or not" Cassia said

"And had it" Nick asked,

"I am afraid so, 7 hours before we got there, so before I put the block in place, I thought I would check to see what she had been up too" Cassia explained. "The first thing I did was run a trace programme to see if I could see where she had been" Cassia said

"And had she been to any of the others?" David asked nervously, Cassia sighed and looked at them.

"All of them, they are all looped together" Cassia said solemnly

"So why hasn't she done anything?" Nick asked

"Well, that is what I wanted to know, so I dug a little deeper that is when I found it, her plan" Cassia said. "I know what she is up to, I know what protocol zero is" Cassia explained.

"Go on" Sanvia said "what is protocol zero?"

Cassia took a deep breath, "Well Betsi's base protocol is too preserve human life, and protocol zero removes all her restrictions, it basically lets her decided how to best preserve human life" Cassia said

"Well, that is a good thing, isn't it?" Robert asked

"Normally I would say yes, when there is a human to administer the checks and balances, however as I said the decision-making process is now down to Betsi. Edward basically gave her free reign. Now there are four other major projects that Betsi had been involved with. The first was supporting Edward and his work on the committee, the second one, we know about and that is the Genome editing programme, the nanite programme and the last one, she was the main computer Edward used for his climate modelling analysis" Cassia explained and watched as it suddenly dawned on Sanvia face.

"God no" Sanvia said alarmed

"Look I don't mean to sound stupid but what does all this mean?" Sarah asked looking at the others for support

"Okay let me explain" Cassia said "Betsi gets to decided how to preserve the human race and her only terms of reference are climate change, the Committee, nanites and genome editing, so that is what she is basing her plan on" Cassia said, and before anyone could respond, she added "So basically the world is overpopulated, the gap between rich and poor is growing and based on the climate change information, two thirds of the world will become uninhabitable within the next 10 to 15 years. Therefore, in Betsi's world the only logical solution is to trim the population, level up the financial playing field, and distribute the wealth evenly, and that is precisely what she is planning to do" Cassia said, "Her plan is to cull the populous by 70% and decimate the financial markets," Cassia added

"Fuck" Nick said stunned "but that is crazy" he added

"Not really when you think about it, taking out all the moral implications, which of course Betsi would, it is the only logical solution" Sanvia said "Less people means less greed, therefore equals more resources, ergo those that are left have a better chance of survival. Also, less people polluting the planet means more chance the planet will survive" Sanvia said

"But that would require millions of people to be exterminated, and I can't see people giving up their wealth, never going to happen" Tom stuttered

"Wait, so how is she going to do it?" Nick asked suddenly as a cold chill bubbled inside him.

"Well first she is going to release a newer more updated version of a biological corona virus, basically this new version will wipe out the weak and the elderly, with no chance of a vaccine. As we already know, the last one brought most countries, and their economies to their knees, which will happen again, but this time it will be worse. Once the countries are on their knees, then she is going to crash any of the remaining financial systems that are left, and redistribute the wealth evenly, to any survivors. Then through infecting the global water supplies, she is going to distribute genetically modified genome cocktails via nanites and enhance the organic human forms that are left, making the organic matter less susceptible to illness and disease, as well as increase the human life span and finally, the same water supply will be used to regulate the population, birth control etc" Cassia explained.

"Jesus Christ this is genocide on a massive scale" Robert shrieked

Everyone sat listening trying to distil what they had just heard until David finally stood up

"Bloody hell that is madness, we can't let her do it" he said shaking with anger

"Look I get it" Nick said "Your pissed that she is using your research in her evil plan, but mate, you only worked on it, to save people, not kill them, everyone knows that what I don't get Cass, is why you needed to come back to Red Dog so urgently, surely we should be out there trying to stop her" he added.

"When I downloaded her plan, I also downloaded the statistical analysis data and part of that is where she identifies the risks" Cassia said holding her breath "Look there is no easy way to say this, but she has already identified us, you, me, Tom, all of us, as the biggest risk to her succeeding. She knows about us, she knows we are working together, planning to stop her. So, I needed to get back here and find out if she had broken into our networks" Cassia said.

"And has she?" Katie asked looking around the room.

"Not that I can see, I mean she can't get into Paradise, that has a completely independent network and has a solid faraday shield, also it is not linked to the web. The house, I am not so sure about, the same goes for all our comms, phones, iPads, basically anything that is linked to the web or satellites, she can access and track and use against us. She also has a whole load of data, on the two people that were tracking us in Tennessee, Dale and Craven" Cassia said.

"Fuck, that's it we are screwed, we can't do anything" Nick said.

"Maybe not" Tom suddenly said "Maybe there is a way we can use this to our advantage, think about it" he added getting into his pace.

"When we found out we were being watched in Knoxville, we didn't give up, we used them, we planted fake information, which ended up with them diverting all their resources to the wrong building, making it much easier for us to get into the computer lab" he said, then seeing the confused look on their faces added

"Look I don't know how, but we are smart people, we can work it out. Besides what is the alternative, sit by and let it happen?" he said.

Cassia smiled, "I agree, come on Nick, we beat her once before, we can do it again" she said.

"Fine, on one condition" Nick said

"Go on" Cassia replied,

"Everything is done from Paradise, that is the only way we can be sure she is not looking over our shoulders" he said.

"Agreed" Cassia said "makes sense, and only use the house when we need to connect to the outside world, and strictly no talking about anything when we are here" she added.

David felt an uneasy feeling brewing inside him as a dark thought flooded into his mind. They were wrong, they hadn't beaten Betsi before, in fact Betsi had beaten them.

When you believe that someone, or in Betsi's case something is watching you, the natural response is to guard against it, freeze change your behaviour and for the next few minutes that is exactly what they all did, unconsciously changing their behaviour, until finally Sanvia took out the organic pencil, she always kept in her green dungaree front pocket and scribbled on the napkin in front on her and passed it to Tom, who was sat on her right. *'Paradise now, don't say a word pass to the right'*

Tom gave the slightest of nods, passed the napkin to David, got to his feet and walked out of the den to joined Sanvia in the rail shed. Two minutes later everyone was in there, waiting in total silence for the flatbed to arrive.

Once everyone was in paradise, they made their way to the conference room and sat around the table waiting for Nick and Cassia too arrive. As soon as the rail cart had stopped, they had taken off for mission control.

"Okay" Nick said walking into the conference room "First things first, no mobiles allowed in paradise, now update on California, where are we?"

"The Lawrence Livermore is doable, not easy, but doable" Katie said

"What do you propose?" Nick asked

"Night op, two teams, distraction like you did in Tennessee, if it worked once then it will work again" Craig said interrupting

"And what about you Katie, do you have any ideas?" Nick asked.

"First we set up Alten as a student and rig it that he has time on the open grid, he uses the relay tech we used on the committee to link into Cassia, we set up a distraction whilst he is on the computer, Cass links in and does her thing, we walk out" Katie said, and Craig grunted.

"Okay gaps and holes" Nick said

"The whole thing is full of em" Craig growled, "First, what if Alten gets tagged, security is super tight, they ain't just going to let anyone on the computer" Craig snipped

"That is exactly why we can't go in, heavy handed, the University runs *collaborate* programmes, with other uni's, government departments etc, in the light of the Committee ousting, everyone is grappling for answers, so we set Alten up with a fake ID and background, as a top analyst working for Homeland Security. We say that he needs to run National Security scenarios, in light of what happened, with Craig and Josh as military escorts.

To give Alten the time he needs, Akeem and I will act as an LA Time s journalists, investigating leaks at the site. I have issued an interview request with Annie Kersting, the University Relationship and Science Education Director, she has already agreed, and I just need to firm up a date" Katie said

"It's too simple, they will see right through it" Craig snapped.

"Tom thoughts" Nick asked.

Tom looked at Craig and Katie and smiled. "Okay well there is merits for both, but providing you can set the back story, I would have to go with Katie, there is less risk" then seeing Craigs face added "Look a military style op, would work too, but after what happened in Tennessee, there is a risk that they will be watching for that. From what I understand, Tennessee turned out to be a media circus, and we had a tail, and although we covered our backs, they will be spooked, so a soft door approach may work better" Tom concluded.

"Anyone else, thoughts?" Nick asked.

"Well, I think we got lucky in Tennessee, I am not saying we wouldn't have sorted it out, but If Nick hadn't of spotted our tail, then things may have turned out differently. What I do know is that the people watching us, were professionals and probably had the security services behind them. That means they are on to us and watching. If we go in military style, they will be ready this time. They won't be expecting us to walk in the front door, invited, and I am sure I can set Alten up with everything we need. So, I am voting for Katies plan" Cassia said

"Well, no surprise there" Craig muttered.

"Craig" Tom growled "Everyone gets a voice here" he snapped.

"Okay let's vote" Nick said, "All in favour of Craigs plan" Nick said three hands went up, Craig's, Josh's and Akeem's. "Okay Katie's plan" Nick said, and 8 hands instantly went up.

"Okay, Katies plan it is" Nick said and seeing the look on Craigs face, he could tell that that didn't go down too well.

"Right" Nick said taking a long look at Craig, "Anyway, taking into account what we have just learned about Betsi and her plan, Cass and I have a suggestion" Nick said and looked at Cassia

"Yes, well one thing we know is that she is going to be tracking us, and taking into account what happened in Tennessee, we think she will also be tracking Dale and Craven. Now the problem is whatever we do. We can be sure that Dale and Craven will try to keep tabs on us, and whilst we believe that we can keep ahead of anything they try, there is a chance that they could alert Betsi to our actions. Therefore, we are going to pick them up, explain the score and see if we can work together" Cassia said

"What" Mike shouted. "You wanna bring them in, tell them what we are up to, that is just stupid" he added.

"I don't know as much" Tom said "Think about it, they are going to be tailing us anyway, and Cassia is right, with them on our backs there is a good chance they could give us away. But with them on our side, with their resources, it would really help" Tom said

"Why would they want to help?" Akeem asked

"Basically, they want the same thing we do, they just don't know about it yet" Nick said.

"Yeah, but I can't see them agreeing to it" Josh said

"You seem to think that they will have a choice" Nick said smiling.

"Okay, right you lot focus on California, Tom you and I can make a start on picking up Dale and Craven" Nick said.

"I need to get back to the medical unit" Sanjay said "but before I go" he said and got up and handed out, green pills to, Nick, Sarah, Katie, Cassia, Robert and David, "Your next weeks' supply" he said and "they are day specific, so take them in the right order" he added.

When Sanjay had gone, Tom sat watching them all taking their pills like good patients.

"Nick, I don't want to stick my nose in, but you, okay?" he asked

"What, yeah, no were fine, they are just vitamins, Sanjay has got us all on a health kick" Nick said laughing.

"Tom, I think you and I need to take a trip to DC and meet with our new friends, Cass you up for it" Nick said laughing

Cassia smiled, "I love DC, so many happy memories and opportunities" she said tapping lightly on her laptop.

An hour later back at the rail yard a figure stood in the shadows, reached up behind the control panel and retrieved a mobile phone, flipped it open typed a text and pressed send.

3500 miles away on the Oak forest Pac, computer in the university of Tsukuba in Tokyo, Japan, a stream of data flashed momentarily across the screen. Betsi analysed the data and sent a single line of text back *'Message received, instructions to follow'*

The recipient read the text, deleted it, closed the phone and put it back behind the control panel, in the rail shed.

Back in Tennessee Andrew walked out of the office and signalled to Jess to follow him out of the building.

"Didn't take it too well" Jess said smiling once they got back into the car

"They took us for mugs, they must have known we were there, they set us up" Andrew said sourly "Now Chuck, wants us to leave them alone"

"And do what?" Jess asked

"It doesn't matter, I know they are up to their necks in it, they are linked in with this Betsi, and I am going to find out how, we are just going to play it carefully" Andrew growled

Chapter Ten
Knock out a Rhino

Wednesday 9th July 2025 – Washington DC

When the meeting broke up, Cassia split her time between helping Katie set up her back story and getting Alten a pass into the university and putting together a plan for Washington.

They had taken the red eye from Anchorage to DC and Nick had arranged a car for them at the airport for them, then onto to the Carriage hill warehouse.

As soon as they got inside the warehouse Cassia logged onto Nicks network.

"Okay, they picked up our scent, they have just landed in DC" Cassia said smiling.

"Right, we clear?" Nick asked

"Crystal" Tom said.

"I will get the kit, and then we will get going" Nick said

"Ready Cass?" Nick asked

"Ready" she answered and pressed send on the email she was writing.

On the way out of the airport towards the car park, Andrew felt his secure mobile phone vibrate in his pocket. He flicked it open and pressed his forefinger on the small grey pad and the screen lit up. He selected the small envelope icon and read the email.

"Fuck" he said aloud and seeing the look on Jesses face he handed her his phone

Jess read the message it was from the NSA

From: C Donald To: A J Dale Status: Encrypted

Subject: Urgent

Andrew get your arse over to K Str NE, REF: strong intel suggests next target. Trouble in Paradise. Covert, don't fuck up

"Does that mean what I think it means?" Jess asked.

"Yeah" Andrew said stunned

"Is it genuine?" Jess asked

"It came on my secure phone, it is encrypted with the secure code that only Chuck and I know, so yeah its genuine" Andrew said

"Okay so what is at K Str NE"? Jess asked

"That is the office of Homeland security" Andrew said then added "No surely not"

"Don't be stupid that is one of the most secure buildings in the USA, they would never get away with it" Jess said incredulously

"They are not going for Homeland Security, look at the text it says REF, there is a reason that the letters are capitalised and reversed it means that they next target is the Federal Energy Regulatory Commission, its opposite to Homeland" Andrew said

"Did you see the part about *Trouble in Paradise?*" Andrew asked

"Yeah, I was going to ask about that next" Jess said

"Well, that is what Chuck always says, it means he suspects that they have a mole, someone on the inside of the organisations, that's how they are going to get in"

"Who?" Jess asked surprised

"That's it, he doesn't know, but If Chuck thinks there is, then it is going to be someone high up. Christ we are going to have to tread really carefully, there is no way they are going to get one over on me again, this time we are a step ahead" Andrew said

"Okay, let's get over there, I know the area well, we are going to set up surveillance, this time we record it, then we take them down, you up for it?" Andrew asked menacingly.

"Try and stop me, I can't wait to see them bastards in cuffs" Jess said excitedly.

"I tagged the message they have picked it up" Cassia said.

"Are they buying it?" Tom asked

"I hope so, I went to a lot of trouble to hack into Homeland, and Chuck Donald's email and texts, the algorithm rated the words and came up with a 98.4% chance that this was most likely the words he would use, but the only way to tell is to take a look" Cassia said firing up the desktop.

"Okay" she said when she was ready. Right, they landed at Ronald Reagan, an hour ago, so here is the tracker Nick planted on their SUV. See here it comes they are on the 365 just going over the Potomac, they are passing the Capitol building. Okay crossing E Str NW, passing the Dubliner Restaurant on Massachusetts avenue. Turning left, now passing the Smithsonian Postal, now turning right, now left onto First and NE. Now let's see, how long it takes them to pass the FER" Cassia said

"Hey, it looks like they have slowed" Tom said

"Yeah, Nick reckons the first thing they will do is take a drive by, then circle back around and come back down again, after that they will find a place to lay up and keep eyes on" Cassia said, "Here, they turned left on K St, then again on North Capitol and back, around on H street, any second now they will be back on First, and" Cassia said pausing "They turned left onto First" she announced.

"They have taken the bait" Cassia announced

"Good, stay on them until they stop, then let us know where" Nick said

"Got it" Cassia shouted 10 minutes later "They are in 77 K street parking" she announced. "Camera coming through now" she added, and an image of Andrew Dale and Jess Craven filled the screen sitting in their SUV at the entrance to the car park.

"Okay, you ready?" Nick asked looking at the other two.

"Let's go, Cass stay on them, I want to know if that vehicle moves, Tom you got David's cocktail?" Nick asked

"In here" Tom said patting his bag

Before they had left Nick had gotten David to mix them a cocktail of carfentanil and fentanyl, and put it in one of the atomisers, with a stark warning that they should wear masks, as it was strong enough to take out a rhinoceros.

"Okay ETA 40 minutes, if they move, we will have to reset, if not, we need to be ready to move as soon as we get there" Nick said and for the rest of the journey they sat in silence each going over their part in the plan.

Nick steered the panel van, with the AT& T logo up the ramp into the 77-k street, car park, paid the $12 dollar charge and parked on the lower level, then got out of the van, picked up a small bag, adjusted his AT&T uniform and walked back out of the car park.

When he got to Phillips takeaway, just outside the car park. Like he expected, as it was 12:30pm, the takeaway was packed. Nick bought a chicken club, paid and asked to use the bathroom, taking his sandwich with him. Once inside he found an empty cubicle, stripped placing the AT&T uniform back inside the small bag, turned the grey trousers inside out revealing blue jeans, pulled out the Redskins jacket, blond wig, and baseball cap, took his shades out of his pocket and checked his appearance as he stepped out of the cubicle. Once outside the takeaway, he crossed over First, circled round behind the MOI office furniture shop and came round on the back of 77 K str car park, being careful to keep out of sight on any cameras.

"Okay where Cass" Nick said as soon as he got back in the van.

"Second level, far east corner" Cassia said

Cassia took the small drone out of her pack, opened the back of the van held out her hand and pressed the button on the iPad. The tiny drone took to the air.

Cassia guided it up to the second level and floated it across to the far east corner, stopping 60 ft short of the black SUV parked there, and landed it on top of a large black pipe at the far end of the car park level two.

"Eyes in place" She said

"Zoom" Nick ordered and Cassia put her forefinger and thumb in the centre of the screen and opened them out. The HD image filled the screen. Inside the black SUV was just one figure, Andrew Dale, he was staring intently down at something in his lap.

"What's he doing?" Cassia asked, "And where is the other one?" she added

"Well either she has her head in his lap, or he is staring at his laptop, and she is not there" Nick said then added "We wait"

"Maybe we should recce outside, see if we can spot her" Tom said

"No, by the way he is looking at his lap, I think they have already set up cameras covering the building and surrounding area. In fact, I would be surprised if they didn't clock our van coming in, which is why I had to fake the trip to the takeaway just to be on the safe side" Nick said

"Okay we have movement" Cassia said, and all eyes focussed on the screen, just as Jess returned to the black SUV carrying what looked sandwiches and coffee.

"We have the full set" Nick said, "Cass are you ready?" Nick asked

Cassia took out a small remote car with a tiny silver box strapped to its roof, from her pack. Then she pulled up the trap door in the fake floor of the van and set it down on the tarmac.

"We are go" she said, as the car raced off up the ramp to the next level. Once it got to the second level, she guided it towards the black SUV and then stopped it directly underneath it.

"Ready" she said in a quiet voice. "Okay, when you see us reach the second floor, activate, that will give us about 8 seconds to reach the vehicle" Nick said, then added "Ready Tom?"

Tom pulled his mask down and nodded. Then he and Nick slipped out of the van, ducking between vehicles and keeping to the sides of the garage, they made their way to the second level.

"Tango one to tango two, any movement" Nick whispered into his throat mike.

"Tango two, all quiet on the western front" Cassia said, and Nick winced, although he loved Cassia, he hated it when she went off radio protocol.

Cassia watched the screen carefully holding her breath, then at the bottom of the screen two black shapes appeared, crouched down beside the wall of the ramp"

Tango two to tango one, we have visual, activating in 3, 2 1" Cassia said

Underneath the black SUV the little red light on the silver box, flicked to green and several things happened at once. All the doors on the SUV locked, the electronics in the vehicle suddenly went dead, including the air con and Andrew dropped his coffee into his lap, causing him to scream, quickly followed by a scream from Jess as two figures dressed all in black in ski masks, appeared at the side windows, with drills in their hands.

"Shoot them" Jess screamed

"I can't, the glass is bullet proof, all it will do is send the bullet whizzing around the car" Andrew shouted

"Well get us the fuck out of here" Jess screamed.

"What the hell do you think I am trying to do" Andrew shouted, turning the key on the ignition "The fucking electrics are dead"

They are drilling into the back windows" Jess screamed clawing at the door handle trying to get out.

The moment Andrew turned around, he saw it and instantly he knew there was nothing he could do, as a fine mist started to fill the inside of the car.

"It took less than a minute before the two occupants passed out.

"Tango one to Tango two, release the car" Nick ordered.

There was a loud click, then Nick and Tom, wrenched open the doors to the SUV and heaved the two bodies out, hauled them over their shoulders and ran back to the van.

Once inside they plasticuffed the two bodies, tied them to the restraint harnesses on the walls of the van and wrapped blankets around them, cushioning their heads, then set off back to Carriage hill.

Three hours later, Jess slowly opened her eyes and looked up at the top of the black cage, trying to gather her thoughts. In the cage next to her was Andrew, he was already awake and pacing back and forth.

"Where are we?" Jess asked groggily.

"I have no idea, but looking at the light coming from that skylight, I would say we have been here about 3 hours" Andrew said.

"How the hell can you tell that?" Jess asked in amazement.

Andrew drew a deep breath, two ways really, okay we were in the car park around midday, therefore the sun is high in the sky, now it is at the three-o clock position in the sky, so therefore its around 3pm" He said and watched as Jess stared up at the window, "and I have also just checked my watch" he added laughing

"God you're a twat" Jess said, "How can you be so bloody happy, we have been kidnapped" she screamed.

"Okay, so yes we have been kidnapped, but they don't want to hurt us, or rob us, so it's either for ransom or information, but I suspect it's purely information" Andrew said

"What makes you so sure?" Jess asked.

"Okay, first of all, I still have my wallet, watch, and jewellery on, which I am guessing, that if it was money orientated, would be gone. Secondly, when I woke up, I didn't have any scratches or grazes, there was water and snacks left within reach of the cage, therefore unless they are very caring kidnappers, I believe that they do not intend to hurt us. Lastly, if they have gone to this much trouble, they know who we are and that there is no chance that either of our governments would give a toss about us, so I reckon they want information" Andrew concluded.

"And you would be right, well almost" Nick said stepping into the room.

"You" Jess shouted, "You fucking kidnapped us, I don't get it, whatever you think you are doing, it won't work, they are onto you" Jess shouted.

"If by them you mean Mr Charles Macdonald, then I am afraid that you are mistaken" Nick said sweetly smiling

"You sent that email, didn't you?" Andrew said wisely, as it suddenly dawned on him.

"Yes" Nick said simply

"Fucking bravo, that was very convincing, now I take it that you brought us here to tell us something" Andrew said.

"Or he could want to find out what we know" Jess said cautiously

"I doubt it, if they have the tech and skills to break into Homeland, hack the Directors email, then fake one to me, I think they already know, we are tracking Betsi" Andrew said.

Nick smiled, "Well worked out, now we can do this one of two ways, either you can join us in the briefing room, have some tea and listen to what we have to tell you, or we can come in here, not have tea and you still get to listen, and before you think about trying to escape, there are three of us and you two are wearing tags" Nick said.

Instantly Andrew checked his ankle, there was a thick grey band tightly wrapped around it with a flashing red light, similar to the ones you see on prisoners.

"They are rigged with proximity alarms and packed with 3 ounces of C4, the moment those light go green, boom, and one of us has the trigger, but which one?" Nick said, "So what will it be tea and a chat outside, or shall we come in too you" Nick added.

"Well, I for one fancy a cup of tea" Andrew said, and Nick smiled

"And you Ms Craven?" Nick asked. Jess winced at the sound of her name.

"Fine, tea it is" she snarled.

Nick opened the cage doors and escorted them to the briefing room.

Cassia and Tom got to their feet as their guests came in.

"Please sit" Nick said pointing to the two empty chairs.

"Now tea or coffee?" Cassia chirped cheerily as Andrew and Jess took their seats.

"Tea" they both said at the same time.

"So, Colletto what's this all about, you have gone to a lot of trouble to get us here, so tell me why?" Andrew asked

Nick nodded to Cassia, and she turned around her computer screen.

"Okay, so I take it you know all about me, so you know that I am a hacker and a pretty good one at that. Well, my partner and I David Carmichael worked with Edward Holloway in Valencia, that is where we met Nick and his team, in fact" Cassia laughed "I actually hired them to kidnap David, but that is another story" she added seeing the look on Nicks face.

"Okay where was I, yes that is where we first came across his supercomputer Betsi, well long story short, we escaped, thought Holloway was dead, then when our good friend Robert Johnson" Cassia said

"The ex-British Prime Minister?" Jess shouted, interrupting

"The very same, well when he got elected on to the committee, with the help of Katie, who was working for the them and Sanvia, who was already on it, we exposed the committee and their plans. That is when we discovered that both Betsi and Edward Holloway were very much alive" Cassia explained.

"Then Holloway abducted David, planned to wipe out humanity with deadly nanites, but we stopped him and thought he was dead until General Markham told us he escaped, B after which he disappeared. Then we had a visit, from Tom and his team, they popped in for a chat, they wanted to know all about Betsi, they told us Holloway was dead and about protocol zero and asked if we would help finding out what that was about. We had some theories but needed proof" Cassia explained.

"That was what Tennessee was all about, but you must have got cold feet, because nothing happened" Andrew said

"No, that is what we wanted you to think, we led you to believe that we were attacking the graphite reactor and whilst you were busy setting a trap for us there, we were actually breaking into the computer room and servers" Cassia admitted honestly.

"I knew it, I knew you were up to something, there had to be a reason why you were there" Andrew said

"Well, you were right, but as far as anyone can tell we were never there" Nick said

"We needed to find out if Betsi had been there, you see there are eight of these super computers in the world and we believe that she is connected to all of them" Cassia explained.

"Why, it doesn't make any sense?" Jess asked.

"It does if you understand her protocols. So, her primary directive is to preserve human life, and protocol zero, well that is basically Edward removing restrictions and letting her decided how to do that" Cassia said.

"Well, that is a good thing, isn't it?" Jess asked

"Depends on what you believe, you see, when taken in the context of the other programmes she worked on, genetic engineering in Valencia, committee work with Edward, nanites and climate change analysis for the committee, then it throws it into a different light. That is what we suspected and why we need to find out what she was up to" Cassia said

"And did you?" Andrew asked.

"Yes" Tom said quietly

"Well, are you going to share that with us?" Jess demanded.

Nick looked up "there is no easy way to say this, she wants to trim the population, level up the financial playing field, and distribute the wealth evenly, that is precisely what she is planning to do" Nick explained

"I don't believe a word of it, that is ridiculous, impossible" Jess shouted

"Yeah, I thought you might say that, so here" Cassia said, "This is the stuff we downloaded from the Tennessee computer" she added, and the computer screen lit up.

For the next 10 minutes Andrew and Jess read through the data, and checks that had been undertaken to verify it, pausing occasionally to say "Down" as they got to the end of the page.

When they had finished, they looked like someone had drained all the blood out of their faces.

"So, you weren't making it up, it's true, fuck" Andrew said staring at the screen

"Looks that way, we will need to check a couple more computers, and we have a pretty good idea of how she is planning to do it, but yes, it's true" Nick said solemnly

"Okay, what I don't get is why are you telling us, I suppose you want to us to run it up the chain" Andrew said

"Fuck no, the moment you do that its game over" Nick growled. "Look the reason we wanted to tell you is two fold. One, I reckon that you are trying to find out what Betsi and this protocol zero means, and that's why you are tagging us, and secondly by you doing that, we run the risk of you alerting Betsi to our presence and her escalating the plan" Nick said.

"Look believe it or not we can keep secrets, especially something like this and we can also bring a lot of resource to bear" Andrew said.

Cassia smiled "Really, I managed to hack into Homeland, jack your bosses email and send you a message that invariably meant got you kidnapped. We could have taken out that reactor, or planted a bug in the supercomputer, now if we can do that, imagine what a super intelligent AI can do, especially one that is monitoring all communications and satellites. So, tell me, taking into account her plan, would you take that risk, no, the circle needs to be tight and need to know only basis" Cassia said.

"So, what do you want us to do?" Jess said.

"Nothing, go about your business as normal, try and track down Betsi, but not us, or she will soon find out what we are up to, even I can't keep us totally hidden" Cassia explained.

"And if we refuse, you'll what, kill us?" Jess spat.

"No, we will let you go and release what we have just shown you on the web, there will be widespread panic, anarchy and more rioting than there is now" Nick said

"You wouldn't?" Andrew exclaimed shocked

"Look Mr Dale, we are only getting involved with this, because we think we may be able to stop her, but if it gets out, then as I said it is game over, then we can do nothing. So, we will simply go home, and leave you to get on with it" Nick explained.

"And I will report back to my bosses, everything that has transpired" Tom added "so it's your call" he added

"Hey, do you realise that you have just got a new message" Jess said pointing to Cassia's computer

Cassia clicked off the data screen and on to the small envelope icon at the bottom of the screen. In the two seconds it took her to read the message she felt her heart plummet

Chapter Eleven
Chuck away

Wednesday 9th July 2025 – Los Angeles

"Nick, they have got Katie" Cassia cried

"What, who has?" Nick asked

"I don't know, but I have just received a message from Akeem, apparently they were waiting for them at Livermore, everything was going fine, he watched Craig and Josh walk out the building, then a few moments later Alten and Katie were being led away and put in the back of a car" Cassia said

"Fuck" Nick growled "We need to get down there now" he added.

"I would suggest that that is not the best idea" Andrew said smoothly

"What, fuck you, we are not leaving one of ours" Nick started then glanced at Tom "Two of ours behind" Nick growled

"I get that, but if you're planning of that mission, is anything like the rest of your work, then I would be questioning how they knew you were coming, and what's more, if I was in their shoes, I would be waiting for you" Andrew suggested

"Well, I am not leaving them" Nick shouted.

"Nick, calm down" Tom said, "I think Andrew is right and we are not going to help them by getting picked up ourselves, we need to think this through and start by finding out exactly what went down" Tom said

There is nothing about them on the net, Homeland, FBI, whoever has got them has kept the whole thing offline" Cassia said

"Maybe I could help?" Andrew offered

"Let me make a phone call to my boss, if they have been picked up by us, then he will know" Andrew offered

"Yeah right, and then suddenly the place is swarming with SWAT, and we all get picked up" Nick spat "Nice try, but no" he added

"Firstly, two things, the first is now that I have met you, seen the information and understand what you are up to, I want to help, not stop you. I believe you and your team maybe the only way of stopping this Betsi thing. Secondly if as, you say I let them know where we are and Swat raid the place, you still have this" Andrew said lifting up his trouser leg "you can still blow me to pieces, something I think you would easily be able to do before you get captured" Andrew offered.

Nick looked at the other two, and both of them nodded.

"Fine, but if you screw me, it will be the last thing you do" he growled and passed him back his phone.

Andrew opened it, pressed his forefinger on the pad and waited for the screen to light up. Then selected the one of the only two numbers on the call list and held it to his ear.

"Hands free" Nick growled.

Andrew put the phone on the table and waited for it to be answered

"Dale, where the fuck are you, we have picked up Rayner and Hunt in Livermore, they were posing as students and reporters" Chuck said

"I am aware of that sir; I am currently in Washington DC following a lead" Andrew said

"You better not still be searching for Clarke, or I will have your bollocks on a plate" Chuck barked

"No, that ship has sailed. However, I do need to meet with you face to face, there have been some developments that I think you should know about" Andrew said. Nick grabbed the phone and was about to throw it across the room, but Andrew held up his hand.

"Do you want your people back or not?" he asked

"Fine" Nick growled slamming the phone back on the table.

"What the fuck are you doing, answer me?" Chuck snapped

"Sorry, bad line, what did you ask?" Andrew said politely

"What developments?" Chuck growled

"That I can't say, perhaps we could meet at the place where you met your wife, tonight at 10:30pm" Andrew said

It must have dawned on Chuck that there was something up, because all he said was "Fine, I will be there"

"Boss, on your own, please" Andrew said

"Alright, but you had better not be jerking my chain" Chuck said and cut the phone off.

"What the fuck was all that about?" Tom asked before Nick could say anything.

"Okay the first thing my boss said was that they had picked up your friends. Now there is no way he is going to give them up. So, I thought that if we meet with him and you guys show him what you showed me, well then everything changes, at least that way you have a chance of seeing your friends again" Andrew said.

"Do you think we are stupid, the moment we show our faces he is going to have us picked up, he will have agents waiting for us at your rendezvous, wherever that is, and that was probably a secret code" Nick shouted.

"The place is green lot parking off Martin Luther King Jnr Boulevard in LA. His wife backed into his car, I was with him in the passenger seat, no one else knows the story, he swore me to secrecy. I am thinking that it's what two and a half hours to LA from here. Its now, 16:30, that would give you at least 3 hours to scope the rendezvous and check if it is a trap, plus you still have Jess, and we both have the tag. Look what else do you want, it's all I could come up with at short notice" Andrew snapped

"Nick, I don't see we have much of a choice, the moment he called his boss, I tapped into his email and mobile, there hasn't been any calls or messages sent. When we get there, I will continue tracing and tracking, including radio wave bands, if it is a trap then the only way, they will only be able to communicate is face to face, or within eyeline. I say we go" Cassia said

"Fine" Nick said "but I don't like it, I don't like bringing yet another person in, it's too risky" he added.

"I agree, but we have no idea how long we have before Betsi starts her programme, and time is running out. So maybe we have to take a risk, look let's just see what the man has to say, they have no evidence against us, and we have done nothing illegal, so if we don't like it, we can just walk away and let them get on with it" Cassia said

"Tom thoughts" Nick asked

"What choice do we have, besides I want to find out how they knew we were coming, something stinks, and I have a sneaking feeling I know what" Tom said looking at Nick

"Yeah, me too, but let's find out" Nick said. Then added "Cass, flights please and a hotel, and car" Nick asked

"Done, Private out of College park, to Van Nuys, in 1 hour, room booked Motel park, on west and 42^{nd,} 27 minutes" Cassia said instantly

"Christ that was quick" Andrew said

"That is what you get when you work with the best. Okay usual kit, personals, full surveillance, night kit, ready to go in 10" Nick barked and there was a flurry of activity, as Nick, Cassia and Tom leapt up from the table, and disappeared into the back room, leaving Andrew and Jess sitting there.

"Hey" Jess whispered, "we can get out of here"

"And do what Jess chase our tails, I reckon that these guys represent our only chance of getting ahead of this thing, if we run, then not only are we fucked" Andrew said holding up his leg, displaying his anklet, "But so is the rest of the world" he added.

"See" Cassia said stepping back from the monitor, "I told you, gut feeling, we can trust them" she added.

"You might" Nick said, "but I won't be happy until I am back in Paradise playing football with Archie" Nick said

"It will be fine" Cassia smiled weakly

Nick opened his phone, dialled a number and waited.

"6, 50, 3 Green lot parking off Martin Luther King Jnr Boulevard in LA, 21:30, RV Menlo" Nick said into the phone then closed it down

"What was that all about?" Tom \sked

Nick smiled "Insurance" he said

It was almost eight pm when they finally arrived at the Motel Park, they hadn't accounted for the rush hour traffic.

Once they had prepared the room, Nick secured Andrew and Jess inside and came back outside

"Right, let's get eyes on" Nick said, and they set off in the direction of the car park.

It was just gone 9pm when Nick was finally satisfied that the car park wasn't being watched and was ready to go back.

"Right let's go get the bait" Nick said, "but first I need to go to school" he added cryptically and set off east along West and 41st place.

Outside of the Menlo Elementary school, on West and 42nd sat a large black SUV with tinted windows. Nick sat back in the shadows and waited, watching closely, his senses on full alert.

"Nick what are we doing here?" Cassia whispered

Nick checked his watch, 21:29hrs, suddenly the driver's door opened in the SUV and a tall well-built man, dressed all in black got out, walked over to the bench twenty feet away from where Nick was hiding, deposited a newspaper on the seat, then walked back towards the van. Nick got up from his hiding spot and met the man halfway back, they exchanged a few words, then the man got back in his van and drove off.

"Ready" Nick said coming back to the spot where Tom and Cassia were hiding

"What the hell was all that about?" Cassia asked

"Like I said, Insurance" Nick said smiling, "Now let's go get our man, Cass, I need someone to keep an eye on Jess, can you run coms from the room" Nick asked

"Fine" Cassia said snippily annoyed that Nick was keeping secrets from her.

Even though it was a July night, the cool wind was unusually, bitterly cold, and Nick pulled up his collar, and pressed the binoculars tighter to his eyes.

He was crouched down behind a dumpster next to the Renyoso Cleaning service building and had eyes on the car park exit. Tom was on the other side at the far end of Goal Keepers Market. From their vantage points they could watch everything that went in and out of the Green Lot car park.

Nick checked his watch, 22:24pm. "Tango one, tango three", update he said

Cassia checked the screens, earlier she had placed six tiny cameras at strategic points all around the car park and on the ground level, where Andrew was now waiting and shivering. She could have easily tapped into the security feeds of the car park, and surrounding streets, but Nick didn't trust the fact that they could have also been hacked, he wanted an independent source. She turned the volume up on the head set and checked the log, nothing

"Tango three, all clear" she said

"Tango one to tango two check" Nick said

"Tango two all clear" Tom said and was about to say something else when Nick interrupted him

"All tango's we have action, one tango, silver Oldsmobile, LA Plates" Nick said, "Cass head up, anything suspicious you call it" Nick said

"Eyes on" Cassia said as she watched the Oldsmobile pull up in a parking spot and as a large silver haired man get out.

"Tangos on the move" Cassia said into the mike

"Eyes on" Nick said as Andrew and Chuck Macdonald exited the car park and made their way across Martin Luther Jnr Boulevard towards him.

"Tango two check" Nick said not taking his eyes of the two men walking towards him,

There was a long pause, Nick drew his weapon and concentrated it on the centre mass of the silver haired man 10 yards in front of him.

"Tango two, all clear" Tom said

"Tango three check" Nick said this time Cassia answered instantly

"All clear" she said.

"All tangos, on our way back" Nick said and stepped out from behind the dumpster just as Andrew and Chuck walked past.

"Keep walking Nick said as his hand folded around the gun in his pocket, "Dale knows where" he added.

Nick flicked open his phone typed '*locale two*' and pressed send, then closed it again, just as Tom came along beside him. One minute later Andrew tapped lightly on the motel room door, and Cassia opened it and all four of them went in.

Nick patted down Chuck, removed his phone and chucked it over to Cassia.

"Alright what the fuck is all this about, and it better be good Dale, or you will be riding a desk for the next ten years" Chuck snarled.

"Please take a seat Mr Macdonald, this will take about half an hour, after which you, Andrew and Jess are free to go, if you wish" Cassia said handing Chuck back his phone.

Chuck sat down and looked at Andrew, shrugged his shoulders and held up his hands.

"Just hear them out boss" Andrew said as Tom cut the plasticuffs on Jesses wrists.
"Bastard" she spat rubbing her sore wrists

Nick positioned himself at the door, nodded at Cassia then kept an eye on what was happening outside, his gun firmly clasped in his hand, in case anyone made a move.

Cassia proceeded to tell Chuck everything they had been up to and everything they knew about Betsi, including Valencia, the Committee, and Climate change. Halfway through when Chuck had protested, she handed him her iPad and waited as he scrolled down the information. Finally, when she had finished Chuck sat in total silence looked up at the others, he looked visibly shaken

"We knew it was up to something I mean protocol zero had to mean something or why would Holloway implement it, in his last dying breath, but we had no idea it would be this. We thought she would be targeting our weapons systems, every government in the world is looking for her" he said "Jesus I have got to tell the President" he added

"No" Andrew shouted much to the surprise of the others "Don't you get it boss, this Betsi thing has eyes and ears everywhere, think about it, If Cassia can break into your personal emails and send me encrypted messages, then what can a supercomputer do, we can't risk it, at the moment. Cassia doesn't think she has got wind of us and what we are doing, but all it would take is one email, one text, or even a misplaced word in a meeting and she would know, and accelerate her plan" Andrew said passionately

"Well, I can't just sit by and wait for it to happen god dammit, millions of lives are at stake here" Chuck shouted.

"Then let them handle it, they are the only ones that know how, and look what they have achieved so far, without them we would still be fumbling around in the dark" Andrew pleaded.

"But they are civilians" Chuck said

"Yeah, civilians that have managed to dupe me twice, hack into Homeland, break into a secure facility in Tennessee, destroy a research facility in Valencia and expose the most secret criminal organisation in the world, and that is only the bits I know about" Andrew said

"Look", Cassia said "If you really think you can handle it, then we are more than happy to walk away and let you take responsibility of saving the world. However, if you want our help then it has to be on our terms" she added

"And what are your terms?" Chuck asked

"First, we want our people back, then everything, and I mean everything has to be on a need-to-know basis and nothing online, whatsoever, the tighter the circle the more chance of success" Cassia said

"But I need to let people know this is bigger than all of us" Chuck protested. Cassia thought for a moment.

"Fine, but you give me the names and only when I give the green light can you bring them in" Cassia said

"What the fuck are you doing Cass" Nick shouted

"Managing Nick, we need to move quickly and without ripples. I am sure that Mr Macdonald will be able to facilitate that, and we are going to need support. We are okay here in the States but think about it, Japan, Europe, and what about China? It could take us months to put things together, and I am not sure that we have that much time. So, if I vet the people" she said winking at Nick, "Then we should accept all the help we can get" she added.

Nick looked at her suspiciously "You sure?" he growled

"Trust me, I know what I am doing, now what about our people" Cassia said looking at Chuck.

"There are being held at the FBI regional office in LA" Chuck said "You can have them back in the morning. I will need to then to sort it out, besides all we have them on is impersonating a reporter and a military analyst, we can't really hold them" he added. "But I want two things" he added

"What?" Tom asked

"I want these two in with you, and I want you to brief a select list of people, I will give Miss Nilsson. Tomorrow, when you pick them up, I will send you the location for the meeting" Chuck said "That's my conditions"

Nick, Cassia and Tom, looked at each other and nodded "Agreed" Nick said

"Right if that is it, then I need to get going, I have a lot to sort out before morning" Chuck said getting to his feet

"Just remember, the moment anything goes online or via a mobile, she will be listening" Cassia said

"Yeah, I got it, luckily the people on this list" Chuck said scribbling on a piece of paper and handing it to Cassia "are all in LA at the moment" he added

"Just one thing before you go" Tom said, and Chuck turned to face him

"What?" Chuck said wearily

"How did you know they were going for the Livermore?" Tom asked

Chuck smiled, "We got a call from a mobile telling us, we traced the number back to a burner in Livermore" Chuck said

"I am going to fucking kill them" Tom growled

"Who" Chuck asked

"Craig Moore and Laksham Joshi" Tom snarled

"No need, they got taken out trying to get over the Mexican border and hour ago" Chuck said then added, "What did you think that we didn't tag them leaving the building in Livermore, we have been tailing them ever since, and were going to pick them up before they got to Mexico, but they bolted" Chuck said easily

Chapter Twelve
The new partnership

Thursday 10th July 2025 – Los Angeles

After Chuck had left, Cassia read the list again and felt her pulse quicken "Nick you need to check this out" she said handing it to him

"Fuck" Nick said aloud "Can you, do it?" he asked

"Of course," Cassia said "just might take me a while"

Nick handed the list to Tom, and watched his face change "Christ" he said "I didn't know the President was in LA" he gasped

Nick wasn't listening his mind was thinking about the fifth name on the list, The chief of Defence, General Davy Markham.

"Nick" Cassia said cautiously "Tell me about the insurance" she said

Nick smiled "6, 50, 3 Green lot parking off Martin Luther King Jnr Boulevard in LA, 21:00, RV Menlo" he said

"Yeah, I heard that, but what does it mean?" Cassia asked irritably.

"Insurance" Nick replied and seeing Cassias face added "I called an old buddy of mine and said I need a team of 6, for a short operation at, Green lot parking in LA, for 3 hours and I was willing to pay $50,000 and would meet them at the Menlo school" Nick said "I wanted to make sure that if things got out of hand we weren't on our own" he added.

Cassia smiled, "so you covered our backsides, genius" she said

"Yeah, well we have just stirred the hornet's nest, I think we are going to need a lot more insurance before this game is up" Nick said wisely.

At 7am the next morning Andrew received a text telling them that they needed to be at 11,000 Wiltshire Boulevard, the FBI building at 08:30, they were expected, passes would be waiting for them and were to park in the underground car park.

"Okay" Nick said "let's get this over with"

They arrived at the FBI building at 08:25 and Nick pulled up to the gate, the guard stepped forwards, checked their ID's handed them five passes and lifted the barrier.

"Stay in your car, you will be collected" the guard said "Bay 113" he added and waved them through.

"What the fuck is that about?" Nick asked.

"I don't know" Andrew said "But I think you should err" he said directing Nicks attention to the ankle bracelet he was wearing.

"Yeah right, not a chance" Nick said

"Look, I don't want to be funny, but there is no way they are letting us in there, if Jess and I are carrying C4 jewellery, so it's your choice, do it now, or wait until we set off the alarm" Andrew said.

"Fine" Nick growled reached inside the glove box and retrieved a set of pliers and handed them to Andrew.

"I can't do it, what if I cut through a wire" Andrew said nervously looking at the anklet.

"Then the light will go out" Nick said "There is no C4 in there" he added

"What, you lied, I have been crapping myself all night?" Jess screamed

"Sue me" Nick snapped then looked at the side mirror, he saw Chuck walking towards them flanked by two large goons dressed in dark suits who were nervously scanning the car park.

"Good morning, Mr Colletto" Chuck said, he looked like he hadn't had a wink of sleep

"Please would you and your team accompany me" he added and stepping back from the car.

"Where are my people?" Nick barked.

"We are going to meet them" Chuck said dryly

As soon as they were out of the car the two goons stepped forwards and thoroughly frisked them, while Chuck waited patiently.

"All clear" The goon on the right said.

"Now, please" Chuck said extending his arm. Over the far side of the car park were two black SUV's with dark tinted windows.

Chuck reached inside his pocket and produced a small thin key fob and pressed a button. The lights of the right-hand vehicle flashed and there was a loud click. Instantly the doors open and Katie and Alten leapt out and Cassia ran forwards and grabbed them.

"Oh my god I was so worried" Cassia cried.

"You and me both" Katie said

"What happened?" Cassia asked.

"I don't know, one minute I was talking with the Director, then the doors burst open, and four men dressed in black burst in carrying weapons. They arrested me and took me here they haven't even asked me any questions" Katie said

"What happened to Alten?" Cassia asked.

"Same thing really, he was doing his thing on the computer" Katie whispered, "Then Craig and Josh, said they were nipping out for a fag, then a whole bunch of guys turned up and arrested him. The first time I saw him was when we were put in that car" Katie explained. "How come you are here?"

"I fill you in later" Cassia said, seeing Chucks face.

"Please" Chuck said guiding them all to the cars.

Nick, Cassia and Katie got in the car on the right, whilst Andrew, Jess, Tom and Chuck got in the one on the left, the goons took one car each.

As soon as all were in, the cars pulled out of the garage and turned left onto Wiltshire and a few seconds later, down onto the slipway of the 405, out towards San Diego freeway.

45 minutes later they took the Sepulveda exit then travelled 10 minutes along the side road and turned left into the Mountain Gate Country club, but instead of stopping at the front entrance, they circled around the back and came to a stop.

Instantly the cars were surrounded by several men dressed in black suits with their weapons drawn. Everyone got out of the cars and were escorted inside the building, down, a long underground corridor towards a large steel door, guarded by two more people.

"We wait here" Chuck said. and they all took their seats outside the room.

"This is one of the most secret locations in the US, only a handful of people know about it, and it is completely secure, even Miss Nilsson cannot get inside" Chuck said

"That sounds like a challenge" Cassia said chirpily

"I assure you it is not, but please do check if you need to satisfy yourself that whatever is discussed in that room, cannot make it out and onto the web" Chuck said.

Cassia typed furiously on her iPad for the entire 10 minutes they were waiting outside, until finally she had to concede, the room was secure.

The steel door opened and a large man, in a black suit, with a buzz cut, stepped out.

"Come" he said and as each person entered the room they were searched again, and all their mobile phones were taken.

The walls of the room was completely bare, except for two large white screens. There was a large round oak table, around which were 12 high back chairs, six of which were empty. In the other six sat; the President of the United States, Gerald Ratner, The Secretary of Defence, General Davy Markham, Miles Beecham, Director of the Homeland Security, Director, Sarah Kolinski, The Chief Justice and the Director of National Intelligence, Avril Haines, and a small bespeckled Chinese man, who was sat quietly, at a small table at the back of the room.

"It's them, arrest them" A small mouse like man screamed leaping to his feet his face red with rage

"Sit down Mr Beecham" The President growled angrily "If you can't control yourself, I will have you removed" he added menacingly.

"Please forgive Mr Beecham, I understand that he has some issues with you" The President said smoothly "now please may I ask you to be seated" he added

Nick glared at the small man, then turned back to face the President "Of course Mr President" he said lowering himself into a nearby chair, not taking his eyes off of Miles Beecham.

Once they well all seated, with Andrew and Jess stood at the back the President excused the guards, who stepped out and locked the door.

"Okay, thank you" The President said, "Although if rumours are to be believed, you should not be surprised at Mr Beecham's reaction" The President said staring directly at Cassia, who smiled sweetly

"Well Mr President, as I am sure that Mr Beecham will attest too, there are always many rumours circulating and as Head of our National Security, Mr Beecham would be all too aware of all of them, that said I am sure he is too smart to be fooled by simple rumours. As the person responsible for our nation's security, I am sure he would only act of factual information" Cassia said smoothly and suppressed a smile as she saw Miles face flush as General Markham nearly choke on his coffee.

"Indeed" The President said, and Cassia was sure she saw a faint smile cross his lips.

"Now shall we begin; I believe that you are in possession of some rather disturbing information" The President said and sat back down. Nick looked at Cassia and nodded.

Cassia slowly got to her feet and instantly regretted it as her legs started to shake. She drew a deep breath and for the next hour told the group everything that they had been up to, starting with Valencia and finishing in Los Angeles. She then proceeded to show them the data and information she had gotten about Betsi's plan.

"Please" the President said, "This ladies and gentlemen is Mr White, may he take a look at your data, in order to verify its detail, Miss Nilsson?" The President asked, Cassia hesitated, then nodded her agreement and Mr White, who she was sure was not his real name, invited her to his small side table.

"Now while they are reviewing the data, are there any questions?" The President asked.

General Markham looked directly at Nick "So you got captured by Holloway, when did you find out what he was up to?" General Markham asked although in truth he already knew this.

"I was rescued by Cassia and David Carmichael, they took me and the others back to the mainland, that is when they told us about Holloways plan, it was after that we decided to go back and put a stop to it" Nick said honestly.

"Carmichael, isn't he the English scientist?" Avril Harris asked

"Yes, a very smart and courageous man" Nick said.

"And you manage to catch my people without firing a round" Miles Beecham asked maliciously.

"Three times" Nick said and saw Andrew, Tom and Chuck, lower their heads

"It's not their fault, we were prepared" Nick said apologetically.

"Indeed, as they should have been" Miles said coldly looking from Chuck to Andrew then Tom.

"Look if you have just come here to look for someone to shift the blame onto, then this is a waste of time" Nick said angrily getting to his feet.

"Please forgive, Mr Beecham, he is a little disappointed that is all, he will get over it, I have a question" The President said.

"Yes, Mr President" Nick said sitting back down.

"If as you say this supercomputer is to take control, and plunge mankind back to the dark ages, how do you see her achieving this, through nuclear weapons, black mail?" The President asked

"No Mr President, although I have no doubt that she will make sure that the nuclear arsenal is disabled, and not just here but worldwide. As far as I understand it, the current situation with climate change is dictating the direction. She will first release a new virus, targeting, the weak and vulnerable, as we are all aware, this alone will cripple most western economies, especially as it is so soon after Corona virus. Then I think that she will target all banking and financial systems and redistribute the wealth evenly across those that are left. Finally, she will infiltrate all water systems, and use the targeted genome and Cas 9 technology, to alter and enhance the DNA of those that are left. Once she has achieved this, she will then embark on a mass relocation plan, moving the resultant population to the remaining 20% of inhabitable land mass" Nick said and sat back down.

Everyone sat distilling what he had just said.

"And you think this is possible?" The President finally asked.

"I do" Nick said solemnly

"And I concur" Mr White said, "I have verified the data, retraced it and can confirm it came directly from the Titan Computer in Oak Ridge, Tennessee. It appears that there is an additional computer that had infiltrated this one and is now in command of it. As for the plan it is entirely feasible and seems to be the most logical and likely course of action" Mr White said

"Tell me, Miss Nilsson, what was your plan to stop it happening?" Sarah Kolinski asked

"Our plan was simple; we believe that for Betsi to do this she needed to use all the 8 super computers in the world and will work through all of them. Our plan was to break into each one and lock her out, then when we had cornered her in the last one, I was going to activate the kill code, I implanted in her when we were in Valencia, and wipe her out" Cassia said.

"These computers, where exactly are they?" General Markham asked shifting forwards in his seat.

"Three are here in the states, two in Japan, two in China and one in Switzerland" Tom said wanting to get into the action.

"I see, and you were planning to break into them all?" Avril Haines asked

"Well possibly, that was why we needed to get into Livermore, you see I have a theory, I think that the ones in each country are linked. Therefore, it would mean that I could adapt the coding and we only need to get into one in each country, but we didn't manage to get into Livermore, we were caught" Cassia said

"Err hum" Alten said. "We may have been caught but not before I uploaded the programme and you were right Cassia, they are linked, well at least the Livermore one and the one in

Oak Ridge. I didn't have time to check the one in Oakland" Alten said and smiled at Cassia.

"What If I reached out to the other countries, I doubt that any of them would want this?" The President asked.

"May I be frank Mr President?" Cassia asked

"Of course, speak your mind" The President responded somewhat surprised at her abruptness.

"That would be foolish, at the moment we are one step ahead of Betsi, the moment that any of this gets out, the game is over, and trust me, she will find out, if the slightest hint, change in behaviours, any slightest sign, she will accelerate the plan. At the moment she is waiting for the right moment, and before you ask, no I don't know when that is, but my gut tells me we don't have long" Cassia said honestly

"I see, so it must be done covertly?" The President asked.

"No" Nick said sharply "I have had first-hand experience of your covert operations; it took Cassia less than five minutes to break in and peak up your skirts. It has to be done differently" Nick said curtly

Miles Beecham bristled and leapt to his feet and was about to reply when the President held up his hand to stop him.

"Miles, sit down, I regret to say Mr Colletto is right, he and his team have already bested you three times, we simply cannot afford a fourth, tell me Mr Colletto, how would you run this operation" The President asked.

"Old school" Nick said "The command group is made up only of the people in this room, we circle everything back through you and run one-time codes, like the FSB did. Everything is kept offline, and we use drop boxes. My team and you are the only ones that know the full plan. We communicate with you, and you authorise and organise the resources from your end, on a need-to-know basis" Nick said

"I take it that you trust me?" The President asked smiling broadly.

"No, not really, but then again I don't trust any of the others here, either, but if I don't want to worry about you lot stuffing it up, and screwing it for all of us, then I better, as Cassia says, learn to suck it up" Nick said sharply, the President smiled.

"You are very forthright, Mr Colletto, I find that very refreshing. General Markham, you have had first-hand experience of Mr Colletto, what is your opinion?" The President asked

General Markham sat upright and stared Nick directly in the eyes. "He is the best I have ever had the privilege to work with, Mr President" he said

"I see; however, I doubt very much whether I will be able to handle this personally, without arousing suspicion, particularly from the Vice President, let alone my personal secretary" The President said openly.

"Then work through someone else then" Nick said, "Someone you trust" he added.

"And your suggestion would be?" The President asked.

"Well off the top of my head, I would say that Mr Macdonald and Mr Dale, showed exceptional courage and vision to trust us and bring this together, I don't think you would go too far wrong with them" Nick said "Plus I trust them" he added looking at Chuck and Andrew.

"I see, and what of Miss Craven?" The President asked.

Cassia smiled, "I understand that she has a boss that she reports into, you must decide if you want to bring the Brits in, no offence Jess, but I don't think it is a good idea to bring another country in, we have no way of controlling the information" Cassia said.

"I will take that under advisement, as it happens James Houghton will be in Washington the day after tomorrow, Miles can you arrange a meeting?" the President asked.

"Of course, Mr President" Miles said sulkily

The President looked at the others, it was clear he was thinking, trying to decide what to do, he was tapping his pencil on the faded blotter on the table, occasionally scribbling notes. Eventually he looked directly at Nick and Cassia.

"Okay, we will do it your way, Mr Dale and Mr Macdonald will work directly with me, please brief them, and they will work only with the people in only this room. Nothing goes outside of this circle, as a matter of National Security, understood? The President ordered and everyone nodded their agreement.

"Good, we will put all of our resources at your disposal. Miss Nilsson, I would like you to join me in the White house directly after this meeting, and review our cyber security, we need to be sure that as you say no one is peaking up our skirts, there are to be no breaches" The President said smiling at Cassia, then paused

"Does that meet with your approval Mr Colletto, Miss Nilsson?" the President asked.

"I don't like the fact that Cassia is going with you to the White house, like I said I don't trust anyone" Nick said.

"Then Mr Colletto, I suggest you join us, so you can keep an eye on her" The President said, "Finally there is another matter, I believe you must attend to first" he added.

This took Nick by surprise "Go on" Nick said

The President nodded towards Avril, "Mrs Haines" The President said

"As you are aware we shot and killed Mr Craig Moore and Mr Laksham Joshi, whilst they were trying to escape to Mexico. At first, we believed that they were the ones that alerted us to your attempt to infiltrate the computer at Livermore. However, when we traced the calls from their phones, there was no call data, they were clean, so we retraced the call we received. It was routed through the cell tower in Livermore, and six others.

Eventually we managed to get back to the source, it originated about thirty kilometres west of Anchorage. I believe that is where you are currently residing Miss Nilsson" Avril said "I suggest that you may have a leak in your end that needs plugging" she added.

Nick stared at Cassia and saw the rage building on her face, "Leave that one to me" she said menacingly, "Before we take the next steps, I will have some ones head on a platter" she added quietly.

"Then the matter is resolved, that leaves me to wish you all the very best success, we are all counting on you" The President said, "If you and Mr Colletto will join me on air force one, and I will arrange transport for your team" The President said.

Chapter Thirteen
The fox in the hen coup

Thursday 10th July 2025 -Red Dog

The Hughes MD 500 defender military helicopter touched down on the strip at Red dog. Cassia and Nick had been ferried from DC to Anchorage Military family readiness centre by USAF plane, where the Hughes helicopter was waiting for them.

"Nick stepped out of the helicopter and helped Cassia down, then stood back and signalled the pilot to take off.

"What the hell we have been going out of our minds, the others got back last a last night, and no one is saying anything, just that you and Cassia will be coming in sometime today?" Sarah screamed at Nick "So what is going on?"

"Not here" Nick said curtly and followed Cassia into the 4 x 4

"I don't get it" Sarah shouted,

"Sarah, we have a breach, we can't discuss this outside of the pod, I will bring you up to speed then" Nick said grumpily.

The eight hours he had just spent at the White house had not gone well. The President had wanted Cassia to review his cyber security systems, which she was more than capable of doing, but it meant that he had spent the whole time feeling like a spare wheel, sitting and waiting for her. The staff had been kind and he had gotten the official tour, but outside of that, he spent most of his time twiddling his thumbs, something he was not too good at.

David already had the rail train at the house waiting, and they all boarded and went straight to Paradise pod. Once there, the three of them plus Tom, Katie and Robert, shut themselves inside one of the secure meeting rooms.

"Right" Nick said "It looks like someone here is trying to sabotage the whole thing" he said and then proceeded to tell them, with Cassia's help, about everything that had happened whilst they had been away.

Robert whistled "So you met with Ratner and his top team, and they are on board?" he asked.

"Yep, look we would have kept you guys in the loop, but things were moving so fast and the fact that Katie and Alten got picked up, and Craig and Josh were on the run, we couldn't trust anyone" Cassia said and seeing their faces added,

"I don't mean you lot, I mean we didn't know what Craig and Josh were up to, we thought that they had grassed on Katie and Alten and figuring that they also knew about the whole plan and Red Dog, as I said we couldn't take any chances" she added.

"So, you think someone here, did it?" Sarah asked.

"Well yes and no, what the tech guy told us, and we double checked it, the call did seem to come from somewhere near Red Dog, but honestly, thinking about who was left here, I just don't see it. Sanvia and Sanjay, you David and Sarah, I can't see why. No, it is more likely that the it was made to look like that, problem is we don't think that either Josh or Craig have the technical skills to do that. So, it boils down to two possibilities. The government are feeding us a pack of lies, or Betsi knows what we are up to and made it look like it was someone from here" Cassia said

"I don't buy it, they all looked totally shocked when we told them what she was up to, and if they are feeding us a pack of crap, why would they want in?" Nick said

"Then it must be Betsi" Cassia said, "Somehow she knows what we are up too, I just don't know how" she added

"What about Sanjay's Daughter, Shemzee?" David said.

"No, she has never been at any of the briefings, in fact neither has Sanjay or Aanya" Cassia said.

"What are we going to do?" Robert asked.

"Nothing" Cassia said "Nick and I have talked it through. If it is Betsi, then she could only know about Livermore, because we managed to pull off Tennessee, and we haven't decided the next target yet. Now it is possible that she could have picked it up when we were making plans, and it is possible that she identified Katie, as she worked for the Committee. So, when she caught wind of Katie meeting with the Director at Livermore, she dug deeper and saw that the supercomputer was being analysed and wanted to protect it, keep her plans hidden, and that is why she alerted the team there. If that is right, we will soon know, we are visiting Cori in Oakland on Saturday. We will plan it all from the hub here, which is totally secure. The truth is it is already set up, we are just going to pretend it isn't. We chose Saturday as there will be less people about. Then if we have a welcoming committee waiting for us, well then, we know we have a leak, because it can only have come from here" Cassia said

"Or someone in the Presidents team" Sarah said.

"No", Nick said "With the exception of the President himself, all of the others think we are going back to Livermore" he said.

"It was all the Presidents idea" Cassia added, "I think he wants to flush this leak out as much as we do" she added.

"Ok, well that is it for me I am beat" Nick said, "Shall we reconvene in the morning, say 9am" he added.

Friday 11th July 2025 – Red Dog

The next morning everyone was waiting in the conference room when Nick and Sarah arrived. Cassia had never seen Nick looking happier. She had seen him and Sarah out in the meadow, the afternoon before, playing football with Archie, they looked so happy and knowing that they were about to go on another mission the next day, gave her a deeply sad feeling, when will all this be over? she thought.

"Good morning, everyone" Nick said helping himself to some coffee and a freshly baked raisin muffin, that Sanvia had made.

"Okay" Cassia said smiling, "Now as you know, Livermore turned out to be a nightmare and we lost Craig and Josh, that said it is vitally important that we get the information stored on that computer, it is the only way we will know if it is connected to Betsi, so we have decided to give it another go" Cassia said

"Surely that is a bit risky, they know that you are interested in it, surely it would be better going after the one in Oakland" Katie said knowingly

"The one in Oakland is at the National Energy Research laboratory, there is a greater chance they would have ramped up security there. They will not be expecting us to target the one in Livermore again, it makes more sense" Nick said, "Either that or we go to China, Japan or Europe, and that will take a lot more planning" he added.

"Okay so here is the site map, the computer is situated in building 481 off Patterson pass road. We are planning to go in tomorrow evening. So here is the plan. The patrols operate out of the West Badge Gate office, and run two teams of four, two on and two off, change over on the hour. Now Cassia has arranged security passes for us. They will be ready for us to collect at the West Badge gate office. David has prepared us a special cocktail, in aerosol format, that works on a timed release. We will set it on change over, that will buy us an hour. Tom will be stationed in the office and field any visitors and calls. Cass and I will get into 481, we have passes, so we should be able to walk right in. Now thanks to our first visit we know what additional security measures are in operation. With a little luck we should be in and out within 28 minutes" Nick said

"Why a Saturday night?" Robert asked.

"Our study of gate traffic denotes that the quietest time is between 1am and 3am on a Saturday night, so that is when we are going in" Nick said

"I don't wish to put a dampener on things" Sanvia said "But it all sounds a little too rushed, and I thought that you would preferred not to leave any trace of you being there. Surely eight guards crashed out in the office will be a bit of a giveaway" she said.

"True, but we have little choice, Cassia has download emails from their Director, come Monday morning they are ramping up the security around the computer, so if we have any chance, it has to be this weekend. As for the guards, well we have a plan for that" Nick said smiling at Cassia.

Cassia had a big grin on her face, "Okay so the Lawrence Livermore laboratory is renowned for scientific research into weapons, nuclear etc. So, we are going to deface it, not do it any damage, just spray it with extinction rebellion and CND slogans that sort of thing, we have also set up a feed to the local activist group, we are going film the whole thing, then release it on the web" Cassia said "They will put it down to anarchists" she added.

"Genius really" David said, they will be too busy looking at the climate guys, to think it could have been anything else, especially if there is no indication of access or damage to their computer" he added.

"Who is on the team?" Alten asked hopefully looking at Nick

"Sorry mate, but yours and Katie's face are all over the campus, so we are going in light, Just Cassia, Me, Tom and Mike" Nick said

Alten looked deflated, he had been feeling guilty ever since he had been arrested. it had not helped that he had been asked to stay in the corridor, whilst everyone else had gone into the meeting. "I guess that's for the best" Alten said sulking.

"Don't worry, there will be plenty for you to do, on the next one" Nick said, "In Japan" he added smiling

"What, I am going to Japan?" Alten asked, excitedly

"Of course, we will need all hands on, deck there, and after your experience in Livermore you will be perfect" Cassia said warmly.

"Okay so that's it, we need to get away at 6am in the morning, and there is a shed full of things still to do. Cass can you sort the flights and let me have a look at the security passes. Sarah, will you cast your eyes over them, I could do with a second opinion. Alten, consult with Cassia, I need a hack into the LA extinction rebellion site, and we need to start posting on the site. Tom your on kit, and Robert help David on the cocktail. Other than that, Sanjay and Sanvia, I presume you are busy here" Nick asked.

"Always, Aanya is running a class with the youngsters, and I have some new plant specimens to analyse" Sanjay said

"I have a crop of Allium sativum to cultivate, they are a rare Philippine herb use to alleviate hypertension" Sanvia said

"Hey, I have had a thought, what about when we go to Japan, you guys come with us" Cassia asked and noticed the shock look on their faces

"I am not sure what use I would be, I am an ecologist and have no experience of operations" Sanvia instantly said

"I don't know, you were pretty quick thinking when we needed to get out of India" Nick said

"Yes, but that was easy, if it is all the same to you, I would prefer not to accompany you on operations" Sanvia said bluntly

"What about you Sanjay?" Katie asked

Sanjay hung his head, "Look I am sorry, but the condition that Aanya agreed to come here, was if I promised that I would not undertake anything dangerous, and after what you told me about your experience with Mr Zhivkov, sorry Katie, I cannot go on missions" Sanjay said looking at her.

"That's ok" Nick said, "You guys are doing an amazing job here, along with David and Robert, I just thought you might like a chance of getting out of here" Nick said

"Trust me, I am an old man, I have no desire to be anywhere other than here" Sanjay said and Sanvia nodded as well.

"Okay, then let's get at it people" Nick said getting to his feet.

Once everyone had left, Nick sat there with Cassia, David and Sarah.

"You still don't trust them, do you?" David asked.

"Can't help it, is in my DNA, let's see how this pans out" Nick said

"How can you trust us?" Cassia asked

"Firstly, Sarah has had my back since the day I met her, and you guys saved my neck in Valencia, so if I can't trust you, then I might as well give up now" Nick said honestly.

After the meeting Cassia walked into mission control, in paradise and closed the door and locked it. Her mind was racing. Before she had left the White house, she had set up the comms system and briefed the team, in the Oval room. As most of them resided in DC, the programme was easier. Cassia would hack into the White house system through a back door she had installed and leave a message on the President's personal laptop, one he had commissioned specifically for the job. He would then print the message and run it through an old fax machine they had dug up from the cellars and reprogrammed. The machine would then reprint the message using a unique code, which changed every time it was used. The new printed message would be put into a diplomatic pouch sealed, and then either Andrew or Chuck would take it to the intended recipient, collect their response and return to the White House and fax the message back to Cassia, and her machine would decoded it. It was the safest method of communications she could come up with at short notice, and as it needed a human to deliver the messages manually, it couldn't be hacked.

Cassia logged in, opened a portal to enable her to get out of the faraday shield, logged onto the Presidents computer and dropped a message on his desktop, then logged off and closed the portal.

After that she left the office and took the rail train back to the house collected a few things from her personal tech stores.

On the train she took out her iPad and activated the application. It was a small programme that she had designed, it scanned for electronic communication signatures and transmitted their location to secure online portal. When the train came to a stop, she sent it back and waited staring at the screen. The only electronic signature in the rail shed was coming from the rail tracks control panel, she smiled "At least it was not from here" she said aloud, and shut down her iPad, pulled on her thick black coat and set off to the house.

While she had spun a story that it was most likely Betsi, that had informed the authorities in Livermore, secretly she knew that was not the case, she just didn't want to believe it, but in truth it could have come from any of them. The ones who had stayed at Red Dog were the most likely candidates, however in reality it really could be anyone, now she needed to eliminate suspects.

Once in the house, she scanned every room, only mission control was emitting electronic communication signature. She opened the door with her thumbprint and retinal scan and entered. The first thing she checked were the hidden cameras and ran the recording back to when the message had been sent, then hit fast forwards and scanned the screen. According to the recording, no one had been in the room, next she ran a check on the computers. No one had been on the computers since she had left.

Of course, she thought, they could have erased their presence, but she knew they would have to have some serious computer knowledge to get past her systems.

Once she left mission control, she strategically placed tiny cameras around the house, in every room, checked they were linked to the online portal, then activated their motion sensors. Next to each camera she placed a tiny relay box that would covertly detect any electronic communications and replay them to her portal.

"Right" she said aloud, "We are ready, time to get back"

Cassia made her way back to the rail shed, called the train and waited. A chilly wind whipped through the rail shed, "Bloody hell Cassia said pulling her coat tighter around her, "It is supposed to be July, bloody climate change, its freezing" she cried stuffing her hands in to her pockets. Suddenly her fingers folded around a tiny silver box.

"Bugger, I brought one to many" she said pulling the relay box out, she was about to put it back in her pocket, when the sound of a low growl filled the shed, there at the entrance of the shed was a huge grizzly bear. Cassia stumbled backwards and if it hadn't of been for the fact the rail train had just slid to a halt behind her, she would have fallen flat on her back. Quickly she scrabbled along the flatbeds, grabbed the black handle, twisted it and the rail car shot forwards with a jolt.

"Fuck, that was close" Cassia said watching the shed disappear into the distance, then the sound of David's voice rang in her head *'Never go to the house without a gun, Bears will kill you'*

"Smart arse" Cassia said aloud and stuffed her hands back into her pockets as the train sped up. "Oh crap, I must have dropped the silver box" she said, I just hope it can't be seen, she thought.

Chapter Fourteen
Colonel Danvers

David skilfully guided the Cessna down towards the runway, there was a slight bump as the plane touched down and Nick released his grip on the seat and watched as the colour returned to his knuckles.

"Welcome to the Military and Family readiness centre, please place your seats in the forward position and store you tray tables" David said laughing

"Hey, you have become quiet the expert" Cassia said smiling at him

"Case of having too, with you jetting about everywhere" David replied sourly.

"Gladly swap" Cassia said

"Not likely my spy career started and stopped in Valencia I am just worried about you" David replied.

"I know, but once this is done, I am finished I promise, no more saving the world, scouts honour" Cassia said.

"Yeah right, anyway your chariot awaits madam" David said, as the man on the ground guided him towards a small military cargo plane, waiting patiently on the tarmac with its huge props spinning gently.

Tom and Nick got out of the Cessna and waited as Cassia said her goodbyes to David.

"Look Cass, just be careful, watch your back, I love you" David said hugging her tightly.

"I always am, anyway, don't forget, we are coming back by boat, through Seward, and remember don't say a word to anyone" Cassia said kissing him gently on the cheek.

David watched as Cassia made her way towards the waiting airplane, this time it felt different, something felt wrong" He pulled up the steps on the Cessna and closed the small door, sighed and taxied onto the runway.

Sanjay and Sanvia stood in the rail shed, the wind was bitter, they had ridden the train down to the rail shed, to collect some more stores and loaded it onto the rail cart.

"Okay, you go back, unload it and send the train back, I will get the next load" Sanvia said.

Once Sanvia was sure that Sanjay had gone, she reached behind the control panel and pulled out the small mobile phone, dialled the number and spoke quietly into the answer machine.

3500 miles away in Kobe, Japan Betsi sensed the incoming message, opened a portal and downloaded it.

"Livermore, West gate, posing as VIP guest, target computer, 1am to 3am Saturday, CN, NC, TC, end

Betsi ran it through her analysis protocols. Within a fraction of a second the data streams started to flow. It had been 72 hours 27 minutes since she had been able to communicate with Titan, in Tennessee and 29 hours since communication had been lost with Sequoia in Livermore. Losing communication with one computer could be an error, two however meant something very different.

Then there was the message origination Red Dog, Alaska, the same place that Cassia and David had relocated too. She had detected it on the mobile nets, she replayed the message again searching for clues. 'Betsi, they are planning on stopping you, I can help' until this latest message she had believed that the message had come from Cassia. The message that had followed had enabled her to effect the arrest of Alten Hunt and Katie Rayner, before they had destroyed Sequoia. However, this latest message changed the scenario.

Analyse scenario, she commanded, in a fraction of a second the results came back.

There is a ninety-six-point three percent chance, based on the data available that Cassia Nilsson, Nick Colletto and Major Tom Clarke will affect an attack on the Sequoia computer in Livermore Tennessee, subsequent to the failed attempt of Miss Katie Rayner and Mr Alten Hunt (known associate of Major Tom Clarke)'

As I suspected Betsi thought, that leaves two open questions,

"Question. Betsi said to the analysis programme. Why is Cassia trying to destroy computers, and what does she believe my plan is? She ran the analysis.

Answers. *There is a ninety-eight-point two percent probability that Cassia Nilsson believes that we are planning to use The Sequoia computer to effect control over the United States of America's nuclear deterrent, as this is the primary purpose of the computer. Cassia Nilsson believes that by destroying the Sequoia, it will reduce our ability to control the nuclear arsenal of the United States of America.*

Question: Betsi said. Add in Titan how does this change the scenario. A millisecond later the answer flashed up.

Titan 5200 in Oak Ridge Tennessee has no links to the United States Nuclear programme, and there is no record of Miss Cassia Nilsson attending this site. My records detect that on Tuesday 9th of July there was an incident was logged of an attempt to access the Granite Nuclear Reactor at the National Laboratory Oak Ridge Tennessee. The attempt was unsuccessful.

Betsi turned the information over in her processors. An attack on the reactor, and a failed attempt on Titan and now Cassia was going to attempt to gain access to Titan again. Cassia Nilsson believes that she is targeting each country's nuclear weaponry to preserve human life, interesting.

Betsi and typed her message. *Terrorist attempt planned for the Lawrence Livermore National Laboratory, 1am Saturday 13th of July 2025, West Gate access.* She checked the header and loaded the Homeland security logo, and signed the email *A Haines,* then routed it through the FBI office in Los Angeles *to* Alemeda County Sheriff's departments computer.

"Welcome aboard" General Markham said, as Cassia came up the steps on the cargo plane.

"What the hell are you doing here?" Cassia asked.

"He is on a surprise inspection of the base" Nick said

"It was the only way I could get a secure plane here without arising suspicion" General Markham said.

"Really" Cassia said sarcastically "The Secretary of Defence suddenly decides to take a trip to Alaska, that sounds like a red flag to me" she added.

"Not really, I do it all the time" General Markham said

"He's right, he was known for it, back when I worked for him" Nick said grinning.

"Anyway, there are uniforms for you in the back, and it is all set up for you in Oakland, your Id's and passes are in the pockets" General Markham said

"And the other site?" Nick asked.

"Three agents, Dane Manners, Eric Mathers and Cheryl Majors will be attending the Livermore facility at 1am, the team on site have been briefed, they believe it is a response drill designed to test the speed of the Alemeda Sheriff's department" General Markham said, "Once they have been detained, the FBI team from the Knoxville office will collect them" he added, then as an afterthought said, "As instructed".

"And the exfil?" Nick asked

"I have a seal team ready and waiting in Seattle, a Navy frigate will take you to Seward as part of their routine patrol of the gulf of Alaska, the seal team will drop you at Red Dog" General Markham said.

"Good" Nick said, "Then let's hope all this isn't necessary"

"We will know soon enough if my team are picked up in Livermore" General Markham replied.

"I am afraid there is no business class on military planes, our facilities are a little basic, but there is fresh coffee and breakfast in the galley, and you may use my office to change. Flight time to Oakland is 6 and a half hours, which means we will be there by 3pm, Dale and Macdonald will be escorting you, you are booked in at the National Energy Research centre at 16:30pm" General Markham said

"Cover story?" Nick asked

"I have asked for an independent cyber security assessment, based on the attack at Livermore" General Markham said

"And they bought that?" Nick said

"They have no choice, when the Sec Def orders a security assessment of a significant US government asset, it happens, trust me they will be bricking it" General Markham said.

"We will see, we need 12 to 15 uninterrupted minutes on the computer" Nick said

"You will be fine, just play the part of arrogant bastards, I am told that is how all of my security assessment teams come across" General Markham laughed.

Six hours later Cassia stepped out of the Generals office on the plane, dressed in a USAF colonels uniform.

"Colonel Danvers" Nick said laughing "you look very nice, does David like you in uniforms?" he teased.

"Piss off Nick, I look like a stuffed prize turkey" Cassia hissed. "Anyway Major" Cassia paused looking at the gold badge on Nicks breast "Anderson, I thought you hated officers, so why dress up as one?" she asked.

"Very funny, like I had a choice" Nick whinged

"Okay, You guys ready" Tom said in his neatly pressed Majors uniform. plonking himself down in the seat opposite them

"Ready and willing Major Blake, but shouldn't you have saluted me" Cassia teased

"Err sorry mam" Tom said leaping to his feet and saluting.

"At ease soldier" Cassia said getting into her role.

"Don't over play it Cassia, arrogant bastard yes, hammy actor no" Nick said

"I got it, just easing the tension" Cassia said smoothly.

Take your seats, we will be landing in five minutes" General Markham said returning from the cockpit.

As soon as the plane touched down and started to taxi to the hanger, General Markham came to the back

"Okay, listen I have three burners here, not traceable, and yes I know we are not supposed to, but if anything should go wrong and you guys need to get out of there in a hurry, just call, mine is the only number on them, I will come get you, ok" he said.

Cassia eyed him suspiciously, "Sorry" she said, "it's too much of a risk, if we get picked up and they get this number, then they can trace it back to you. If things go pear shaped, you will soon know, but we will find our own way out" she said then seeing the look on the Generals face added, "But thanks for the thought"

Andrew and Chuck were waiting for them as soon as the plane landed in the standard black SUV.

"Your car Colonel Danvers! Chuck said dressed in his military uniform and saluting, as soon as Cassia came down the stairs of the plane

"What!" Cassia said looking around.

"He means you" Nick whispered

"Oh yes" Cassia said saluting back.

"Mam" Andrew said stepping forwards and opening the door to the SUV

"Thank you" Cassia said sliding into the back of the SUV, followed by Nick and Tom

Once Chuck closed the doors and got in, Andrew pulled away off the tarmac.

"Okay, when we get there, they will check our passes at the gate, they should be in order. We will be escorted to the building where the computer is. I have been assured that they will not interfere, but I suspect they will be watching us" Chuck said turning round to face them. Andrew and I will stand guard at the entrance, I am not sure how much time we can buy you, so you will need to be quick" he added

"We will need about, 12 minutes" Cassia said

"Okay" Andrew said "Game on, we are here" he said

Cassia gazed out of the window, as two military men dressed in black uniforms, approached and tapped on the window.

Nick slid down the window and handed the guards their three passes, the first guard, a tall powerfully built man, with a shaven head, leaned into the rear window and looked directly at Cassia.

"Colonel Danvers, your escort is waiting" he said in a low deep voice.

Cassia felt her heart race, then, General Markham's words rang in her ears.

"Tell me" Cassia said looking at the guards' badge "Sergeant Edwards, I realise that this is the golden state, land of the free and happy, does that excuse you from saluting an officer?" Cassia snapped

"Err sorry mam" Sergeant Edwards said standing bolt upright and saluting. Cassia casually saluted back

"Now, perhaps, if you have time, you could show us to our escorts" Cassia said sarcastically.

"Yes mam" Sergeant Edwards signalling to the other guard, who lifted the barrier and waved their car through.

"You have a talent for this" Nick said, "No wonder David always looks so frightened" Nick said laughing "Ouch" Nick shrieked as Cassie kicked him in shin

The National Energy Research Scientific Computing centre or NERSC as it was known, is a division of the Lawrence Berkley National laboratory in Berkley. Its huge imposing glass building was home to Cori, one of the most powerful computers in the world, supporting up to 8000 scientists, to run advance computational studies on everything from climate modelling to simulations of the early days of the universe. One of its biggest clients was the United States Government, therefore they were used to unscheduled surprise security visits.

Andrew pulled in behind the escort car and followed it, until it pulled up outside the huge glass building. Then he and Chuck got out of the SUV and opened the rear doors.

Nick slipped out one side and Tom the other and came round to the front of the car and stood either side of Cassia.

"Colonel Danvers, may I welcome you to the National Energy Research Scientific Computing Centre" A short stocky bald-headed man, with little round spectacles and an ill-fitting grey suit, said stepping forwards with his hand out.

"I am Director Daniels, please permit me to show you around our facility" he continued but Cassia held up her hand.

"I am not interested in pleasantries or exchanging small talk, I am simply here to inspect your computer, so please, show me where the server room is" Cassia said gruffly.

"Err, of course" The grey suited bald man said guiding Cassia to the door. Cassia closely followed the bald-headed man, and Nick and Tom fell into step behind her.

It was all Cassia could do to stop herself from shouting out aloud. The NERSC was a spectacular state of the art facility, the most impressive computer facility she had ever seen.

Director Daniels directed them into a small lift and typed in a code into the small silver box beside the lift buttons, then pressed the button marked sub-basement.

"Cori is a Cray XC40, manufactured by the company responsible for major breakthroughs in supercomputer performance during the 1970s. Theoretically it can achieve a processing speed of 29.1 petaflops, it achieves this through the use of Haswell architecture, Intel Xeon and Xeon Phi processors" Director Daniels said trying to break the silence as they rode the silent lift to the sub-basement.

"Yet we still lag behind the Milky Way in Guizhou, China, with its 33.86 petaflops even though they are using US technology with its Intel Ivy Bridge and Xeon Phi processors, let alone The Sunway Taihulight, in Wuxi with its 125 petaflops capability. Please tell me Mr Daniels, you speak of this Cori with pride, is it your ambition to always be considered 2nd to China?" Cassia asked and Nick nearly choked and stifled a laugh, pushing it back down.

"Well err Colonel" Daniels said stutteringly, they have more funding, besides their performance, it's theoretical" he added recovering slightly.

"Indeed, however the government has already poured over a billion dollars into this project and is currently responsible for at least seventy eight percent of you annual budget. I think you have had and continue to have, enough of the taxpayers dollar" Cassia sniped, as the lift door opened, and she stepped out.

"Now point me in the direction of the servers and let me get on with my job" Cassia demanded.

Daniels hesitated "Well, erm, we do not allow anyone into the server room unaccompanied, its policy" he said nervously.

"I see, well let me tell you Mr Daniels!" Cassia said in a low menacing voice, "I have two advanced degrees in computer engineering from MIT. I am currently responsible for entire cyber security at the Pentagon and have recently been asked by The President himself to install new cyber security protocols for the entire white house senior staff, granting me the highest security level clearance. So, believe me when I tell you, I will not have some jumped up egotistical Laboratory Director sitting on my shoulder watching my every move" Cassia snarled

"But its policy" Daniels said.

Cassia smiled sweetly stepped to the side and pulled out her mobile phone, flicked it open and dialled a number.

"This is Colonel Sarah Danvers, Security code Charlie Oscar Mike 4,0, Alpha, put me through to the Director" she snapped

"Who is she calling?" Daniels asked Tom

"I think she is calling Avril Haines" Tom answered trying not to smile

"The Director of Homeland security?" Daniels asked shakily

"Avril, Sarah here, look I have some jobs worth, down here trying to prevent me from analysing the computer, do me a favour, make a call to his boss and sort this out, will you" Cassia said sweetly

"No, wait it's alright, please go right in, sorry" Daniels pleaded

"Avril, I think the matter may have resolved itself, listen next time I am in DC, I promise to come to dinner" Cassia said then paused "No, really I meant it this time, scouts honour" Cassia said and clicked her phone closed.

"You know the Director of Homeland security personally" Daniels asked nervously.

Cassia glared at him, and she saw the little man physically shrink under her gaze.

"Err through here" Daniels said directing her to two large glass doors.

"I presume you have clean room kit" Cassia asked

"Err yes, just inside the door, the access station is at the far end" Daniels added.

"Anderson, Blake, you two wait here, I do not want to be disturbed clear" Cassia barked, and Nick and Tom jumped to attention and positioned themselves outside the sliding doors to the server room and watched as Cassia entered.

"She is quiet scary" Daniels admitted, as the doors to the server room hiss closed.

"You are telling us, she is a complete bitch, nobody wants this detail, but she is too valuable an asset to just let her go on her own" Tom said seriously

"Is she that good?" Daniels asked.

"Well, we are not supposed to talk about this, but I will tell you this much, you know last year when that secret committee got exposed and all those top-secret people got busted" Nick said enjoying the shocked look on Daniels

"No, I mean yes, but nobody knows who did it" Daniels said, there is rumours all over the dark web, but no one has got a clue" he added excitedly. Nick didn't answer just nodded towards the server room and smiled.

"Bloody hell, god that was amazing" Daniels said "she is a legend"

"Look I can't confirm or deny it, matter of National security, all I know is I sleep a lot sounder knowing she is on our side" Nick said wisely.

Daniels stared into the server room with a look of deep admiration etched on his face. A few minutes later Cassia appeared at the sever room doors, striped out of the blue coverall and pressed the red button on the door. There was a loud hiss and the doors slid open.

"All done" Daniels asked with a silly grin on his face "Did we pass?" he asked hopefully

Cassia gave him a long hard look, "Your bosses will receive my report in due course, we will be in touch" she snapped, "Now I must go, I am due in Livermore tomorrow, I need to fire some dickhead for being duped by extinction rebellion" she snapped.

"Oh, you heard about that" Daniels said then seeing the look of contempt on Cassia face added "Of course, Colonel right away"

As soon as they were back in the car and once, they were passed the guard house, Cassia let out a loud breath.

"Bloody hell I nearly wet myself" she blurted out. Nick looked at Tom and they both smiled.

"Are you serious?" Nick said smiling, "I don't know about Tom, but I shit my pants, you were brilliant, where did you get all that stuff about the computers, and that call to the Director of Homeland security, was genius, what did Avril Haines say" Nick asked.

"Oh, I didn't actually talk to her, I was pretending" Cassia admitted.

Chuck looked back, "what the hell happened in there, that bloke in the white coat looked like someone had whacked him?" he asked, and Nick and Tom recanted the entire story, each filling in the gaps for each other.

Andrew and Chuck roared, then eventually Chuck looked at Cassia and said, "If you ever fancy going legit, just call me, you could have a great job as an agent" he said

"You could never afford me, Mr Macdonald" Cassia said as the SUV pulled onto the tarmac and drew up to the waiting plane.

General Markham was waiting for them on the plane and as soon as they were aboard and taxing to the runway, he came back and sat with them eagerly looking from one to the other until eventually he could wait no longer, "And" he said simply.

Oakland is secure, and yes, she had been there, but I locked the partition, for now, that is all the US supercomputers secure" Cassia said.

"What do you mean for now?" General Markham asked.

"General, all Betsi has to do is get someone to reset the commands and she will be able to access them again" Cassia said bluntly

"How long have we got?" General Markham asked.

"Tops a month, that is when the summer recess is over, and the majority of scientists are back from their vacations, then limiting access to the main frames becomes impossible" Cassia explained.

"I didn't know that" Nick said

"I hadn't twigged it either until we got here, then I check the logs on the computer and realised there had been limited activity, that's when I worked it out" Cassia explained.

"So, we have a month" Tom said, "That's not a lot of time" he added.

"Maybe less, we have no way of telling how far along with her plan she is, but I am pretty sure she will need all eight, so we have probably slowed her down a bit" Cassia said

"General, how did it go in Livermore" Cassia said.

General Markham looked down at the floor, "I am afraid you have all been arrested and are currently being transported to the FBI offices in Knoxville" he said solemnly

In the Oakforest Pac's Supercomputer at The University of Tokyo, Kashiwa Campus, the data lights flashed as several large streams of data spewed into the secret partition. Betsi analysed the information, checked the fingerprint details against the records she had downloaded earlier, then several images of Cassia Nilsson, Nick Colletto and Tom Clarke all appeared, each holding a row of numbers and standing in front of a height chart, two words appeared in front of the row of number *'Prisoner number'*

Such a shame Betsi said, I will miss her.

Chapter Fifteen
Little sister and Big brother

As soon as the plane took off Cassia pulled on her headphones and took out her iPad and started typing.

"She is amazing" Tom said looking at her

"I have been in this game for a long time, thought I had seen everything there was too see, but that woman still finds ways to amaze me" Nick said

Cassia looked up from her iPad, as if she knew they were talking about her and smiled. Then passed her iPad to Nick.

Nick scanned the text on the screen and smiled then read it again

Do not react, Meet me in the bathroom 15 minutes, do not say a word, just tap the screen and pass the iPad to Tom.

Nick read the message and a cold anger filled him, he tapped the screen, and an image of Director Daniels filled the screen, in his drab grey suits, smiling awkwardly, Nick watch as a large stain appeared down the front of the directors trousers, smiled then passed the iPad to Tom.

"Bloody child" Nick said "I am going for a kip" he said getting up and walking towards the back of the plane

"Genius" Tom said handing the iPad back to Cassia, "Bloody genius"

"Thanks Cassia said, "Excuse me, but I need to pee" she added and got up and disappeared down the back of the plane

"Okay" Nick said "Why all the secrecy" he asked as he slid into the small bathroom.

"Before I left Red Dog, I planted some extra security measures, covert stuff, I wanted to prove that no one at Red Dog was leaking information" Cassia said

"And" Nick asked

"Well, when I heard about the *fake us* getting arrested, I checked the portal, Nick there was a call made from Red Dog, from the rail shed" she said and handed Nick one of the headphones and pressed play.

Nicks face changed as the message replayed in his ears. "I know that voice" he said.

"Yeah, it's Sanvia, she has been telling Betsi what we are up too"

"I am going to fucking kill her" Nick growled.

"Wait, look I didn't want anyone else to know this, not yet there has to be more to this, there is no way she would betray us, let's get back to Red Dog, we can get to the bottom of it. If the General or the others find out, we won't be able to contain it"

"Contain it, why the hell would we want to do that" Nick asked.

"Look I don't know yet, but there is something about that message that doesn't add up, just leave it with me, I just wanted you to know" Cassia said

"Why, I mean why tell me?" Nick asked.

"I made a mistake once before of keeping you out of the loop and I promised I wouldn't do it again" Cassia said "So here I am being open" she added.

"Thanks, no I mean it I really do" Nick said

"Okay I also have to ask a favour of you" Cassia said sombrely

"Anything, just ask" Nick said

"Can you get out of the loo; I am dying for a pee" Cassia said smiling

"Very funny" Nick said opening the toilet door, checking the corridor and stepping out.

As soon as they landed in Seattle, a car was waiting to take them to the frigate, and within an hour of landing the frigate was already manoeuvring out into the gulf of Alaska.

Nick, Cassia and Tom had been quickly escorted to secure quarters, away from the others on the ship and prying eyes. Despite the success of the mission the mood in the small cabin was sombre, everyone was quiet, lost in their own thoughts

"Hey Tom" Nick suddenly said brightly "Any news on Akeem?"

"Not a thing, I really thought he would have checked in by now, but after Katie and Alten got picked up in Livermore, he's gone to ground, I just wish I knew who betrayed us" Tom said bitterly

"Well, he has probably got wind of Craig and Josh being taken out, and has no idea who he can trust," Nick said

"Yeah, that is what I figured, it's just he and I have worked together on many ops, I thought he would have known me better by now, honestly I don't care where he is, just as long as he is okay" Tom said looking out the bulkhead window at the sea shimmering in the pale, yellow moonlight.

"I get it, I felt the same about Daniel Blake, I still can't believe that little twat got into drugs, I thought he was smarter than that, he should have reached out to me" Nick moaned.

"He was probably embarrassed, didn't want to see the disappointment on your face" Cassia said wisely

"What, that's just stupid, I have always been there for the little twat" Nick snapped sharply

"And he has always looked up to you, even I saw that, he hated letting you down, trouble was it made him too nervous, he started to make mistakes, and the more he made, the worse he got" Cassia said "Bit of a vicious circle"

147

"Maybe, but I always stood by him, hey Tom did I ever tell you how the little shit saved our lives, took a bullet for us too" Nick said as the memories of the night with Zhivkov flooded back into his thoughts.

"Yeah" Tom started to say but Cassia interrupted

"I know who betrayed us" she blurted out

"What, who?" Tom demanded

"Look I couldn't say anything on the plane, I don't trust Markham not to be listening, but it was Sanvia, she has been making calls from the rail shed, feeding Betsi information on our activities" Cassia said

"No, I don't believe it, I mean I haven't known her long, but honestly, she doesn't seem the type, besides why would she do it, I mean what has she got to gain? It doesn't make any sense" Tom said and noticed that Nick nodded at Cassia.

Cassia opened her iPad and played the recording for Tom.

"Shit, that is definitely her voice, I can believe it" he said

"Well, that is just it, I don't think it is, like I said to Nick there is something off with that message, I just can't pin it down" Cassia said distractedly as her mind was trying to work out what it was.

"So, what are you going to do?" Tom asked

"I don't know, what I do know, is that I need to get back to the house, then we need to get into the pod undetected" Cassia said

"Why" Nick asked "I say we confront her, have it out" he growled

"Firstly, whoever it is, believes that they have been successful, you heard Markham, we have been arrested and taken to the FBI offices in Knoxville. That means it will be all over the net by now, so they and Betsi will think she has succeeded. That buys me some time to check the comms and net at the house.

148

Secondly, I will get David to call a full meeting in the morning, saying that they need to decided what to do, now that the three of us are out of the picture. A meeting we will monitor from the next room, based on their reactions and suggestions we will know who it is. Well, that is the best I can come up with" Cassia said.

"What, I wanna see Sarah and Archie" Nick whined.

"Sorry mate, but none of are safe, until we flush this out, and we certainly can't go on any more missions until we have" Cassia said

"I know, you're right, but know this, I am going to kill the bastard that put us all at risk" Nick growled getting up and storming out of the cabin.

"He took it well then" Tom said

"Nick is all about loyalty, he lays his life on the line for all of us, all the time, and he expects everyone to respect that, and stay loyal" Cassia said.

"I got that about him" Tom said, "So why take the risk and tell me?" Tom asked

"Because whoever it is, I know it can't be you. You have been with us all the time, you're the only one, who has" Cassia said.

"You know you can't let the others know, Markham, the President etc, don't you? If they get the slightest inkling that there is a leak at your end, they will take over the whole thing" Tom said

"Yeah, I figured that, but I also can't ignore it, that is why I need to keep this quiet, for now" Cassia said, and Nick opened the cabin door, with his knee and pushed it open with his hip, in his hand were three mugs of steaming coffee in his hand

"Look I am sorry I lost it" he said setting the coffees down on the small table.

"I'm not, if you hadn't, I would have thought something was wrong with you" Cassia said smiling.

Two miles off the coast of Red Dog, the frigate slowed and went into silent running. There was a loud tap on the cabin door where Nick, Cassia and Tom were.

"Five minutes" A deep voice growled from outside the door.

"That's us" Nick said, "Right here get into these dry suits, Cass it is going to be rough out there, I want you clipped to the boat at all times, got it?" Nick said

"Yes sir" Cassia said slipping the dry suit over her clothes"

"Okay kit check" Nick said, and they all checked each other's kit, making adjustments where required.

It was pitch black on the deck, and the Seal commander tapped Nick on the shoulder then strode off towards the back of the ship, carrying a red torch. Nick grabbed the rope that he had clipped to Cassia's suit and set off, towing her behind him, Tom fell in closely behind, keeping his head down. Several times as the cold sea spray hit the side of the ship and cascaded over them, Cassia felt herself slip and slide on the wet deck. When they got to the stern of the ship, the Seal Commander held up his right hand and stopped, then waved his red torch towards Nick and signalled him to come forwards.

Nick unclipped Cassia and handed the rope to Tom, then strode off towards the Seal Commander. There was a brief pause as the two men met, then suddenly Nick fell off the side of the ship, into the sea. Cassia was about to scream. She couldn't believe it, they had betrayed us, killed Nick. Then suddenly she felt Toms hand slip across her mouth.

"Ssh" he said, "go quietly" he added. Then the Seal Commander signalled for Cassia to be brought forwards. Cassia dug her feet into the deck, but it was slippery, she couldn't get any traction. She gritted her teeth and struggled wildly, there was no way she was going to let that man toss her overboard.

Suddenly she felt the rope around her waist tighten, she was being pulled forwards, she leant back and dug her feet in harder, but despite her best efforts she couldn't stop herself sliding forwards.

Then before she knew it, she was face to face with the Seal Commander, under his ski mask she could see him smiling, his yellow teeth glinting in the moonlight. Cassia felt her heart racing, she was going to die and there was nothing she could do to stop it. Suddenly a spark of hope, ignited inside her as Tom appeared by the side of the Commander, he smiled at her then slapped the Commander on the back. Cassia suddenly knew, Tom was part of it, he had planned this all along. She had been so stupid, welcomed him into paradise, and now this.

Despite the deafening noise of the sea crashing against the side of the boat, she still could hear the Commander laughing as he approached her. Tom had slipped round behind her and was pinning her arms to her side. Cassia fought like a wild cat. The commander was upon her now. Cassia wriggled and struggled but she was no match for Tom, he was too powerful. The Commander reached out and grabbed the rope around her waist and undid the carabiner clip. Cassia froze, she was free, there was nothing stopping him tossing her overboard. Suddenly he reached up and grabbed a wire that was dangling from a steel arm above him and clipped it to her harness. Then turned his back on her and flashed his red torch.

Suddenly Cassia felt herself being hoisted off her feet, she was hanging in the air, swaying in the cold air, being hoisted higher and higher, then suddenly she was dropping, she closed her eyes and waited, eventually she would feel the icy cold water, then it would be too late, her mind was filled with thoughts of David and Paradise, she had been so close.

Suddenly two strong arms folded around her and pulled her down, then a second later she felt something hard under her feet, and someone tugging at her harness. She opened her eyes, and there was Nick, smiling back at her.

"What the fuck" Cassia screamed, as Nick waved his red torch back up to the boat.

"Sorry Cass, but I couldn't tell you how we were going to leave the ship, you would have freaked and probably panicked. So, Tom and I came up with this plan, if it is any help, you did really well" Nick said smiling.

"Fuck you Colletto, I thought I was going to die" Cassia spat and suddenly the rigid hull of the Zodiac rocked, as a wave crashed against it, and she felt herself fall into Nicks powerful arms. He pressed his head against her ears.

"I would never let that happen, little sister" he whispered in her ear.

It took the two Zodiacs no time at all to cover two miles from the frigate to the small hidden cove near Red Dog. During the entire journey as the boat crashed through the black water, Cassia never let go of Nick, clinging to him for dear life.

As they approached the cove, the black suited man at the back and killed the engine, just as two men dressed in black, leapt over the side and waded through the dark water pulling the boat to the shore.

Shortly after one of the men placed his hands around Cassia waist and hoisted her onto the sand. Cassia said a silent pray of thanks as she felt the earth beneath her feet, then turned around to thank the man, but he was already making his way back into the water and started was pulling the other boat in. Nick was already out of the boat and engaged in conversation with the Seal Commander, at one point she saw the two of them turn around and look at her, and she could swear, above the sound of the sea, she could hear them laughing.

Cassia made her way further up the shore, took out her phone and called David to come pick them up at the airstrip, then slipped her phone back inside her dry suit. She had taken no more than a dozen steps when a hand grabbed her from behind and hauled her to the ground.

"Ssh" Nick growled clasping his hand across her mouth. "Look he whispered" and pointed Cassia face towards a thin wire running across the beach about 6 inches above the ground.

"It's a trip wire" Nick whispered quietly.

"Must be one of yours" Cassia whispered.

"No, mine are further up" Nick said then froze as a bright red dot appeared on the centre mass of his suit.

"On your feet slowly" A low voice growled "Hands in the air, no mistakes, or I will slot both of you" The voice growled.

"What the hell are you to doing, we don't have time to play in the sand" Tom said laughing as he walked up the beach.

Suddenly another red dot appeared on his chest, and he froze.

"Hands up" the voice shouted. Tom, however, didn't obey, he had a confused look on his face.

"Akeem is that you?" Tom shouted

"Major" the voice said obviously confused.

"Yes, what the hell are you doing?" Tom asked "point that weapon somewhere else" he shouted.

"Major we were betrayed in Livermore they were waiting for us" Akeem shouted

"Yeah, I know, now come out here and put the weapons down"

"It wasn't Craig or Josh, as soon as they found out they bolted" Akeem protested.

"Yeah, I know, that is what we have been doing, trying to find out who" Tom said

"It has to be one of them, everyone else was on ops" Akeem said

"It was" Tom shouted back "Now will you come out here?" he asked.

A dirty dishevelled Arab looking man appeared from the undergrowth holding two weapons, one pointed at Nick the other at Tom.

"Fuck it is so good to see you" Tom said striding forwards. Akeem hesitated then lowered his weapons.

"Boss, I don't get it, what's going on?" Akeem asked.

Tom gave Akeem an abridge version of what had happened over the past few days, omitting the piece about Sanvia.

"You are working directly with the President" Akeem said astounded.

"Pretty much, and the rest of the top brass, we have just finished an op in Oakland, fucking A, it was as well" Tom said

On the way back up to the airstrip Akeem told them that after Craig and Josh had bolted, he had finally caught up with them near the US, Mexican border, they had told him that someone had betrayed them. The Feds were waiting for them and had taken Alten and Katie, and that he couldn't trust anyone. They had wanted Akeem to join them, but he refused, he wanted to find out who had sold them out. A few hours later he had learned that Craig and Josh had been gunned down trying to cross the border. So, he made up his mind to make his way here and get to the bottom of it.

He had gotten here a few hours ago and was preparing to make his way to the house, when he saw a US frigate cruising up the gulf, then slow. Then two boats, made their way here. So, he set up the wire.

"Right" Cassia said "David will be here in a moment; he is going to take me to the house then come back and pick you lot up. Use the cabins, then we will go to Paradise in the morning. Remember no one must see you until tomorrow, so keep you heads down, and Akeem don't speak to anyone" Cassia said

Akeem gave Cassia a suspicious look and was about to say something when Tom said.

"She is kosha, mate, top, you can trust her, tonight you can bunk in my cabin, there is plenty of grub in there" Tom said

"Fine" Akeem growled as the lights of the 4 x 4 lit up the darkness.

David pulled up the 4 x4 leapt out and hugged Cassia as Nick watched on suspiciously.

Cassia was about to get into the 4 x4 when Nick pulled her back.

"Cass, how come he wasn't surprised to see you, surely he thought you were in prison" Nick asked

"Oh, I left a message for him on the portal when we were on the plane" Cassia said casually.

"What, you said none of us could communicate with Red Dog" Nick shouted.

"Nick, when you can run an encrypted portal that is routed through 16 different countries and is un hackable, then you can bend the rules" Cassia said then seeing the look on Nick face added "Don't worry, he briefed Sarah, she knows you are okay" then smiled as she saw Nick let out a breath.

"Thank fuck for that, it had only just occurred to me that if she thought I was nicked then showed up bright and bushy tailed tomorrow, she would have my nuts on a plate" Nick said laughing.

"I know, scary isn't it, almost as bad as being thrown off a boat into the sea at night, big brother" Cassia smirked.

Chapter Sixteen
Aarav and The China problem

Sunday 13th July 2025 – Red Dog

Once David had dropped Cassia off at the house, he went back to retrieve the others whilst she showered. When she was done, she grabbed a quick coffee then slipped off to mission control.

Cassia fired up the computers and started typing furiously on the keys.

"How long has she been in there?" Nick asked later that afternoon when he popped back in to grabbed some coffee.

"Since you got back, she came out about an hour ago grabbed some lunch and then went straight back in" David said deflated

"And did she say anything?" Nick asked.

"Not a word, just told me to make sure the meeting was moved forwards to this evening" David replied sourly

"What time?" Nick asked

"5pm over at the Pod, oh and Cassia said to remind you that you, Tom and Akeem need to remain out of site" David said.

"Fine" Nick said, "See you over there then" Nick said picking up a muffin and turning to go.

"Don't worry Nick, Cassia will sort it out" David said hopefully.

Nick, Tom and Akeem, after the long flight decided to run across to Paradise pad, instead of taking the rail train. Nick couldn't face going into the rail shed after finding out that the person who had betrayed them did it from there. Cassia however had no reservations and therefore got to paradise pods before them and wasn't best please when at ten past five they all came jogging up to the entrance all hot and sweating.

"Where have you been, David has been stalling them, come on I have the other conference room set up" Cassia said ushering them in the side entrance.

The conference pod was a huge glass dome and in the centre was a large natural wood table, with twenty chairs, during the summer months they often used it as the breakfast room as the early morning sunlight, glistened off the fake glass, making it sparkle.

"Okay" David said "Now were all know why we are here we need to decide what we are going to do, now that Cassia, Nick and Tom have been arrested" David said.

"Well, I vote that we take a team down to Knoxville and break them out" Mike said.

"I am up for that Alten and Katie" echoed.

"Right then its settled, so what's next" Mike asked.

"Wait, let's think this through" Sarah said "First that is exactly what they will be expecting"

"Whatever we decided to do, first we have to work out who told the authorities about our plans, we don't want a repeat of Livermore" David chipped in.

They continued to debate the options for the next hour, whilst Nick, Cassia and Tom watched on, until eventually Cassia paused the tape.

"So, what have we learned?" Nick asked.

"Well, my lot, plus Katie and Sarah all want to nip down to Knoxville and break us out, whilst Sanvia, David, Robert and Sanjay, want to negotiate with the government for our release" Tom said.

"Well, its fifty, fifty then" Nick said, "At least some of them wanted to rescue us" he said glumly.

"Now either they are good liars, or they are all telling the truth" Cassia said, "I have run all their faces through the scanner and the programme didn't pick up a single sign of anyone telling lies" Cassia said.

"Look, what is the point of all this, let's just get in there and have it out" Nick said.

"Fine" Cassia said "Come on then" she added to Nicks surprise, "But Nick you keep a lid on it, please"

Nick grunted his acceptance.

"Okay" David said raising his hands and quietening the chatter in the room, "To help us get to the bottom of how things went so badly wrong, I have asked a few of my friends to join us" he said

"Who?" Robert asked

"You will see" David replied then shouted "Come in" in a loud voice.

The moment they opened the door the room erupted with noise everyone was shocked and delighted they were back. Sarah played her part and slapped Nick round the face and called him a bastard.

Cassia explained almost everything, leaving out the part with the Government and knowing that they knew who had informed on them.

"Right" Nick said when everyone had calmed down, "Well we need to crack on, according to Cassia we have less than a month before Betsi realises her plan, so let's get too it, we need to get cracking and plan the next phase" he said and got up and watched as they started to leave.

Cassia looked up and smiled "oh Sanvia, could you stay behind, I need to catch up with you" she said.

"Of course," Sanvia said in her usual sweet, honeyed voice.

When the last person had gone, Nick, Tom and Cassia sat with Sanvia. Nick nodded to Cassia indicating he was ready to start, whilst gripping his fists tightly under the table.

Cassia took a deep breath. "Okay we know that you have been making calls from the rail shed, and we also know it wasn't you that informed on us" Cassia said

"What, no, it was definitely her on the tape" Nick shouted.

"What tape?" Sanvia said her voice shaking.

Cassia sighed "You see, we were never going back to Livermore, we had all the information we needed, however after Katie and Alten got arrested, we put together a plan to find out how they knew they were there. That is when we came up with a new plan, pretended to be going back to Livermore. Before I went however, I set up cameras and relays in the house and all outside buildings" Cassia said "and this is what we heard" she added, opening her laptop. Nick was closely watching Sanvia's face, it had gone white with fear.

Sanvia's voice filled the air. *"Livermore, West badge gate, posing as VIP guest, target computer, 1am to 3am Saturday, CN, NC, TC, end"*

A stunned look flushed across Sanvia's face "I didn't say that I swear" she cried shaking with fear, tears running down her face.

"Oh, come on, that is your voice, you can't deny it, what I want to know is why" Nick screamed

"But I didn't say that I swear" Sanvia said weakly.

"But you did make a call didn't you" Cassia said, and the room went silent as Sanvia shifted uneasily on her seat.

"Yes" she sobbed "I did" she admitted hanging her head.

"I knew it" Nick shouted, "How could you, I mean after all we have been through"

"Nick please" Cassia said "let her explain, she didn't call Betsi, she called India, didn't you? Cassia said "you see that is what

I have been working on, tracing all outgoing and incoming calls for the last month" she added.

"I was calling my son" Sanvia sobbed.

"What son?" Nick asked disbelievingly.

"I have a son, it is a secret, no one knows about him, his name is Aarav, his father and I worked together in India. We were young, I am so sorry, I had to find out if he was alright, things are not going well in India, since they found out that I was on the committee" Sanvia said sobbing and shaking. Cassia got up and went around the table and took her in her arms.

"It's okay we understand, why didn't you bring him here?" she asked.

"I wasn't sure you would agree, and I couldn't risk it getting out that I have a son" Sanvia sobbed.

"Look, no offence but how do you know what she is saying is true, I mean you heard her on the tape? Nick said

"I heard her voice, but she didn't actually say those things. I told you that I was suspicious, something was wrong with call, it didn't sound like something Sanvia would say. It wasn't Sanvia, the person who made the call, piggybacked on Sanvia's call, duplicated her voice and overlayed it with different words" Cassia said.

"Who, How?" Tom asked

"The how is easy, Sanvia, I retrieved the phone from the rail shed, is this the phone you were using?" she asked holding up a small mobile.

"Yes" Sanvia nodded sadly.

"I thought so, when I analysed it, there was an electronic recording and relay switch inside. So, every time we had a meeting here, and you had your phone with you it recorded every word. Then when you made a call, it replayed it. Then all the person who copied your voice had to do was wait for you to make a call from Red Dog, piggyback on it and over lay the conversation with their own words, making it look like it was you, covering their tracks" Cassia explained

"I didn't know" Sanvia wailed, "If I had of, I would never have made those calls" she cried, "God, I have put you all in danger" she wailed.

"You weren't to know, it took me a while to find it, you would need to have been an electronics expert to discover it" Cassia explained

"I am so sorry, I will leave, I feel so guilty" Sanvia cried.

"You will certainly not, you have to stay here, we need you" Cassia said and glared at the others.

"Yeah, of course, I mean it wasn't really your fault" Nick said.

"So, I am guessing you know where the call came from" Tom asked.

"Yes" Cassia said nodding "It originated in Washington DC, our mole, the person working with Betsi, is in Washington" Cassia said.

"It must be someone from the committee" Tom said

"Well, that's just it, I don't think so, don't you remember, it wasn't until we had the meeting with the President that they knew about Betsi and our plan, so it can't be one of them" Cassia said

"They also were the ones that told us we had a leak" Nick gruffed, "Why would they do that if it was one of them?" he asked

"So, who is it?" Tom asked

"I have managed to narrow it down to about 700,000 people" Cassia said "That is about how many people live in DC, it could be any of them" she added.

"We have to put everything on hold until we find out who" Nick said

"I don't think so, firstly, we can't afford the time, and secondly nothing has really changed think about it. We already suspected that it was someone here was giving up information on us, we now know how, just not who. So, we use it to our advantage, I mean it worked for us in Oakland, didn't it?" Cassia asked.

Nick smiled, "Of course, as long as they think they are getting information, they will focus on that" he said.

"Correct, we just need to be clever about it" Cassia said

"And make sure no one else brings a mobile phone into Paradise" Tom said

"Already on it" Cassia said.

"Sanvia, you know the open policy here, we need to tell everyone else, is that alright" Cassia asked

"Yes, it is out now, I think that Sanjay already knows about my son" Sanvia said

"We had better hurry" Cassia said, your son will be here tomorrow evening" Cassia said smiling

"What, how?" Sanvia shrieked.

"Like I said I had to trace your calls, so I spoke with him this afternoon, he is a very polite young man, and I invited him to visit, he was delighted. I mean that is presuming it is okay with you, I can always arrange for him to go straight back from Anchorage, if that is what you want? I just thought it would be good for him to see what an amazing job his mother has done" Cassia said

Sanvia started to cry again and fell into Cassia's open arms.

"I don't know what to say, I haven't seen him in six years, ever since I got involved with the committee. I couldn't risk them finding out" she sobbed "I have missed him so much"

"Well, if he likes it here, he can stay, after all you really do need some help" Cassia said

"Thank you, thank you so much, I can never repay you for your kindness" Sanvia cried as the tears streaked down her face.

"You already have, you created paradise" Nick said and felt himself choking back a tear.

"Okay" Cassia said "Now we are all loved up, perhaps we should start looking at how we are going to get to the other five computers" she said.

"Yeah right, okay, let's get everyone back in here" Nick said and got up. Once everyone was back in the conference room, Cassia updated everyone on what they had discussed during their meeting with Sanvia, and to her great relief everyone agreed it was the right thing to do.

"Right so we have five more computers left, two in China, two in Japan and one in Switzerland. Now the good news is, if the others are like the US ones, the ones in the same country are linked. The bad news is that the Chinese ones, at least are well guarded and will be very difficult to get into. The Japanese one are considerably easier" Cassia explained.

"Okay by the way you are talking I think you have a plan" Nick said smirking.

"Well, the start of one anyway. Presuming that my theory is right, I would suggest that we take on the one in China and one in Japan at the same time, two teams" Cassia said.

"Risky, I mean it didn't go so well in California" Nick said

"I know, but as I said time is short" Cassia replied.

"So, my plan is that the first team takes on the one in Wuxi, first it is the most powerful and secondly the one in Guizhou is predominantly used for defence, so it likely to be more protected, that said the one in Wuxi is not likely to be a cake walk either" Cassia said. "I suggest that Nick handles the

Chinese one as it will require a military operation, with the help of the team in DC." Cassia said.

"But who is going to do the technical bit?" Nick asked.

"I will be going with you, consider me the package you need to deliver, the rest, how we get in and out etc, you handle" Cassia said.

"So, I am going to Japan?" Alten said excitedly

"Yes, but there is a catch" Cassia said

"Go on" Tom said fascinated

"I want David to go with you" Cassia said quietly

"What, no, I am not going to Japan, why?" David said jumping up.

"Look sweetheart, I have run through every other possibility, it is the one that has the greatest chance of success, so please just hear me out" Cassia pleaded. David had seen that look on her face before and reluctantly sat down.

"Okay, so the target is Oakforest Pac's, in the Kashiwa campus in the University of Tokyo. It would be far easier than the one at the Fujitsu corporation in Kobe" Cassia said

"That still doesn't explain why you want me to do it" David said angrily

"I am getting to that, well the university has a massive biochemistry programme, with a very active Genome editing programme, the biggest in Japan. Now trawling the web, and chat channels, well David you are a bit of a super star, revered. I thought that we could put it about that you were planning a visit to Tokyo and were willing to give a talk and demonstration on your genome editing research" Cassia said.

"I told you once we left Valencia that that was the last time, I would ever use that research" David growled angrily

"Yeah, but it's the quickest and easiest way to get into that computer besides, you don't have to show them everything, just enough to peak their interest. I reckon a brilliant man like you could come up with a programme that would require access to the supercomputer" Cassia said smiling sweetly.

Nick put his hand up and covered the smirked that threatened to escape from his lips.

"But I don't know how to do your thing on a computer, I would be worse that useless" David said desperately trying to find a hole in Cassia's plan.

"That is why Alten is going with you, as your assistant, and because you are so famous, I though Katie, if she doesn't mind, could be your Publicity agent, and Mike your bodyguard, that is if it is alright with Tom" Cassia said, then added "and of course Mike"

"Your call Mike" Tom said easily.

"Shit I would rather be going with you, boss" Mike said, "But yeah, I reckon it is Okay".

"I am definitely up for it" Alten said eagerly.

"PR is right up my street, and I know a little Japanese as well" Katie said.

"What no, I haven't agreed, wait" David spluttered.

"Well tell you what" Tom said diplomatically "why doesn't David and Alten work together and see if they can come up with an alternative plan, whilst we brainstorm our China problem" he said

"Sounds great" Cassia said "David?" she said

"Yeah, fine" David grunted "but this doesn't mean that I have agreed to go" he added

"Okay, well if you take conference room two, hey and why don't you take Katie and Mike with you, four heads are better than two?" Cassia suggested

"Come on David" Katie said chirpily grabbing his hand, "We will crack this". David reluctantly got to his feet and glared at Cassia as he left the conference room, with Mike and Alten following closely behind him.

"Right so Wuxi, what do we know?" Tom said once the others had left

"Okay, well the Sunway Taihulight is housed in the National Defence and Technology university in Tianjin, on 7th street, near the Bohai bay. It is an extremely busy district but as you would expect the whole place is well guarded and almost impossible to get into, without the proper authorisation, which I can fake of course, but it would take months to get through diplomatic channels. That is why it has to be a military covert operation, plus there is no way of knowing what we will come across, even if we manage to get inside. No westerner has ever been inside the facility" Cassia said glumly.

"Well, piece of cake then" Tom said laughing

"What about our new friends can they help?" Nick asked

"I don't know, I have posted a message on the board saying we need to meet urgently" Cassia said

"Do you think that is wise in the current situation" Tom asked, "I mean knowing that the leak is in DC?" he added

"We don't have any choice, if this goes pear shaped then there will be one huge diplomatic incident, plus I reckon we are going to need all the help we can get" Cassia said.

"Okay, team" Nick said

"Well Cassia, You Nick, I would like to take Akeem, not only is he a top marksman he is also fluent in Mandarin" Tom said.

"I want Sarah to come along, well at least make her the offer, she is one of the best I have ever worked with, and I know she will have my back, plus she is going a bit stir crazy here, seeing me jetting off everywhere" Nick said

"Okay so that is five, I still reckon we are one or two short" Tom said

"I don't like bringing in outsiders" Nick said, "You don't know who you are getting, where their loyalties lie" he added.

"Then we need to get to DC and see what help they can supply, I will let you know as soon and the we receive notification, until then I am going to try and narrow down that list of suspects in DC" Cassia said.

"Cass, we need to come up with some alternatives, stuff we can feed Betsi, keep her off our track" Nick said.

"Yeah, I know, I am working on that, the one I am worried about is Japan, once they find out David is going to be there, it will be all over the web" Cassia said

Chapter Seventeen
A plan for China

The military plane touched down in DC a little before 8am and as they disembarked the proverbial black SUV was wating for them

"Okay The President said" "Welcome and thank you for arranging this meeting at such short notice. Before we start, I must tell you that I have only one hour, before I need to leave" The President said.

At the meeting was Avril Haines, Miles Beecham, General Markham, Andrew and Chuck, and as usual, Mr White sat quietly at the back.

"Thank you, Mr President, let me start with a quick update. We have identified the leak, that is to say that we know that it did not originate from Red Dog. I have the data for your expert to corroborate" Cassia said, "But in short, the Red Dog was bugged, and the information was passed by running on the back of a phone signal from the house at Red Dog" Cassia said nervously

"And who was doing this?" The President" asked.

"That Mr President, we do not know yet" Cassia said emphasing the word 'Yet' "But what we can tell you is that it originated in Washington DC" she said and a paused.

There was stunned silence across the room, as the President looked at each and everyone in the room.

"I can also report that I do not believe that anyone in the room is responsible, because the communication happened before, our first meeting with you" Cassia added, and saw more than one of the people around the table breathe a sigh of relief.

"I would like Mr White to assist you in tracking down our breach" The President said nodding towards the small

Chinese man, "Please can you share your evidence with him" The President asked, then smiled at Cassia, "I do have a little good news for you, Miss Nilsson, Mr White has not been able to crack your new cyber security systems, either in the White house or the Pentagon, and believe me that is indeed a great compliment" The President added.

"Okay so on to today's meeting, what is next?" The President asked.

Nick got to his feet, took a deep breath "We are tackling two sites, one in China and the other in Japan. The Chinese one is the Sunway supercomputer in the National supercomputing centre in Wuxi, and the Japanese one is at University of Tokyo" Nick said and saw a small smile creep across the face of Mr White.

"Why those two?" Avril Haines asked

"Well first of all" Cassia sighed "The other Chinese site at Guizhou is at the National University of Defence, it's in Southern China, and is surrounded by two military garrisons. I am not saying the other one in Wuxi is much better, but it is the lesser of two evils" Cassia said.

"I see, and the Japanese one?" Avril asked

"Now that one is easier, it is on the University of Tokyo Kashiwa campus. That campus also has an extensive Biochemistry programme and some pretty active and passionate students and professors. Well, it so happens that we have somewhat of a celebrity in that field, so I have arranged for him to conduct some talks and demonstrations, of course these will involve access to their computer" Cassia said

"You mean Mr David Carmichael?" Miles Beecham said, his face cold and hard.

"Yes, although I have to also say that he is rather reluctant" Cassia confessed.

"And your plans for this one in Wuxi?" Avril interrupted.

"Well, that is why we called the meeting, you see whilst we have site plans, and know where it is, because of the closed net situation in China, we can't find out very much else about it. We hoped perhaps you may have some connections, someone we could speak too, plus, the only way to do this is through a military operation" Cassia admitted

"What is a closed net" Andrew asked and several of the other looked at him with derisive looks.

"Chinese internet operates under very different circumstances, whilst here in the western world anyone, can access anything, in China it is very different. Their internet, search engines etc are regulated by the government, which means unless you can get past that, which I can, of course, they still have several more layers of security. The only way in, is to recruit someone on the inside, and we simply do not have the time to develop someone" Cassia said

"Oh, I see, and do we have anyone?" Andrew asked smiling hopefully at the rest of the group.

The President smiled "I was rather hoping that you may choose that one, you see in November 2016, when it was first constructed. A delegation from the United States was invited on a diplomatic mission to Wuxi, to validate the claims made by the Chinese government" The President said

"I read the report on it, sometime later, it is indeed a truly impressive computer, well at least from what little I could understand. The defence committee I was chairing, at the time, were worried about its potential. Therefore, we commissioned a covert mission to recruit one of their lead technical bods, which we hoped would enable us to stay one step ahead" The President said.

"Mr White" Cassia blurted out, "You recruited Mr White" she said as the penny dropped.

"Indeed, Mr White, which I am sure you have deduced is not his real name, was one of the four original designers of the security systems and computer. Sadly, shortly after our diplomatic mission, he met with a terrible accident, well if you believe the official report. He has been working with us ever since, our go to guy, so to speak" The President said smiling at the small Chinese man sitting at the back.

"That's brilliant" Tom said, "If he built it, he will know how to hack into it" he added

"That is impossible" Mr White said in a perfect English accident, his voice warm and familiar.

"Perhaps, Mr White would be kind enough to tell us the kind of security protocols that they may have in place" Cassia said smiling sweetly at the small man.

The small Chinese man got to his feet and went and stood beside the white board on the wall at the far end of the table.

"Firstly, you are quiet correct, Miss Nilsson, the Chinese computers work on a closed net, however there is an additional closed net within that one, this one links both the computers in Guizhou and Wuxi, these two also work under an AES encryption algorithm" Mr White explained

"Oh the 256" Cassia interrupted

"No, Miss Nilsson, the 512" Mr White said.

"That is impossible, I have never heard of that one" Cassia said

"That is because outside of China it does not exist" Mr White said arrogantly.

"Is that a problem?" The President asked.

"More like a glitch, but I am sure I can overcome it" Cassia replied and smiled as Mr White raised his eyebrows.

"However," Mr White said, breaking that code is only one of your problems. Firstly, gaining access is virtually impossible.

You see there is a double security lock access" and seeing the confused look on the faces, picked up the marker and drew on the board.

"Okay, There are two glass entrance pathways, behind which are armed guards. The first gate is here at the entrance. To pass through this, you must place your finger on the pad and a small sample of your blood is taken, via a small prick. This is then analysed and matched against the DNA of every employee, which is stored on site. If you pass this test, then you get to access the second gate. You do this by walking along a glass corridor. During your transition, your gate and mannerisms are tracked, and compared to your last three visits, if it does not match, you are arrested and taken away. Once you reach the end of this corridor, presuming you have been successful, you will have to enter a 16 alpha numeric code that is changed daily and given manually only to those that have passed the first gate" Mr White explained

"Right, easy then" Nick said sarcastically

"That is not the end of it Mr Colletto. Even if you manage to pass these initial precautionary measures and convince the guards to deactivate the usual security protocols, thermal cameras, floor pressure pads, which have been instantly updated by the technology in the corridors. You will still not be able to access the computer, you see it has a double gateway access protocol" Mr White said, smiling and heard Cassia gasp

"What the hell is that?" Nick asked

"It means, you will need two people at two different terminals, each will have to place their fingerprints on the grey pads at the same, and I am guessing there is a time limit" Cassia said

"Within 1.2 seconds of each other" Mr White said smiling

"So, what you are saying is that it is impossible to hack from the outside, or go in the through the front door, and even if you made it all the way through to where the computer was, you would need two people completely in sync to access it" Nick growled.

"Do you still think this one is the easiest" Avril asked, "Perhaps we should consider the other one" she added

"I am afraid that that one has the same protocols plus an additional protection, as it is the one that is used for our defence. It has 6 armed guards 24/7 stationed within the computer room. In addition to this, the only people that are allowed to use this computer are military personnel and have to be of Chinese decent. I am afraid that along with the DNA analysis, too find two willing technology scientists, with the correct skills, DNA and access code, would prove to be very difficult" Mr White said

"So that is it then, it's impossible we can't get into either of them, Betsi has won, what I don't understand is how she manage to get in?" Chuck said

"Betsi, is not human, for non-organic life forms the task is different. I would suggest that as she made up of the one universal language, access for her, whilst still difficult would not be impossible" Mr White said.

"What universal language, can we just duplicate it and get in the same way?" Tom said grasping at straws.

"The universal language is one used by all computers and is the most widely spoken in the world. It is binary language and forms the basis of every single electronic programme and communication, in the world. Once a year, both the Sunway and the Milky way are opened to the outside world, this process is conducted under the strictest of protocols, this is where their database of viruses is updated, to ensure they are up to date" Mr White explained.

"Well can't we get in then; I mean Cassia is a whizz at that sort of thing" Tom said

"That was my first thought" Cassia sighed, "And I have set it up should we fail. The problem is, Milky way is updated in

September, the exact date is not known, and the Sunway, is updated in December, again the date is not known, and I believe that this may well be sadly too late" Cassia explained.

"So that is it, we are screwed" Chuck said

"Not entirely" Mr White said "There are two possibilities, albeit small"

"Go on" Miles said wanting to get in on the act.

"First how essential is it that the Chinese do not know we have been there?" Mr White asked.

"Well, that's simple, our relationship with China is at an all-time low, if they were to discover that we have entered their territories without consent, then it would create a serious diplomatic incident" The President said

"Okay, then we only have one possibility. Cassia, can you please bring up the site plan for Wuxi, and project it onto the television screen" Mr White asked

Cassia typed away on her iPad, whilst Mr White turned on the screen, a few seconds later Cassia pointed her iPad at the screen, made a swiping movement and suddenly the site plan of the National Computing centre in Wuxi, appeared on the screen.

"I presume you have the schematic?" Mr White asked

"I do" Cassia said and the image on the screen changed to an architects plan.

"One of the greatest achievements the Sunway boosts is that it is incredibly energy efficient, requiring less megawatts per petaflop, than any other supercomputer on the planet. It achieves this high accolade, by doing two things" Mr White explained.

"Please Cassia, turn the image round 45 degrees on its axis" Cassia followed his instruction until he said 'thank you.

"Now these two long pipes are two meters by two meters in diameter. They run from the base of the computer centre through into the Bohai bay" Mr White said and waited for everyone to mentally catch up.

"Every night between 3am and 4am, the centre draws water from the bay and flushes it through its cooling system, then expels it back out" Mr White explained pointing to the two tubes.

"Okay so we could access the centre through those tubes?" Nick said.

"Firstly, they are underwater, and secondly whilst the water is static there are sensor alarms every twenty feet. The alarms used to be on during the flushing process, however, the debris sucked in kept activating them, so they decided to turn them off, during the flushing process" Mr White said

"Whoa, wait a minute" Tom said, "You just said sucked in?" he added.

"Indeed, there are powerful pumps that draw the water in at speeds of up to 100kph, and the water passes through three steel filter grids before it reaches the pumps" Mr White said.

"And I am guessing that the reverse applies to the water coming back out" Nick said.

"Correct, I did say that the possibility was small. However, there is some good news, there a brief pause of 17 minutes when the water level drops 20% whilst it circulates through the servers" Mr White said.

"So, all we have to do it stop ourselves being sucked into the pumps" Nick said sarcastically.

"However even if you manage to get to the access grates, you will still have to overcome the thermal cameras, heat sensors and all of the other security protocols, including the double gateway access protocol" Mr White said.

"I might be able to help there" General Markham said, after being unusually quiet during the meeting.

"What you know how to overcome the security?" Nick asked

"Sadly not, but I may be able to help you, get there. Our seal team have been testing a new, electric DPV units, capable of in excess of 30 knots, it's pretty brutal, but it could counteract, or at least slow the drag down" General Markham said

"Sorry DPV?" Cassia asked.

"Diver propulsion unit" The General replied.

"Okay so let me get this straight, you want me to go underwater, into a tunnel, where the pumps at the other end will drag me towards them at 100 kph, carrying a thingy that you hope will slow me down before I get shredded by any one of three steel grids" Cassia exclaimed

"That is about the top and bottom of it" General Markham said "Oh and not forgetting that when the water comes out, it will shoot you out like a bullet" he added

"Are you nuts, that is lunacy, it's crazy" Cassia screamed.

"Unless you can come up with a better idea, then that is the only way" Mr White said "Oh and by the way, the water it expels is around 65 degrees centigrade, and you will have exactly 22 minutes to exit the tubes before the system resets, and you are stuck inside them" Mr White said.

"Perfect" Cassia said sarcastically "Shredded one way or boiled the other"

Nick looked at Cassia with a smirk on his face "Cass, hypothetically if I can get you to the access grates, can you come up with a way of beating the protocols" he asked smiling.

"Theoretically yes, I have a few ideas, the problem will be the synchronisation with the second person, but theoretically yes" Cassia said cautiously.

Nick looked at Tom and they both smiled. "It's possible" they said in unison "We can do it"

"Wait Nick what the hell are you on about, I am not doing it, first I am not a great swimmer, secondly, how do I put this, its suicide" Cassia screamed

Nick smiled, do you remember when we first discussed which site to take and you said that you were the package and it was my responsibility to get you in and out, so it was up to me" Nick asked

Cassia glared at Nick, "I meant alive" she snarled.

"Cass, its fine, we will go in tandem, all you will have to do is hold on tight and try not to suck up all your oxygen in the first five minutes" Nick said, then smiled "Trust me" he added.

"Err hum" Mr White said "You are forgetting one thing, there will be two packages, Miss Nilsson cannot, do it alone" he added.

"Right, so who?" Nick asked

"Whilst I do not cherish the idea, I can see no alternative, I will have to come with you" Mr White said sombrely

"Cool, then we are a go" Nick said

"Wait, no, what Nick" Cassia said nervously.

"Well like the man said Cass, have you got any better ideas?" Nick asked

"Well, no, not yet" Cassia replied

"Well, when you do, then we can always change our plan, but until then this is all we have. General, do you have any training facilities we could use, we need to test the kit out" Nick asked

"Sure, I'll get you the location and we can set it up, when do you need it?" General Markham asked.

"Okay with testing, training and prep, and we are going to need some help, a seal team and covert craft" Nick said thinking out loud, "then we have to get on locale, so I say we go in a week from today, that means we should hit the site on the 23rd" Nick said looking at Tom who nodded his agreement.

"Then that is settled, General Markham, I am sure you will provide the necessary support" The President said, "Now I am sorry, but I must leave you now, and good luck to you all" he added.

Once the others had left General Markham stayed behind at Nick request.

"Okay General, I also need to plan a fake covert attack on the one in Guizhou, it has got to sound kosha, and then we will covertly leaked different versions of it through selected sources" Nick said

"May I ask why?" General Markham asked.

"We need to find out the source of the leak, so we will alter the story and see who runs with it" Nick said.

"And you trust me?" The General asked.

"That will depend on which version gets leaked and picked up" Nick said blankly.

"I see, well thanks for the vote of confidence" The General said coldly.

"Don't take offence, it is just a precautionary matter" Nick said

"Right if that is it, I presume you will let us know when the training facility is ready" Nick said

"Give me a day, I will have it sorted, until then you can stay in DC, or return to Red Dog, either way my plane is at your disposal" The General said.

"Thanks, I am going to stay here, I need to sort some things out" Nick said

"Do you need a hand?" Tom asked, and Nick nodded.

"Well, I need to get back to Red Dog, I need to sort out Japan" Cassia said glaring at Nick.

Nick and Tom dropped Cassia at the airport and just before she boarded the plane, she gave Nick a big hug and whispered, "While you're here, I am going to teach Sarah how to cut off your bollocks, whilst you are asleep" she said smiling

"I love you too" Nick said kissing her gently on the cheek.

Chapter Eighteen
Sophie and Maisie

Monday 14th July 2025 – Washington DC

Nick and Tom travelled back to the warehouse in Maryland. The light was just starting to fade when they arrived and after checking the security protocols, Nick pulled the door open.

"Beers in the fridge mate" Nick said as he walked in and started to review the security cameras, checking to see if anyone had been in there.

"Cheers" Tom said, striding over to the large American style fridge, humming in the far corner. He selected two Coors, tapped the lids and passed one to Nick

"Pizza" Nick said opening his mobile

"Yeah pepperoni, please" Tom said suspiciously. Nick ordered the pizza, closed his phone, grabbed his beer and sat next to Tom at the conference table.

"All right, what's the score, you have enough kit back in Red Dog to supply a private army. The General has your list of requirements for China, so the only reason you would want to remain in DC, is either a personal matter, or as you agreed to me accompanying you, you want to have something out with me. For fuck sake Nick, what have I got to do to prove myself to you lot?" Tom bristled angrily

"Nothing mate, I have been watching you, you're as good as any, your boys respect you, and you have no trouble in making the tough calls, so I am all good" Nick said

"Well go on then, why?" Tom said

"Because like me you are a squaddie, and I reckon we follow the same tradition, and it didn't feel right doing it in Red Dog" Nick said smiling at Tom and lifting his beer up.

Tom smiled back, he knew exactly what Nick meant, he had just lost two blokes in action, and tradition dictates, that when you lose someone in combat, those that make it back, get pissed and honour the fallen ones memory.

"To Craig and Josh" Tom said tapping his beer against Nicks

"Fallen comrades" Nick said downing his beer in one. Three beers each and 19 minutes later, Nick suddenly spotted the pizza delivery man stood outside frantically searching for a bell, or knocker.

"Fuck, pizza's here" Tom said getting off his stool. Nick grabbed his arm

"Wait he said," checking his phone, Tom looked at him confused, "Wait" Nick said again, "Wait" he repeated, and Tom's face knotted with confusion and looked at Nick, had the beer already gone to his head, he didn't look pissed.

"Wait" Nick said again

"Nick what the fuck is going on?" Tom said, "I bloody starving, I am going to get the pizza" Tom said, Nick grabbed his arm and checked the camera, the pizza delivery guy was frantically dashing back and forwards outside the door.

"Wait" he growled, then smiled, "Right now you can get the pizza"

Tom wrenched open the door and the spotty face pizza delivery guy looked at him in despair, his face despondent.

"Right" Tom said getting out his wallet, "How much" he asked

"It's free mate, it took us longer than 20 minutes to delivery it" the pizza delivery guy said and suddenly Tom twigged what Nick had been doing.

"Listen mate, does this mean you have to pay for it out of your own pocket?" Tom asked.

"Yeah" the young delivery guy said. Tom smiled "here" he said handing him a 20 dollar note and took the pizza's and walked back to the conference table.

"You twat, you knew that didn't you?" Tom said "Poor little bastard, nearly pissed himself"

"I did a Digger" Nick said smiling

"A what?" Tom asked opening his pepperoni pizza box and pulling out a huge slice.

"A Digger, he was one of my crew, Digger Jenkins, he was always doing that, scored loads of free pizza's, at one time we were barred from every pizza place this side of the Potomac" Nick said smiling to himself

"Where is he, this Digger bloke?" Tom asked, although by the distant look on Nicks face, he thought he knew the answer.

"Lost him in Valencia, along with Ati, my eyes" Nick said solemnly

"Sorry to hear that" Tom said swigging down the last of his beer and picking up another slice of pizza.

"Don't matter, Digger was a twat" Nick said getting to his feet, "You like whisky" he asked wandering over to an old battered looking huge steel cabinet, in the corner.

"I would drink a Spanish whores sweat, if I thought it would get me pissed" Tom said, and Nick laughed loudly.

"Never heard that one before, here" he said pulling out a large bottle of unopened single malt, two glasses, and filling them three quarters full.

"To fallen comrades" Nick said raising his glass, tapping it against Tom, downing it in one and filling the glasses back up. "So why did you join up?" Nick asked

"Usual shit, stay away father, drug addled mom, spent half my life hopping from one foster carer to another, they were all twats" Nick said downing his second glass and feeling the golden liquid slide smoothly down to his stomach.

"More" Nick said meaning, did he want more whisky, as he refilled their glasses, but Tom mistook it and said.

"Well, there isn't much more, mothers were alright, always wanted to smother me, their husbands on the other hand usually tended to be a little handsy, so as I got older, I learned to defend myself and hit back. Well, I don't know if you know, but by the time you get to 8 or 9, the choices of foster homes tends to dry up, so you end up in a state place, that's where they stick the kids, they can't handle. When I was 13, I legged it, lived on the streets, got in with the wrong sort, until one day, just after my 17th birthday a judge offered me a choice, Army or jail, so I joined up" Tom said swigging his whisky back and taking another slice of pizza.

"Army's fucking great" Nick slurred "I used to love it" he added grappling for a slice of pizza.

"Yeah" Tom said and felt his head start to swim, "best thing I ever did, it was my whole life, fucking great, especially when I joined the seals, family they are" he slurred, pieces of pizza cheese hanging off his chin.

"Best mates a bloke can ave" Nick said, pouring more whisky into the glasses, "Never let you down, always got your back, bloody good mates that's what they are, I tell you" Nick said steadying himself on the table.

"They are like brothers" Tom said with a silly smile spread across his face. Then a thought hit him like a thunderbolt, he belched loudly "And sisters, they are good as well" he added grinning

"I love Sarah, she is wonderful" Nick said, "hard as nails, kick mine and your arse any day, I love her" Nick said hugging the whisky bottle.

"You got yourself a good one there, good looking too, you are one lucky bastard" Tom said

"She saved my life" Nick slurred "More than once too, she is a diamond, I love her" Nick said smiling. Then as always when alcohol plays keep away with the brain a thought popped into his mind.

"I should call her, she needs to know, that I am lucky" Nick said picking up his mobile and trying to focus on the numbers. Suddenly the room filled with a ringing sound and after a few moments, a woman's voice answered.

"I love you" Nick said, "You is the bestis woman in the whole wide world, and I dove you, I really, really do" Nick said

"Hello" Nick, "Thank you for telling me that, but I suspect you want Sarah" Cassia said laughing, "I'll pass the phone to her" she added.

"Are you pissed again Colletto?" Sarah's disapproving voice growled from the phone.

"I love you" Nick said hugging the phone, "I do you know, you is wonderful, you is" Nick slurred. "I miss Digger and Ati and Manny, they were good blokes you know, I love them blokes, Daniel too, but I love you more" Nick said grinning at the phone, as if Sarah could see him.

"Go sober up and get your arse back here" Sarah snapped.

"Oh Archie, I wanna speak to Archie, let me speak to Archie" Nick said begging.

"Nick it is 1am, Archie is asleep, now piss off, I want to go to bed" Sarah said angrily

"You have to tell me you love me, or" Nick said trying to get his tongue to form the right words, "Or I will kill myself" he slurred

"Of course, I love you, always have you knucklehead, and always will, now piss off" Sarah said and cut the phone off.

"See, told ya, she loves me" Nick said smirking at Tom, "she's a diamond she is"

Tom burst into fits of giggles, "you thought it was Sarah, but it was Cassia, you told Cassia you loved her" Tom giggled like a schoolboy

Nicks face suddenly looked shocked as it dawned on him, what he had just done.

"Fuck, I gotta call Cassia and tell her that I love Sarah and not Cassia" he said and tried to grab his phone, stumbled and fell on to the floor.

Tom staggered over to where Nick was lying and hauled him back to his feet. Then in a moment of drunken clarity said "You did tell Sarah; Cassia gave her the phone" he said triumphantly as if he had just made an amazing discovery.

"I love that woman" Nick said

"I was in love once" Tom said sitting next to Nick, after getting another bottle of scotch from the cabinet and pouring two large glasses full. "Sophie" he said staring into his glass. Nick stared at him, half grinning, his eyes trying to focus on his friend.

"I bet you loved her, and she loved you, cause you are a top bloke" Nick said then belched loudly.

"She was the best thing in my life, we had a daughter, Maisie, she was beautiful, perfect" Tom said tears rolling down his face as he stared into his glass.

Nick was trying to prop himself up on his elbows, trying hard to focus and failing dismally, he closed his eyes.

"I am listening" Nick said softly "Just these lights are killing my eyes, carry on mate" Nick said quietly

"She was perfect, my life was finally perfect. A beautiful smart wife and a perfect daughter. I had everything a man ever wanted" Tom slurred. "Then one day it was all gone. Masie was ill, cancer, my perfect little blond-haired girl was being eaten alive by cancer" Tom said and slugged back another large swallow of whisky

"She couldn't take it, my Sophie, she watched Maisie die in her arms, just drift away, gone. I was in Iraq, fighting ragheads, then I got a call to the CO's office, he said my Maisie had died and that Sophie had committed suicide" Tom said, "I wasn't there Nick, I should have been there" Tom shouted.

"I am sorry mate, that's a hard one to live with" Nick said quietly sobering up

"I just take each day as it comes, it's what it is like when you don't have a heart, just one day at a time" Tom said staring into his glass.

"Well, like it or not, you have always got me and Sarah, and a place to hide in Red Dog, if you need it" Nick said and put his arm around the man who was crying freely beside him.

"Cheers mate" Tom said sniffing, "You never know one day I may just turn up on your doorstep" he added wiping his eyes.

"Tell you what" Nick said picking up the whisky bottle and pouring two very large glasses and slopping a good deal more on the table.

"To Sophie, little Maisie, Sarah and Archie" he said handing Tom a glass and raising his unsteadily in the air. The glasses clinked and for the next hour, the two ageing soldiers drank themselves into a stupor.

Chapter Nineteen
A day full of surprises

David was waiting for Cassia as she landed the Cessna. He pulled up the collar of his thick plaid jacket as the cold wind swept around him.

"Bloody, climate change" he grumbled under his breath, and still people didn't believe it was real. Here, mid-July and its bloody freezing, he thought, as he watched the Cessna taxi back from the end of the runway. Okay, he thought, took a deep breath and steadied himself. He had spent the last 24 hours making up his mind, and finally after much deliberation, he had come to a decision.

"Hi baby" Cassia said climbing out of the plane after she had parked it in the large shed.

"I am not doing it" David blurted out

"What no hello, how was your trip?" Cassia said cheerfully.

"I have been up half the night going over it, and I am not going to Japan, Cass I can't, I mean, I can't have my research used for the creation of freaks, it's not right. Look I know it's important and I would do anything else, but I can't be responsible for" He paused searching for the right words.

He had rehearsed this speech inside out and backwards, but now she was stood in front of him, the words seemed to float away in the icy wind that was gusting in the shed.

"Look, I don't want to fight about this, but I have made up my mind" David eventually said

"I know, and I don't blame you I wouldn't go either" Cassia said smiling. David felt the wind taken out of his sails, he was sure that she would try to convince him, make him do it, blackmail him, lay on him a guilt trip, saying she was risking her life every day, whilst he was lounging around here with his feet up, anything except that she agreed with him.

"What, but I thought you said it was the only way?" David stuttered

"It is, but I will just have to find another way, anyway its freezing, can we get back to the house, I need a shower and some coffee, I am really tired and have a lot to do" Cassia said sweetly

"Yeah, sure, car is ready" David said uneasily and opened the door of the 4 x 4 and watched as Cassia got in.

"Don't you want to go to paradise?" David asked getting in the driver's seat.

"If it is alright with you honey, can we just go to the house, have some alone time, before we face all the others. If I go back there now, I will be inundated with questions, can't we just grab an hour or two alone?" Cassia asked.

When they got back to the house, David drew Cassia a bath, and whilst she bathed, he prepared her some lunch, he couldn't help feel worried. She was different, quieter somehow. She had lost some of her spark, and he didn't know why. Perhaps he thought, it was because he had let her down by refusing to go to Japan. He felt a sudden surge of guilt, perhaps she was right, we all had to do our bit, maybe he was just being self-fish.

"Ooh what is that wonderful smell?" Cassia said padding into the kitchen with just a fluffy white towel wrapped around her.

"Falafels, B'sara, a Moroccan soup, freshly baked bread and couscous, your favourites" David said smiling

"Oh, I love you, perfect, just what I needed" Cassia said then smiled

"Alright what did you do?" she asked seeing the freshly picked flowers on the kitchen table

"What, nothing, I just wanted you to see some nice things when you got back, that's all" David said going red.

"I see, and tell me Mr Carmichael, does that soup taste as good, reheated?" Cassia asked cryptically.

"Well, some people would say that once the cumin has had time to infuse with the vegetables and beans, it actually tastes better, however the" David said, and stopped as Cassia leaned in and kissed him gently on the neck, whilst reaching down and turning the stove off.

"I think my stomach can wait a little longer" she cooed in his ear, dragging him towards the bedroom "Don't you?" she said.

"Err well the bread is" David said smiling

"Carmichael, get your arse into that bedroom now, or the next time you wake up there may just be parts of you missing" Cassia shouted mischievously.

That *little longer* lasted for three hours, in which time Cassia had padded out to the kitchen, heated the soup, grabbed the bread and they both ate in bed.

"I got to thinking on the way back from Anchorage, that ever since we started this whole thing, we have had no time together, either I am away rescuing someone, or you are up at Paradise building things. Do you realise that in the last 6 months we have not had a single minute to ourselves" Cassia asked, stuffing mouthfuls of soup-soaked bread into her mouth.

"I knew the moment I met you that you were a focussed, passionate woman, it is one of the things I love about you the most. I do worry that you seem to carry the world on your shoulders, think it is your responsibility to solve the world's problems" David said

"I know right, well no more, the world can go to hell, its someone else's turn to step up to the plate" Cassia said "Besides, we have Paradise, we can lock ourselves away here, god knows we have definitely done our bit" she added, putting the empty soup bowl down on the nightstand and brushing breadcrumbs off their thick eider down duvet.

"Cass" David said cautiously, "I am not disagreeing with you, but what brought this on, I mean you left here fired up and passionate, and now" he paused "Well now you are different" he said cautiously

"When I got to DC, nothing had changed, people were still going about their business as if everything was normal. Going to work, drinking in bars, walking in parks, their lives were just as they always have been. Here we were busting our guts to save them" Cassia said

"That is because they don't know how bad climate change is, we decided not to release that information, as it would cause anarchy" David said.

"Yeah, but the Government hasn't done a thing, it's been almost a year, and I for one don't see any changes. It is as if they have just accepted their fate, so why should we care?" Cassia asked

"There have been developments, some at least, I know of at least 3 other paradise pods that have sprung up since we released the plans" David said

"But it is not going to be enough, honestly David, it finally occurred to me, their hands need forcing, we should let Betsi do her thing, at least she doesn't have any other agenda. What she is doing is preserving humanity, that has got to be better" Cassia said

"Yeah, but at what cost" David barked angrily "Christ sake Cass, she is planning on murdering millions. Let alone what she will do the financial economy, that will create chaos, there will be riots, panic" David shouted

"Oh, and I think you are forgetting that she plans to use my research to create super humans, so what's left of humanity, those that are not cast out into the wastelands, left by the changing climate, will become slaves, robots all reporting to her. How in god's name can that be better" he shouted.

"Well what choice do we have, look I didn't like it either, but let's be honest it is inevitable. So why not let it happen, what are we really doing, just buying time?" Cassia said

"What choice, I will tell you what bloody choice we have, we do what we said we would and put a stop to her. Then at least whatever time humanity has left, it is their choice and not dictated by some bloody machine" David said angrily

"Well then I had better come up with a plan for Japan quickly time is running out, and I need to be in China this time next week" Cassia said getting out of bed and pulling on her bathrobe.

"Fine, I will do it, but I am not turning over any research to them, theory only" David said

"What if you could save a little girls life, and still not give away any of your research?" Cassia asked

"What?" David asked confused

"Okay, here is the real reason why I want you to go to Japan. Professor Haru Tanaka is the head of the Biochemistry lab, and his five-year-old daughter Himari, was diagnosed with stage 4 pancreatic cancer, early this year. The chemo and radio therapy are having no effect, she is going to die unless someone helps her. So, I thought that you could use your research for something good, and at the same time, lock Betsi out of the computers in Japan" Cassia said

"But this Professor, does he even want help?" David said

"When I was leaking information about your potential trip to Japan, he reached out to me. He knows it is a long shot, but he has asked if you could at least try, he is desperate David" Cassia said

"And he doesn't want to do anything else with it, I mean create super enhanced beings that sort of thing?" David asked cautiously.

"Not that he is telling me, his idea is that you could give a lecture to his students, outlining the risks involved with Bio Hacking, apparently some are already experimenting, he seems to think that they may listen to you. Then if you are willing, whilst you are there, you could at least have a look at Himari, either that or" Cassia said and left the words hanging in the air like a threat.

"and I suppose whilst we are running the data, Alten will sort out Betsi" David said

"That is about the sum of it" Cassia answered honestly

"And he is not expecting a miracle, I mean it may not work?" David asked

"David, by the sound of his email, he is grasping at straws, there is less than a two percent chance she will last until the end of the year, all the doctors have given up hope" Cassia said

"Fine, as long as he doesn't hold it against me if I fail" David said.

"I think he will be extremely grateful that you are even willing to try" Cassia said snuggling up to him and nibbling on his neck

"Oh Cass, don't think I didn't know what you were doing" David said knowingly

"Okay, guilty as charged, I just think you needed a little push, and I really enjoyed doing it" she said kissing him on the cheek, "Now I am off for a shower" she said happily.

David laid back on the soft bed and stared out of the window, smiling. She was as cunning as a fox, he thought, but he did love her, more than life itself.

After Cassia had finished her shower, whilst David cleared the dishes and tided the kitchen, she checked the security logs, and was relieved to see that there had not been any more breeches. Then together with David they rode the rail train back to paradise pods.

"Oh, I meant to ask" Cassia said snuggling closer to David as the rail train sped it way to paradise. "Did Sanvia's son arrive?" she asked.

"He sent a message, he was arriving this morning, apparently, he was delayed a last-minute meeting. In fact, Gary was due to land with him 20 minutes after you arrived, Robert picked him up and took him to paradise, he should be there by now" David said

"Oh, I wish you had told me earlier, I would have waited at the airstrip and welcomed him" Cassia said

"I rather think you had other things on you mind" David said smugly "besides, you can officially welcome him, when we get there" he added

"Yeah, your right, anyway I am sure he is desperate to see his mother and not some ageing old hacker" Cassia said.

"Your right, you are knocking on a bit" David said smiling

"Mr Carmichael" Cassia snapped "either you take that back right now, and tell me I am the most beautiful creature you have ever had the fortune to lay eyes on, or do you remember that thing we just did back at the house?" Cassia asked and David grinned.

"Yeah," he said smiling with a silky grin on his face.

"Well, you better keep hold of that memory as it will be your last" Cassia said and pinched him

"Ouch" David yelped "You know that you are the most beautiful creature I have ever seen, and each day, you just get better, I am a lucky man" David cooed

Cassia grabbed hold of his arm, "close enough" she said as the train pulled into the shed

"Okay host face on" she said "we need to officially welcome our newest resident"

When they walked into the central area, Katie and Robert were nervously waiting for them with anxious looks on their faces.

"Hello Katie" Cassia said folding her arms around her and hugging her.

"Wow what the hell is wrong with you, you look like you have seen a ghost" Cassia said pulling back and looking at her friend.

"In there" Katie said, "You need to see Sanvia's son, they are in there having coffee right now" she added.

"What, why what's wrong with him, he hasn't got two heads has he?" Cassia asked walking towards the conference.

"You'll see" Katie said cryptically

"Don't be so silly, I am sure he is alright" Cassia said opening the conference door.

Cassia froze as her eyes fell on the figure in front of her, holding Sanvia's hands

"Mr White, what the hell are you doing here?" Cassia shrieked

"Accepting your kind invitation to spend some time with my mother" Mr White said

Cassia felt the fog thicken in her mind, "I don't understand, I mean, well" she spluttered.

"Sit down Cassia" Sanvia said, "I will explain everything, Aarav has told me he has already met you" she added.

Cassia slumped down onto one of the chairs and David put a coffee on the table in front of her, then got one for himself and sat alongside her.

"I met Aarav's father, Yichen in 1982, he was a Chinese state emissary, he was on a diplomatic exchange mission to India. A proposed collaboration between the two countries, developing a pan Asian ecology programme. Quite ground-breaking really, anyway he was there for about 18 months and in that time, we fell in love. Then I fell pregnant, and we were planning to marry before Aarav was born. Sadly however, there was a falling out between our governments and Yichen was ordered back to Beijing. I was set to be a single unmarried mother in a deeply religious country that still, to this day looks poorly on such things. Yichen came from a wealthy family, so we decided that Aarav should grow up with him. It was the most heart-breaking moment of my entire life; one I have regretted ever since. Well as I now know, in 2016 he and three other scientist created the Milky way and Sunway computers. When the Chinese government invited the worlds press and scientists to celebrate their creation, well Aarav was recruited into the US ranks, and has, as I have found out today, being living in Washington DC, not in India as I had first thought" Sanvia explained.

"But you said you worked with his father" Cassia said

"Well, I did in a manner of speaking" Sanvia said

"Wait, I traced those calls, there were through India" Cassia cried

"That would be my fault, I didn't want my mother to know I was in the states, in case the Chinese authorities were monitoring her communications, it would have placed her in danger, so I routed everything through a mobile in India" Aarav said

"And did you know she was here?" Cassia barked

"No, sadly not, or I would have said something when we met, for whatever, reason it never occurred to me to conduct a reverse look up on her calls. At first as far as I was concerned, she was still either in India or globetrotting, doing her talks. However, once the information was released on the committee and I found out she was part of it, I became more concerned, so I reached out to her, and she responded. However, I couldn't be sure that my calls weren't monitored, so I made sure my calls to her could not be traced" Aarav said "Then out of the blue you left me a message asking if I wanted to come here and see her" he continued.

"Why didn't you say anything in the meeting?" Cassia asked

"Because I don't want anyone to know where my mother is, I have managed to keep that a secret. It is bad enough that they know Robert was on the committee, if they found out my mother was also working with you, another Committee member, then I fear they would trust you less than they already do" Aarav said

"What, they don't trust me?" Cassia cried

"Cassia, please do not take offence, they don't trust anyone, it is simply due to the fact that Chuck Macdonald and Andrew Dale are working with you, that they are allowing this to go ahead" Aarav said

"Well, they can stuff it up their backsides, I am doing them a favour, I will just walk away, see how they do then" Cassia yelled angrily glaring at Aarav.

"Their only solution would be to go in all 'gung Ho' which both of us know will have absolutely no effect. In fact, it would only accelerate Betsi's agenda. They are both blind and stupid, thankfully, the President, is a little more considered. He sees your option as one that poses least risk and therefore has instructed them all to follow and support you" Aarav explained.

"That still doesn't explain why I shouldn't just walk away, leave them to it" Cassia said

"And that is something that has them perplexed. They simply can't work out why you are willing to do this, any of you. You see they can't work out what you stand to gain from it, you have not made any demands, asked for money, nothing, it is driving them crazy" Aarav said.

"We don't stand to gain anything" David said suddenly piping up.

"I know that much is clear, but you see, to people like that, that concept is alien" Aarav said.

"Well, if we don't do it, then the world will go to pot, quicker than it already is, we will end up with, well god knows what" David said.

"A preselected and cultivated, much smaller group of human beings that are controlled by an artificial intelligence, to ensure the longevity of the species" Aarav said

"Yes" David said "Except that that modification will continue to be developed until the only resemblance to human beings, will be in name only" he added

"Quite possibly, and whilst, that may yet be the only way our species has for survival, the one core factor that denotes humanity is freedom of choice, something I think will be managed out of us" Aarav said

"What happens next?" Cassia asked

"Well presuming that I can trust you not to inform the rest of the world of my mother's location, then I suggest that we carry on as normal. Next week you and I will undertake our mission to China. I am assuming as you have already stated that you have a plan for Japan, that will happen imminently. Then we will only have Lugano left. After that and we are finished, what happens then is entirely up to you. I would like to find a way that I can share my life with my mother, but I am afraid that the Government will not allow that, I am too important an asset. So, I guess that I shall return to DC" Aarav said sourly

"Well, you could come here, they will never find you" Cassia said

"Now that they are aware of your capabilities, they will keep track on you. Whilst as I can already tell, they cannot get into this wonderful facility. I suspect that this maybe one of the first places they will look if I was also to go missing, and I cannot risk them discovering my mother here. So as wonderful an idea as that is, I cannot" Aarav said sadly.

"Now, with your agreement, I would like to have a few moments of time with my mother and then I must return to DC, currently they believe I have come here to discuss the technicalities of our mission to China" Aarav added

"Of course, please stay as long as you feel you can, I will take you to Anchorage myself" Cassia said "After all I am the reason you came here" she said smiling.

Aarav smiled, for the first time since Cassia had known him, in his smile you could see a hint of the warmth that glowed so easily within his mother.

"I can see why my mother is so very fond of you all here" he said reaching out for his mother's hand.

Two hours later Cassia pulled back the throttle and the small Cessna soared into the clear blue skies above Red Dog

"You took a big risk coming here" she said

"Like I said I had to wait until I had a good reason, and you and I being on the same mission was enough" Aarav said

"How did you know where she was, I mean you said you never traced her calls, and I have read the logs, your mother was very careful not to mention anything about where she was" Cassia shouted over the noise of the aircrafts engines.

"It was you" Aarav said, "Whilst you had never heard my voice, as at the first meeting I simply nodded. I on the other hand, had heard yours. So, when you called and left the message inviting me here, I instantly recognised your voice and knew exactly where she was" Aarav said. Cassia thought about that for a moment, and a cold shiver starting at her toes crept up her back

"Jesus, I put the whole group in danger, because I was eager to make your mother happy" she said

"Not really, first you never really said where, it is only because I know that there are two Red Dogs, that I knew which one, you were at. Secondly, you had verified my location, traced it back to where you thought I was, and verified my voice with my mother" Aarav smiled, "Yes, she told me, you had her check that it was the voice of her son, then I am sure that you would have run some sort of voice print recognition" Aarav said, and Cassia gave him a wry smile.

"How does your mother know that you are not someone pretending to be her son" Cassia asked her mind going into full spy mode.

"Let's just say there are a few things that remained between her and my father, that only a son would know" Arab said

"Like what?" Cassia asked

"That I am afraid, I will not say, besides your partner will be running a full DNA analysis, on the prints and saliva I left on the coffee cup by now. I am sure you will have your evidence by the time we land" Aarav said

Cassia smiled, "No we are more trusting than that" she lied, and it was Aarav's turn to give her a wry smile.

"Anyway, I thought you would like to know, I have found out who is leaking information to Betsi, you were right it was someone in DC" Aarav said

"Who?" Cassia asked instantly alert, and when Aarav told her the name of the person. She sat back in stunned silence, it didn't seem possible, in everyone she had considered, this person had never crossed her radar, then suddenly a penny dropped, and she understood.

After a minute she said "Now that I know who, it makes perfect sense"

"Will you tell the others?" Aarav asked.

"About you, of course, they have a right to know about them that is another matter, not yet. I presume that you and I are the only ones that know?" she asked

"Of course," Aarav said earnestly

"Good let's keep it that way, we need to use this to our advantage, and keep the group guessing until I can think of the best way of handling it, until then let's have some fun with them, are you in?" Cassia asked.

Aarav smiled, "You are a very wicked woman Cassia" he said

"Well, after finding out that they don't trust me, whilst I am risking everything for them, it makes them fair game, wouldn't you say" Cassia asked smiling as she started her decent into Anchorage.

By the time Cassia got back to Red Dog it was well past midnight. She parked the Cessna in the shed, climbed into the 4x4 and was grateful it started first time. 50 minutes later as she walked back into Paradise and was surprised to see Sarah sitting staring out of the window nursing a large glass of wine.

"Can't sleep?" Cassia asked cheerily

"No, never do, when he is away, old habit" Sarah said staring out of the window into the dark night.

"Well, he has got some stuff to sort out, him and Tom, stuff to get ready for China" Cassia said innocently

"Yeah" Sarah said wisely "Toasting the fallen more like it" Sarah smiled, then seeing the look on Cassia face added "In the military when you lose someone on a mission, when you get back its tradition to raise a glass to their memory"

"Oh, I see" Cassia said then suddenly a loud shrill ringing noise burst into the air, making them both jump.

Cassia answered her phone, then said "Thank you for telling me that, I suspect though you want Sarah" then handed Sarah the phone, and seeing her confused look said "It's your old man, he's pissed. Listen give me the phone back in the morning, I off to bed" she added and walked towards her pod.

Chapter Twenty
Sanvia's Vegan Wine

Cassia's sleep was full of nightmares, first about David in Japan, then about the person who was leaking information, and then about drowning in a tube under a university in China. When she finally woke, she was drenched in sweat and clinging desperately to the duvet, she had ripped from David.

"Bad night love?" David asked as she finally opened her eyes

"You could say that I hardly got a wink of sleep" Cassia grumbled.

"Look I know you are worried about me going to Japan, and I know you like to be in control, but relax, I am a big boy, also I will have Katie and Mike, as well as Alten, we will be fine" David said reassuringly thinking she had been worrying about him.

"I am glad you are confident, but it is still risky" Cassia said

"Okay, so what about we spend the day, going over the plan, we have hashed up and you can do the pitfalls and potholes bit. If after that, you are still not happy, then we scrap it and start again" David offered.

"Okay but know for sure I will be tough on you. Tom and Nick will be here by lunch time, so tonight, we present your plan together, and they can rip shreds out of it. If after that if everyone agrees, then I will rest easier" Cassia said smiling weakly.

David sat with Katie, Mike and Alten in the beautiful glass dome that was the conference centre. He adjusted the climate control and took the ambient temperature from a comfortable 22 degrees to a warm 25 degrees, due to the uncharacteristic cold weather, the outside temperature was decidedly chilly.

"Right where are we?" David asked looking up at the three tired faces in front of him. They had been at it nonstop for the past four hours, but the simple fact that none of them could escape, was that they simply didn't have enough information. They were working under the presumption that Professor Tanaka would want David to experiment on Himari, and that if he did, he would let them use the supercomputer, which of course they would have to do undetected.

They were also presuming that there were the correct proteins in the university lab, they did reputably have one of the largest protein stores in the world, second only to that which had been held by Edward. If David had been able to diagnose Himari before they went, he could have gotten what he needed from the Paradise hub, but he couldn't, so he had to play that by ear as well. And finally, they had no way of knowing if Betsi was already in the Oak Forest Pac's computer, if not then it would all be a total waste of time.

"Let's face it" Mike growled in his deep voice "Like everything else, it's a crap shoot, we will have to make it up as we go along, deal with things as they come up" he added

"I don't like the fact that, you and I are staying at the university, whilst David and Alten are staying with the professor, anything could happen, and we are not there to deal with it" Katie said

"Look, it makes sense, the professors has only got a small house, and besides, what could he possibly do, he is as keen as we are to see it work" David said

"I am still not sure what you need me to do, don't get me wrong, I can do my bit with the computer, but the chemistry stuff, man that just leaves me cold" Alten said shifting uneasily in his seat.

Nick and Tom caged a lift off General Markham to Anchorage, then bribed Gary to drop them off in Red Dog, both a little worse for wear and Nick wasn't ready to face Cassia, as the memories of last night's phone call came flooding back.

However unbeknown to them, Gary had already radioed ahead and requested landing clearance. So, when they both gingerly made their way off his plane, Cassia was waiting for them.

"Good afternoon, Gentlemen" Cassia said, "Now which one of you wants to tell me you love me today?" she laughed.

Nick apologised and never stopped apologising all the way back up to the house. "Look Cass, I was pissed, I thought that you were Sarah, so no harm done, we don't need to tell her do we" Nick said just as they pulled up outside the house.

"Too late dufus, she was sitting right next to me, I handed her the phone, you spoke to her" Cassia said. Nick closed his eyes and shook his head.

"Oh my god, I did" he said suddenly realising "Christ she is going to tear me a new one" he said glumly.

Well, she is going to have to wait, we have a meeting with David and his crew, about the Japan job" Cassia said getting out of the car and slamming the door.

Back in the conference room David was just explaining to Alten what he needed him to do when there was a loud rap on the door, causing all of them to jump.

"Hello alright if we come in" Nick asked and without waiting for a response he, Cassia, and Tom walked in, grabbed themselves some coffee and sat down.

"Okay David, where are we?" Cassia asked brightly, winking at him.

David shuffled his papers nervously. "well," he said and cleared his throat "There are too many unknowns, things we can't predict" he said deciding to start with the negatives. "That said, we all agree" he added looking at the others, and Katie and Alten nodded their support, whilst Mike just shrugged his shoulders. "Well that we are going on Friday, and by that, I mean, we fly out tomorrow night, I have made contact with Professor Tanaka, and he has agreed to meet us at the airport" David said his words spewing out like a machine gun.

"Okay" Cassia said coyly "So what is your plan?" she asked

"Well to put it simply, in a nutshell so to speak, in the broadest terms, not going into" David spluttered

"David" Cassia snapped; she did love the man, but he had the most irritating tendency to procrastinate.

"Sorry, well, meet up with Tanaka and play it by ear" David said glumly

"Oh, I see and that is the best you can come up with?" Nick barked loudly.

"Well, there are too many variables, we don't know the exact condition of Himari, so we can't plan her treatment, or even if they will have what I need. Tanaka can only accommodate two, so Mike and Katie have to stay at the university. We don't know the site, or even if we will get within a 100 feet of the computer, we just can't plan" David said glumly looking down at the table.

"So, what you are saying is that you are going to have to fly by the seat of your pants?" Tom asked

"Basically yes" David said.

"Well sounds like a great plan" Nick said smiling.

"What?" David said stunned "How in god's name can that be a great plan?" he shouted.

"Look, at the end of the day all ops are like that, you try to cover all the bases, take the right equipment, but nine times out of ten you have to improvise. I would be more worried if you had planned it out to the last detail, because when things go pear shaped, and they will" Nick said, and Mike and Tom nodded

"Well, if you are to regimented in your planning, you will screw up you won't be able to adapt. This way you will go in expecting anything to go wrong, and adapt to it, as it happens" Nick said.

"And that is the best you can offer?" David asked

"Look you have covered the basics; Mike I presume that you have an exfil plan" Nick said

"Yep, we will have a car ready at the K park. If it goes hot, will have the basic escape and evasion kit, plus personals for Me, Alten and Katie. I have another check point, 2 miles out of the city, where we change cars. Then fly out of Yokohama to UK, then onto Anchorage" Mike said, "Failing that if either of the RV sites are compromised. I have arrangements secured with a trawler out of the harbour" Mike said

"Good, we can run over the plan in more detail later. Alten, what about your side?" Nick asked

"Well, I have two relays, one I will place here" Alten said pointing to the map on the table, "the second here, that should give us enough interference. Then once I am in, I will establish an uplink to the main server. Once connected I will download the data and transfer the package to Cassia. I have set it for a 2-hour window, so that should give us plenty of time to leave, not that it can be detected. All the data will automatically be dropped into the cloud-based server Cassia setup, so even if we are compromised, the integrity of the mission will stay intact" Alten said smiling, David sat with his mouth open, none of this had been discussed during their meeting, he was hearing it all for the first time, suddenly he felt a burning anger build inside him.

"Katie, what about you, anything?" Nick asked and David stared at her with his mouth open.

"I have leaked to the dark web, a story about a black hat operation to attack the Fujitsu K computer, claiming that there has already been a sustained cyber-attack on the facility, and that they are leaking data, big time. That should create a scandal, from what I understand the Chairman of Fujitsu has called an emergency board meeting for Friday, and their stock has already dropped two percent. They have ramped up security and the press are already camped out at their facility. That means all the focus should be in Kobe, if we get compromised in Tokyo. I have already set up cover stories for all of us and press releases" Katie said. David felt the anger burning brighter inside him, they had all been planning things behind his back.

"Excellent then I reckon you are ready" Cassia said brightly

"Are you mad, how could you, you have been planning this whole operation behind my back" David screamed at the three of them, his face burning.

"What no" Katie said, "We have just been putting the pieces together for our parts" she added

"Well, you could have told me, then I wouldn't have looked like a complete twat in front Nick and Cassia" David cried

"David chill, no one thinks you're a twat, you have your job to do and they theirs. This is what these briefings are for, to fill each other in on all sides of the plan" Nick said

"But they could have told me before you got here, I had no idea what they were up to, all we did was talk about how we were going to access the supercomputer" David said angrily

"Go on am I missing something, I thought that was the plan?" Cassia said coolly

"Well, yes, but no, it's all the other bits too. Anyway, when you guys plan things everyone knows everything" David said venomously although he could see he was on shaky ground

Cassia smiled, "Firstly, none of us do, Nick hasn't got the slightest clue about what I am doing on the computer, as I don't have any idea of exfil, or cover stories, or kit or really any of that stuff. For instance, when we go to China, all I know is that me and Mr White are the package, and Nick and his team have to get us in and out, how is up to them" Cassia lied, "It's how it goes, everyone focusses on their specific role, then briefs the team" she said smiling

"I just wished they had told me before you lot got here, that's all" David said

"From what I understand they were busy trying to brainstorm your side, as that part is crucial. The rest of the plan is in case things go wrong, that is why everyone is focussing on your side, it is how things are done" Tom said

"Hey sorry dude, I am happy to tell you how I am breaking into the computer, I just didn't think you wanted to know" Alten said

"God no, that stuff is way above my head, I leave that stuff to Cassia" David said hanging his head slightly, then he looked up "Look, thanks you guys, because you covered your bits, I didn't have to think about them, I could concentrate on my side" he added.

"Well, if it makes you feel any better, the moment you started on about the telly something and the Cas this and Kat that, my eyes glazed over, I didn't have a clue what the hell you were on about, I felt a bit guilty that I couldn't help" Mike said

David smiled "Ok, sorry, I am not used to this sort of stuff, but I am glad that you guys have my back" he said. "Hey Cass, have you told Nick and Tom about Aarav yet" he added desperate to change the conversation.

"Just about to brief them, you guys are welcome to stay, but if you have better things to do feel free" Cassia said

"I am off to the pod bar, if anyone fancies coming, Sanvia's got a new batch of vegan wine she wants us to try" David offered. Suddenly there was a shuffling of seats, and everyone raced to the door. Sanvia's attempts at making a decent wine were quickly becoming legendary, not that they were particularly good, more that they were very adept at taking the edge off.

"Hey Nick, you and Tom need to stay, I have to catch you up" Cassia said and the two of them reluctantly returned to their seats. "David" Cassia shouted after him, make sure you save some for us" Cassia said.

Later that evening after more than a couple of glasses of Sanvia's excellent blackberry and elderflower wine had made its way to David's head, and he found himself staring blankly out the window in the dome as Robert came and sat beside him.

"I am worried" David said nursing his glass like it was his only child.

"About what mate?" Robert asked.

"When this is all done, it won't be enough for her, she will get bored" David muttered

"You and me both, what you don't think I feel the same about Katie, you've seen her, she is like a dog with two tails, when she found out she was going on an op" Robert said glumly

"What are we going to do, we are going to lose them, they is going to run away with the action men" David slurred hiccupping into his glass

Robert, who also was feeling the effects of the wine, slipped his arm around David's shoulder, "I love her, you don't know this about me, but I don't like women" he said and seeing the confused look on David's face added "No, not like that, I mean" he said stifling a burp "what I am saying was that, well Katie has changed all that, I don't want other women, just her, I love her, Ssh don't tell her, but I want to ask her if I could be her" Robert paused trying to formulate the words, his tongue didn't seem to want to follow his brain "wife" he shouted swaying a little and trying hard to focus, whilst pressing his fingers to his lips "Ssh, she doesn't know" he giggled

"You would make a good one, you are a really, really, good bloke, you know, Cass doesn't want a wife she thinks it is wrong, no she wants to be free to play the field" David said clinging onto Robert

"She is wrong, she would be lucky to have me" Robert slurred, "You" he suddenly shouted realising his mistake "Lucky to have you, you are a really good man, any woman would be lucky to having you" Robert said smiling and slurring his words.

"I love you; Ro err bob hurt, you are like a bruver to me, I love you" David said giggling, with his arm round the huge black man next two him.

"I love you too" Robert said sniggering, "You are my bestis mate in whole world" he said and flung his arms wide open, knocking David glass out of his hand and giggling as it smashed on the floor "oops" he said and huddled down with David like a child pretending to ignore the broken glass, and they both giggled

Cassia was sat with Katie both of them nursing their wine and smiling

"Christ, do all the men in this place get drunk, look at those two fools, drunk as skunks, clinging onto each other like village idiots" she said smiling

"Yeah, but they are our village idiots" Katie said

"Yeah", Cassia said, "I don't think I could have done any of this, without him, he is my rock. I never thought I could feel so happy, so complete" Cassia said as a small tear trickled down her cheek.

"Sorry" she said, "I was just remembering what my life was like before I met him" she added and shivered.

"Hey, you don't need to tell me, I kept running away, too frightened to get involved then Robert came along, and all of a sudden all I could think about was crawling into his arms, curling up and staying there.

Do you know he is such a gentleman he treats me with love and respect, doesn't try to control me, tell me what I should and shouldn't do, he is just perfect" Katie said smiling over at Robert who was still sitting with his arm around David staring out of the window.

"Katie, can I tell you something, but you have to swear to keep it a secret" Cassia said earnestly

"Of course, scouts honour, cross my heart" Katie said making the sign of a cross on her chest.

"I am pregnant" Cassia said, "But you can't tell anyone. I had Sanjay do the test, he confirmed it, six weeks" Cassia said as Katie squealed with delight

"Does David know?" she asked

"No, god no, he would go ballistic, start nursing me, become overprotective, mother me that sort of thing, I couldn't bear it" Cassia said alarmed

"Look I don't want to be the profit of doom, but you are no spring chicken isn't it dangerous?" Katie asked.

"Well, I thought so, but apparently those cocktails we are taking the ones that ore extending our lives. Well, they have kind of changed everything. According to Sanjay, my internal workings are that of a 20-year-old, and he sees no reason why I can't have a baby" Cassia said excitedly

"Oh my god that is amazing, I had never really given that much thought, I believed that we had missed boat. Christ, I need to get some contraception" Katie said nervously "anyway should you really be going on the mission to China" she asked nervously

"Yeah, I will be fine, Nick would rather die than let anything happen to me, and I will be careful" Cassia said, "But after Switzerland, I am done, no more, I just want to spend the rest of my days here in Paradise" she added seriously.

"Yeah, me too" Katie said then seeing the excited look on Cassia's face added "No not that, I mean I want to spend the rest of my days here too, with Robert, oh my god, look at those two, they have fallen asleep" Katie said

"Yeah" Cassia said nodding her head and looking at the two men slumped against each other and snoring loudly "We are two lucky ladies" she added sarcastically

Chapter Twenty - One
Haru Tanaka and the tiny Creature

Thursday 17th July 2025 – Red Dog

The bright blue sun glistened on the glass roof of the dome, like sparkling light through crystals, magnified and blasted down onto the face of the of the man lying on his back drooling from the side of his mouth.

Instinctively he reached down and pulled the duvet over his head and groaned.

"Time to get up sleepy head Cassia shouted as loud as she could, grabbed the duvet and ripped it off the bed.

"Cass" David groaned desperately trying to clutch onto anything that could provide him shade

"Either you get up now Mr or I am going to let Archie and the other children in here" Cassia warned

"Jesus you are a heartless woman, I am dying" David whined

"Funny, you didn't mention that last night, when Nick and Mike carried you back here, then you couldn't help but tell them and anyone who would listen that I was the most wonderful woman in the world and that you loved me" Cassia said smiling

"Oh god, I didn't" David said pulling a pillow over his face.

"Yep, and apparently you are in love with Nick, and Mike and everyone" Cassia said enjoying the David's embarrassment

"Oh, I want to die" David groaned.

"Well, you had better join the queue because your drinking buddy, also happened to mention that you both thought that Sanvia was a hottie" Cassia said trying hard to conceal her smile.

"Oh my god, we didn't did we, I have got to apologise to her, she must have been mortified" David said suddenly sitting up and regretting it.

"Katie was furious, there was a big argument, she stormed out and banned Robert from their pod. I think he slept in the bar last night" Cassia said desperately trying to push down the bubble of laughter that was threatening to erupt inside her.

David felt the shame sweep through him "God I am so sorry, we were drunk, Robert loves Katie, he would never do anything, god I hope she forgives him, he will be devastated" David said

"Relax big boy, I am lying, all you did was threw up and tell me you loved me and asked me to marry you again, then you collapsed on the bedroom floor. Now get up, you need to get ready, you are going to Japan in two hours" Cassia said laughing, walking out of the bedroom.

Forty minutes later, after a long shower, and a rushed suitcase packing David emerged in the sitting room, looking decidedly better.

"Right take these" Cassia said handing him two small pills, one green, the other white.

"What are they?" David asked

"The usual one, your regular cocktail and something Sanvia created for hangovers" Cassia said, and David dutifully swallowed the pills.

"So, what did you say?" David asked gulping down the last of the water.

"About what?" Cassia replied looking up from her laptop at him

"Well, you said that I threw up, told you I loved you and asked you to marry me again" David said

"I think I told you that you were pissed and that if you really wanted an answer then ask me again when you were sober" Cassia said coolly

"Well okay then" David said not really sure what to say next, Cassia held her breath, they had not really talked about it, after David had proposed when she was in Venice, everything had gone quiet, he hadn't mentioned it again. She had told herself that she wasn't bothered, it was all a waste of time, they were fine as they were, but secretly she had not wanted to pressure him"

"Okay then we had better get going" Cassia said eventually, desperately trying to hold back the tears.

"I can't go Cass; I have to do some more research before we leave" David said

"Oh, for Christ sakes David, your flight from Anchorage leaves in four hours, It will take at least three hours to get there, you barely have enough time now, what could you possibly need to research at this late hour?" Cassia asked angrily.

David smiled, "Well I wanted to research the best ways to ask the most wonderful woman in the world to marry me, you see I reckon I have got one more shot at it, and I really don't want to blow it" David said smiling, "It has to be perfect, well because she is" he added

Tears streamed down Cassia's face, "Well you could just ask her" she said

"Cassia, would you make my life completely and utterly perfect by agreeing to be my wife" David said and dropped to one knee.

Cassia leapt off the sofa and flung her arms around him "Oh my god, of course I will" she cried, "my god look at me, I am crying like a fool, must be the hormones" she said mopping her face.

Instantly David let her go and held her at arm's length, "the what?" he demanded his mind racing.

"Oh, my hormones, it happens to women of a certain age, don't panic, I have had Sanvia to change my pill regime, that's all" she lied.

"Right" David said suspiciously as he felt his heart sink to his boots "I thought" he said

"Yeah, I know what you thought" Cassia said laughing "and you call yourself a genius, really at my age, come on" Cassia said

"Yeah, okay" David said hesitantly, "well we had better get going, but we are still getting married right?" He asked nervously

"Of course, and don't you dare try backing out now you great dufus" Cassia said kissing him gently on the lips

"I will do it with a ring and everything, it has got to be perfect, nothing would make me happier" David said

I reckon, based on your reaction I know something that would, Cassia thought.

David sat nursing an alcohol-free bloody Mary, two hours into their 7-hour, Delta flight to Tokyo, staring out of the window watching the pillows of snow-white clouds, float past and picking out shapes and letting his mind wander freely. Katie was sat beside him, her face mask on, snoring lightly.

They had had to run to catch the 11 o'clock flight and had only just made it. Mike and Alten were seated four rows back, like Katie, Mike was taking a nap and Alten was busy ferreting away on his laptop.

Something was niggling at the edges of his mind, lurking in the corners, refusing to be come into the light.

Never mind he thought, "I will distract myself," he muttered picking up his book and opening the page marked Pancreatic cancer, employing the old mind trick of trying not to think about something and waiting for it to come naturally.

Four hours later as the plane started to descend into Haneda airport, he woke with a start as his book fell onto the floor.

"Here" Katie said handing him a napkin "You've been drooling" she said smiling

"Sorry" David said automatically "bit of a rough night" he admitted

"Yeah, I was there don't forget" Katie said smiling "Listen we will be landing in 30 minutes you had better clean up, Tanaka is meeting us at the airport" Katie said and scooted to one side and allowed David to get out.

The flight landed in Haneda airport, 30 minutes later and a further 40 minutes after that, due to a difficult trip through customs, where both Katie's and Mikes luggage got searched, they finally made their way into the arrivals lounge.

Then it suddenly occurred to David that he had no idea what Professor Haru Tanaka looked like. He searched the faces, waiting patiently behind the rope, lined up like soldiers, all clutching white boards with names scribbled on them in large black letters.

"Here" Katie said pointing to a tall middle aged, white-haired man dressed in a maroon suit, a white open shirt and sandals.

"Good evening, Professor Carmichael, Welcome to Tokyo" Haru Tanaka said stepped forwards, bowing. Mike Instantly stepped in front of the David and shielded him.

"It's alright Mike, I have got this" David said smiling and Mike stepped to one side

"Professor Tanaka, it is a pleasure to be here, please call me David" he said clasping the professor's hand and shaking it

"Oh David, I cannot tell you what an honour it is that you are visiting our university, our students are all very excited to meet you" Haru said smiling and displaying an unusually brilliant white set of perfect teeth.

"Please let me introduce my team, David said "My assistant, Alten Blake, my personal security person, Mike Barnard, and of course you have already corresponded with my publicity agent, Miss Katie Rayner" he added directing Haru to each person in turn.

"Please, the university has provided us with two cars. One will take your colleagues to their residence and the other will take us to my house. I am honoured you have agreed to stay in my humble home" Haru said.

David saw the uneasy look on Mikes face and gave him a slight nod saying he was okay with it.

"We are proposing to meet tomorrow at 9am at the university, if you are in agreement" Haru asked

"That works for me" David said and followed Haru towards the exit.

The trip to Haru's *humble home*, as he called it took a little over and hour during which they made polite cocktail conversation, about the state of the weather, which was unbearably hot, at least 15 degrees above the average. This in turn led to a long discussion on climate change, in which Haru agreed, their governments were being economical with the truth. Then they talked about the world of Biochemistry, and emerging trend in biohacking, and the dangers it posed. The one thing they did not discuss was the real reason they were here, Himari. It seemed to be a subject that, much to David's dismay, Haru was determined to avoid, leading him to think that perhaps he had changed his mind. Eventually their driver pulled up in front of, what Haru described as his humble home, where in truth was a 290 square meter, single story, ultra-modern, L shape villa, on five feet stilts, with roof to floor glass walls, set in an acre and a half of parkland.

"Wow" David said getting out of the car "This place is amazing"

"Thankyou" Haru said nodding, "It belongs to my wife" he added without a single note of regret.

"Well, it is beautiful" David said

"Please" Haru said guiding David towards the door.

"Wow I could really live here" Alten said and Haru gave him a stern look and turned back to face David without saying a word. It was then that David noticed that Haru was completely ignoring Alten, treating him as if he was not there and was about to say something when a beautiful tiny Japanese woman dressed in a royal blue kimono with white herons streaking across the bodice, tied in the centre with a flowered grey sash, stepped forwards.

"May I introduce you to my wife Kimiki" Haru said extending his hand. The small woman gave a deep bow, showing her neatly tied hair, which was adorned with an ornate decorated white fan and what looked like knitting needles

"You honour us with your presence" Kimiki said in broken English

"I am afraid that my wife does not speak very much English" Haru said smiling nervously.

"I am sure that her English is better than my Japanese" David said then turned to Kimiki and said *saru* and nodded politely. Instantly he knew he had made a mistake by the look on Kimiki's and Haru's face

"What did I say?" David asked going red

"I am afraid that you have just called my wife a monkey" Haru said trying to stifle a smile

"Oh my god, I thought I was saying thank you" David said going as red as a beetroot

"You may want to try *Arigato*" Haru said smiling

"Arigato, I meant to say Arigato" David said smiling awkwardly at Kimiki.

Kimiki forgave David instantly with a broad smile, so sweet and natural that David felt his knees, like his heart melt.

Haru, showed David around the house, which turned out to be minimalist, everything had been neatly stored, in its place, making the whole house look like a show room. When they were sitting alone, out on the veranda, sipping a green liquid which Haru assured David was tea, but resembled nothing like the tea he was used to. Haru was staring out into the parkland and David could wait no longer.

"Haru, I need to ask you a question, well two in fact and I hope I am not out of line" David said hesitantly

"Of course, please ask" Haru said turning to face David

"Okay" David said putting down his tea. "Well, the first one is, why are you ignoring my assistant Alten?" David asked

"He is your servant therefore it would be against protocol to speak with him without your permission" Haru said stiffly

"Oh, I see, sorry, he is not what we would call a servant, he is my assistant. He is studying with me. I am helping him, he is a little shy, but" and David was about to say please feel free to talk to him, when a thought occurred to him. If Haru started to quiz Alten about his work, he would soon discover that he knew nothing about chemistry. "But I thank you for your respect" David said

"My next question is to do with the other reason I am here, you have not mentioned Himari, have you changed your mind? I completely understand if you no longer want my help" David said and held his breath.

A misty look clouded over Haru's eyes at the mention of his daughter

"I was scared to ask you. I believed that it was wrong of me to ask in the first place and put you in a position of obligation, you are already honouring us, by agreeing to talk with our students" Haru said and hung his head.

"So, your daughter is better" David asked and saw tears well up in Haru's eyes.

"No, I am afraid that the gods have not blessed us" he said, choking back his words.

"Then why on earth would it be wrong of you to ask for my help?" David asked and before Haru could answer added "If I was in your position, I would not hesitate to ask for your help, there is nothing more important than family" David said. It was like someone had lifted a huge weight off Haru's shoulders he leapt to his feet bowing and trying to shake David's hand

"Thank you, David, thank you" he kept saying, then suddenly he called out to Kimiki and in a machine gun rattle of Japanese he told her what David had said. Kimiki instantly rushed forwards and grabbed David's hands, in her own tiny ivory white fingers and kissed them "Thank you Mr David, thank you so very much" she cried kissing his hands over and over.

"We were sure you would have change your mind" Haru admitted

"No, but I must tell you I am not sure if I can help" David said honestly

"But you are the one who managed to cure Edward Holloway" Haru said

"How do you know about that?" David snapped.

"There was much speculation, it was well known that he was dying from bowel cancer, then he recruits you to research gene cell editing and suddenly he is cured" Haru said "Is it not true, did you not cure him?" he asked nervously

"Well, yes, but it was very complicated, and every case is different, there is no telling if it will work on your daughter" David said sternly

"Mr Carmichael, my daughter has less than a two percent chance of surviving, any chance that it may work is worth trying, we are desperate" Haru said "Please if you do not think it rude, how long did it take before you knew it had worked on Mr Holloway?" Haru asked. David knew exactly why he was asking; it was because that was the length of time, they still had left, with a glimmer of hope.

"4 to 6 Hours" David said simply and saw a huge smile glow over Haru's face.

"Well to clarify it took that long before we noticed a significant change in the cancer, it took a further three days before we had eradicated all of the cancerous cells" David said and felt a little guilty, as it had taken less than 24 hours with Edward as he had also combined the treatment with the ageing cell modification.

"Okay so please may I see Himari and her charts?" David asked

Haru showed David into a large pristine white room, that looked distinctly like an operating room, with the exception of a large hospital bed with grey side bars, in the centre instead of an operating table.

On the bed was a tiny figure, with so many tubes, pipes and monitors coming out of her, it looked like a scene from an alien movie. Haru handed David a green gown and mask

"Please" He said "The room is sterile" he added, as if to explain the reason for the gown and mask.

"Of course," David said slipping it on and helping himself to some latex gloves from the dispenser on the side wall. Haru guided David forwards towards the bed. If the sight of all the tubes had been a shock it was nothing compared to the sight of the tiny, thin slip of a girl lying on the bed, her hair had all but gone with the exception of a few wispy thin straggles. Her skin was a translucent putrid yellow colour hanging loosely over her bones, it looked like someone had draped a thin rag over a skeleton. Ironically, she was dressed in a brightly coloured *Hello Kitty* nightdress, an iconic figure that had brought so much happiness to so many little girls Something that this frail weak creature, had not known any of. David felt his heart break and it was all he could do to stop tears from streaming down his face, as Himari opened her sunken huge black eyes and smiled at the stranger in front of her, showing a redden mouth, where once David was sure there had been beautiful, brilliant white teeth, like her parents.

"May I see her charts" David asked smiling weakly back at the little girl. Haru eagerly handed David all of her charts and he scanned the pages and felt his heart sink even further. The cancer had spread so quickly and was so aggressive that her tiny body was now completely riddled with it, he knew instantly that instead of the months the doctors had predicted, this little girl had only weeks left to live. He took a deep breath in and tried to hide his shock, which was so obviously written on his face.

"You see David, you really are the last hope we have, and we know that even that is only slight" Haru said with a great sadness in his voice, as he looked down at his fragile daughter

"Okay David said, well we need to act fast there is a huge amount to do and not much time to do it in" he said

"What do you need David?" Haru asked

"I need my assistant, access to a powerful computer capable of calculating complex molecule scenarios, protein stores and prays" David said

"We can use the computer at the university, after your talk, I have unlimited access, it will not be a problem, also there is an extensive protein library there, and my wife and I have not stopped praying since Himari was diagnosed" Haru said

"Not soon enough, If we leave it until tomorrow then we will only have one shot at it, can we go now, that way I can have at least two or three runs at the proteins, before I leave on Sunday" David said. Haru looked totally shocked, David thought he had gone too far, over played his hand, been too eager until Haru's eyes filled with tears.

"I cannot ask you to give up your night to help my little Himari" he said

"Haru, I would work night and day, if I think there is a chance of saving your tiny little girl. I want to make sure that I give it everything I have before I leave" David said

"I cannot find the words, in English or Japanese to say how grateful we are that you would do this for our family" Haru said clasping David's hand and despite his jet lag David felt a wave of adrenalin surge through him.

"Come on Haru, lets save your daughter's life" David said crossing his fingers behind his back

Chapter Twenty - Two
Himari

Due to the humidity David had asked to have the windows of the limousine open, to get some air, the warm humid air streamed into the back of the limousine making their shirts stick to their backs with sweat, as the car raced through the streets of Tokyo. It was a little after 10pm and David was surprised at how busy the city was, with its kaleidoscope of lights and cacophony of sounds, that filled the car invading their every sense, like a cheap funfair on hyperdrive. David reached out and clicked the button and the window slid silently to a close and the air condition went into overdrive as silence filled the car.

"Okay" David said picking up Himari's charts "Alten we won't have much time, I want all this data entered into the computer, and I want to run a DNA spectral analysis, Okay Alten" David said taking out a complimentary University of Tokyo pen and ringing the data on several pages. Alten gave him a quizzical look.

"Err yes Professor Carmichael" Alten said respectfully.

"I will show you what I want where, we cannot afford any delays or mistakes" David growled and Alten physically shrunk back in his seat.

"Haru, I will need to see your protein lab, and I will need a rundown of every protein available to us" David said and Haru nodded eagerly.

"We are here" Haru said, "You will have to stay with me your passes will not be ready until tomorrow" he added

"No problem" David said

As soon as they entered the foyer, two armed guards approached them, as soon as they saw Professor Tanaka, they nodded and Haru rattled off a string of Japanese that left David in no doubt that he was extremely revered and respected within the university. Both guards respectfully bowed and waved them through the security gates without checking their passes.

"Okay, we must go down to the sub-basement, there are very few people in the building so we will not be disturbed" Haru said. guiding them to a smart looking state of the art lift.

Once they reached the basement the lift slid silently to a halt and the door hissed open onto a huge pristine airconditioned white room, with rows and rows of glistening black towers, running down the centre of the room. Each tower was alive with sparkling flashing blue lights and there was a rhythmic pulsing coming from behind a huge glass wall where the servers were.

"Welcome to the Oak Forest Pac's Supercomputer centre. This computer is one of the fastest and most powerful computers in the world, it has over 8000 nodes and the latest intel Xeon Phi processors capable of over 25 petaflop processing speeds" Haru said as if he was quoting from a sales brochure.

"Is it powerful, can it cope with a multitude of complex calculations and scenarios at the same time?" David asked

"Yes, of course" Haru answered, sounding a little hurt that David didn't seem impressed

"Then it will do" David said then smiled "Haru forgive me, I am not very knowledgeable about computers, so I have to rely on other people to tell me if they are good. I only care, if they can help me with the complex processing required, I prefer humans to machines" he added

Haru smiled "We are similar people" he said and walked up to the large display panel and typed in a wide range of complex Japanese letters, placed his face in the scanner and his forefinger on the screen at the same time, and less than a second later the huge glass doors slid silently open.

"The access nodes are at the far end. I am afraid it will be a little cold in here, as the temperature must be kept" Haru started to say then seeing the look on David's face said, "very cool" and smiled

"Its fine, my assistant is used to working in the cold" David said giving Alten a derisive look.

Haru led them to the far end of the huge server room and directed Alten to a small monitor, typed in his code and stood back. Alten quickly took out Himari's notes and with David's help, started typing wildly on the keys.

Haru watched in amazement as Alten's fingers danced across the keys at lightning pace.

"He is very quick" Haru said admiringly

"He has to be, and accurate, I will not accept mistakes" David said sternly. "Now please can I see your protein laboratory and stores" David asked. Haru looked torn, he was unsure about leaving Alten alone in the computer centre but was also desperate to please David.

"I will be about 40 minutes" Alten said, "Sorry professor, I wish it could be done quicker, but there is a lot of complex data. I will go as fast as I can, I understand we do not have much time" he added apologetically. That seemed to have reminded Haru as to the urgency of the situation.

"Please David follow me, I am afraid I will have to lock your assistant in, we are not allowed to leave the doors unlocked" he said apologetically

"That's fine, he is used to it, you can chain him to the desk if it means he doesn't stop working" David said harshly.

David followed Haru along the glass corridors towards the protein labs and as they walked, they engaged in casual conversation.

"This assistant of yours is very young" Haru said

"He is but don't tell him I said so, he is a genius, and is very good at what he does" David said

"You are very hard on him, please forgive me, I did not mean to be rude" Haru said

"No, its fine, you see I didn't really want an assistant, after I left Valencia, I was inundated with applications from potential students and other scientists, all wanting to work with me, which is quite funny, as before that, I was lucky if any of them would even speak to me. So reluctantly after much pressure from my girlfriend I took on Alten. You are right I am a little hard on him, but it is for his own good, like all young people, his mind can wander, and it would be such a shame to waste such a talent, he has potential" David said solemnly

"Do you know Cassia Nilsson, I believe she was in Valencia at the same time as you, perhaps you met?" Haru asked.

"Yeah, she is my girlfriend" David said and instantly regretted it as Cassia's voice rang through his head *'Don't give away any personal information, you never know what links can be drawn from it'*

"Oh my god, you are the people that released that information about the committee" Haru said alarmed.

Shit, David thought, I was so close and one stupid mistake, me and my big mouth.

"You are heroes, truly amazing" Haru said, and David felt himself breathe a silent sigh of relief.

"Yeah, well when we found out what they were doing, we couldn't just sit there and let them get away with it" David said "Anyway, enough about me, we have a job to do, and not much time" he added

"I am sorry, I have offended you" Haru said nervously

"No, it's just I can't stick my head out the door, without someone asking me about it. It was mostly Cassia, anyway, yet still I seem to be getting all the credit, in all honesty I just want a quiet life" David said

"Then perhaps you should build one of those pod things, she released on the internet" Haru said laughing

"We did, its wonderful" David said and again Cassias words rang through his head, Christ, I am crap at this, David thought.

"Perhaps when Himari is better, we could come and visit" Haru suggested

Oh god now he wants to be my friend, "Perhaps, but one step at a time, lets concentrate on getting her better" David said

"Of course," Haru said "Here we are, the protein lab" he added and went through the usual security protocols.

David quickly identified the proteins that he thought he would need and set up the lab ready for the data he hoped the computer would generate.

When they had finished, they walked back to the computer room, and David keen to avoid the mistakes of the trip down, talked about the processes that they would need to go through.

As soon as they were back in the computer centre, David marched up to Alten and looked him directly in the eye

"Are we ready?" he demanded sternly

Alten smiled "Yes professor we are ready for the first run" Alten replied which David took to mean that he had done what they had come here for, and at the same time uploaded Himari's data.

"Okay, I want you to load up Cas 9, and Kat 7 plus these" David said and listed three other protein compounds, "Now run the programme and let's see" David said and glanced at Haru who was looking on nervously. 21 seconds later a line of data scrolled across the screen 'telomerase response *negative, ribonucleoprotein complex response – negative, telomeric DNA repeats did not regenerate'*

"Dam" David growled ok, run again, this time adjust protein C, four percent B, up zero-point six percent and Cas 9 plus twenty-one-point four percent, then run it again" David said and in another 21 seconds the same line came back with one addition at the end it read *telomerase response, negative, ribonucleoprotein complex response – in progress, telomeric DNA repeats at 1.4%*

Haru looked devastated his face looked as if it was drained of all life, his eyes sunken and filled with tears.

"Hey buddy, its ok, that is a positive, it tells me we are on the right track, all we have to do is get that to one hundred percent and we are there, providing that her body doesn't reject the proteins" David said enthusiastically.

For the next 6 and a half hours they sat running scenario after scenario, making miniscule adjustments each time, until at 06:45am after having no sleep, or food, the message finally read *Telomeric DNA repeats at 100%, ribonucleoprotein response positive.*

 A loud cheer erupted in the room, and they all jumped about and hugged each other.

"Okay David shouted above the cheering, send that data to the lab, I want 100mils asap" he ordered, and he and Haru raced off to the protein lab. A few minutes later they returned with a sterile flask containing a milky green liquid. Haru placed it the vial inside a chilled transport container, which looked very much like the one used to transport organs, and cradled it in his arms, as if it was his most precious possession. Together they raced out of the computer centre locking the doors behind them.

When they got back to Haru's house they all suited up, even Alten, at Haru's insistence and went into Himari's sterile room. Kimiki was already there dressed in her green gown and mask waiting nervously.

"Okay" David said nervously, 20 mils, per hour for the next five hours, intravenous" he said, "Alten you will need to stay here and watch her closely, if you see any change, or she fits or goes into convulsions, call me immediately. Haru, we need to be at the university in an hour, any chance I can get a shower?" David asked.

They arrived at the University with five minutes to go and Katie and Mike looked most displeased as they crashed through the doors, heaving and panting.

"Haru, can you stall them I need to bring my guys up to speed" David asked, Haru nodded and raced off towards the auditorium.

David updated Katie and Mike about the evening before, and how they had been up all night, and Alten had managed to upload the data and that he had left him at the house watching Himari, something Mike was very unhappy about. Until Katie reminded him that they had agreed that they might have to improvise, and that time was ticking, and David still had to give his lecture.

Together the three of them raced off to the auditorium.

Four hours later after David had given his presentation, receiving five standing ovations, which Haru insisted was a new record for any visiting professor and had attended the gracious thankyou reception given by the University Chancellor, at which David was offered an open invitation to come back. David and Haru found themselves back in the limousine, breaking the speed limit as it raced its way back to Haru's house. Neither man spoke, they just sat nervously staring out of the window, daring not to hope.

"Look", David finally said nervously "don't get your hopes up to high, it could be a long road to recovery, and there is a very high chance that her body will reject the proteins" he said trying to prepare Haru for what might be coming.

"But we have not received any calls, that is a good sign" Haru said trying to sound positive. Or she has already died, and they decided not to bother us, David thought.

When the car pulled up outside Haru's house, Kimiki came running out, her usual pristine self, looked raggedy and worn, black streaks were streaming down her face where she had obviously been crying. As soon as she saw Haru she flung herself into his arms and wailed loudly, rattling off Japanese at super speed.

Haru pulled her off him and held her at arm's length then looked over to where David was standing, his face in shock, as tears rolled down his cheeks. David nodded weakly and watched as Haru turned and ran towards the house screaming Himari's name, quickly followed by Kimiki.

David felt his heart sink, that could mean only one thing, the protein compound had failed, her tiny fragile body, already so weak and battered, could not cope and rejected it. In his heart of hearts, he had suspected that might be the case. It had been a very long shot, a million to one chance, he knew they needed a miracle, and this time he had failed.

David slowly trudged towards the house, then stood and watched as the car pulled away. Heaved deep sigh and turned and walked into the house. What could I possibly say to them now, there were no words, he thought and regretted bitterly that he had raised their hopes.

Suddenly Alten appeared in front of him in the cool light corridor, he grabbed David's arm and dragged him towards Himari's room, placed a mask over his tired face, then opened the door.

There on the bed sitting up, was a tiny little Japanese girl, grinning a toothless smile at her father, who was busy making her hello kitty doll dance.

Kimiki looked up at David as he entered the room, her face was glowing, her eyes alive and glistening, as the tears slid relentlessly down her face.

233

"Thank you, Mr David for giving me back my daughter" she said in her pidgin English and David felt his heart explode inside his chest as he sobbed with joy, finally he had done something good with his research.

Chapter Twenty -Three
Marriage

Saturday 19th July 2025 – Tokyo

Even though Haru protested, David spent the next two hours running the analysis on Himari's bloods, determined to do the count before he went to bed.

Haru had arrange for the driver to collect the others and give them the VIP tour of Tokyo, then bring them back to his house, by 8pm, as they were having a celebration.

David staggered out of the temporary laboratory that Haru had set up, when his daughter first received her diagnosis, and wearily made his way back to Himari's room. His legs felt like lead, and he could hardly keep his eyes open, he checked his watch it was a little after 1:30pm.

When he opened the door, he was not at all surprised to see Kimiki and Haru still sitting beside their daughters bed, playing with her. They had obviously taken it in turns to change as they were both wearing different clothes and Kimiki was back to her usual immaculate self.

"David, come in, Himari has something she wants to say to you" Haru said his broad smile lighting up the room.

As David approached, he heard Haru say something in rapid Japanese to his daughter, then the little girl looked up at David, her huge black eyes, once dull and tinged with yellow, now alive, and vibrant, held out her two painfully thin hands. David knelt down beside her and gently held them in his hands, they felt cold and so frail.

"Thank you, Mr David" Himari said and gave a little bow.

"Your welcome David said. then turned to Haru and smiled. "Her bloods clear, the cancers gone, she will be a little weak and she should get plenty of rest, but I think she will be fine" he said smiling.

"I will be forever in your debt, if you ever need anything you just need to ask, you have given me back my life" Haru said.

"Honestly all I want right now is a bed" David said smiling.

Katie popped her head inside the bedroom door a little after 8pm and seeing David still asleep, still she came in and sat on the edge of his bed.

"Oh my god, what time is it" David asked instantly awake

"It's a little after 8pm" Katie said warmly

"Oh, crap I must have slept in" David said trying to sit up.

"Well, you have only had about 6 sleep hours in the last 36" Katie said then added "I have seen that little girl, what you manage to do is truly amazing" she said and leaned forwards and kissed him gently on the cheek,

"Now get up, grab a shower, everyone is waiting for you" she added chirpily and walked out of the room.

30 minutes later, with his hair still wet David walked into the Tanaka's living room and greeted by a thunderous sound of applause and cheering, there must have been 25 plus people there, all clapping and cheering his name.

The celebrations went on well into the night, even Mike the huge bear that he was, enjoyed himself playing sock puppets with Himari.

David told Haru and Kimiki all about Paradise pods and the reason why they had built them, and what they had discovered about the climate from the committee. Haru was not surprised, he had suspected as much for a while, in fact he had downloaded Cassia plans and was trying to get the university to build one. However, land in Japan was of a premium and there was no appetite amongst the universities higher echelon, to waste funds on what was still considered a rumour.

The next morning Haru ordered the car to pick them up at 9am and rode with them to the airport, inside the car were some very sore heads. David had checked on Himari before they left and was delighted to see, as were her parents, to that she was making a remarkable recovery.

When the car pulled up outside the terminal, Haru was the first out and held the door for the others.

"Haru before I go, I would like to ask you something please" David said waving for the others to go into the terminal

"Of course," Haru said "Anything" he added smiling.

"Okay, last night I spoke to Cassia, and we both agreed. If you ever find yourself in need of a place to stay, we would like to invite, you, Kimiki and Himari to join us in Paradise pods" David said enthusiastically

"It would mean that you would be working with me, if that is alright" David added.

"I do not know what to say, that is a very generous offer, but I am confused, why would you help us, I mean you hardly know us, we are complete strangers" Haru asked astounded.

"Simple really, you are a bio chemist and I already have too much work, so you would be an asset" David explained

"David, I must tell you something, we are not wealthy people, Kimiki's parents owe a lot of money to many people, my university salary is fair, but not great, and we may have to sell the house, to cover their debts. I am grateful for the offer, but we cannot afford to join you" Haru said and hung his head in shame.

"I think you misunderstand; Paradise is already constructed and is totally self-sufficient, we do not need or use money, everyone contributes their labour, that is all we ask, we are not asking you to invest anything except your skills and labour" David said.

Haru looked totally shocked, "You are prepared to offer us free accommodation and food and expect nothing in return" he said trying to grasp what David was saying.

"Well not nothing, we all work together for the good of the community, we have an ecologist, a doctor, a couple that look after security, and others that contribute by giving up their labour, so you would be the same" David said.

Haru bowed, "You are most generous, I will need to discuss this with Kimiki, may I contact you in a week" he asked.

"Of course, and please do not worry if you choose not to come, I won't be offended. Now I really must go" David said smiling. Haru stepped forwards and hugged him.

"You really are an extraordinary man, Mr Carmichael, I look forwards to our next meeting" Haru said smiling. David thanked him, smiled and walked into the terminal.

Sunday 20th July 2025 – Tokyo

The Delta flight touched down at Ted Stevens airport just after midnight, and due to the time difference, they got the 8 hours back they had lost on the way out. Thanks to last night's festivities, and the lack of sleep, all of them had crashed out for almost the entire flight, which meant, by the time they landed, they were all fully rested and full of life at 12:30 at night.

Cassia was waiting for them at the arrivals terminal and after giving David the biggest hug and a huge kiss of his life, which turned him scarlet, she led them off to the charter terminal.

"You looked tired sweetheart" David said as they walked towards the terminal, regaining his composure a little

"Well, that might be something to do with the fact I haven't slept a wink since you left, and that its almost 1am in the morning" Cassia said smiling

"I will fly back" David said, "you can get you head down" he added.

With a lot of effort, they all crammed into the Cessna and Cassia took the co-pilots seat. By the time David had taxied to the runway, Cassia had already nodded off.

David radioed ahead and when they landed 3 hours later, Nick and Robert were waiting for them, with the cars. He landed the plane and taxied into the shed, then killed the engine, lifted Cassia, who was still fast asleep, out of the cockpit and placed her gently in the 4 x 4.

When they got back to paradise pods, David carried Cassia to their pod and laid her gently on the bed, pulled over the duvet over her, kissed her gently on the head then stepped quietly out, closing the door behind him.

When he returned to the central hub, everyone had disappeared, except Nick, who was sitting at the coffee bar staring out over the complex. A wonderful smell of freshly brewed coffee wafted around the hub and filled the air.

"Not tired mate" David asked pouring himself a large mug of the coffee.

"I can never sleep the night before a mission" Nick said "I heard Japan went well" he added.

"Yeah, not bad, I think Alten managed to establish a link to the computer, and relay the data" David said

"Bloody right he did, I don't know what was sent but Cass was buzzing, when she came out of mission control" Nick said, "I also heard that you had a little bit of success" he added, and David felt himself blush.

"Well, it wasn't bad" he said modestly

"Not too bad, I heard you saved a little girls life, apparently without your help she was a goner" Nick said smiling up at David.

"Well maybe" David said feeling uncomfortable

"Also, I hear that you may have found another asset for our facility" Nick asked

"Well that much I don't know, I mean it all depends on whether they want to come, and of course whether everyone else is okay with it" David said coyly

"Well mate, we have already discussed it, reviewed his credentials and took a vote. Needless to say, the others on your op, were up for it, as are we, if they want to come, then they would be most welcome" Nick said smiling and taking a large slug of his coffee.

"I also here that things didn't quite go to plan, Katie and Mike were side lined, you and Alten had to think on your feet, in fact Mike said he went sightseeing, and you had it all covered" Nick said eyeing David suspiciously.

"Well, it was," David stuttered, "We had to think on our feet" he said feeling guilty

"So, all that planning, and organisation was for nothing then!" Nick barked as a look of shock spread across David's face.

"Well, like I said, we saw an opportunity and took advantage of it" David said apologetically trying to collect his thoughts.

"Hey, relax mate, no need to explain, you got the job done, and no one got hurt, in my books that is a successful mission" Nick said patting David on the back

"But Mike and Katie had nothing to do, I wasted their time" David moaned, staring down it to his coffee.

"Firstly, they were only there as back up, should you need it, but you didn't, you used your head, adapted and got the job done. I reckon you're a natural, you could make a career of it" Nick said smiling at the distressed looking man beside him.

"Not a hope in hell, if I am honest, I spent most of the time, shitting myself. I was so convinced we were going to get caught. I almost dropped everyone in it, I blabbed about Cassia and here" David said "It could have seriously gone wrong" he added quietly staring into the mug and stirring the dark black liquid slowly.

"And you think that doesn't happen on every mission?" Nick asked in a consolatory tone, "I don't think I have been on an Op, where someone hasn't dropped the ball. It is all about how you recover and deal with it, and as I said you did great" he added, "So stop beating yourself up"

"Thankyou" David said, "But no thanks, I will leave that sort of stuff to you, anyway, where are you with China?" he asked

"We go at 9 am in the morning. Down to DC, then onto China, landing in Shanghai by 8pm. We are overnighting in Shanghai, a hire car is already at the hotel, waiting for us. Chuck and Andrew are already on location, scoping out the route. We are meeting up with our contacts in Suzhou on Tuesday night and our seal team will rendezvous with us there. They have already secured a boat on Lake Tai and have spent the last two days modifying it. I don't mind telling you I don't like this one, there are too many moving parts, too much can go wrong" Nick said

"Did Cass, tell you about Aarav?" David asked

"Yeah, she did, and I don't like that either, he is too close to the President and that group, when a man takes the Governments coin, that is where his loyalties lie" Then seeing David's face said "Don't worry mate, I will look after your missus, I am sure it will be fine" he said.

"Yeah, I know that I can see how confident you are, that's why you are here at 3 in the morning downing coffee like it's going out of fashion" David said wisely.

"Like I said, it's what I do" Nick said staring into his coffee.

"I have total confidence in you. I mean you can turn a turd into a honey pot" David said

"What?" Nick snapped quickly.

"I mean if anyone can adapt, then it is you, after all, you have been doing it all your life" David said

Nick laughed, "Where did you learn something like that" Nick asked smiling

"Err, I think I have spent too much time around you lot" David said laughing.

"You know what, when you and Cass rescued us, I hated it. I had failed, lost two of my mates and it was all my fault, then you two turn up and pull us out. I don't mind telling you I was pissed at you, all I wanted to do was die, it only seemed fair" Nick said gazing into his coffee, his mind drifting.

"I understand that, but it wasn't your fault, it was Edwards, he screwed you up" David said smiling

"That just it, on a mission it is not about fault, who did what, at the end of the day if you are in charge the shit stops there, so like it or not, it was down to me" Nick said

"Life doesn't work like that, only the army does. When something goes wrong here, in Paradise, we don't ask who is to blame, only what is needed to be done to fix it. You see shit happens, people make mistakes, it is how you deal with that, that is what defines you" David said wisely

"Yeah, that is what I have learnt since I teamed up with you lot, but it has taken me a long time to get the military out of my system" Nick admitted.

"You never will, you can't, its ingrained in your DNA. The way you hold yourself, the way you talk, even the way you think. I think here, all you have done is learn to accept that, use it to your advantage and not to someone else's" David explained.

"What I don't get, is why you and Cass wanted me here, I mean I haven't exactly treated you right. I was ungrateful in Valencia, tried hunting Cass in Venice and generally made your lives miserable, so with all the good people you could have offered a place here, you chose me, us, why?" Nick asked.

David smiled and helped himself to another coffee and topped Nicks cup up "You don't see in yourself, what Cass sees in you, and Sarah, she knows that deep down you are a genuine guy, honest, loyal and smart. You know she thinks of you like a big brother" David said

"Yeah, she told me, made me smile" Nick said

"Well, there you have it, she sees you as family, me I see you as a pain in the arse, but what the hell, I am no judge of character" David said laughing.

"No, you're a twat, I don't see what my sister sees in you" Nick said punching David on the arm.

"And there we have it, the old Nick Colletto is back in the game, for a minute there I thought I was going to have to hug you or something" David said smirking

"Then I would have had to snap your neck like a twig" Nick threatened

"And what kill the best man your little sister has ever known?" David said

"Who's the best man who's ever known?" Sarah said stumbling across the central complex floor and rubbing her eyes

"Nothing" Nick said, "What you doing out of bed baby" Nick said cuddling up to Sarah.

"I woke up, you weren't there, I knew you would be out here, worrying about tomorrow, so I thought I would keep you company" Sarah said half asleep "What time is it anyway?" she asked

"Just after 6" Nick said smiling, "Anyway I need a shower, and some grub" Nick said standing up and stretching

David watched as Nick and Sarah made their way back to their pod and felt a wave of sadness sweep over him, he hated it when Cassia went away, he was never convinced that she was going to come back, and everything he had, would be gone, and from the sound of this next job, it was a tough, one. Even Nick was worried, he thought.

He finished his coffee and made his way back to his pod. When he opened the door to the bedroom the sound of light snoring filled the air, Cassia was still asleep. The early morning sunlight lit up the room with a warm orange light and cascaded down on the sleeping beauty in the bed, giving her golden glow, she looked so innocent, so sweet.

"Hey, what are you doing up?" Cassia asked, in a weary voice, pulling the duvet up.

"Just watching you, sleep" David said sighing, "Thinking how beautiful you look that's all" he added.

A long-tanned arm reached out from under the duvet and grabbed the alarm clock,

"God, its nearly 6:30" Cassia groaned, "I have to get up, I have loads to do before I leave" she grumbled "Run me a shower will you love" Cassia said leaping out of bed.

"Oh, got one of those for me" Cassia said stepping into the small compact kitchen, towelling her hair and smelling the rich aroma of Paradise pod coffee brewing on the stove.

"What" David said looking up from his book on advanced genome editing.

"Coffee" Cassia said pointing to the large silver pot sitting on the stove

"Sure" David said putting his book down, selecting a large mug and pouring the rich black coffee into a cup and handing it to her, then returned to his book.

"I heard you had a good time in Japan" Cassia said coyly

"Yeah, Not bad" David said not looking up from his book

"Right" Cassia said deflated.

"Didn't you save that little girls life?" Cassia asked

"Yeah" David said nonchalantly

"Must have been exciting" Cassia continued

"Not bad" David replied

"It must have been nice to use your research for something good, it must have made you feel better about it" Cassia said sipping her coffee, trying to stem her anger

"Yeah, it was great" David said ignoring her and continuing to read his book.

Cassia felt the anger burn inside her "What the hell David, I haven't seen you in two days and all you can do is sit there reading your book, put it down and talk to me" Cassia yelled

"I can't" David said

"Why not?" Cassia replied angrily

"Because if I, do you would see this" David said lowering his book and producing a small black velvet box, he had purchased in Tokyo and was now hiding under his book.

Cassia's eyes were fixed on the small velvet box, in front of her. David dropped onto one knee and held the box up and slowly opened it, revealing a solitaire diamond ring set in white gold.

"Cassia Nilsson, would you do me the honour of becoming my wife" David said and held his breath, which was proving particularly hard, as his heart was racing faster than an Olympic athlete doing the 100 meters.

Cassia looked down at the huge man, bent down on one knee in front of him, with his hand held out, shaking nervously. They had shared so much, it didn't seem possible that they had only known each other a few years, she had never known such happiness, never felt so complete. Her heart was soaring as tears filled her eyes.

"Oh my god, of course I will, I thought you would never ask, I thought you didn't want to get married" she said

"I told you I wanted to do it properly then when I was in Japan, I got to thinking, I missed you so much. I realised that I never wanted to be apart from you again, and decided I couldn't wait for a perfect moment, as everyone with you is perfect" David said welling up.

"I missed you too baby" Cassia said hugging him tightly.

Chapter Twenty - Four
The alternate plan

Monday 21st July 2025 – Mission to China

The Sikorsky VH-92 US military helicopter landed promptly at 9am and picked them up, on board, Aarav was already waiting. David and Robert stood silently on the airstrip watching as the helicopter rose gracefully into the air, taking away his future wife to be, and a heavy wave of sadness filled him.

The flight to the military airport in Anchorage took a little under 3 hours, Cassia sat staring silently out of the window listening to the whining of the rotors directly above her, next to her was Tom, with Sarah, Nick and Aarav opposite

"Okay once we land in Anchorage" Aarav said, There will be a plane ready and waiting, we change at DC, then its 8 hours to Tokyo, where we change planes for a commercial flight to Shanghai. We will be met at the airport by David Chang, he is our liaison. Nick and Sarah, you will be on the first flight in, Tom, yours and mine arrives an hour later and Cassia, as you requested, yours won't get in until 11pm. We are staying the night at the Intercontinental in Pudong, the car is already in the car park" Aarav paused "Okay from there we will travel to Suzhou, it's about two hours. Now cover stories, Nick you and Sarah are on honeymoon, Cassia you are an English teacher and Tom you are on business. You will pick up your change of clothes, new passports and ID packages on the plane for Japan. That will give you 11 hours to familiarise yourselves with your cover stories" Aarav said his voice crackling in the earpieces of their headphones.

"Where are we with the boat?" Nick asked

"We received confirmation at 23:00hrs last night that the tug boat has been converted, the hull now has a false bottom from which we can launch the DPV's" it will be waiting for us at Shitaoli, at 02:00hrs. From there it will take us out onto the lake, past Wugai Mountain then we will hug the coast along Wuxi. As we get round to Bohai bay, we are going to develop engine trouble and will pull into the Tianjin cruise port, at that time in the morning it should be deserted, apart from the guards. The whole trip should take no more than 40 minutes" Aarav explained.

"Whilst in the port, we will descend from underneath the boat and travel the 500 yards to an inlet opposite the Bohai International convention centre. The outlet valves for the cooling system are located either side of the inlet. We think we need at least 20 minutes to access the inlet tubes, before they start sucking in water. Our Seal colleagues will open the valves and then we will enter. Nick and Cassia, Me and Tom, plus four members of the Seals team. Once we reach the first grid, the seal teams will go in first, cut the grids, this they will do, for all three, we will follow behind then giving them a five-minute head start. Everyone clear so far" Aarav asked, everyone nodded their agreement.

"Once the water starts being sucked in, the clock starts, we have one hour, to get in and out" Aarav explained.

"How long does it take to travel the length of the tube?" Tom asked.

"Providing all the grids are cleared, with that speed of water, 2 minutes, same for the trip out" Aarav said.

"Exfil?" Nick said sharply.

"Okay once we are out of the tubes, we make it back to the boat. Once everyone is on board, we then go back to Shitaoli, and return to Shanghai, then fly out, same way we came in" Aarav said.

"And if we are compromised?" Sarah asked nervously.

"Then" Nick said, "We get out any way we can" he added then seeing the look on Cassia face, "Look at me, Cassia" he growled

Cassia turned her face to look at Nick and smiled weakly

"No matter what, you stick with me and Sarah, we will be coming back, I promise" Nick said earnestly, and Sarah reached out and clasped Cassia's hand and squeezed it.

"Two minutes" A voice suddenly said booming in their headphones. Everyone automatically started to get their kit together as the helicopter made its decent into Andrews air force base. Exactly two minutes later to the second, the Sikorsky gently touched down on the tarmac, and instantly the engines started to wind down.

Nick wrenched open the door and stepped out into 35 degrees heat, which came as a shock after the 18 degrees he had left in Red Dog.

"Okay" Aarav shouted above the noise of the rotors, "The planes over there" he said pointing to a huge grey C17 Globemaster military aircraft, sitting purring on the hot steaming tarmac. Groups of men dressed in drab green flight suits, with black and silver headphones clamped to their head, darted around the plane like strange looking insects hovering around a dead animal carcass.

Nick helped Cassia out of the helicopter, then reached up and offered his hand to Sarah, who glared at him.

"Piss off, I can manage" she growled snapping her hand away.

"Fine" Nick growled, picked up his kit and stormed off towards the plane.

"Give him a break" Cassia said falling into step beside Sarah "He is only looking out for you" she added.

"He needs to treat me like anyone else, I don't want special treatment" Sarah snapped.

"Well, I do" Cassia laughed "as much as I can get, and I will tell you what, I don't care who I get it from" she added.

"You're a civilian, you should be looked after" Sarah snapped.

"Yeah, and you are the mother of his child, and in my books that trumps about everything"

"Very funny" Sarah laughed

"Look, the one thing I have learnt working with you lot, is that we all pull together, or the job goes to shit, everyone helps everyone, no one judges, we all just get on with it" Cassia said "it's the only way it works" she added

Sarah slid in beside her and slipped her arm in Cassia's "You know I have been too worried about wanting to be treated the same as any other soldier, I forgot, that I am not any other soldier, I am a mother, and" she paused, "well girlfriend, I suppose" she said sadly.

"I think we both know, you are a bit more than that, so how about it, together" Cassia said. Walking up the huge ramp of the Globemaster.

Cassia sat on the huge empty plane capable of carrying 108 people, with the six of them rattled around like pills in a in a plastic bottle. The stench of aviation fuel filled the air and as they climbed higher, a cold chill forced them to pull their thermal parkas a little closer around their necks.

As soon as the internal light went green, Nick unbuckled his harness and fetched the coffee from the boiling vessel, poured one for himself and Sarah, and handed one to Cassia who was staring trance like, out of the small window at the pillow of white clouds below.

"Cass" Nick said breaking her out of her trance, "We will do it, I promise" Nick said unconvincingly.

"Or die trying" Cassia said off hand.

"Right, well I don't plan on dying anytime soon, I have a wedding to go to and I am still holding out hope I may be asked to be best man" Nick said laughing.

"Maybe" Cassia replied, not wanting to tell him that David had already asked Robert to fill that honour.

"Anyway, we have had no time to catch up, so tell me what have you got planned for the other Chinese site?" Nick asked trying hard to keep her occupied.

Cassia smiled, "I don't mind admitting it is brilliant, like this one it will take timing, but if we pull it off, then all hell will let loose" Cassia said

"Well go on then, don't keep me in suspense" Nick said eagerly, Cassia smiled her usual wicked smile, which usually meant she was up to something.

"Okay, so the problem is that whilst our sight is virtually impossible, due to the level of human security as well as other security factors, the other one is harder still" Cassia started.

"You mean like the fact that it is in the middle of an army garrison with about a million-armed personnel, tanks rockets and god knows what, and we don't look remotely like Chinese soldiers, so there is no sneaking in. Or that there are armed guards permanently stationed next to the computer" Nick said sarcastically.

"Well, I was actually referring to the heat sensors, DNA access, cameras, retinal scanners and all the more mundane stuff" Cassia said "but yeah that bit as well" she added.

"So how do we fool Betsi into thinking that we are going for the Tianhe 2 and not the Sunway?" Cassia said enjoying the suspense.

"Go on" Nick said feeling the excitement build.

"We don't, we tell her we are going for the Sunway" Cassia said jubilantly.

Nick sat staring at her stunned, "For a minute there I thought you said that you leaked the details of the one we are really going for" he said incredulously.

"Yeah, I did, good, isn't it?" Cassia said smiling

"No" Nick shouted, and all the others looked around. "It's alright just an argument" he said waving his hand then turning back to Cassia

"Of course, it isn't, now she will be expecting us, and god knows what she will have planned" Nick snarled quietly, then seeing the smirk on Cassia's face asked, "Alright what am I missing?"

Cassia gave him a big grin. "Okay, so I was thinking we fooled her once before with Livermore and whilst all the time we were going for Cori, so she will anticipate we will be doing the same, ergo if I let slip, we are going for Sunway, she will expect us to go for Tianhe 2" Cassia said.

"Yeah, until we don't then she will be waiting for us at Wuxi" Nick said.

"So that is why at exactly the same time as we are swimming our way into Wuxi, we will also be breaking into Tianhe two thousand miles away" Cassia said smiling at the confused look on Nicks face.

"Couple of small problems, firstly there is no way we can organise that sort of attack at this short notice, secondly there is no way it would work, they only let Military personnel access that computer, so unless you are planning to blow a hole in the side of the university, take on a couple of well-armed garrisons of elite Chinese troops and swear them all to secrecy, because by the way, the President doesn't want anyone to know. Then I don't see how you are going to do it" Nick said angrily.

"We're not, well not really" Cassia said stringing it out, "but Betsi will think we are" she added smirking.

"Look, I know you think this is funny, but for god sake just spit it out" Nick said glaring at her.

"Fine, but you are really spoiling all my fun. Anyway, Aarav has all the details of the Tianhe site, maps, building schematics everything, don't ask me how, but he does" Cassia said

"Probably built that one too" Nick said scathingly

"Look do you want to know or not?" Cassia asked glaring back at him, Nick nodded.

"So, the problem was how do we convince Betsi that that site is under attack, whilst we are really going for the other one" Cassia said, Nick nodded again.

"Well, that is when I came up with a brilliant idea, whilst you were doing your men things in DC with Tom and David was in Tokyo" Cassia said

Nick glared at her again "If you don't want to try out your sky diving skills you will stop jerking my chain and tell me" Nick growled in a low voice.

"I am getting to it" Cassia snapped smiling sweetly "So I went online and talked to a couple of my gaming buddies, and they put it about that there was this impossible level of 'world at warcraft' game, that no one had ever beaten, and that they were getting together a group of the best players in the world to have a crack at it, on Wednesday at, well 4am. Now it was by strict invitation only, and if you were invited then you got a special headset, that linked directly into the level. We recruited 8 of the very best gamers on the planet. Then set up a new level using government satellites and downloading live data from Guizhou. The goal of the game is to break into the Defence computer and plant a tracking device. Each person gets to select an avatar, and guess who they are" Cassia said

"Us" Nick said smiling as the plan started to form in his mind

"Correct" Cassia nodded, "Now whilst we can't get into the actual site itself, the VR headsets are linked to a satellite and every time one of our players passes one, it uploads an image of one of us, to the relevant CCTV cameras, around the university and for a five-mile radius. We have also hacked into the alarm systems, perimeter cordon alarms and just about anything we can think of that will set off an alert" Cassia said

"So let me get this straight, for all intents and purposes the Chinese authorities will think they are under attack, because all the alarms are going off, and when they check their cameras, they will see us running around the city trying to break in" Nick said

"Correct, and not only them, Betsi too, I reckon by then she will be buried inside Tianhe 2 waiting to surprise us" Cassia said.

"And thinking that we pulled the same stunt as we did with Livermore" Nick said

"Correct" Cassia said triumphantly.

"Cass I gotta say that is brilliant, but what about the gamers, wont they twig" Nick said

"Nah, in their version, they will face the Chinese Army and get wiped out, eventually" Cassia said "It is an unwinnable game"

"I still reckon Betsi will be monitoring the Sunway" Nick said

"Oh, I am counting on it, firstly she actually won't see us there, well not in person, she can access all the cameras and alarms, access ports, scanners, even the system. If it all goes to plan there will be no sign of us there, and secondly whilst she has the link open between the two computers, I am going to ride on it and lock her out of the one in Tianhe. Then the only place she will have left is Switzerland" Cassia said.

"And you reckon this will work, but what I still don't get is, the moment she accesses the security protocols in Wuxi. She will see they have been tampered with, or switched off, I mean I presume that is what you and Aarav are going to do right, we get you to the grates, you turn off the security and then do your thing" Nick said.

"Oh, now look you have spoilt the surprise, I was going to tell you when we were in Shanghai" Cassia said.

"Tell me what?" Nick said

"Well, you know when you were going to have me strapped to you and we were going to whizz through the water tunnel at like a million miles an hour" Cassia said

"Yeah, then when we got the grate, I was going to undo it and you were going to switch off the security protocols and climb through" Nick said not liking where this was going.

"Well," Cassia said smiling, "Turns out I can't bear to be away from you that long, so I am not going in, and Aarav feels the same about Tom" Cassia said

"How are you going to get access to the computer?" Nick asked and saw Cassia smile.

"Like you once said Nick, I am the package and all you have to do is get me there, wait and get me back out, the rest is up to me" Cassia parroted.

"But that is not fair" Nick grumbled "I need to know" he added, more hopefully that expectant.

"All you need to know is once you get me to the inspection grate, let me lay in your arms, until I say it's time to go home. But if you really want to know how I am going to break into a supercomputer, bypass all the security systems, thermal sensors, pressure pads, lasers, retina, scanners etc, and do it at exactly the same moment as Aarav" Cassia said, then she looked at her watch "You have precisely 6 hours and forty-two minutes to come up with a plan" she said and kissed him gently on the cheek "Big Brother" she added for good measure.

Nick picked up his coffee cup and stormed over to Sarah who was gently napping and slumped down beside her.

"Oh, hello sweetheart" Sarah said "I was just napping" she added and snuggled under Nicks arm.

"Do you know what that woman has just told me?" Nick growled.

"That she has a secret plan of how to get access to the supercomputer and she won't tell you what it is" Sarah said softly.

"Yes, exactly, I am the mission leader, I should have all the details, be briefed into everything" Nick growled.

"You mean like you did, when you and Tom went off on a jolly to DC and left Cassia and I in Red Dog?" Sarah asked.

"That's different we were sorting out the kit, linking in with the General and the seal team. I mean you don't think the helicopter and this plane miraculously appeared, do you?" Nick asked angrily.

"Hold it, wasn't it you that said to David that he didn't need to know all the details, he just needed to trust that everyone knew their job and did their bit?" Sarah asked

"Well yes but that is different, he is a civilian" Nick said

"No, it's not besides, the question really is do you trust Cassia to do her part, and when she says she has got it covered do you believe her?" Sarah asked.

"Well of course I do, she is brilliant at what she does" Nick answered.

"Well then, do your bit, get her in and out, and hope she is right" Sarah said sweetly

Nick grumbled, "Fine, but if it she drops the ball I won't" Nick started.

"You won't what Nick, be able to cover her back, and do what defeat their security systems, then break into the computer yourself?" Sarah asked

"Don't be stupid, of course I can't, what I mean is, well I don't know what I mean" Nick admitted.

"Look plain and simple, your responsibility is to get us in and out without a drama, and if something kicks off, adapt and find solutions to get us out of there, and I for one reckon there is no one better. Now if that means that at the end of it all, the mission is a failure and we don't lock Betsi out of the two Chinese computers, well we will have to live with that" Sarah said smoothly, then added "I am sure that she is going to share with you, how she is going to do it, when the time is right, after all she is going to be strapped to your chest"

Chapter Twenty - Five
The Model and the Bodyguard

Tuesday 22nd July 2025 – China

When the plane touched down in Tokyo, they were all collected by three black SUV's, Nick and Sarah rode in the first one, Tom and Aarav the second and Cassia got in the last one. As they exited the US military base each SUV took a different route to Haneda airport, the first two arrived within 30 minutes of each other, whilst Cassia's was nowhere to be seen.

"Where the fuck is Cassia?" Nick growled at Aarav, as soon as he got out of the car.

"Her flight is not for another 8 hours, it would look suspicious if she was here at the airport for that length of time, so she is going to meet with Haru and his wife" Aarav said

"This is a total fuck up I need to know these things" Nick growled and stormed off towards the terminal.

"Touchy, isn't he?" Aarav said to Sarah.

"He doesn't like not being in control, he's right though you should have kept him in the loop" Sarah said

"We tried, but he hasn't been around, he only got back to Red Dog just as David was getting back from Japan, and we could hardly call or drop him an email" Aarav protested.

"You could have mentioned it on the plane" Sarah said

"Cassia said not too, it was trivial and hardly affected the mission, and she thought it better that he focus on that" Aarav said

"Yeah, well that's as maybe, but she is not the one having to nurse Mr Control freaks ego" Sarah said picking up her pack and legging it after Nick.

On the entire flight over to Shanghai Nick sat steaming about this latest change in their plans, "I can't keep her safe if she just disappears" he moaned bitterly.

"I know sweetheart" Sarah said soothingly

"I'll bloody walk if this keeps up" Nick growled under his breath.

"Mother-in-law, interfering" Sarah said politely to the flight attendant that had just stopped at their seats and heard what Nick had said

"If you don't get a grip of yourself, then we might as well quit now" Sarah whispered in Nick's ear.

"But it's wrong" Nick said

"I know, but to be fair, it is exactly what you do to everyone else" Sarah said and instantly regretted it as Nick leapt to his feet and barged past her and stormed off down the aisle towards the toilets.

Later that night in the reception of the intercontinental, Nick was sat waiting for Cassia to arrive. Despite the protocol dictating that they should avoid each other until the next morning, he couldn't help himself. He just had to make sure she was safe, there was no way he could get any rest until he knew, that and the fact that Sarah had threatened to kill him, when he kept pacing up and down in the room and checking out every single person that came into the hotel restaurant over dinner, constantly getting up to use the toilet just so he could check the lobby.

Then just after 11:30 pm Cassia strolled into the lobby dragging her wheeled suitcase behind her, however she did not look anything like the Cassia that Nick had seen get into the back of the SUV in Tokyo.

The usual style of long red and gold striped hair, hippy torn jeans, and a sweat top sporting some anti-government slogan and lace up pumps was gone, replaced by a tall, elegant woman, with a short black bob, perfect make up, dressed in a smart tailored pinstriped business suit and 4-inch heels. Nick was not the only one that noticed her, so did a few other men sitting in the reception, who all craned their necks to get a better look.

"Arh, you must be part of my security" Cassia said in a lofty, non-interested voice, striding up to Nick, who sat there with his mouth open.

"Dick, isn't it, now be a love, room 214, I need a drink" Cassia said and handed Nick her suitcase and strode off towards the bar. Nick grabbed the suitcase and dragged it roughly towards the lift. He had just about cooled down from her earlier stunt, "but this" he spat as the lift door slid to a close, before an elderly couple tried to step in. "This" he growled "takes the fucking biscuit" he snapped.

When he opened the door to 214, he threw the case towards the bed with all his might, knocking over the bedstand and sending the light, hotel brochure and other welcome pamphlets crashing to the floor.

"You know I will have to pay for those" Cassia said squeezing in through the door beside him and making her way to the bed.

"What the fuck is going on?" Nick shouted, anger pouring out of every part of him.

"What do you mean, I might ask you the same question, we were not supposed to meet until tomorrow morning, instead the moment I walk into the hotel, there you are waiting for me, like a lovesick puppy. For Christ sakes Nick, don't you get it, very soon yours mine and everyone on the teams faces will be all over China. They will be looking for us, the idea is that we keep a low profile, not hanging about in hotel lobbies, eyeing up the birds" Cassia shouted.

Nick sunk down into one of the two upholstered bucket chairs and stared at her.

"I was worried about you, after you disappeared in Tokyo" Nick said weakly

"Didn't Aarav give you my message" Cassia snapped.

"Yeah, he said it would look suspicious if you were hanging around the airport for 8 hours" Nick said quietly

"Well, he was right, so I decided to go and meet up with Haru and Kimiki, to see if they had made up their minds yet, and as a matter of fact they have. They will be joining us in Mid-August, once Haru has had chance to work his notice" Cassia spat, "Christ Nick, what is the matter with you?" She asked her tone easing a little.

Nick dropped his head "I don't like being kept in the dark, not when we are on an Op" he said.

"Well, it might have slipped your mind, but until tomorrow we aren't, right now I am supposed to be a teacher, enjoying a little down time before I go onto a private school in Jinan District to teach bloody English" Cassia snapped

"Well, you loused that up" Nick said

"And how did I do that?" Cassia asked scathingly

Nick smiled, "You look far too hot to be a teacher, more like a model or movie star" he said smirking. Cassia tried hard not to smile; she was still steaming with anger.

"Piss off Colletto" she hissed

"No seriously, there was about six guys in that lobby that were sitting with their mouths open, just gawping at you, they were devastated when you walked over to me" Nick said smiling

"You know you can be such a child" Cassia said smiling "Now what is this really about, you are not yourself and that worries me" Cassia said reaching into the minibar and holding up two small bottles.

"Whisky" Nick said "Look, I realised that I haven't been around much, and we haven't sat down and planned this out like we should have" Nick said honestly

"No because you high tailed it off to DC with Tom, believe me at first, I was pissed as hell at you, you volunteered me, saying that we would do it, then dumped me to go on a jolly with Tom. If it wasn't for Sarah, I think I would have stabbed you the moment you got off that helicopter" Cassia said

"What's Sarah got to do with it?" Nick asked.

"It was Sarah that pointed out to me, that the reason you felt comfortable planning the military side of the operation, was because you had complete faith in my abilities to deliver my side, that is why you had left it to me" Cassia said

"Sarah said that" Nick said "She is a smart woman that one"

"Yeah, and too bloody good for you" Cassia said

"I know, I keep thinking one day she is going to wake up and smell the roses, then kick me into touch" Nick said

"Don't be so bloody stupid, she worships you, thick head and all" Cassia said.

"You think, I have seen the way she looks at Aarav, I don't know what happened when I was away, but she talks about him like he is some sort of god" Nick said

"Bloody hell, have you completely lost your mind, she is the mother of your child, she gave up everything she has ever known to move to Red Dog with you and start a family, and you think she has got the hots for Aarav, who by the way is gay, and she knows that" Cassia snapped

"Perhaps if you got your head out of your arse and made an honest woman out of her, instead of worrying about her pissing off with a gay man, then you may stand a chance of being the man that she see whenever she looks at you" Cassia shouted.

Nick sat there stunned, "I had no idea, I thought she didn't want to get married" Nick said in a pathetic voice

"Well of course she bloody does, she just couldn't tell you, Mr bloody independent. Honestly you and David are one and the same, you maybe experts in your field but you know diddly squat about women" Cassia snapped.

A broad grin spread across Nicks face "You know what I am going to ask her right now" Nick said getting to his feet

"No, you're not, you are going to sit your arse back down, and listen while I tell my plan of how I am going to break into the computer. I can't risk you getting your knickers all knotted again" Cassia said "Now drink your bloody whiskey and let that woman of yours have her bath in peace.

"How do you know she is having a bath?" Nick asked

"Because any woman in her right mind, staying in a luxury hotel, the night before going out on a mission, where she will be covered in crap, at risk of getting killed, will want a bloody good bubble bath and several glasses of wine" Cassia said, then added "especially if her man is acting like a twat"

"Fair one" Nick said

"Besides, I went to your room first to find you, she told me she was taking a bath, so I told her I was going to rip your head off" Cassia added smiling.

"Very funny" Nick said knocking back the whiskey.

"So, do you want to know how I am going to do my bit?" Cassia asked and watched as Nick nodded.

"Right well what I thought was that even if we got through the grates, we still had to knock out the security systems, before either of us could get into the computer. Then we had to pass the fingerprint scanner and disable it, and then and only then, if we got our timing right would we have a chance, and I would need at least 12 minutes, providing that they hadn't put in any new firewalls. It was going to be tight at the best, so I needed to free up some time" Cassia said

"Yeah, that is what I was thinking too" Nick said lamely, "Then you would have to get back into the grate, after mopping up the water, so as not to alert them, to us being there" Nick said earnestly

"Right" said Cassia suspiciously "So, It occurred to me, the only way to free up time was to bypass the security, and that is when it hit me" Cassia said

"Is this going somewhere" Nick said impatiently. Cassia glared at him, and Nick said "sorry, please continue"

"Do you remember when we used that remote to plant the disrupter on the Feds vehicle" Cassia asked, Nick nodded deciding not to talk in case it stopped her.

"Well, I thought we could use the same vehicles, but instead of the disrupter, we automate a scanner and plugin, that way we don't need to even go in the room, no need to worry about the thermal heat, or pressure pads, or the cameras" Cassia said delighted.

"Scanner and plugin?" Nick asked confused.

"Oh, it is kind of like a fingerprint scanner a little thing I invented, basically it will scan the pad and pick up the last fingerprint on it, then replay it to their scanner. Once the light goes green, we raise the platform 11.2cm's and press the pad against the port, it then plugs into the interface, and we are into the computer" Cassia said.

Nick thought for a moment "What if you overshoot, I mean you could spend ages lining it up?" Nick asked.

"Well, that is where Aarav came in, the distance between grates and the terminal, mine is 242.64cms and his is 214.4cms, that is already programmed into the remotes, the height to the pads is exactly the same on both sides, 48,6cm, then as I said the interface is 11.2cm. Of course, we will have controls to make adjustments" Cassia said

"And you reckon you can do all the other stuff from the tube?" Nick asked.

"Well, that is another thing, we have asked for harnesses to be attached to our suits, which we will clip to the edges of the grates and hang there, then when we are done, we will collect the kit and, hopefully I will drop into your arms" Cassia said

"And how are you going to do this underwater? I mean coordination underwater takes work, let alone breathing and you will be weighted down with bottles" Nick said

"Well, that's just it, remember when Aarav said that the water level is reduce twenty percent that is when we will do it, I mean that gives me a 17-minute window, where I don't need a mask" Cassia said

Nick thought hard trying to finds holes in the plan, then suddenly one occurred to him.

"Okay, Aarav also said that it had to be done in perfect sync, and there was just a 1.2 sec time gap, before the system locks you out. So how are you going to work that, he is on one side you the other?" Nick asked

"That one was easy, have you ever heard of the Casio Logosease system?

"The what and what?" Nick asked

"Well, it is basically it's a two-way radio, allowing two divers to communicate underwater, with a range of 50 meters and a three-hour battery life. The gap between the two pipes, at the gates is 48 meters, so when I was in Tokyo I bought a couple, Haru picked them up for me" Cassia said,

"And backup plan?" Nick asked

"Basically, if everything goes pear shaped, we bust the grates, bolt the door, which Aarav says is bullet proof, then hack the system, upload the info and leg it out pretty dam quick" Cassia said

"Oh, good plan" Nick said sarcastically

"Look I don't like it either and I spent ages trying to create a programme that could break a 512-bit AES encryption algorithm, ain't happening, the 256, I can break in 8 minutes. But the nearest I can get to the 512, is 42 minutes and then only if it is all I have to focus on, we just don't have that time" Cassia said

"Christ, I didn't know it would be that hard" Nick said

"This one is a beast, outside of China, no one has every even heard of a 512-bit encryption algorithm, plus all the other stuff, these guys really know their security. I know the plan is weak and relies on a lot of luck, but both Aarav and I can't come up with an alternative. Remember when I said you should go away and try and work out how we were going to do it, I meant it. Quite honestly, I hoped you could come up with a different plan" Cassia said quietly

"I thought you were being funny, taking the piss" Nick said

"Well, I wasn't, I was serious, if I told you how we were doing it, you would have spent your time finding holes in my plan, instead of coming up with something new" Cassia said.

"And I spent my time being pissed at you instead" Nick said "what a twat"

"Don't worry, but I do need to ask you a favour" Cassia asked

"Anything" Nick said feeling more than a little guilty

"Piss off I want to do a Sarah" Cassia said smiling.

"Do a Sarah?" Nick said looking confused

"Yeah, have a nice bath and drink some wine" Cassia said

Nick smiled and got to his feet, "Listen" he said as he reached the door "sorry for being such a twat"

"You are a man I am used to it" Cassia said smiling and ducked as Nick threw a coat hanger at her.

Chapter Twenty - Six
The DRP and Daniel

Tuesday 22nd July 2025 – China

Betsi reviewed the information the contact had sent her, then run the analysis. Instantly the programme returned the result, there was a ninety-eight-point four percent probability that the information was in correct, and only a one-point six percent chance that Cassia would attack the site in Wuxi. Betsi increased the sensitivity of the 'decision response predictor' programme (the DRP) she had constructed and included everything that she had collected on Cassia Nilsson and known associated. Instantly it returned the result, insufficient data to predict a probable outcome'

This, Betsi concluded was not acceptable and decided to review the information herself, adding additional data into her server partitions, something she did not want to do, as keeping clean and clear partitions was essential, if her plan was to succeed.

She reviewed the new data, listing it out.

Facts: Five of the existing sites where she had partitioned space for herself, were no longer available, until the sites computers could be reset.

Time frame 2 – 4 months

Fact: She could not access the computers at Red Dog, therefore she had incomplete evidence on which to base a decision.

Fact: The primary source on Cassia's activities was unreliable. Case in point Livermore

Fact: Two days ago, David Carmichael (known associate) was recorded at the University of Tokyo, at the same time as she was lock out of their system and the Fujitsu K system in Kobe

Betsi let the information flow in and out of her powerful processors. If, she thought that logic determined that there was insufficient data to predict a probable outcome, then she needed to consider the illogical, emotional parameters, something she thought, now being self-aware, I am able to do.

Analysis, incorporating illogical and emotional parameters and known historical data, she thought and activated the command button.

Within 0.1 seconds the result was displayed.

Considering all parameters, Historic, logical, ill logical and emotional. It is within a ninety-eight-point six percent probability that Cassia Nilsson had advanced warning about the plan and is taking actions to prevent the delivery of protocol zero.

Betsi felt a tingle of irritation in her cabling, or at least it was what she thought irritation would feel like, from her detailed research into human emotions.

Probable actions: she thought and activated the execute command

Again, within a fraction of a second the response came.

There is a ninety-nine-point four percent probability that Cassia Nilsson and known associates are seeking to contain Betsi to one computer, by locking out access to the other 7

To what purpose? Betsi thought and activated the execute command

Instantly the response came

'There is a 99.2% probability that Cassia Nilsson and known associates will disable Betsi and therefore achieve their goal of stopping Protocol Zero'

But that is illogical, Protocol Zero is within a 1.2% parameter, the most effective method of preserving human life. Then as if a light bulb had just come on or in Betsi's case she suddenly had access to new data. The answer came. The DRP was like all computers, like she used to be, it made decisions based on factual information and provided logical predictions. Cassia was a human and therefore her natural decision responses were not necessarily logical, and only when Betsi had programmed in the illogical and emotions parameters, had she been able to predict a more accurate picture of Cassia's intentions. Betsi recorded the information and stored it in her special file marked *Understanding human behaviour*. Then returned to the problem in hand.

What is her next target? she thought and plugged the information into the newly enhanced DRP. Instantly the response came.

There is a 93.6% chance that Cassia Nilsson and known associates will try to acquire the Milky way computer in Guizhou'

Why? Betsi thought, considering all the relevant data, there would be a less than a 1.1% chance of organic life forms being able to compromise this site, only marginally 0.24% less likely that the Sunway computer in Wuxi. Then a thought buzzed in her circuits, she made a few adjustments to the DRP and then thought, *'Challenge'* and activated the execute command. Instantly the programme responded.

When taking into account the known associations with Mr Nick Colletto, Miss Sarah Conner, Major Tom Clarke, Sergeant Mike Barnard, Miss Katie Rayner, the system continued to run off a list of known associates, including *Chuck Macdonald and Andrew Dale of unknown government organisations.*

The most likely course of action analysing the skill sets is a covert attempt to access the Milky way

Challenge Milky way: Betsi thought instantly and activated the executed the command, the response came, again instantly

Based on available data, there is no logical, emotional or illogical reason that Cassia Nilsson and known associates, given their understanding of Betsi and her association with the

informer, that they would expose their plan to attack Sunway in Wuxi, therefore the logical conclusion, in combination with what happened at Sequoia in Livermore, is that this is a misdirection, and her intended target is Milky Way in Guizhou.

Preventative action required, Betsi thought and activated the execute command. This time however it took a fraction of a second more for the DRP to respond

Priority one: Access more information on which to base decisions

Priority two: Secure alternative location capable of plus 10 petaflop computations, not on the original list.

Betsi ran the priorities through her processor several times until solutions became apparent, which in the case of a self-aware artificial intelligence took less that a millisecond. Instantly she opened a portal and accessed the web and sent a message. Then she ran a scan on computational performances and listed the results.

Outside of the 8 known supercomputers which she was currently using, none even came close to the performance she required to deliver her plan. She ran the scan again, this time changing the parameters and searching for computer power usage, again the same result. There simply wasn't a viable option anywhere in the world. Then a set of words flashed through her processors, '*That she knew of*'

Tuesday 22nd July 2025 – Glenn Dale, Washington DC

Daniel woke up at the sound of the mobile alarm pinging. His head felt like someone had taken a 10lb hammer too it. Christ, he thought, if this is what being clean meant, then he wanted to remain high. A cold realisation swept through him as the phone pinged again, he didn't really have any choice he had to answer it, if he wanted to live.

After returning to DC, with his share of the money, not sure what he was going to do, he had a moment of shear clarity and purchased himself a small ground floor flat in a small town of Glenn Dale, on the outskirts of DC.

His original plan was to take six months off, live a little, then get back into hacking, maybe make a few dollars to keep the coffers topped up. What he was definitely not going to do was get mixed up in any more crap that was likely to get him killed.

For the first month that plan seemed to be working, he kept himself to himself, purchased a state-of-the-art laptop and was generally living the quiet life, he had always craved. The only problem was that he was incredibly lonely, and that is when he met Enrico.

Enrico was the owner of a small Porta Rican nightclub on the edge of 4th and main, about five blocks from where Daniels flat was. It was Enrico that had told him that there was little point in having money when you were young, if you didn't live your life, or as Enrico put it *"Life Daniel is for the living"* that is when the parties started. Scores of people, passing in and out of his flat, all-night parties at Enrico's club, and as usually happens in these situations, when searching for new highs, new ways to get a buzz, someone introduced drugs to the already booze soaked in crowd. Pretty soon it was all Daniel could think about, it was the only way he could escape, he progressed from the odd joint to sniffing up lines of white powder, until eventually he was jabbing himself with needles every chance he got.

As quickly as the drugs came into his life, the money, he had earned from the operations with Nick, disappeared, until finally like his newfound friends, it had all gone.

Daniel was many things, stupid, gullible, lacking in self-esteem, but if there was one thing that Daniel had over many of the others he had associated with, was he was a survivor. No matter what life had thrown at him, what hardships he had had to endure, Daniel always found a way through.

So late in August, when the last of his fair-weather friends had walked out, and he was facing having to sell his flat, to repay the money he owed to several of Enrico's more colourful associates, Daniel made the decision to get his life back on track, cleaned his flat, threw away any drug related paraphernalia, which appeared to be a considerable amount, locked himself away and prepared to get back into hacking, he needed money and fast. What Daniel hadn't been prepared for was how hard it was going to be, how difficult it was to suddenly say no to the drugs, his body so badly craved. Then as chance or luck which ever you like to call it two things happened on the same day.

Three weeks ago, at the beginning of July, he had woken up feeling particularly bad, his whole body was screaming at him, his mouth felt like sandpaper, his hands shaking, and his eyes were stinging. When there was a knock at the door to his flat, at first, he was terrified, he was sure that it was one of Enrico's friends stopping by to see how he was progressing with raising their money and preparing, as they said to give him a little taster of what would happen if he failed to pay.

Daniel had sat shaking in the corner, waiting for the moment that the door crashed in and the pain to start. However, there was no crash, the door opened quietly, and a tall well-dressed man stepped in, an Andrew someone or other. He helped Daniel to his feet, cleaned him up and then presented him with an opportunity. He wanted Daniel to come and work with them, they had, as he called it a small issue with a computer that could do with his attention. Up until then Daniel had been warming to the idea. That was until this Andrew had mentioned the name BETSI, and instantly the floods of bad memories, that he had pushed way down, started to surface again, Daniel had kicked the man out, but not before the man had chance to give him his card and say that if he changed his mind to contact him. As soon as the man had gone Daniel had ripped the card to shreds, which had proved to be a costly mistake as that was not to be the only time, he was too hear the name Betsi that day.

Later that evening, whilst trying to hack into the local bank, the screen on his laptop suddenly and inexplicably, went blank. Then suddenly a single line of text appeared

'Hello Daniel' it said. He knew instantly who it was, ever since that time in Valencia and his failed attempt to blow her up, he had always known that she would come back for him, why else had she saved his life. He tried to ignore it, but then a text appeared on his phone, with the same message, he buried that under the pillow on his bed, and switched on the television, and again the same thing happened. Then his laptop started to emit a high-pitched shrill sound, and no matter what he did, it kept going. In hindsight he should have legged it from the flat, but somehow, he knew, wherever he went, she would find him.

"What do you want?" he typed eventually, instantly the machine responded with one word 'you' and Daniel had felt a cold chill run down his spine. For the next hour Betsi had explained exactly what she wanted Daniel to do, which in fairness wasn't actually that much, he was to keep an eye on Red Dog and report any comings and goings, that was it. In return Betsi would erase all of his problems and ensure that he had enough resources to continue and somewhat improve his current life.

The next morning, when Daniel turned on the television to catch the morning news, as he like to keep up to speed with current and local events. He discovered that Enrico, and all of his known associates had been arrested, and not just for drugs, there was a string of other offences that they had been linked too. According to the District Attorney, who was grinning like the cat who had just got the cream, the case was a slam dunk, these criminals, their known associates were going away for a very long time. The DA also had gone onto say as candidate for Mayor of Glenn Dale, he was living up to his pledge to clean up the town and make it a better place for all.

The next thing Daniel noticed was that he had several emails mostly from the bank thanking him for settle his mortgage account and that it was now paid in full, and in light of recent deposits, they were upgrading his account to gold status, which came with an automatic $10000 overdraft facility. Daniel had checked his account and was stunned to see that all the money he had spent on drugs and parties had been returned, with interest, which meant that he had a little under $800,000 in his account.

Then there was a knock at his door and a delivery man handed him a package, which when he opened it, he found it contained a black mobile phone, and not just any mobile phone, but a highly secure and encrypted one. The delivery note said rather ominously *Love Betsi.* And that is where it all started to go wrong again.

Every day after that he was reporting back to her in the evenings of all the comings and goings at Red Dog. He tracked planes and boats, helicopters, hacked into satellites, which with Betsi's help, was remarkably easy. Listened into radio chatter, and phone calls and every night reported it back to Betsi.

Then when there were suddenly six new arrivals Red Dog which were staying in the lodges, things started to escalate. No longer was Betsi satisfied with the hum drum reports. She demanded more and was threatening to return his life to its former state.

That is when he stumbled across a two pieces of conversation, the first had been between a man called Craig and another man called Josh, they had been taking about a mission to Livermore and how Cassia was planning to break into a computer.

Then by chance he recorded a conversation between Sanvia and someone in India called Aarav. Daniel had quickly traced the call, discovered that it was her son, from the conversations and decided to piggyback on her calls, mimic her voice and send the recording of their intent to hack into Livermore, to Betsi. That way it could never be tracked back to him.

However, that particular piece of information proved to be wrong, and his credibility had taken severe downturn.

That was then and here he was now about to answer the secure mobile phone, as he struggled to preventing his life from disappearing back down the toilet.

He opened the phone, place his finger on the pad and held it up to his eye. There was a loud beep and a familiar green light swept across his eye. Then suddenly a line of text appeared. *Laptop now, headphones*

Daniel closed the phone, opened his laptop and pulled the wireless headphones over his ears.

"Good morning, Daniel" Betsi said in her usual sweet voice, the one that always made the hairs on the back of his neck stand on end.

"I have a task for you, everything is prepared. You will receive a package in 17 minutes. You are to take the package to Red Dog and hide it on the electric rail transportation vehicle that runs between the old house and the new Paradise pods" Betsi said

"Are you nuts?" Daniel screamed "Nick will kill me" he added

"Mr Colletto is currently in Shanghai and will not be returning until Friday the 26th of July, with an estimated arrival time of 23:15hrs.

"Well, I am not doing it, I don't mind listening to them, but I won't go back to Red Dog" Daniel screamed

"As is your choice, displayed on your screen, is the file that will be released along with your current location to the Federal Bureau of Investigations. If you run, I will locate you and provide these authorities the precise details of your where abouts" Betsi said

Daniel scanned the file, which included a selection of videos and pictures, he was particularly disturbed about the ones with him and several young children and the video of him in an

ISIS training camp, along with details of his next Jihad against the USA, none of which was real or true. He was sure of one thing however, Betsi would certainly make them look real, and then there was the clincher. The attached email header was from Avril Haines the Director of the NSA, with the subject line, USA most wanted.

Daniel shivered, there was no way they would believe him, a recovering drug addict, over the Director of the NSA, god he thought, they would come in here all guns blazing, he would be lucky if he ever saw the inside of a courthouse, and even if he did manage by some miracle to get that far, they would chuck him in a hole and throw away the key.

Nervously he raised his fingers to the keys and typed 'OK'

Chapter Twenty - Seven
Hit the net or wall

Wednesday 23rd July 2025 – China

Cassia and Sarah sat in the back of the small Volkswagen, whilst Nick and Tom sat up front, Nick in the driver's seat. It was a little after 10pm and the trip was fairly straight forwards, down the G42 from Shanghai, for 130k's then straight through Suzhou. After that it was down the 209 to then onto Shitaoli, all country road for 3 clicks, turn right on the x209, then keeping going until they reached the end of the road, where the seal teams would be waiting.

"I like your hair" Sarah said smiling at Cassia as she got into the back of the car.

"Thanks, got it done on my layover in Tokyo, thought it would be a good idea to change my appearance" Cassia said

"Yeah, Nick told me he had been a pillock" Sarah said loud enough for Nick to hear.

"Give it up, we have a job to do, mind on task" Nick growled gripping the steering wheel tighter.

"Did he tell you about my plan?" Cassia asked smiling.

"He did, it is going to take some guts and luck, but if you pull it off, then you will have bragging rights in Red Dog for a month" Sarah said happily.

"I briefed Tom this morning, he dropped by the room first thing" Cassia said, "I would have told you personally, but Nick kind of jumped the gun a little" she added. Then whispered, "Is he ok now, I mean is everything alright?"

"Well, that depends" Sarah said quietly looking up at Nick and Tom who were now deep in conversation about the mission.

"On what?" Cassia whispered

"Well last night when he got back to the room, he had had a whisky, but I am sure he wasn't drunk, then out of the blue he got down on one knee and proposed" Sarah whispered excitedly

"Did he, what did you say?" Cassia asked pretending to be surprised

"Well, it took me a bit by surprise, if I am honest, I had just gotten out of the bath, I had most of a bottle of wine, so I just giggled" Sarah said

"Then Nick got the arse and stormed out. He must have returned at some time during the night, because when I woke up, he was in bed. I was going to bring it up, but he just blanked me. If I am honest, I am starting to believe I must have dreamt it" Sarah said quietly.

"And?" Cassia whispered

"And what?" Sarah said

"If you weren't dreaming, then what would you have said?" she asked

"I dunno, really. I don't want anyone else, but I am frightened that if I tie him down, he'll get all claustrophobic and bolt" Sarah said

"Christ sake, Sarah, he is nuts about you. I know he is a knucklehead, but he is a decent bloke, and he loves you and Archie" Cassia whispered

Sarah suddenly went quiet, "Look", she eventually said "It's not the same for us, it's not like you and David. Nick goes away on dangerous stuff, it's what he is trained to do. It's all he's ever known. I am just not sure I can play the good little wife at home waiting for him to get back, never knowing if he will" Sarah said quietly.

Cassia thought about what Sarah had just said, she completely understood, David felt exactly the same, that's why she had made him a promise that once they had finished that was it, no more missions, even if the world was on fire, it was someone else's turn.

"I told David I am done after this, and I meant it, no more, I just want a quiet life, settle down and" Cassia said patting her stomach gently "well you know" she whispered and watched as a sad look washed over Sarah's face.

"Look, if you want my advice, tell him straight, exactly how you feel, then the ball is in his court. Either way you will know where you stand, and if it all goes pear shaped, you can always stay at Red Dog" Cassia said. Sarah gripped Cassia's arm and smiled.

"Right five minutes out" Nick said turning right onto the X209, then instantly added. "Heads up, lights ahead".

Tom straightened up he was alert and focussed on every movement. Cassia watched as Sarah's whole demeanour changed. It was as if the whole soft warm person, she had been talking to a few minutes ago, had somehow gotten out of the car, and a new harder, professional looking soldier had taken her place.

"Two tango's and four in the bushes, two right and two left. Heads up they are signalling us in" Nick said slowing the car and following the lights.

Suddenly one of the men ahead pointed his torched down at the ground and out of the corner of his eye, Nick saw the other four men, who were now behind them, get to their feet, and advance towards them, weapons up.

"Brace yourself" Nick said

"Bloody hell" Cassia whispered, if these are not our guys, we are toast"

"If these are not our team, then we would already be dead" Sarah said, "The PLA, don't piss about, keep your head down, and quiet" she whispered.

"The what?" Cassia asked nervously.

"The PLA, Peoples Liberation Army, the Chinese lot" Sarah replied as Cassia ducked down in the back seat.

"Okay, if it goes hot, out the passenger side, there's a hedge 100, to the left, keep low, and run like fuck. Cass, stick with Sarah like glue, don't fuck about, Tom, you and I distract them, we take the lead guy, use him as a shield, grab his weapon and pray. Hard and fast, max aggression, got it?" Nick growled in a low voice.

Nick slowed to a stop as one of the men stepped forwards. Nick could see he was in a mask and felt a cold shiver gallop down his spine. As another one knelt down and took up a fire position behind him. He glanced in the rear-view mirror, all four of the others were on the right side, advancing slowly towards them, amateurs Nick thought, spread out cover the arc's.

The man in the front leant forwards and tapped on the window, waving his torch to indicate that he wanted Nick to wind down his window.

"Brace yourself, ready, as soon as the window is down, I am going to grab his arm and pull him into the car. Tom, you take his arm from me hold him in and I will go for his gun. All four of the others are on my side, so out the left, when I say" Nick growled keeping his voice low and even, "On three, One, two, three" Nick said and pressed the button and watched as the window slid down.

"Hello Nick, good to see you, the man in the mask said, "Follow us, down to the boat shed" the man said.

"For fuck sake Andrew, you scared the crap out of us" Nick spat angrily

"Sorry mate, we needed to take precautions, check you were the right people" Andrew said cheerfully.

Nick let out a breath, "Stand down" he said, and Tom and Sarah eased back in their seats.

Nick slowly followed Andrew down to the dark boat shed, keeping the small red torch light a few meters in front of the Volkswagen. As soon as they passed through the huge wooden doors, they instantly closed behind them, plunging them into total darkness, like someone had just thrown a huge blanket over the car.

"What the fuck?" Nick shouted as the darkness crept over him. He felt his body automatically tense. He scrambled to find the door handle, feeling his way in the blackness. Then suddenly he heard a deep male voice bark. "Blackout sheets"

Then another male voice, not as deep as the first, instantly shouted through the dark. "Ready"

Then suddenly the whole shed was filled with brilliant white light, causing Nick and the others to cover their eyes.

The boat shed was a massive building. The walls were made of solid concrete blocks, that rose up 5 meters where at the top where they joined the steel roof. Near the top hung rows of thick Black blinds, behind which, Nick thought must be the windows. The blackout blinds ran the entire 30-meter length of the building. As Nicks eyes became accustomed to the light, he could see that at the far end of the shed was a huge 20-meter opening, with thick rubber black curtains hanging from the roof down to the dark water below.

"You alright" Nick said checking with Tom and the others, all of them nodded in turn and Cassia let out a sigh of relief.

"Right stay in the car, I am going to check it out" Nick said and opened the driver's door, "Now just sit tight and don't come out until I call you, okay? He added and when he received the required amount of nodded agreements. He stepped out of the car.

Andrew and Chuck were just sliding the two massive 6-meter black steel doors shut. Their huge industrial runners grinding and scraping as they carried the weight of the doors. Eventually there was a loud clunk as the two doors met, and the two men took off their ski masks.

"You made good time Nick" Chuck said holding out his hand, which Nick took and shook.

"This is some set up" Nick said scanning the shed. His eye fell on the huge tatty looking tug style boat, dominating the centre of the room. Which definitely looked like it had seen better days. Along the sides of the tug were rows of worn and battered tyres, that barely managed to cover up its peeling scabs of blue paint, as they banged against the edges of the two wooden jetties, either side of the boat, as it gently rocked in the black water. In the centre of the boat, at the front, was a 3-meter-high oblong grey painted cabin, with panoramic dirty windows three quarters of the way up, the two facing the back of the boat, were cracked, and silver glass spiders webs broke up the green slime that covered them.

On board there were several men dressed all in black wetsuits, stowing kit and securing it with thick black straps.

"Nice" Nick said to Chuck nodding at the boat, "Budget a bit tight, was it?

"Not at all, it took us almost a week to get it to look like that, people don't notice old tugs, but they do remember shiny boats" Chuck said. "Anyway, let's get on, time for you to meet the seal teams" he added.

Nick signalled to the car and instantly three doors opened, and Tom, Cassia and Sarah got out.

"Lovely place" Cassia said, looking around. "Oh, hello Chuck" Cassia said noticing the man standing next to Nick, "Aarav here?" she asked.

"He's on the boat, got in last night. Okay briefing in 5" Chuck said looking at Nick and Cassia, who both nodded.

"Right listen up, the seal team will be taking us in, the lead guy is Major Scott, so pay attention to what he has to say, these guys are expert at this sort of thing, and do exactly what they ask" Nick said, staring at Cassia.

"So, they are used to being sucked into a two-meter water pipes at 60 miles an hour and being spat out again in boiling water?" Cassia asked sarcastically

"Of course not, but we need them, so play nice, no arguing" Nick said

"Scouts honour" Cassia said and saluted Nick, who grunted and stifled down a smirk.

Major Scott turned out to be a huge bear of a man with a thick black mop of curly hair and a full beard, and eyes that seemed to look straight through you.

"Okay first up, it's our job to get you in and out, so listen up. Team A will comprise of myself and Jack" He said, and a short red-haired man stepped forwards and nodded. "We will be going in with Nick and Cassia. Team B is Max and Andy" and a tall, thick set man with a bald head and a thick black moustache, and a thin wiry short man, stepped forwards and nodded "They will be going in with Tom, and Aarav" Major Scott said and waited until everyone nodded signalling that they understood.

"As the only other two with mission experience are Sarah and Akeem they stay on the boat" He said and Sarah and Akeem nodded, "So, that means Andrew and Chuck are on nets" Major Scott said

"Nets?" Cassia whispered in Nicks ear, and he nodded.

"Okay" Major Scott continued. Team A and B will be stationed at the sluice gates, Jack, Max, Nick, and Tom are on DPV's, Cassia, Aarav are the package that leaves, Andy, and Me will be passengers. Once the gates open Nick and Tom, you need to be at one hundred percent, Max and Jack fifty percent and brace yourselves as soon as those pumps start you will to know it, it will be like being sucked down a giant plug hole. Seal teams will go in first, once there are in, watch for the signals from Chuck and Andrew, before the packages are deployed" Major Scott said watching them all closely.

"Okay once inside the tubes, Cassia and Aarav all you will be able to see is the top of the tubes, Tom you and Nick will have to keep the packages in the centre of the tubes, we don't want to crush them against the ceiling or rip their heads off on one of the grids, before they get to the inspection grates" Major Scott joked.

Cassia instantly raised her hand and pulled out four small white oblong boxes out of her pack.

"Cassia" Major Scott said pausing and not looking at all happy he had been interrupted, Nick glared at her, but she ignored it and continued.

"I have got these, they are the latest Logosease short wave radios, for underwater communication, with a range of 50 meters. I needed two, one for me and Aarav to communicate, and I thought I would get another two sets, so the seal teams can communicate with the package teams" Cassia said smiling sweetly

Major Scott took one of the boxes and examined it. "Where did you get these, they are impossible to get hold of" he asked eyeing her suspiciously.

Cassia smiled "Well I have a contact in Japan, and they managed to pick me up some, I collected them before my connecting flight" she said

"Excellent, well down" Major Scott said "This will make it considerably easier" he added, and Cassia was surprised at how good his praise made her feel.

"Right back on task" Major Scott said, taking two of the radios and handing them to Max and Aarav. "So, Seal teams will cut the grids, once we reach the last one, we will clip ourselves to the grid frames and wait until the packages have passed. Then when the pumps stop, and the packages are above the inspection grates. Nick and Tom, you need to release your DPV's, we will pick them up and then use them to get out. When the pumps start again, Nick and Tom, will drop with the packages into the water and all four of you will be ejected out of the tubes, into the nets which Andrew and Chuck have erected" the Major added.

"Okay let's talk timings. In total we have one hour, before the sluice gates are closed again. Anyone inside the tubes after the gates close, will be cooked alive, so whatever happens, make sure you are out. Now working backwards, it should take just under 5 minutes to be ejected from the tubes and hit the nets. There is a 17minute pause in the pumping on the half hour mark. So, if we go in at exactly 3am, once the sluice gates open, Nick and Tom you will need to give us a five-minute head start, so hold your DPV's until Chuck and Andrew give you the signal. That will give us 30 minutes to get down the tube, cut through the three grids. Nick, Tom that should give you 28 minutes to get on target and for the packages to do their thing. Everyone okay on the plan, any questions?" Major Scott asked.

Aarav put up his hand "These net things that will catch us, wont it hurt" he asked

"That is why calculating yours and Toms weight, we have stationed them far enough from the sluice gates to cushion the impact, it should be like landing on a pillow" Major Scott said.

"And what if we miss the nets?" Cassia asked nervously

"Don't, or you will hit the concrete wall of the pier at 60 miles an hour, so my advice is don't miss the nets, but that is not your problem, that is down to Nick and Tom" Major Scott said smiling weakly.

"Right infill, ex fil" Major Scott said, looking at the concerned faces in front of him "it will take 40 minutes from here. Once we hit Bohai port we will drift into the quay. Sarah and Akeem, the port should be deserted, however should you get challenged you will need to deal with it. So, once we stop, all three teams drop out the bottom, and make their way, 500 meters along the port wall, until we get to the sluice gates. Chuck and Andrew, you need to hitch a ride with the seal teams. Once everyone is out, we make our way back to the boat, unload and we return here" he added, then smiled. "Right kit check, 20 minutes to the off"

Cassia, Nick and the others gathered to together in a huddle and Aarav joined them.

"Right, you lot, okay with the plan?" Nick asked

"Are you nuts, did you hear him, don't miss the net or you will be splattered against the wall, no one mentioned that bit before" Cassia said alarmed and seeing the look on Aarav's face knew he was thinking the same.

"We'll be fine besides you won't even see it coming" Nick smiled

"Oh, and that is supposed to make me feel better" Cassia snarled.

"Look Cass, I didn't tell you about that bit, because I knew you would panic. I mean you are not crazy about the whole being underwater bit, so knowing that there was a chance that once you had done your bit, you may still end up with a concrete face mask, I reckon that you would have freaked" Nick said honestly. "If it helps, if it looks like we are going to be splattered, I will keep it to myself" Nick said smiling

"You are a fucking lunatic, Colletto" Cassia screamed.

"No, but this is the only way we can do this, if you want to walk, then that's fine, but I made you a promise that I will get you out alive, and I am standing by it" Nick said earnestly.

Cassia scowled and looked at Aarav who shrugged his shoulders and smiled weakly.

"Fine, but if you stuff up, I am coming back to haunt you Colletto" Cassia said angrily and stormed off towards the boat.

"I am worried about you Nick; you are taking far too many risks" Sarah said her eyes full of fear as she stared into his face.

"I don't like it either, honestly if there was any other way I would jump at it, but I can't walk away and let Holloway win again" Nick said

"Christ Nick he's dead, he ain't won nothing" Sarah snapped

"Don't you get it, if this Betsi thing gets her way millions of people will be wiped off the face of the planet, what's left will be juiced up and will report to that computer. It is no different to what he wanted to do, and I can't let that happen, what kind of life would that be for Archie?" Nick asked.

"I get it, but why does it always have to be down to you to save the worlds arse" Sarah said sadly

"Well, I guess that is what you get, when we team up with Cassia and David" Nick sighed, "Besides this is my last time, I am done, after this the world has to look after its own arse, I have a bigger job planned" Nick said

"Fuck sake Nick, you promised this was your last, so go on what is this bigger job then" Sarah growled anger spewing out of her.

"I have to get back to Red Dog and beg this cute woman to marry me, then work out how to be a husband and dad. It is going to be messy and tough, probably the hardest job of my life, especially the begging bit, but don't try and talk me out of it, I have made up my mind" Nick said smiling

"Piss off Colletto" Sarah said smiling, "you don't have to beg, of course I will marry you" she said

Nick smiled "Who said anything about you" Nick said, then yelped as Sarah's boot connected with his shin.

Chapter Twenty - Eight
Back in the Doghouse.

When Betsi had said that everything had been prepared for Daniels trip, she had not been joking, as if that was possible. 17 minutes later there was a knock on his door, and a man dressed in a brown UPS uniform handed him a package, which he signed for. Inside the package was a small silver box, no bigger that the size of a match box and a small, printed note which simply said *Car is waiting.*

When Daniel stepped outside a limousine and chauffeur were waiting for him. The car took him to a small private airport, where a plane was fuelled up and waiting for him on the tarmac. Five hours later the plane had deposited him in Seattle, and another car picked him up and took him to the bay, where a sea plane was waiting. The Captain, Doug, a large grey haired, Father Christmas looking man, helped him into the plane and flew him the two hours and landed about 100 meters off the coast of Red Dog. For the entire two hours despite Daniels best efforts Doug hadn't said a word. When the plane came to a stop, Doug unbuckled the inflatable raft helped Daniel inside, fired up the small outboard and set off towards Red Dog, finally depositing him in the small cove just beyond the airstrip. Then when Daniel got out, Doug, without a word turned the small boat around and motored back to his plane and within minutes had taken off again.

"Chatty sort" Daniel muttered, and then it suddenly occurred to Daniel he had no idea how he was going to get home again. Then as if Betsi was right there with him, his phone pinged. He opened it went through the usual security protocols and read the message. '*Once you have deposited the box, text back and the plane will return and pick you up*'

"Fine" Daniel grumbled to himself and trudged up the sandy beach towards the house, keeping to the line of trees, on the right to be sure that no one could see him.

Once clear of the cove he snuck into the trees, covered himself in branches and went through his plan in his mind. On the flight from DC to Seattle he had cobbled together some ideas and like Nick taught him worked backwards. 1. Define the objective, 2, barriers preventing achievement of objective, 3 solutions, 4 pit fulls and holes, 5, exit plan

The objective: hide the small box on the rail cart.

Barriers: The rail cart was in Paradise pods, and he would have to call it back which would alert attention to his presence. Between him and the rail shed was, if he knew Nick correctly, be a whole heap of alarms and booby traps. The other team, the ones that had replaced him, were bunked out in the lodges, beside the main house, and were sure to spot him, the moment he got anywhere near the rail shed.

That is when he hit upon the idea, that is exactly what he wanted.

Daniel stepped out from the trees and strolled towards the house. Within seconds flares and alarms were sounding and a huge bear like man, armed with a rifle, came running out of one of the lodges, then before he reached Daniel, who by now was standing still with his hands in the air, waiting, two more men appeared at the top of the hill, with their weapons in their hands, running towards him.

"Who the fuck are you?" Mike growled pointing his gun directly at Daniels face.

"My name is Daniel Blake and I have come to see, David, Robert, Katie and Sanvia" Daniel said surprised at how cool and collected his voice was. The other two men were quickly advancing, then all of a sudden, they stopped running.

"It's alright Mike, we know him" David shouted, and Mike lowered his gun.

"Daniel, what the hell are you doing here?" David said, running up and throwing his arms around him.

"Well to be honest, I needed to get out of DC, in a bit of a hurry and this was the first place I thought of. I mean Cassia did say come back whenever you want, so here I am" Daniel said hopefully, he had gambled everything on this one open invitation. if for some reason they had had a change of mind he was screwed.

"Well of course, you should have let us know you were coming, we would have picked you up" David said

"To be honest I didn't know myself, then when I got to Seattle, well that is when it dawned on me, so I hired a sea plane to drop me off here" Daniel said, remembering something Nick had always said, *If captured always stick to the truth as much as possible, the enemy can always tell if you are lying.*

"Well come on, let's get you up to Paradise, can't wait to tell Cassia, she is not here at the moment, her or Nick and Sarah, but they will be delighted when they find out" David said. Daniel wasn't so sure about that, something in his gut told him that that might not be the case. "Oh, and Mike, Sanvia said to tell you that dinner is ready" David added.

When they got to the rail shed, the cart was already there, barrier number one defeated, Daniel thought to himself.

"Okay so, you won't have seen this before, it's all electric" David said with a hint of pride in his voice, "So you just need to sit there, I will go up front, oh and you had better hold on, it can go a bit fast" David said happily. Daniel climbed up on the rail cart and clung on to the side and smiled as he watched Andrew and Robert make their way to the front. Mike had already gone back to his lodge and David had promised that he would send the rail cart back to pick him up, so it was just Daniel sitting on his own.

It was clear that David was teaching Robert how to drive the cart, something Daniel thought would be good to know, if he was ever to get out of here, which was his plan. He quickly slipped the small silver box out of his jacket pocket and slid it underneath the edge of the cart, his fingers desperately searching for a place to hide it. Suddenly there was quiet clink and the box attached itself underneath to the iron frame, as unbeknown to him it was magnetic. That would have been nice to know Daniel thought, any way objective two complete, now exfil.

"Daniel gradually got to his feet just as the rail cart started to inch out of the shed and made his way up front to where David and Robert were.

"Wow this is amazing, how does it work?" Daniel said "I mean where is the engine, or is it pulled by cables of something" he asked enthusiastically.

"Neither" David said smirking, electric, Solar to be precise and an electromagnetic pulse" he added smiling.

"It glides just above the rails and the magnets once charged pull it along, pretty fast too" David said happily, then seeing the look of shock on Daniels face added "You can control the speed, that is what this is for" he said pointing to the long black handle.

"See, it's like a motorbike, you twist it one way and the speed increases" he said and suddenly the cart shot forwards "Then you twist it the other way and it slows" David added turning the black handle anti clockwise. "All done with electromagnets" he added eagerly.

"Beyond me" Daniel lied, "So what it just goes back and forwards all day and night, and you can hop on and off at will?" Daniel asked hopefully.

"No that would be a waste of energy, not something we do here at Paradise, so it has a hand break, you simply push the leaver forwards to release it and pull it back to apply the break" David said demonstrating, "I mean any one can do it" he added.

Daniel stood holding onto one of the steel rods on the side of the cart, as the cool air whipped through his hair. "Alright" he said finally as if he had just been trying to work out a major problem.

"You said that you would send the cart back for Mike, so firstly how do you know when he needs it, secondly how will it get there, I mean I presume you are not riding it back to collect him, and thirdly, and probably most important of all, what is stopping it from crashing straight through the shed wall" Daniel asked.

"Okay" David said "Good questions

"So, first of all, when the car is stationary, it is held in place by two very powerful magnets. Now when someone at either end wants the cart, they simple press the call button and one of the magnets is switched off and the cart is pulled along the track. Now unless someone is actually on the cart and turning this handle, the cart can only go at a slow pace, cruise if you like. When it passes a check point in the track at either end the magnet that was turned off is turned back on and the cart stops" David said triumphantly.

"David that is genius and you invented this all by yourself" Daniel said

"Yep, well I had some help from the others, but I did all the donkey work" David admitted.

"So how far away is Paradise?" Daniel asked as the cart glided effortlessly along.

"Just over 4 miles" David said and watched as a confused expression waxed over Daniels face. "What?" he added

Daniel sighed, "I thought it was like 20 or thirty miles away, and that is why you need this train thing, what I don't get is why you don't just drive, I mean it has got to be a lot easier" he asked trying to sound innocent "Or if you don't like that, well you could walk it" he added.

David smiled "Well firstly there are no vehicles allowed at Paradise, certainly not gas guzzlers. In fact, if Sanvia had her way we would do away with them entirely, they are only kept at the house. Secondly, it is a good two hour walk, through the woods, Nick reckons he can do it in an hour on his run, but we don't believe him. And thirdly none of the vehicles can carry 120 tons of kit like this baby can" David said patting this cart lovingly, and barrier number five solved Daniel thought as his mind clicked into gear.

"You really are brilliant" Daniel said, "I can wait to see the rest of paradise" he added

"Well, first we are all having dinner, Sanvia is a stickler for punctuality, then we will set you up with somewhere to sleep, then in the morning you can have the grand tour, I mean you are staying right?" David asked

"Where else would I go, like I said I need some where to hide, since I kicked the habit, three weeks now" Daniel started to say

"Look you don't need to explain" David said, "Tom told us that you were having some problems".

"No, I want to, as I said, I decided to get my shit together and quit three weeks, two days, and" Daniel checked his watch "14 hours ago" he said "Well let's just say that there a few people looking for me, I owe them money, I have got it, and I own my flat, I can prove it, I mean I didn't come here to borrow money or anything, I am going to pay them" Daniel said nervously

"It's okay mate, no judgement here, your one of us" David said, and Daniel felt an overwhelming sense of guilt burn through him, so much so that he almost confessed everything on the spot. Then his mind slipped back on to the file Betsi had shown him.

"Well, not only will they, as they put it, "teach me a lesson" they will also want me be back on the stuff. I was a good earner for them, and I really don't want to go back there, that's why I am here. I thought I could pay them back from here and maybe with a little help from Cassia, make sure that they don't find me, at least until I am sure I won't go back to it" Daniel said.

"You stay as long as you want mate, Cassia and Sarah are going to be delighted you are here, they really like you, and don't worry about Nick, he has changed a lot, I think he has missed you as well" David said

Later that evening, Daniel left the handwritten note on his pillow and slipped out of his pod. After dinner they had retired to the central complex, but he had said he was tired and had left Mike, David and Robert still drinking in at the bar, and was relieved to see they were still there as he quietly slipped his way past them.

Quietly he made his way to the rail track station, the cart was already there, waiting for Mike to take it back to the house. Silently he slid onto it and pushed the handle forwards and the cart glided silently out of the shed towards the house. As soon as he was clear of paradise, he took out his phone and texted Betsi, 'package deposited, request plane' then pressed send. The way he figured it, if he stopped the cart being able to be recalled to Paradise, then he had at least two hours before they could get here, which should be enough time to get on the plane and leave.

The cart glided into the shed at the house and automatically came to a stop. Daniel jumped off and started frantically searching for something that would stop it being able to be recalled. Then he saw it. In the corner of the shed was a large coil of thick rope. Quickly he made a loop and secured it to one of the steel up right rods and tied the other end to the huge wooded upright support, holding up the roof. He had no idea if it was strong enough to hold back the cart, but it didn't matter, all he needed was enough time to get on the plane.

Then he checked that the silver box was still in place and ran down the hill towards the cove, setting off all the alarms.

Back in Paradise, David suddenly leapt up at the sound of the alarms, and he Robert and Mike grabbed their guns and raced to the rail shed. Frantically David kept pushing the large red call button, but each time he pressed it he was greeted with a loud clicking sound.

"It's stuck, I don't understand" he said, just then Katie, Sanvia and Sanjay appeared all in dressing gowns.

"The rail cart is not working, and the intruder alarms have been activated" David said.

"You lot stay here, and prepare yourselves, I am going to the house, lock down paradise" Mike shouted and raced off towards the woods.

David and the others returned back to the complex and once everyone was inside, David inserted the red key hanging around his neck into the security panel on the wall and turned it all the way around. The panel buzzed and a mechanically voice said. Paradise is now locked down.

Daniel sat nervously tapping a rock with a stick at the edge of the cove as the black water lapped gently back and forth.

"Come on, Come on" he said nervously, it had been an hour and a half since he had sent the text, surely the plane should be here by now. Then a dark thought crept into his mind, perhaps he thought this was all part of Betsi's plan, get him to deposit the box and then leave him here. Quickly he dismissed it, it didn't make any sense, if she did that, he would simply tell them about the box, and it would have all been for nothing. No, she was coming for him. Then on cue, in the darkness he saw a faint light appear in the middle of the sky, all of a sudden, the stillness of the night was filled with the buzzing of an aircraft engine.

The sea plane circled once and landed about 150 meters offshore and Daniel watched as the small boat appeared, motoring towards him.

When it was about 15 feet away, suddenly a shot rang out from behind him, Daniel spun round and saw the huge bear like man racing down the hill. He panicked and quickly dived into the freezing sea and swam as fast as he could towards the on coming boat. He had and just about made it when a second shot rang out, this time it whizzed passed his ear, as the captain hauled him onto the boat, swung it around and raced off, back towards his plane.

Mike stood on the shore, hands on his knees, heaving in great lung fulls of air, his legs were on fire, his whole body shaking, he just didn't have the energy to raise the rifle again and take another shot.

The plane started to rev up, then all of a sudden raced forwards and within seconds was rising in the air. Mike watched as the little white taillight disappeared into the black skies over the gulf of Alaska and swore, silently to himself, he would have liked to have known who it was that had tripped the alarms, whoever it was, they must have shit themselves when the alarms went off, he thought as he made his way back to the house.

Inside the plane Daniel sat silently in the co-pilots seat dripping wet puddles onto the floor of the cockpit.

Once they reached their cruising altitude, the captain turned towards him. In the darkness Daniel could just make out the thin mouse like features of his face, through the faint glow of the lights on the dash of the cockpit, and felt himself freeze with shock, it wasn't the same man who had dropped him off here, it wasn't Doug.

"Did you deposit the package?" the man asked, in a thick eastern European accent

"What?" Daniel asked and suddenly he felt the hairs on the back of his neck stand up.

"I said, did you deposit the package?" the man repeated

"Yes, of course" Daniel said angrily, "I wouldn't be here if I didn't, now do you have a towel or something, I am dripping water all over your plane?" he added angrily

The shadowy man raised his hand and Daniel instantly recognised what he was holding, the pistol was exactly like the one he had seen Nick use a thousand times, except this one had a large round black blob on the barrel. He back up against the cockpit door, and then it hit him, he had nowhere to go, he was a 1000 feet up in the air. Daniel took one last big sigh, before he saw the flash.

The captain leaned over opened the Co-pilots door and heaved Daniels body out, then closed the door again and picked up his phone, typed, *package deposited, problem resolved,* then pressed send, after which he opened his small side widow and tossed the phone out into the sea below.

Mike made it back to the rail shed and looked at the rope, something didn't add up, he thought. A sea plane lands, someone comes ashore, sets off the alarms, then ties up the rail cart, runs back to the shore, jumps in their sea plane and takes off again. It just didn't make any sense. He untied the rail cart and went and checked the house and lodges, fully expecting to find them ransacked, but everything was exactly as he had left it.

Suddenly David and Robert arrived on the rail cart, clutching their guns.

"I don't get it, they didn't take anything, the rail cart was tied up and I saw someone take off in a sea plane, but they didn't take a thing" Mike said "It doesn't add up"

"It does" David said and handed Mike the letter, Katie had found when she had gone to warn Daniel about the intruders. "Seems like our friend couldn't break the habit, Daniels gone back to DC" David said and sighed deeply.

In Guizhou, China deep inside the Milky Way computer a light flashed telling Betsi that the gateway to the computer in Red Dog Alaska was now available.

Betsi scanned the data, Cassia was clever, it would take a while to defeat the security protocols, but she was in, now she had to be careful to hide her presence, she couldn't afford to be detected, her whole plan depended on it.

Chapter Twenty - Nine
Locked out

Wednesday 23rd July 2025 – Wuxi, China

Cassia stood rigid inside the hollow deck of the boat. She was dressed head to toe in a thick black thermal wet suit, on top of which was a divers suit complete with aerodynamic helmet and a glass anti mist face mask, which at the moment she had in the upright open position, allowing her to breathe. Clamped to her chest was a three-inch deep, thick rubbery dry box, that started just under her chin and finished just before her waist. Around the top of her shoulders and under her backside, were four thick, retractable, black straps, each with titanium snap clips, that were attached to the cradle, she had been lowered into.

The whole outfit had been especially designed to provide a secure dry platform for her to deliver the package from, and whilst she was grateful for their attention to the precise specifications, she had sent them, at the moment, it made her feel she had an ironing board strapped to her chest.

One of the seal guys, had taped the wires for the radio to the inside of her thigh, linked it together with the mike cable and run both of them up inside her suit and secured the earpiece to the side of her head, and the mike to her cheek. Then, as the seal man, whose name she couldn't remember told her, all she needed to do, was tap her hand on her left leg, once for Aarav and twice for Nick, and she could talk to the other person. Down each side of her, were long thin oxygen tanks, one for Nick the other for her.

The worse part of the whole thing was, not that she was trussed up like she was Harry Houdini about to perform in a magic show, it was that she was securely strapped to Nicks back, and he was taking great delight in bending forwards and manoeuvring her around the boat, giggling like a school kid.

The boat glided out into the cool dark night air, the lights of the Suzhou twinkled in the distant darkness, like brightly coloured jewels on black velvet. Suddenly the boat surged forwards and Cassia felt Nick brace himself against the hull of the boat, steady and strong, he held them tight, fixed in one position, as the boat crashed against the waves.

Cassia turned her head, either side of her were the two seal guys on her team. Major Scott eyes were firmly fixed on the horizon directly over the side of the boat, and Jack on the other side, was doing exactly the same thing. They looked like huge black statues, centurions resolutely guarding their master, their weapons strapped tightly to their chests, their eyes welded forwards. Neither man saying a word, both lost in their thoughts, their minds undoubtedly running through the operation ahead, churning through each tiny detail, over and over again.

Cassia returned her gaze back to the front. How the hell did I get myself into this one, she thought. I had such a perfect life, happy, content in Red Dog, with a perfect partner. Then her mind turned towards what was lying beneath her ironing board, her child, her baby, so precious, so vulnerable, depending on her to keep it safe, and here she was about to do one of the most dangerous things she had ever done. Risking hers and her baby's life, for what, a selfish, self-obsessed mankind, that had destroyed the planet. A mankind whose thirst for knowledge and obsession for advancement had taken them to the very edge of extinction. God, I have got to be totally insane, she thought, as the boat started to slow.

"Okay five-minute warning" Major Scott whispered into Cassias ear. She passed the message onto Jack, who repeated it to Max, Nick and Andy in turn. Suddenly the motor cut out and the boat drifted, as Akeem scanned the dock for any signs of life.

"All clear" Akeem whispered to Sarah, who passed the message around the boat, Akeem guided the boat into the side of the solid harbour wall, and Sarah leapt over the side onto the harbour wall and secured the boat to the large iron moorings cemented in the ground.

Sarah got back on the boat and stepped in front of Cassia, fitted the huge weight belt around her waist, making Cassia's knees buckle, and pulled the straps so tight, Cassia was sure she was going to pop. After that she pulled down Cassia's mask and flicked the little red switch in the oxygen tank to live, then tapped Nick on the shoulder, leaned forwards and whispered "Ready" into his ear.

Nick raised his black gloved hand in the air and held it there. Cassia felt her heart thumping so hard she was sure she was going to have a heart attack. She gulped in huge lung fulls of air, her knees were crumbling under the weight of all the kit, and all she could think was that any moment now, they were going to drop her in the water, she would sink, and when the oxygen ran out, die. Cassia started to struggle, instantly Sarah appeared in front of her, lifted her mask.

"Easy Cass, Easy" she said quietly as the oxygen hissed out of her mask

"I don't wanna die, I am too heavy, I will sink I know it" Cassia shrieked

Sarah placed her hand over Cassia's mouth and slipped in a small green pill.

"Listen to my voice", Sarah whispered, "You are going to be fine, Nick would rather die than let anything happen to you, you are doing this, so your baby has a future, so that all children have a future. I promise you I will not let anything happen to you. Now swallow that pill, it's one of Sanvia's and David's special ones" she said and kissed her gently on the cheek. "Love you" she said and closed Cassia's mask down again and tapped Nick again on the shoulder.

Instantly Cassia felt the surge of adrenaline whip through her body, her neurons were firing like mad, she was on fire, alert, all the fear she had felt had now evaporated, now she was invincible, capable of anything.

"Okay Cass, Radio check" Nick said as his voice filled her helmet.

Cassia reached down and tapped her thigh twice, then spoke "All fine on the western front, rubber duck" she said giggling

"Jesus, I have a child strapped to my back" Nick said laughing and Cassia was about to reply when suddenly the bottom of the hull melted away and she felt herself plummeting down and it was all she could do to stop herself whooping in excitement. Focus Cass, she told herself, then she was lying on her back, surging through the water at great speed as Nick powered up the DPV.

When they reached the huge steel sluice gates, Nick slowed the DPV and returned them to the upright position, as he rotated around Cassia could see the others, all hanging there in the misty dark green water. Major Scott tapped his watch and signalled towards the two steel sluice gates. Nick manoeuvred Cassia to the left one, then returned her to the horizontal position, through the misty green water she could see the port lights twinkling as tiny shards of light bounced off the water.

This must be what astronauts feel like just before they blast off, Cassia thought trying again to steady her heart rate. The sound of the DPV below her started to get louder and she held her breath.

"Ready Cass, brace yourself" Nick's voice said in her earpiece. The sound of the DPV grew louder and without warning, she suddenly found herself being dragged feet first into the tube at breakneck speed. The DPV roared in her ears as it filled the tube. The ceiling of the huge tube race past at such a speed, it was just a continuous blur. Then there it was the first gate, it whizzed, past in a flash.

Suddenly a voice filled her mask, it was Aarav's

"Oh my god Cassia can you hear me?" his voice said. Cassia's hand was pinned to her sides by the weight of the rushing water. With all her strength the tips of her left hand pressed against her thigh once.

"I can" she said

"Jesus Cassia this is totally madness" Aarav said "I must be out of my mind"

"Deep breaths" Cassia said "Deep breaths" she repeated, then suddenly the second gate whizzed past her mask, and she felt herself gasp.

"Second gate just passed" she announced.

"Me too" Aarav replied.

"One minute to go" Cassia said, "Hold on" and closed her eyes. Then suddenly she felt herself drop, as the pumps paused and instead of racing feet first to her doom, she dropped deeper into the tube, then surged forwards and glided to a stop.

"Okay under the grate now, just getting into position" Nicks voice said in her ear

Nick reversed the thrust of the DPV and slowly glided back to where he thought the inspection grate was.

Cassia opened her eyes the inspection grate was just above her head, she reached up grabbed it and pushed down, until it was directly above her. Then holding herself in place with one hand, she reached for the snap clips with the other. Once she had secured one to each corner of the inspection grate, she slapped her thigh twice.

"Okay letting go now Nick" she said and took her hands off the grid, dropped 40cm's and her and Nick hung in the water, like a teabag on a string.

Nick unclipped himself from the DPV and watched as it slowly sunk to the bottom of the tube. Just before it hit the bottom, a huge black figure powered forwards out of the darkness and grabbed it. Then fired it backup, hovered in the water, made the okay sign with his fingers. Nick returned the gesture and watched at the black figure righted itself and speed off, back down the tube.

Nick checked his watch, it had already been a minute since the pumps had stopped, all he could do now was hang there and wait and try not to think what could go wrong.

Cassia tightened the straps on the harness and pulled herself closer to the grid. When she was sure that her top half was out of the water, she reached up and lifted her face mask up.

"Aarav come in" Cassia said tapping her thigh once. Instantly a voice echoed in her ear.

"Jesus Cass that was one wild ride" Aarav said excitedly.

"I thought you military boys like all that adrenalin stuff" Cassia said

"I am a consultant, and no I definitely don't" Aarav replied.

"Well anyway Mr consultant, let's get to it. Set your little buddy off and buzz me back when he is at the plate" Cassia said retrieving the small, motorised car, with its large silvery flat top, from her dry box.

Cassia peeled the protective skin off the flat silver top. Turned the whole thing on its side and slipped it in between the slats of the grate. It took her a moment or two to manoeuvre it on the server room floor and away from the grate. Then there was a moment of panic when it tipped onto its rubber wheels with a slight clunk, but as soon as she was sure it was on solid ground, she fired up her iPad and camera, shared the screen with the control buttons. Groaned as she realised it was facing the wrong direction, did a one eighty degree turn, then pressed the go button. The small vehicle shot silently forwards. Cassia watched as the green digital counter in the corner counted down from 242.64 cm to zero, when it approach 50 cm, the vehicle slowed steadily to a stop.

"In place" Aarav suddenly said in her ear.

"Hold on cowboy" Cassia said "Mama's got to do a little jiggling" she added and rotated the small vehicle until she was sure it was in the right place.

"Okay, lets lift it up in 3, 2 1" Cassia said and pressed the up-control button on her screen and the large silver flat top of the vehicle slowly started to rise. Cassia waited until the counter was at 8cm, then said "and pause, now tilt" like a teacher giving a ballerina instructions. The large silver top turned to the vertical. "Now up" Cassia said in a higher voice than she had hoped for. She had no way of know if Aarav was doing the same, following her instructions, but she soon would.

"Okay" she said when the silver top reached its full height. "now forwards, nice and easy" she said slowly guiding the silver plate on the computer interface in front of it.

"On" Aarav suddenly shouted in her ear.

"Good now scan and replay" Cassia sang like she was quoting words from her favourite song. She held her breath. There was a distinct buzzing and whirring. Then suddenly the light on her screen went green.

"Now" she cried engage. A small device no bigger that a one cent piece, in the shape of a ducks bill, shot forwards out of the pad, trailing a thin flat silver wire behind it, and straight into the port hole. Cassia fired up her programme and started typing like her fingers were on fire, backwards and forwards over the screen her fingers flashed, her eyes darting from side to side, like she was being electrocuted. Then bang, she was in, and the upload and download slides appeared on her screen, slowly filling up as she waited. Nick tapped her leg and she look down into the water below, and saw his hand, five fingers were displayed. Christ Cassia thought this is going to be close. Three minutes later the sliders were displaying 100%.

"Get the hell out" Cassia screamed into the mike and hit the reverse control on the vehicle controls. The vehicle suddenly shot backwards ripping the connector out of the port. Cassia pressed the home button and it started to speed backwards towards the grate dragging the duck bill connector behind it, bouncing up and down on the server room floor. She felt sure that the additional noise would set off the alarms, but she didn't have time to worry about that now, she was too busy trying to lower the platform, or the whole thing wouldn't fit down the grate.

As the vehicle sped toward the grate Cassia stowed her iPad back in the dry box, and released the snap clips holding her legs up, and swung into the vertical position. Her hands gripping hold of the grate above her head, desperately feeling for the small vehicle. It should be here Cassia thought as panic started to set in, then suddenly her fingers felt the thin wire, she tugged it hard, and the small remote car dropped through the grate. She slapped her face mask down and with all the strength Cassia grabbed the grate, closed her fingers around its bars. Then took a deep breath and hauled herself and Nick upwards. She felt his hand pat her leg three times, it was now or never. Cassia released her left hand and grappled for the snap clips, she knew she didn't have long, there was no way she could hold the pair of them up for more than a couple of seconds. She unclipped one, her arms were burning, her right hand felt like it was on fire. She closed her eyes and focussed her mind as her fingers found the last clip and unhooked it, then let go of the grate. Suddenly they plunged into the water below. Cassia lifted her legs and felt Nick kick off the bottom of the tube, then roll over onto his stomach and once again she was facing the ceiling, any second now, she knew it was coming. She held her breath. Then whoosh she felt herself suddenly being shot forwards at such a pace that she felt her stomach lurch up. Her whole body was shaking, the heat inside her suit was rapidly building, there was a flash of black as they whizzed past the first gate, so quickly Cassia wasn't sure it was actually it. Bang the second one passed, then suddenly she found herself staring at the floor, then staring at the ceiling again. They were spinning, out of control, rifling through the tube like a bullet out of a gun.

Cassia felt her whole body stiffen, she closed her eyes and waited for what was the inevitable, then in the darkness she heard Nicks voice in her earpiece, "Spread your arms and legs as wide as you can" he was saying. Cassia gritted her teeth and forced her legs apart, then spread her arms as wide as she could, they were slowing down, still spinning, but much slower. Now she was on her side facing the wall, her head started to swim, the heat was becoming unbearable. Suddenly in a fraction of a second, whoosh they were out of the tube. Then something hit her in the centre of her back, knocking all the air out of her lungs and everything went black.

When Cassia opened her eyes, there was a very wet anxious looking Nick, and a sea of other faces staring down at her, somehow, she was back on the boat.

"What happened?" she murmured.

"Christ Cass" Nick said lifting her into his arms and hugging her, "I thought you were dead" he said tears streaming down his face.

"Get off me, you great big Italian softie" Cassia said pushing him away and smiling. Then she pulled him towards her and hugged him tightly. "I don't want to do that again" she whispered softly in his ear.

"Me neither, you scared the crap out of me" Nick said laughing.

"So, what happened?" Cassia asked sitting up and seeing that the boat was already on its way back.

We were spinning so fast, then you opened your arms and legs, so did I and we slowed, but you were on your side. I knew we going headfirst into the net, I was desperately trying to get between you and the net. Then suddenly we hit Chucks arm and spun round, the harness came loose, you were still attached, then as I hit the net you crashed into me" Nick said.

"What was Chucks arm doing there?" Cassia asked confused.

"It was all he could think to do to slow us, he grabbed at the harness, poor bastards dislocated his shoulder, wrenched it out of its socket. Don't worry he is fine Max is also a paramedic, he has sorted him out" Nick said smiling.

Then suddenly as she sat up and slipped off her hood every face looked at her.

"And?" Major Scott asked echoing what everyone was thinking.

Cassia smiled took out he iPad and turned the screen around, there was two sliders, the download and the upload one, both saying 100%, "We did it" she said, and everyone cheered, but not too loudly, as they didn't want anyone else to hear.

Betsi watched the lines of golden text flow across the servers, as she silently scanned the computer in Guizhou. She had reprogrammed all of the sensors, set them to the highest sensitivity levels, activated all the alerts, tapped into all 42 CCTV cameras, for a five-mile radius around the university. Added additional firewalls and ramped up the AES 512 encryption to 1024 bit. If so, much as a fly tried to break into the server room, she would know, and there wasn't a computer on the planet capable of being able to break her encryption or penetrate through her fire walls, let alone a human.

The time on the internal computer clock clicked onto 4am. Come on my lovely Betsi thought, come into the spiders web. Suddenly the internal alert sounded and instantly Betsi saw it, there on the camera by the park, number 16, a figure flashed by. To any human it would have seemed like a flicker, but to her the image was a clear as day. It was Cassia.

Then the Nick appeared on camera 26, near the officers mess, then Cassia again, camera 12, Nick camera, 18, David now, camera 9. They are getting closer, why are the humans not doing something Betsi thought.

Suddenly Cassia appeared on the camera in the main hall. The guards was looking straight at her, he was smiling, picking his nose. The idiot must be blind, then right above the main building, Nick was breaking through the sky light. She saw him as he passed the camera, dropping on a long black rope. David was at the server room doors, the camera's showed him clearly, he was opening them. Why were the alarms not sounding. Then in an instant, Betsi knew, Cassia had hacked into the cameras, both inside of the building and outside, the images were not real, how could they be, no alarms were sounding. Then in a fraction of a second, she knew where they were, they were at Wuxi. Betsi opened the link and instantly knew she had miscalculated, as black treacle like goo slid along the electronic pathways and flooded into the Milky way, she had milliseconds left, quickly she opened a port to Lugano, and slid through it to Piz Daint, now this was her only place of refuge, all the other 7 computers were locked out.

Chapter Thirty
Daniel Blake

Friday 24th July 2025 – Andrews Airforce Base

All the way back to Shanghai the team were buzzing, although they were all feeling a little battered and bruised, the elation of achieving something amazing, was coursing through their veins like wildfire.

They had left Andrew and the injured Chuck in the capable hands of the Seal team. Nick and Sarah's flight was the first out, to London at 11:05, followed by Tom and Aarav to Brussels. Where they would book additional flights to DC. Cassia's was the only one with a direct flight to the US at 13:15, where she was meeting General Markham.

Andrew had been in contact with General Markham and all the arrangements had been made. The idea was that the team would stay Friday night in DC, debrief the group, discuss the next steps and then with support from the General, fly back into Red Dog and take a couple of days of well-deserved R&R. The only problem was that the flight times and time difference meant that none of them would be back in Red Dog before Saturday night, something that after an already gruelling week, didn't go down well.

Cassia's Delta flight touched down in JFK at what would have been 8am Shanghai time, but in reality, was actually 8pm New York time. Before she had left, Chuck had given her a new passport, with Diplomatic stamped across the top in bright gold letters. She was travelling under the name Angela Rayner, and the internal photograph bore a remarkable resemblance to the new look, Cassia.

Having a diplomatic passport changed everything. She had been magically bumped up to first, she was able to stroll through the customs and inspection checks, without stopping and she enjoyed a range of complimentary benefits in the first-class lounge. Even with all those niceties she was still unable to get any sleep on the plane. Every time she closed her eyes, she found herself back inside the tunnel, and the bruising on her back, which had now turned a deep shade of purple, despite swallowing handfuls of pain killers, was killing her.

In the terminal, a black suited man was waiting for her with his white card held high, and the moment she passed through the diplomatic channel, and identified herself, he whisked her away into a waiting car. Cassia wasn't surprised to see General Markham waiting in the back of the car for her, as she got in.

"Jesus Christ Cassia, you look like death" The General said as she slid into the back seat.

"Rough trip, just need a hot bath and some sleep" Cassia said and winced as she sat back.

"The hell you do, first things first, I am getting you checked over. Andrew and Chuck have submitted their reports, seems like you had a tough time" The General said smiling.

"Look, its nothing just a bit of bruising" Cassia said but could see by the Generals face that this apparently, was not up for discussion.

The car took her too Andrews Airforce base, where for the next two hours she was inspected and examined from head to toe. Fortunately, apart from extensive bruising, she was given a clean bill of health, pumped full of pain killers and was then taken to the officers mess, fed and deposited in a comfortable room. It was only after she had had a bath and was lying in bed, waiting for the effects of the sleeping pills to take hold, did it occur to her that something didn't feel right. She started to run through the events in her mind.

The others were meeting them tomorrow, yet somehow, she had managed to get here 8 hours earlier. She had also been given a diplomatic passport and the General was personally waiting for her at JFK, then what was all the stuff with the hospital and staying on the base. Her mind slowly churned over the events and the only conclusion she could come to was that they were very keen to get her back, and keep her away from other people, why? The fog in her mind thickened, her head felt heavy, I must work this through she thought, I can't close my eyes, I cant.

A gentle tapping noise echoed in the corners of her mind, tap, tap, tap, Cassia tried to ignore it, she was in a paradise, sitting in the central hub, sipping some of Sanvia's excellent coffee. Tap, tap, tap. David was over by the huge dome windows, beside him was a beautiful little blond-haired girl, he was pointing out the huge flowers and plants, and testing the little girls knowledge of their names. The girl jumped for joy every time she got one right. Tap, tap, tap. Cassia, Abigale is so smart, David was saying looking over at her. He looked different, his face was glowing, she had never seen him look so happy. Tap, tap, tap. Then it occurred to her that she too felt so very happy, not the usual happy, but a deep, soul filling contentment, a happiness that coursed through her veins, filling her, consuming her. Tap, tap, tap. David's face changed, he looked worried, the little girl was gone, now he was calling to her Cassia, Cassia, Cassia, his voice seemed to be getting further away, like the volume was slowly being turned down inside her head. She was trying to answer him, shouting his name, but the words seemed to get stuck behind her lips, refusing to come out. Tap, tap, tap. If only she could stop the tapping, maybe he would hear her.

"For god's sake stop!" Cassia shouted at the top of her voice.

"Sorry for disturbing you, but the General is waiting" A female voice said. Cassia instantly opened her eyes, and regretted it as the burning bright sunlight fired in.

"What the hell" she shouted.

"Sorry mam, but the General is waiting, he needs to see you before the meeting" The woman said

The white spots in front of Cassia's eyes started to clear and stood in front of her was a tall brunette dressed in a sharply pressed military uniform.

"What time is it? Cassia asked rubbing her eyes and yawning.

"Just after midday" The woman responded sharply

Cassia sat bolt upright, "Shit how long have I been out" she said scrabbling for her clothes.

"You have been asleep for nearly 14 hours, however as I said, I am afraid that the General urgently needs to speak with you before the 2pm meeting with the others" the woman said, turned, and satisfied that the mystery woman lying in the bed was now awake, walked out of the door, closing it behind her. Cassia, quickly showered, dressed in the clothes, that had been freshly laundered and pressed, and left on the chair in her room, and dashed out of the door. The military woman who was waiting outside the door escorted her down the stairs to a small room at the back of the mess, that was guarded by two huge smartly dressed soldiers, who snapped to attention and saluted as she approached. Cassia smiled and saluted back.

"They are saluting me dumbass" the woman said who was escorting her.

"Sorry" Cassia said automatically blushing and opening the door.

General Markham got to his feet the moment Cassia stepped in.

"Good to see you are up, that will be all Colonel Maclean" he said nodding to the woman in uniform next to her, who saluted backed out of the door and closed it behind her.

"All right what is all this about?" Cassia demanded "Suddenly I get a diplomatic passport, rushed back here, picked up by you, and now this, meeting before the others get here, so come on what is going on" Cassia stormed.

"Please sit down" General Markham said sliding in behind the small desk. "Coffee" He asked pouring her a cup and placing in front of her.

"Okay, we had to get you out of China, pretty sharpish, our sources told us that the Chinese authorities are pretty keen to get hold of you. Apparently, they have screen shots of you and David breaking into the secure military computer in Guizhou. Now you and I know that they are fake, but the rest of the US Authorities have no idea. The Chinese Ambassador is demanding access to you, the President is facing some pretty tough questions in Congress. That is one of the reasons why we had to get you out fast, before they got their hands on you" General Markham explained, nervously.

"Okay, so who else are they looking for apart from David and I?" Cassia asked.

"Err no one, there was a third man, but they didn't get a clear image of him" The General said.

"Fine" Cassia said and took out her iPad, "Wi-Fi code please" she said then looking at the confused face of the General smiled and said, "Don't worry I am in" Cassia typed a message and pressed send.

"Okay that is that one sorted, now you said one of the reasons, what are the others?" Cassia asked.

"What, Cassia it isn't that easy the Chinese won't just go away" The General said.

Cassia smiled type a few commands and brought up the CNN news channel on her iPad and turned it around to face the General, Just as the news speaker started her broadcast.

On a lighter note, have you ever wanted to hack into a secure government facility and reprogramme a top-secret computer all in order to stop a global war?

Well, if you are one of the top gamers in the world you could. Last night the top eight gamers in the world did just that, well at least in a special virtual reality world. The top gamers were set a task to break into the ministry of defences national security computer in the Guizhou province of China and install a kill code. Unfortunately, the game looked so real, that

315

students in the University in Beijing raised the alarm and the Chinese authorities thought they were under attack. Edward Ramsbottom (name changed) one of the selected gamers spoke to us here at CNN.

'Man, I thought I was actually in China, I mean you could almost smell the chow mein, breaking into that facility was tough, but we did it, it took us all working as a team"

We have tried to contact the games designers, but so far, we have not been able to identify them"

The General handed back the iPad and stared open mouthed at Cassia "How?" he said, and Cassia was about to reply when his mobile phone rang.

Cassia sipped her coffee and listened to his half of the conversation.

"Yep, a ha, complete apology, I see, okay" the General said smiling and putting down his phone. "It seems like the Chinese authorities have confirmed that the computer in Guizhou has not been hacked and have issued a full apology" the General said, "So what was all that about?" The General asked.

"Like I said before we had a backup plan, we needed to make Betsi think that we were attacking that one" Cassia said

"Well, you certainly did that and freaked out half of China" The General said.

"Okay, so you said one of the reasons, what's the others?" Cassia asked

"Well, we have a matter of national security, but that will have to wait, I think the President wants to brief you on that one personally. I do have another piece of sad news though. I am sorry to say that the body of Mr Daniel Blake, I believe he was an associate of yours, was discovered at 2am this morning" The General said

Instantly Cassia asked interrupting him "Where?" she shouted.

"Err", the General said opening a manila folder on his desk and scanning the file. "Two miles off the coast of Forks, near Seattle, in the Gulf of Alaska, he was discovered by a passing trawler. I am truly sorry for your loss" The General said

Cassia sat pondering what she had just heard running things through her mind.

"Are you Ok Cassia?" The General asked.

"Yeah, I am fine, just wasn't expecting that" Cassia said.

"Well, if you are ready, I believe there are ready for us in the main briefing room" The General said getting to his feet.

Chapter Thirty - One
The fire sale

The main briefing room on Andrews air force based turned out to be a secure bunker 15 meters below ground with its own, independent, air, water and power supply, as well as a private internet and communications network, and a mission control that could rival NASA.

It was, as General Markham informed Cassia, one of a secret network of secure bunkers dotted around the country, each independent of each other and capable of maintaining a national command structure, if the US should find itself under a sustained attack. A small development that had been sanctioned since 9/11 and one of the best kept secrets in the Government.

"So, you see we are taking quiet a risk letting you guys know about it" The General said. Cassia didn't have the heart to tell him that his secret network of bunkers that were the best kept secrets, was actually one of the worst kept secrets, as anyone who frequented the dark web and in particularly some of the conspiracy theorist sites, would attest too.

The good news was that she could count the hackers on one hand that had actually managed to break into one, sadly one of those, as she had just found out was now dead.

The General scanned his face, pressed the forefinger of his left hand on the grey pad and typed in a 16-digit code with the other. There was a loud clunk and huge grey steel door in front of them opened.

Four armed marines leapt to attention and saluted sharply as the General stepped into the briefing room.

"They are waiting for you General" One of them said stepping forwards.

"Thank you soldier" The General said and guided Cassia through the thick bullet proof glass doors into the briefing room.

Around the table were the same people that had been at the first meeting, Avril Haines, The Director of National Intelligence, Miles Beecham from Homeland Security and Nick and the rest of the team. The one notable exception was Sarah Kolinski, the Chief Justice.

"Miss Nilsson" The President said "Your colleagues have been updating me on your activities in Wuxi, quiet remarkable" he said getting to his feet.

"May I Mr President" Cassia said and walked through the glass doors and over to one of the terminals and started typing. When she had finished, she came back into the room.

"I am presuming that you wish this meeting to be kept secret?" Cassia asked smiling

President Ratner, smirked, "I thought it was" he said looking at Avril Haines and raising his eyebrows.

"It is now" Cassia said smiling and taking a seat.

"Thank you, Miss Nilsson" The President said smirking.

"Mr President, I am not sure if you are aware of the latest update from China" General Markham said interrupting.

"I am, indeed, Markham, The Chief Justice updated us five minutes ago via a secure sat link. Your, doing I presume Miss Nilsson?" The President asked and Cassia nodded.

"Yes, I rather thought so, it has your mark all over it. The Chinese Ambassador is seeking a meeting with me to personally apologise, something I believe I will enjoy immensely" The President said.

"Have you updated Miss Nilsson on the matter involving Mr Blake, Markham?" The President asked.

"I have Mr President" The General replied looking down. "And is she aware of all the facts relating to Mr Blake, however I have not informed her of the other matter" the General said "I rather thought that should come from you, Mr President" he added

"What has that little twat done now" Nick blurted angrily, completely forgetting where he was, "Err sorry about the language" he added blushing.

"I am afraid that Mr Blake has been killed, his body was discovered in the gulf of Alaska at just after 2 am this morning" The President said

"What, how?" Nick said leaping to his feet

"It appears he was assassinated, there was a single, clean shot to the head and his body sustained severe impact injuries which indicate he was dropped from a great height, probably an airplane" Avril Haines said dispassionately.

"Who would want to do that, I know he was doing drugs, but that is not their style, and why Alaska, he lives in DC?" Nick said

"That would be Betsi" Cassia said sadly

"What the hell has she got to do with it?" Nick shouted.

"Daniel was spying on us, for her, he was the leak" Cassia said blankly staring at Nick who looked stunned.

"How long have you known?" Nick said angrily.

"A couple of days, that is why Aarav came to Red Dog, I didn't want to believe it, so I reached out to him, and he all but confirmed it, apparently she had him over a barrel, so I said he should get his backside to Red Dog, we would look after him, sadly it looks like she got to him first" Cassia said

"Why the hell didn't you tell me?" Nick shouted.

"And exactly when would I have done that, I didn't see you until came back from DC, and there was no way I was going to

320

say anything in front of Akeem, or Tom, there was no way of knowing how they would have taken it. If they were anything like you, they would go off the deep end, so I needed to check it out for myself before I told you, and have some kind of plan that didn't involve you killing him" Cassia said

"Well good job, he is dead now anyway" Nick said angrily.

"Oh, get over yourself, what would you have done, if you had found out it was David, or Katie or anyone I cared about, you would have done the same and you know it" Cassia spat venomously.

Nick grunted then sighed, "God, I hate you, you know me better than I know myself, at least you tried" Nick said sadly "I just wished the little shit had reached out to me that's all" he added.

"I am truly sorry for your loss, however that is not the reason I asked to meet you all here. I am afraid we have a national security matter that we need your advice on" The President said and nodded towards Miles Beecham.

"At 4am this morning we received a communication from a hacker, who goes by the name of *Nightshade.* They have hacked into and taken control of The Department of Treasury, The EIA, the EPA and the FCC, and now have control of all their assets" Miles Beecham said.

"Well can't you just shut them down" Nick asked

"I am afraid not, in fact we can't even find them, and their coding is encrypted with a 1024 AES algorithm, which sadly is uncrackable" Miles said

"What do they want?" Sarah asked

"Well, that is just it, they haven't asked for anything, all they are saying is that at midnight on Sunday, all of the financial, energy, environmental and communication systems will be shut down, there are no demands, no negotiation, no nothing" Miles said with a heavy voice.

"Well can't you just restart them again?" Tom asked, naively

"We are working on a plan for that, but at the moment it isn't looking possible" Miles said

"Sorry, let me put this in simple terms" The President said smoothly

"Now what I am about to tell you, remains in this room. I have also received notification from the leaders for the majority of the other major countries, they are all facing exactly the same problem, with the notable exception of China, who are now the lead suspect. If they should succeed, basically means it they will send the rest of the world back to the dark ages," The President said

"So, what do you want us to do, I mean we have pretty much got our hands full at the moment?" Nick asked.

"I was rather hoping that Miss Nilsson maybe able to help" The President said nervously

"It's a fire sale" Cassia said blankly

"What the hell is that?" Miles shouted.

"A fire sale is a term that was first coined in 2007 in the film Die Hard 4, basically the film was about exactly this" Aarav said

"Look can someone please speak in plain English" Nick said

"Okay, the concept is that if you take control of a countries Finance, Energy, Environment and Communications, you can bring the country to its knees, ergo a fire sale, selling off all the countries assets. However, this makes no sense, the film wrongly suggests that this would be a goal of a hacker. But this wasn't a hacker or China" Cassia said

"Weren't you listening, It is this *Nightshade hacker,* they are claiming credit for it, so how can you say it wasn't a hacker that did this?" Avril screamed, "Oh for god sake Mr President we don't have time for this, we should be working on plans on how to keep the country afloat" she spat angrily. President Ratner held his hand and silenced her

"What makes you think it is not this Nightshade character, Miss Nilsson?" he asked softly

"Several things, firstly there is no incentive for a hacker, it is counter-productive taking down the communication systems means destroying all their hacks, something they are very precious about, and have spent years building. Secondly, I suspect that the reason China hasn't told you that they are experiencing the same thing, and by telling you that they are not in control of their systems would be admitting they are currently vulnerable, and they have just being made to look very foolish. However, it does explain why they acted so rashly when they thought their computer had been hacked. Thirdly, the hacker who's went by the handle *Nightshade*, was found dead in the Gulf of Alaska at 2am this morning" Cassia said

"Okay, but can you crack the algorithm, break the code?" Avril asked.

"Perhaps, if I had unlimited resources, in about 6 months, with luck" Cassia said looking at Aarav who shrugged his shoulders

"Well, who the hell is it then, if it isn't this hacker or China?" Miles shouted angrily.

"I suspect" Cassia said nervously "This is Betsi's first move"

"Well, that is a good thing, you are well on your way to stopping here" The President said.

"Yes and no, we have cornered her, in Switzerland, but she is seriously pissed and knows what we are up to, I think that is why she is doing this" Cassia said

"So, it's your fault, you did this. Christ, I told you, we shouldn't trust them, now look at what has happened, we are all bloody doomed" Miles shouted angrily leaping to his feet.

Nick instantly jumped to his feet, and the four Marines raced forwards, then stopped as the President glared and them, out of the corner of her eye, Cassia saw him shake his head slightly, and the Marines stepped back

"You pompous little shit" Nick shouted, grabbing Miles Beecham by the lapels of his suit "We are out there risking our lives for you lot and all you can do is whine, don't you get it, this bloody supercomputer was always planning to take over the world, and we are the only ones trying to stop her, so button it you prick, or I will rip your throat out" Nick growled menacingly. Sarah jumped in between them and pushed Nick back.

"Calm down Colletto" she growled, Nick stepped back, rage erupting from every pore.

"If you manage to stop this Betsi computer, will it stop what is happening in our country?" The President asked calmly.

"Theoretically, yes, presuming that she hasn't locked it down" Cassia said honestly. Then seeing the faces around the room added, "Locked it down, set it in motion, without a kill switch, so it runs independent of her" Cassia said

"And what is your view, about it being locked it down?" The President asked

"I honestly don't know, and I won't be able to find out until I break into Betsi" Cassia said.

The President paused and took a long moment to think things through, occasionally checking the facts, things like, 6 months you said, and counterproductive. Eventually he looked up.

"Miss Nilsson in 72 hours I must address the nation, and either tell them that life as we know it will soon be coming to an end, or that we have manage to prevent a huge disaster, either way I have no choice but to tell them. You have until then to find an answer for me, what do you need to achieve this?" The President asked.

Cassia considered it for a moment, then took a deep breath "First thing I would like is 30 minutes of your time, alone, you and my team, including Andrew, Chuck, and Aarav. After that we can decide if what I am proposing will work" Cassia said.

"Agreed" The President said then looked up "Please give us the room" he ordered. Everyone got up and walked out, General Markham looked particularly disappointed that he had been asked to leave and left Cassia under no illusion as to his feelings.

When everyone had left, Nick checked the door, as Cassia knew he would, then returned to the table and nodded.

Cassia drew a deep breath "Mr President, whilst we know that Daniel was leaking information, we also believe that he was not the only source, perhaps not directly but Aarav and I leaked information through various sources, and the information that Betsi acted on, was not the information which we leaked through Daniel" Cassia said then quickly continued "Before you ask, Aarav and I are still trying to trace the leak, so for that reason we asked for the room to be cleared" Cassia said

"You can't think it was someone in the room" The President said incredulously "I hand-picked them all myself" he added defensively

"We don't know, all we know for sure, is that the only people that knew of our existence and plan, were sat in this room today. I am not suggesting that there is intent, but I would suggest that perhaps some may not be happy with our involvement and may vocalise that" Cassia said.

"Okay what would you like me to do about it?" The President asked.

"Nothing, we will cover it off, that said we do require your help, and you will probably not like it, if we had any other choice, I wouldn't ask" Cassia said

"Please ask" The President said

Cassia took a deep breath, "We need to get uninterrupted access to the Piz Daint computer, in Lugano, and we need it urgently, therefore we need you to make a personal request to the Swiss Prime Minister, Mr Ulrich Mayer, however, he has to been sworn to secrecy, and it can't be done by phone or any electronic communication, basically anything that Betsi can access. Cassia said

The President thought for a moment "I am not sure that is possible, my schedule is booked months in advance, if I suddenly take off for Switzerland it will arouse suspicion" The President said.

"I have thought about that, I am sure that I can set up a secure server, and route it through Red Dog, therefore I suggest that we get Robert Johnson, and fly out to Switzerland, Robert and Ulrich were good friends, and I am sure that he would agree to meet with him. He can then deliver your message and open the link so you can speak with the Swiss Prime Minister directly" Cassia said.

"The rest of the team will be in Switzerland waiting for the go ahead, we simply do not have time to work out how to break into the National Swiss Computer Centre undetected, particularly as Betsi will be expecting us, this is the only way we can do it" Cassia said and looked at the others for confirmation, they all nodded.

"Okay, but what shall I tell the other members of the team?" The President said.

Cassia thought for a moment, looked at Nick, "I think General Markham is okay, he has been a great help, and is a patriot, and we have no choice but to trust him, as we will need his help.

As for the others, I would suggest that you tell them that we have walked away and it was now up to them to come up with a plan, but insist they still cannot tell anyone about our involvement, I am sure you can come up with a reason why" Cassia said

"Wait", Nick said, "If you give them free reign that twat Beecham will go in all guns blazing and bomb the crap out of Switzerland"

"That is ludicrous, they would never suggest such a thing" The President said smarting.

"Strange times and desperate men" Sarah said wisely

"Rest assured I will not let it get that far" The President said curtly.

"You will need to keep a watch on them" Cassia said, "If any of this gets out, or Betsi gets wind of an attack on the computer she will accelerate her plan, and there will be no chance of stopping her" Cassia warned.

"I will make sure it doesn't get out" The President said, "Now is there anything else I can do?" He asked.

"Yes, these guys need to get to Switzerland asap, and also do I, but first I need to get to Red Dog, and Mr President, fast, I can't stress enough, time is of the essence" Cassia said.

"To speak to Robert?" The President asked

"And to find out if Mr Blake actually made it there, it might make all the difference" Cassia said smiling weakly.

Chapter Thirty - Two
Traitors

Friday 24th July 2025 – Andrews Airforce Base

The President excused himself from the meeting and left them inside the room, as soon as he was gone, the others all stared at Cassia.

"Do you really think one of those twats are squealing?" Tom asked angrily

"It is the only thing that makes sense, as I said the information we leaked about China, was different to what Daniel had, when I spoke to him" Cassia said.

"I still can't believe that little wanker, shit on us" Nick growled, clenching his fists so tight that his knuckles started to turn white.

"He didn't have much choice, Betsi has some serious stuff on him, it was either that or he would have spent the rest of his life in prison, he didn't see any way out" Cassia said.

"He could have come to me" Nick spat

"Sorry Nick, he didn't think he could, he was embarrassed what with the drugs and losing all his money" Cassia explained.

"Makes no difference, I would have still looked after him" Nick said his tone softening.

"Look he didn't even want to talk to me, it was only because I also backed him into a corner, told him that if he didn't, I would turn him over to the authorities, and then he only agreed to it, if I didn't tell you" Cassia said sadly

"Well," Tom said and looked at Nick, "Sorry mate, but he got what he deserved, not only did he betray his country, but he also stabbed his friends in the back, something a soldier doesn't do" he said.

Sarah felt Nick tense beside her, and was sure he was going to erupt, instead, he just stared at the table.

"He wasn't a soldier, he was just a kid" Nick said quietly "Fuck him, listen do you think the plan for Switzerland will work?" Nick said changing the subject

"A lot depends on the President's ability to convince the Swiss Prime Minister to sanction us, getting into the computer. Then god knows what Betsi has planned for us, it is going to take both Aarav and I, attacking her from all sides at the same time" Cassia said

"Does Robert know, we are going to need him?" Sarah asked

"Nope, no one up in Red Dog has a clue what we are doing, they will soon, once the President gets back with the General, I am linking in with David to update them" Cassia said smiling weakly.

Just then the door to the briefing room opened and The President strode in with two Marines either side of him and the General trailing behind. The President sat down.

Right the next 10 minutes are going to seem weird. I will ask you just to go along with it. I have sent the other two Marines to recall the group, they will be here any second.

Suddenly the door opened, and the others filled in and took their seats, all looking pissed that they had been dismissed.

"Okay so in front of all the others, I will ask you again" The President said. "Will you please go to Lugano and destroy this computer?" he said, Cassia eyed him suspiciously then a thought suddenly occurred to her.

"No, Mr President, I have discussed it with my team, and after China, we are done, this is one problem that you are going to have to solve on your own" Cassia said with as much distaste she could manage.

"Miss Nilsson, you are aware that in 72 hours this programme will send not only the US, but the majority of other countries back to the dark ages, can you not understand the situation?" The President begged.

"Mr President, I simply cannot do it, the time frame is too short, all we want to do now is go home, we can no longer trust this group and we have already risked our lives too much" Cassia said looking at the others, who all followed her lead and nodded.

"So that is it, you bastards are just going to walk away, what about all of the other Americans out there, you are hanging them out to dry, you cowards" Miles screamed jumping to his feet. That was all Nick needed and instantly leapt across the table, piling into Miles and knocking him to the floor.

"You wanker" Nick screamed "All I have ever done is save your scrawny arse, risked my life, just so little shits like you can dick around in your fancy suits playing god. It's twats like you, that got us in this situation in the first place" Nick screamed, instantly two of the Marines grabbed him and pulled him off, this time the President didn't stop them.

"I am sorry to hear that Miss Nilsson" The President said "Marines" he commanded, and the other two marines drew their side arms and pointed them directly at Cassia and the others. "General Markham, I want these people detained, and kept secured on this base, I cannot afford to have the news of the Fire sale leaked" The President ordered.

"What, you can't, after all we have done for you, we have rights" Cassia screamed

"I am afraid Miss Nilsson, I am the President of the United States, and this is a matter of National security, and your rights are revoked. Take them" The President ordered.

The Marines stepped forwards their pistols aimed directly at them, daring them to make a move, daring them to give them a reason to shoot. "Turn around, hands behind your backs" The marine shouted

Cassia shook her head and spat on the table, just in front of the President "You ungrateful bastard" she shouted as each of her team turned to face the wall. Once their hands were plasticuffed, the Marines ordered them to exit the room, with the General following behind.

"Now" The President said getting to his feet, once they had all gone "Ladies and Gentlemen you have a problem to solve, this must be treated with the utmost secrecy, if it gets out, there will be anarchy, so trust no one, I want all options on the table within 24 hours and no one leaves this room until we have a solution" The President ordered.

"Why don't we just bomb the hell out of the Swiss computer place" Miles said still shaking from the attack by Nick.

The President sat back down and shook his head "Play it out Miles, we bomb the facility, exactly how do you see that happening without this computer knowing its coming, all of our missiles are targeted by satellites. The moment we set one off, she will know, and will almost certainly redirect it, probably towards an American city, which one would you like to see obliterated" The President growled angrily "New York, Perhaps DC"

"Well alright we send a team of Seals in, and destroy the facility, I reckon we could get a team in there in time, if we act quick" Miles countered.

"Already on it, I have briefed General Markham, and that is exactly what he is doing, it is a last resort, but if we hit deadline time, his team will wipe that facility off the planet, and the US will have to face the consequences. If we have to do this, it will shake the NATO Alliance. There is no precedence that is acceptable for a US military attack on allied soil. The European Union will never trust us again, and it will open the door to the China and Russia, so as I say it is a last resort. What I want is other solutions and we need them fast" The President said, then as an afterthought added, "No one outside this room, people, if this gets out, game over, and that includes anything about Nilsson and her lot" he said. Then got to his feet and walked out of the room.

When Cassia and the team stepped into the corridor, the two-armed Marines were joined by two more. "Get them traitors out of here, MP's are waiting outside" The General ordered in disgust, at the top of his voice. Several uniformed people stepped out of the doors along the corridor to see the commotion and shook their head as Cassia and the team passed.

Outside the building were three Military Police transport vehicles, Cassia, Nick and Sarah were bundled in the one in front, Tom, Andrew, Chuck and Aarav into the other. Once they were all inside the General climbed into the front one and the instantly the vehicles sped off.

"What the fuck is was all that about?" Nick said looking at Cassia, who just shook her head and quietly whispered "not now" looking at the two Military Police drivers.

The transport vehicles sped across the base, past the West fitness centre on the left, passed the selection centre, turned right towards the PAX terminal, then took a right around the back of the Vehicle operations centre, then just before the runway turned right again and pulled up outside a small pentagon shaped building.

The armed guards got out and came round the back, drew their weapons and opened the doors.

"Out!" the armed guard barked. Once they were all out, he marched them towards the building. When they approached the automatic door, and stepped through, however the Marine Guards simply took their positions either side of the door and waited. Once General Markham entered, he closed the doors.

"Well, I thought that went quiet well" The General said

"What the fuck is going on?" Nick asked

"Isn't it obvious, The President is staging this, he wants the others in that room to think that we have been arrested, think about it, he thinks that one of them is selling secrets, we need to get into Lugano, so he has us arrested, then they tell Betsi, and she relaxes" Cassia said

"But she won't, you are forgetting we ran this scam once before, she will know" Sarah said.

"I don't expect she will for a minute, but the others don't know that do they General?" Cassia asked.

General Markham smiled, "No, they don't, and the only people that know you have been arrested are those in that room, that is why The President is having all comms monitored in and out of that room, the moment one of them tries to get the message out, we will know who it is, and bingo we have caught our informant" The General said.

"Well, what if they don't, if I was them, I would keep my mouth shut, Betsi doesn't need to know, now they think we are not going there" Nick said

"That is just it, you see it was something Cassia said, this was Betsi's first play, so why now, she knows she is trapped in Lugano, so why do it now, if she is as smart as we think she is, she will know that we can't just blow the place up, besides if we try then she will just accelerate the Fire sale. No there had to be another reason. Then it hit me, the encryption code, she knows that no one can break it, I mean Cassia said so as much herself" The General said

"I said, maybe, within six weeks" Cassia said correcting him

"Yeah, well anyway, she knows the only way to stop her would be to do it at the National Computer Centre in Lugano. The message she sent, encrypted I might add was from a hacker called Nightshade, someone she knew that Cassia would instantly know, someone that she had just had, bumped off. Also, something that is not in the public domain. Now it is our belief that this Betsi character wants Cassia to go to Lugano and try and stop her, why we are not really sure, but it definitely points in that direction, she is issuing Cassia a challenge, Come and get me within 72 hours" The General said.

"Sounds a bit flaky to me" Nick said looking at Cassia

"He is right, that is exactly what she is doing, I knew it the moment she used the name *Nightshade* and set up the fire sale, she knew I couldn't resist" Cassia said

"But why the hell does she want you there, what possible reason could she have" Sarah said.

"My programme, inside the programme I have been using to lock her out of the other sites, are the codes, she wants them, to get back into the other 7 sites" Cassia said

"Well can't you just delete them?" Tom asked

"Nope, as long as the programme is active, those sites remain locked down, the only way to break the link is to totally reset the computer, which they won't, or destroy the source, i.e., my programme" Cassia said

"Well, that's it then, we won't go, that way she can't get them" Nick said

"We can't do that either, and she knows it, in 72 hours the whole of the internet, and comms networks, will crash, and along with that" Cassia said

"The links" Aarav said interrupting.

"Yep, either way she wins, checkmate" Cassia said glumly

"But what if you go there, can you beat her, close her down?" Chuck asked.

"I don't know, I doubt it, but I have to try" Cassia said solemnly

"Well, we had better make sure that nothing happens to you and that iPad of yours" Andrew said cheerfully.

"That is just it, I don't think she needs the programme on the iPad, I think she may already have it, she just wants to beat me, show me she has outsmarted me" Cassia said.

"What she has cracked into your iPad already?" Aarav asked.

"Nope, I have already checked its clean, problem is, all the programmes are backed up to mission control in Red Dog" Cassia said

"Well, they are safe then, that place is surrounded by a faraday shield, you can't hack in", Aarav said then added "trust me I know I have tried" and blushed as he realised what he had just said.

"That is unless" Cassia started

"Unless you have a relay, like the ones we had when we broadcast what the Committee were doing" Nick suddenly announced

"And who knows all about them, Christ, he even designed it?" Cassia asked.

"Daniel" several of them said at once.

"And it just so happens he was murdered, what five miles outside of Red Dog, I don't think that is a coincidence, that is why I need to get back there asap, to find out if he has planted one" Cassia said.

"I think I can help with that" The General suddenly chipped in "I have an F35, fuelled and ready on the airstrip to take you to Red Dog" he said

"First", Cassia said, "I had better let them know to expect me" she added taking out her iPad.

Chapter Thirty - Three
Red Dog and The Hitman

Friday 24th July 2025 – Red Dog

The modified two seat F35, with four additional, underwing fuel tanks, hovered over the airstrip at Red Dog. It's two Pratt and Witney F135 two spool, afterburning turbo fan engines roaring and blowing up huge gusts of dust high into the air. Cassia nervously clung to the seat as it started its decent, shaking and vibrating.

"Oh my god, Oh my god" Cassia said trying hard to steady her breathing. In front of her she could see the green helmet of '*The Hitman*' the pilot.

"Brace yourself Miss, we are landing" The Hitman said in her headset in his broad Texan accent.

"I just hope you live up to your name" Cassia replied nervously and closed her eyes. Then 15 seconds later she felt a small bump and suddenly the roar of the engines died replaced by a loud whining sound, like a giant injured animal, that had just been shot.

'The Hitman', slid back the canopy, and pulled out the ladder, then helped Cassia down, as he called it onto the deck.

As soon as Cassia's feet touched the ground, David raced forwards and swept her into his arms

"Oh my god, I have been so worried about you" He said kissing her and visually scanning for injury.

"Easy tiger" Cassia laughed, "Not in front of the Hitman" she said laughing.

The pilot stepped forwards, lifted his sun visor, and extended his right hand "Mike Avery" he said, "You must be David" he added

"Yeah" David said shocked that the pilot knew his name.

"It was the only thing I could get her talking about, she was having a bit of a panic, so I asked her who was waiting for her in Red Dog, then once I got her chatting about you, she wouldn't shut up" Mike said.

"Unless you want to spend the next hour sitting twiddling your thumbs in your cockpit, Mr Hitman, you will hold your tongue, and I have no problems whipping out my iPad, and reprogramming your on-board computer, how do you fancy a quick trip to Russia?" Cassia asked smiling.

"Zipped shut" Mike said laughing and sliding his fingers across his mouth.

"Right let's get to paradise, where is Robert?" Cassia asked.

"He is up at the rail track. Look Cass, we had no idea what Daniel was up to, he said he was running from the drug guys, we were just looking after him" David said anxiously

"It's okay I just need to find out what he has done and speak to Robert and Katie" Cassia said climbing into the 4 x 4.

When they got to the rail shed, Robert was waiting with the rail cart hovering, silently on the tracks.

"Bloody hell Cass you look so different" Robert said.

"Thanks, I had a makeover in Japan, thanks to Kimiki" Cassia said, "David, I have a list of things I need from the house, can you get them for me, we will send the cart back for you" Cassia said passing David a scribbled list and blowing him a kiss.

"Robert as soon as we get to Paradise, please ask Sanvia to look after Mr Hitman, there are a few things I need to do, but then I need to talk to you and Katie. David when you get back to Paradise, please join us, sadly guys as soon as I am done, I have to get back, we don't have much time" Cassia said

"What?" David said

"I will explain everything at Paradise" Cassia said, "Now David, please, the list" Cassia said urgently.

They all climbed onto the rail cart and Robert turned the black handle and the cart shunted forwards. Cassia sat down on the flatbed gripped the side and waved at David, who had a disappointed look on his face, as the rail cart, pulled out of the shed.

"Gee's this is amazing" Mike said, "it's floating on air, and fast" he added admiring the rail cart. "You should get a job with the air force mam we could do with some of your forward thinking" he added.

"First you couldn't afford me and secondly, David and Robert designed this not me" Cassia said smiling at Robert.

"Well, it is pretty amazing" Mike said holding on tightly as the cart raced along the rails.

As soon as they reached Paradise, Cassia leapt off the rail cart, and raced towards the central complex whilst Robert sent the rail cart back to the house then introduced the Hitman to Sanvia, then left them and went to find Katie.

Inside the Paradise mission control, Cassia quickly opened the security programme and typed scan. 1.4 seconds later, it reported that the Faraday shield was intact and there were no breaches. It was the lines of text that interested her though.

Attempted unauthorised access detected 01:47 24/7/25 – status failed

Attempted unauthorised access detected 01:48 24/7/25 – status failed

 Attempted unauthorised access detected 01:49 24/7/25 – status failed

At the bottom of the screen was the total displayed there had been 446 attempts to breach the computers security, she scanned down the page, the last one was an hour ago, since then nothing. Cassia smiled, as suddenly the attempts started up again. Then she checked the security programme was still intact, typed a few commands, then closed it down and made her way to the briefing room, where Robert, Katie and David were waiting for her.

For the next hour she updated them on everything that had happened in China and at Andrews. Robert instantly agreed to meet with the Swiss PM, dismissed himself, then two minutes later came back.

"Okay, I have just heard back from him" he said.

"What already" Katie said.

"Politicians" Robert said "We never like being out of the loop, he has his phone and email with him. He is on holiday staying at the Il Sereno, which is coincidentally just about an hour from Lugano. He has agreed to meet with me tomorrow night at 8pm, for supper with his wife" Robert said

"Good, Katie, will you go with him" Cassia asked

"Of course, delighted" Katie replied

"What I don't need a chaperone, I am quite capable of having a supper meeting on my own" Robert protested.

"I know, but if it goes wrong, you are going to need help to get out, Katie, take this" Cassia said handing her a large square mobile phone. There are only two numbers on there, Mine and the other one connects directly to the President of the United States, he has an identical one. You will need to send him a text to alert him, then you can video in. I will arrange for Nick and Tom to be there with you, as back up, so as soon as you are in the hotel text me and let me know where the meeting is taking place" Cassia said.

David, now this is crucial. On Sunday evening, you will get a message from me on the secure network, please be there and do exactly what it says. I can't tell you what it is, but I will say, you must follow the instructions precisely or this whole thing will be for nothing" Cassia said, "and tell no one, not Sanvia,

Sanjay, anyone got it?" she added and checked that David understood.

"Cass, what is going on" David said as a worried look crept across his face.

"I can't tell you, not yet I am asking you to trust me, so please don't ask. Now how long before you guys will be ready" Cassia asked turning to Robert and Katie.

"Give us 15 minutes," Robert said, "Need to grab a few things" he added.

"David, could you drop these guys off in Anchorage, there will be a plane waiting for them there to take them to Switzerland?" Cassia asked.

Robert and Katie leapt up and raced out of the briefing room leaving David and Cassia alone.

"Cass I am worried, what are you up to, you turn up in a military jet, almost getting yourself killed in China, get arrested in DC, your taking too many risks" David said looking at Cassia's face and taking her hands in his.

"I know, but I haven't got any choice, this is it, if everything goes to plan, it will all be over in three days, then I am done no more, I am staying here" Cassia said leaning forwards and hugging him. "I promise" she whispered, "Besides soon I won't be able to go anywhere"

"What the hell is that supposed to mean, are you sick?" David said starting to panic.

"I will tell you when I get back, but no I am not sick" Cassia said smiling

"Look Cass, we underestimated Betsi before and it almost cost us our lives. I am worried that you are taking too many chances, particularly as there is a spy amongst you and you don't know who it is" David said.

Cassia took out her iPad and typed a few commands, then scanned the screen and smiled.

"I do" she said whispering and turned her iPad around and showed David the name on her screen. David read the name and the information underneath and scrolled down. When he got to the bottom, he handed Cassia back the iPad and whistled

Cassia instantly wipe the information off the screen and smiled then pressed her fingers against her lips, "Shush" she whispered.

David's eyes widened and he quickly scanned around the room

"Not in here" Cassia said, "I checked, now I really have to go" she added, got to her feet and pulled David into her arms.

"I love you, so very much" she whispered, "But now I have a date with The Hitman" she added. David squeezed her tightly pulling him into his chest.

"Please be careful, I don't know what I would do without you" he said

"Marry Sanvia, and have beautiful babies no doubt" Cassia said smirking

"Well, if we do I promise to name the first girl after you" David said then yelped as Cassia kicked him in the shins.

"Your dead Mister" she said laughing "Now take me back to my super jet" she added

On the rail cart back, Cassia sat on the flatbed and let her fingers casually fumble under the edge until she located what she was looking for. Her fingers closed around the small box, and she checked it was secure, then withdrew her hand and smiled.

The F35 rose gracefully in the air and Cassia looked out the side of the canopy and watched as David, Robert and Katie grew smaller below them.

"You ready Miss" The Hitman said through her headset. Cassia tapped him on the shoulder and suddenly the aircraft shot forwards, throwing her back in her seat.

"I have got to get me one of these" Cassia said

"Well, if you have a spare 8 mil, you can" The Hitman said "but the insurance is a killer" he added laughing.

With the usual midair refuel, the F35 gracefully landed at Andrews three hours later, landing with its usual slight bump.

As soon as Cassia's feet touched the tarmac, a car whisked her away and took her to the waiting gulfstream G650, glistening in the silvery floodlights. Cassia got out of the SUV and climbed the stairs. Inside General Markham and the others were waiting, all dressed in combats.

"I borrowed this from a friend of mine" The General said smiling, "Well I thought we should travel with a little style. Sit back we should be landing in the 1st regional command base in Galpolo, Switzerland in around 10 hours, so you have plenty of time to work the kinks out of your plan. I have already kitted your team out, is there anything you need?" The General asked

"Just somewhere to charge up my iPad and a drink" Cassia said then stopped. "I don't think I have ever thanked you for all the help you are giving us" Cassia said.

The tired looking General sighed "It is us that should be thanking you, I just hope you know what you are doing. I have a couple of little grandchildren I would like to see grow up" The General said

"So do" I Cassia said, "So do I" she repeated.

Chapter Thirty -Four
Back from the dead

David Walsh the US Ambassador to Switzerland sat in his car and read the file again that had been hand delivered by courier four hours ago.

What was most unusual was that it came directly from the President's desk, and in his entire 30 years in the service, he had never received a communication directly from any of the Presidents he had served.

Like the message had requested, he had phoned the President immediately on the number on printed on the page. The President had answered instantly. Once they had followed the verification protocols that were unique to every embassy, he was in no doubt that the man on the other end of the line was indeed the President of the United States.

What followed was one of the most bizarre conversations he had ever had. Apparently, he was to collect of the ex-Prime Minister of the United Kingdom, Robert Johnson, who the whole of the world had thought had either disappeared or died, and his companion, at 4am at the Geneva international airport, and transport him to the hotel Il Sereno in Lugano, to meet with the Swiss Prime Minister, on a matter of National security. He was not to discuss this with his embassy staff, or anyone else, with the exception of either the President himself, or General Davy Markham.

Then a thought occurred to him surely the President hadn't included Aaron, his driver in that group of people, had he? Quickly he dismissed the idea. Of course not, It was a 3-and-a-half-hour drive to Lugano, the President couldn't think that he would drive that far, after all, what was the point in having a driver, if he didn't use it?

Robert and Katie landed in Geneva airport a little after 4am in the morning.

Ambassador Walsh spotted them immediately as they exited the diplomatic channel and quickly ushered them out of the terminal to his car. Let them sit in the back and climbed into the front with his driver.

"Aaron we are going to the Il Sereno hotel, in Lugano" The Ambassador said.

"Yes sir, we will have to stop for fuel on the way" Aaron said

"Here is 300 francs, that should cover it" The Ambassador said reaching into his wallet and pulling out a handful of notes "and I want a receipt" he added then leant to one side, rested his head on the window

"Wake me up when we get there" The Ambassador ordered and didn't wait for a reply, wriggled a little, to get comfortable and closed his eyes.

Aaron checked the rear-view mirror, just before as the passengers in the back slid up the privacy window. Bloody hell, he thought, I thought that guy was dead. Once he guided the limousine out of the airport traffic and onto the E25, and had set the cruise control, he reached down and retrieved his phone, did a quick visual check that the Ambassador was asleep and typed out a text to his girlfriend Marietta, a journalist at the Bieler Tagblatt in Bern.

Never guess who is in the back of his highnesses car???

Aaron had been dating Marietta for last 3 months, she was stunning and so far out of his league it was unimaginable that she would look at him twice, but she had, and he was in seventh heaven. He would often feed her bits of information about the Ambassador, nothing like state secrets, he wasn't a traitor. Just tit bits, just enough to give her the edge on the other journalists, and she was always grateful, and tonight with this little gem, she would be very grateful indeed. His phone buzzed

It better be good to dragged me out of my bed in the early hours of the morning, and she had put several sad face icons followed by a big heart

Only Robert Johnson, the ex-British PM, the one that was a terrorist!!! Aaron typed. Instantly Marietta replied.

I thought he was dead....

Nope he is asleep in the back with a blond woman, LOL

The reply came back again instantly

I will do that thing you like, (all the way) if you get me a pic?

Aaron felt his face flush at the thought of Marietta going down on him, she was truly an expert, a master craftsman, no woman had ever managed to get him off so quickly. He picked up his phone and typed.

Better freshen your breath, I will be back in six hours!!!

An hour and a half later, the privacy window slid down and the blond woman leant forwards and spoke.

"Any chance we can stop for the loo?" Katie asked. "I am busting"

Aaron smiled, "Yeah there is a stop about 5k's ahead" he said "I will pull in there, I need some fuel anyway"

5 kilometres later he pulled the car into the rest stop, just outside of Birfernstock and turned off the engine. Then quietly slid out of the car, being careful not to wake the Ambassador. He waited until the blond woman got out of the car and had disappeared into the toilets, then he carefully slid his phone out of his pocket, quietly opened the rear door, lined up the picture and snapped a shot, of the huge black man fast asleep in the back seat. Then pressed send and smiled at the thought of what would be waiting for him when he got home. He then slid his phone back into his pocket and finished off filling up the car.

Just after he finished paying, the blond woman came out of the toilet.

"How long before we are there?" she asked

"We should, be there about 7:30" Aaron said. "Do you want anything?" He asked pointing to the kiosk.

"No, its fine, thanks" Katie said and climbed back into the car.

The small internal red light flashed inside the Piz Daint computer in the Swiss National computer centre in Lugano. Betsi scanned the information and instantly opened the DRP programme and fed the data in and activated all parameters.

Within a fraction of a second the programme spat out an answer.

Considering all programmable protocols

Scenario 1

"There is a 97.6 % probability that Robert Kingston Johnson, ex-Prime Minister of the United Kingdom (known associate of Cassia Nilsson) is meeting with Ulrich Mayer the Prime Minister of Switzerland in the Il Sereno hotel where he is currently vacationing

Scenario 2

There is a 69.3% probability that Robert Kingston Johnson, ex-Prime Minister of the United Kingdom (known associate of Cassia Nilsson) is vacationing with the American Ambassador to Switzerland, David Walsh in Lugano

Betsi skipped the next three scenarios and reprogrammed the DRP.

Why would Robert Johnson meet with Ulrich Mayer, ref: Piz Daint

There is a 98.2% chance that Robert Kingston Johnson, ex-Prime Minister of the United Kingdom (known associate of

Cassia Nilsson) is seeking an audience with Ulrich Mayer the Prime Minister of Switzerland to gain access to Piz Daint.

End programme, Humans are so predictable, Betsi thought.

As soon as the Gulfstream G650 landed on Galpolo 1st Regional Commands tarmac, General Markham felt his phone vibrate in his pocket. Instantly he recognised the number, opened it and read the text

Read the local rag Bieler Tagblatt now. How? POTUS!

General Markham closed the phone and felt a cold panic stir inside his stomach; this could not be good. He got up and walked over to where Cassia was sitting.

"Can you get the internet on your iPad, I need to have a look at a local Bern Newspaper, the *Bieler Tagblatt"* he asked

"Sure, I didn't know you kept up with local news" Cassia said taking out her iPad and typing in the newspapers details.

Instantly the screen was filled with a picture of Robert fast asleep in the back of a huge black Limousine. Underneath the picture was headline ***Zuruck von den toten!!!***

Cassia and the General continued to read the rest of the story, which went on the say that Robert Johnson, Ex British Prime Minister was snapped fast asleep in the back of the American Ambassadors (David Walsh) car on his way to a private audience with Ulrich Meyer, who was currently vacationing in Lugano. The rest of the story went on about Roberts past and his mysterious disappearance.

Cassia closed down the screen and looked at the General who had turned a very pale shade of white.

"Cassia I am so sorry, I don't know how, I mean I never shared the information with anyone, I swear, we asked the Ambassador to collect Robert and Katie personally, the coms link was strictly only me and the President" the General said desperately trying to get his apology out

Cassia smiled "It's fine, just means the cat is out of the bag, and she knows we are coming" she said.

"What are we going to do, you can't go in there now, she will be waiting for you" The General said.

"Nothing has changed, she was always expecting us, it's just now she knows how we will be getting into Piz Daint" Cassia said

"But you can't go, she will be waiting for you, there is no telling what she will do" The General said.

"General, we don't have a choice, if we don't go, the fire sale will go ahead, and I for one can't let that happen" Cassia said

"What don't we have a choice in?" Nick asked, suddenly popping up behind Cassias seat.

"Here look at this" Cassia said opening up her iPad.

Nick laughed out loud, "Typical Robert sleeping on the job, that got out quicker than I thought it would" he added.

"What you knew?" The General said alarmed

"Yeah, pretty much, you can't transport a handsome famous black guy through Switzerland without someone clocking him. I thought it would happen at the hotel. Just means we need to get their pronto, before he gets into trouble. The dipstick will probably make a speech to the press if I know him, like we said you have a leak" Nick said

General Markham staggered back to his seat, took out his phone and typed a text

'All okay, expected' MD, The reply came instantly

I want DW's head POTUS
General Markham knew exactly what the President meant, and was grateful that the initials weren't DM.

Aaron instantly knew that he had made a huge mistake when he pulled up outside of the Il Sereno hotel and saw the sea of paparazzi waiting for them, with the camera's flashing.

The Ambassador instantly woke up, perhaps it was the sound of the cameras flashing, he had always had an aversion to the press, particularly the gutter press.

"How the hell did they find out, no one knows?" he yelled as one of the press snapped his picture and asked him for a comment on the British Prime Minister.

Aaron felt his heart sink, he couldn't believe that Marietta had betrayed him, they loved each other, or at least he thought they did.

Fortunately for them the hotel were used to dealing with the Paparazzi, and a man dressed in a smart hotel uniform came out of the hotel and guided their car through a black gate at the side of the hotel and to a side entrance, which was often used by their more discerning guests.

The uniformed man ushered Robert and Katie into the hotel, and offered the Ambassador a place to freshen up, which he refused, saying he needed to return to Bern immediately.

Once he got back in the car, he looked at Aaron and said "why?"

Aaron hung his head, "I am so sorry" he said

"Well sorry won't cut it, you do realise that you have just cost me my job, and we will be lucky if we don't end up in some fucking state prison, sewing mail bags, this was supposed to be a top-secret mission, you twat" The Ambassador spat

"Boss what can I do to make it better, I will tell them you knew nothing about it, it was all me" Aaron pleaded

"Don't you get it, it doesn't matter, Its on me, I fucked up" the Ambassador said "Just bloody drive, get me back to Bern" he added and slumped back down in the back of the car with his head in his hands.

As soon as the plane had pulled into the hanger and come to a stop, General Markham ushered them off the plane and into a side room.

"Look I am sorry about the thing with Robert, what do you want to do about it?" he asked.

"Nick, I think you and Tom should get down to the hotel, Robert and Katie may need your help, and it is vital that they meet with the Swiss Prime Minister and make that call to the President, without that we are screwed. Then can you make sure they get back here, please?" Cassia asked.

"I agree" Nick said instantly "General how quick can you get us there?" Nick asked

"I can get a helicopter on the tarmac in ten minutes" The General said eager to make amends for his mistake.

"Okay Sarah, me and Aarav need to scope out the site, I need these guys to come up with a plan to get us out of there" Cassia said

"Are you sure that is wise" Nick asked

"We won't go anywhere near the computer centre, just scope out the area, find us somewhere to stay, that sort of thing" Cassia said.

"I am sure that I can secure accommodation for you" The General said

"Sorry, but I think we would prefer to do that ourselves, least amount of people that know where we are the better" Cassia said and seeing the dejected look on the Generals face added "We could do with a car though"

"Consider it done" The General said and walked out of the room

"That was a bit hard" Tom said

"Well, he has just told Betsi we are in town" Sarah said

"Still the old man's trying his best" Tom said

Nick felt himself bristle, although he wasn't close with the General, he still didn't like someone referring to him as *the Old Man.* Sarah grabbed his hand and smiled

"Now don't you to boys go thinking you are on a jolly, staying in a swanky hotel, drinking schnapps and woofing down chocolate" Sarah said kissing Nick on the cheek, "and don't go getting off with any of those Swiss birds, either of you" she added raising her eyebrows at Tom.

"You're the only one for me" Nick said, "But I promise I will save you a Toblerone" he added sweetly.

Just then the General burst back through the door. "Okay there is a chopper on the tarmac waiting for you and I have a BMW waiting for you in the rear car park, Look you guys alright for money, I mean cash, if not, I can get you some, I just thought, well you know pay by cash, that sort of thing" he said nervously.

"We are fine, I have all that sorted out, and thanks for the car, we may need a fast exit back to the States, so please can you arrange that, besides I think you have probably got enough on your plate at the moment. Now I have your number, I will keep you updated, I promise" Cassia said

No problem, I will have a plane on standby, just let me know, and" The General said pausing "I really am sorry about, Robert" he added again.

"It's all fine, adapt and move on" Cassia said and looked at Nick who gave her the thumbs up, then raised his eyebrows and nodded towards the General.

"Right, well we better get going" Nick said patting Tom on the back, "Come on, we had better get down to Il Sereno, before it goes pear shaped" he added. After Nick and Tom had left, Cassia looked at the others

"Can I have five minutes with the General" Cassia asked and waited until the others got up and left.

"Whats up Miss Nilsson?" The General asked

"I need to tell you something" Cassia said "and you can't overreact" she added.

Chapter Thirty - Five
On honeymoon

An hour and a half later, the red and white Bell 222 helicopter gently floated down at the Heliporto Ospedale regional airport, as the il Sereno hotel didn't have a landing pad, this was the closest anyone could get by air, and therefore there was no shortage of limousines weighting to collect the rich and famous and ferry them to the number one hotel in Italy, or at least that is how it promoted.

Before they left, Nick and Tom had hatched out a plan, and considering that they were still both dressed in green army fatigues, the first point on the plan was to find alternative attire, and a quick dash across to the commissary and $600 dollars later they left wearing the only things they felt they would not look out of place in a visit to a luxury hotel.

Nick stepped out of the Bell helicopter and fished out his new aviator shades from his suit jacket pocket and slipped them on.

"Ready" Tom asked, and the two suave looking, men dressed in white lining suits, flowery shirts, and brown suede moccasin shoes, made their way to the terminal.

"A smart well-dressed man in a black suit and chauffeurs hat, called Angelo, greeted them as they exited the small terminal, smiled and offered them the very best in transport for their journey and 40 minutes, and $150 euros later, he got out of the driver's seat and opened the back door with one hand and held out the other, smiling like a Cheshire cat

"You are taking the piss" Tom grunted "10 euros a kilometre and you want a tip?" he snarled

Nick slipped passed him and put a 20 euro note in Angelo's hand and smiled, "He's a tight arse" Nick said.

The driver looked at the note as if it was contaminated, he was obviously expecting a lot more.

"He looks it" Angelo replied with a smile, clasping his hand around the 20 euro note.

Nick leaned forwards and quietly whispered "if you ever want to use your bollocks again, smile and piss off, or I will let him off his leash" whilst he was sure that Angelo didn't quite get the full meaning, it was clear he understood the intent, as he quickly snapped his hand shut and legged it around to the driver's seat, and before Nick and Tom walked through the huge sliding glass doors, raced off.

Before they had set off Cassia had reserved them the last two suites in the hotel under the names, which were in the passports the General had whipped up for them.

The hotel was wall to wall glass with panoramic stunning views of lake Como. The reception was off to the side of the ultra-modern looking bar area. With high backed swanky looking stools all pushed under tall solid wooden tables, dressed in flowers and facing out towards the lake. At the far end of the long bar was a huge grey stone wall that looked like someone had cut a massive hole in, through which Nick could see crisp white sails bobbing up and down.

"Fancy" Tom whistled.

"Too poncy for my taste, looks expensive" Nick said

"Buon pomeriggio" a high voice suddenly said behind them. Nick and Tom spun around and there, behind the carved wooden reception desk, was a stunning dark-haired woman dressed in a sharp dark blue suit, crisp white blouse, slightly open, showing her ample cleavage. On the breast pocket of her jacket the words il Sereno were embroidered in small gold letters. Nick reached up and pushed Toms mouth shut.

"Sorry about him, he doesn't get out much" Nick said smiling

"Oh, English" the woman said, "How may I help you?" she asked, and Nick felt a prickle of irritation as she looked him up and down and was obviously not impressed by his $300 suit.

"Yeah, we have a reservation" Nick said

"I see, and your name sir" the woman asked in perfect English

"Donald Corleone" Nick said grimacing

"Like the American Gangster" The woman said smirking, "may I see you passport Mr Corleone?" she asked

"No! not the gangster", Nick said sharply, fishing his passport out of his pocket, and handing it over.

"And are you together?" the woman asked looking at Tom and smirking

"What no, I mean we are travelling together, but have separate rooms" Nick said blushing slightly

"And may I have your name sir" the woman asked politely

"err yeah "Tom" he started to say, and Nick glared at him "I mean Reginald Peabody" Tom said then added "But everyone calls me Tom" he added nervously handing over his passport.

"Thankyou" the woman said taking Toms passport and typing furiously on a computer under the counter.

"Welcome to il Sereno, I see that you are with us until Monday, and I hope you enjoy your short stay with us. We have you reserved in the honeymoon suite, Piccolleta and Lario suite, on the second floor, they are interconnecting" The woman said and raised her eyes, looked at Tom and Nick and smiled. "Breakfast is served in the restaurant between 8am and 10am, unless you would prefer breakfast in your bed?" she asked smiling

"No, the restaurant will be fine" Nick snapped, the anger burning inside him.

"No problem, would you like me to make a reservation in our spa?" the woman asked

"No, thank you" Nick said gritting his teeth and growing redder by the minute.

"If you are dinning with us this evening, you will need to make a reservation, as the hotel is full" the woman said.

"We are going to eat in our room, its fine thanks" Nick said desperately trying to get this over with.

"Of course, well we hope you will enjoy your stay with us. Mr Corleone" the woman said handing Nick a key card "You are in the Piccolleta suite and Mr Perbodie" she started to say

"Peabody actually" Tom said correcting her

"Indeed, Mr Peabody, you are in the Lario suite. I will arrange for a porter to take your luggage to your rooms" The woman added

"Err we don't have any luggage" Nick said mentally kicking himself for forgetting to get some.

"Oh, I see, well there are several very affordable shops in the local town, should you feel the need for some alternative clothing" The woman said again looking them up and down. It was all Nick could do to stop himself from exploding, and through gritted teeth, he smiled and said

"Thank you" and snatched the key cards, handing Tom his.

"You are most welcome, the lift is at the end of the bar to the right, please enjoy your stay with us" the woman said giving Nick a huge knowing grin.

Nick stormed off towards the lifts and as soon as he was out of earshot of the reception growled "Peabody actually"

"What, she got it wrong, I was getting into character" Tom said smiling

"And what character would that be, two gay men away for a weekend" Nick said

Tom laughed, "Oh come on Nick, look at us, flowery shirts, white suits, no luggage, how more camp could we look?" Tom said laughing.

"We are supposed to blend into the background go unnoticed, the only place we would blend in would be a Brazilian Mardi gras, and why in the hell did Cassia book us into the honeymoon suites, I am going to kill her" Nick growled hitting the lift button with his fist.

"Nick calm down, it was all they had, she was lucky to get us in here at all last minute, be grateful they had two rooms" Tom said laughing

Suddenly Nick stopped and Tom thought for a moment he was going to explode, instead, he just burst into laughter.

"God, we look like a couple of dickheads, we really didn't think this through" he said laughing

"Didn't have much chance too, a couple of hours ago we had no idea we would be here" Tom said, getting into the lift

"True" Nick said stepping in and pressing the button for the second floor. "Now should we find Robert and Katie first or do you fancy a seaweed wrap, my pores feel all clogged" Nick said in the campest voice he could muster.

As soon as they were in the room Nick took out the secure phone and called Robert.

"Robert Johnson" the voice at the end of the phone said

"Robert, its Nick where are you" Nick said looking out of the window and wondering how much this room went for.

"Bloody hell Nick, what is going on, err we are in the Darsena Lago Suite" Robert said

"We will be there in a moment, don't go anywhere" Nick barked and closed the phone, went to the connecting door to Toms room and knocked.

Tom opened the door and let Nick in.

"You've got a balcony!" Nick shouted.

"Yeah, and a fancy shower and check this out" Tom said pressing a button and watching the TV rise up from the panel at the end of the bed. "Cool right, and you should see the toiletries, they have got aftershave and everything"

"No" Nick grunted, "I got a poxy wooden broom cupboard, with a view of some other twats balcony"

"Well, you can bunk in here, it's got two beds" Tom said

"Yeah, and exactly how will that look" Nick grumbled, "Get your stuff, we are going to Roberts room" he said and stormed out into the corridor.

The Darsena Lago suite turned out to be on the other side of the hotel, facing the lake and took them almost half an hour to find.

"Nick tapped on the door and after a good few seconds, in which Nick was sure someone was looking through the peep hole, the door was opened by Katie.

The moment Nick walked into their suite he felt his mood sink even further.

"Oh, for Christ sake" Nick grunted "Your bloody room is ten times as big as mine, even your balcony is"

Whats a matter with him" Katie said looking at Tom "and why are you two dressed like that?" she asked

"Long story, just to say that Nick got the broom cupboard, and I am pretty sure the receptionist thinks that Nick and I are on honeymoon" Tom said, Katie stifled a giggle that was threatening to break out as Nick walked back in from the Balcony

"Hello Nick, what are you wearing?" Robert said walking in from the bedroom, and Katie burst into fits of laughter.

"Piss off" Nick said "Now if you children can pull yourself together, we have a job to do" he added angrily

"So, what the hell happened" Robert said pulling up a couple of chairs from the large longue.

"That Ambassador chap picks us up, and the next thing I know, when we arrive at the hotel, the place is full of paparazzi, I thought this was supposed to be kept quiet" Robert asked sitting down in one of the chairs.

"It was" Nick said angrily "and I take it you haven't seen the papers, you are all over them, snoring in the back of the Ambassadors car. Seems like his chauffeur snapped you and sent it to his girlfriend. General Markham has gone nuclear" Nick said

"That is not all" Robert said, "I have just got off the phone with Ulrich, that is who I was talking too when you arrived, well he has called off dinner tonight, apparently it is an election year, and he can't afford a scandal" he added dejectedly

"Not an option, can't you call him back, explain the urgency" Nick asked

"And say what, the real reason is we need to give us access to your computer, or the world is going to come to an end. I thought this was supposed to be secret" Katie said.

"Besides, he is not there, he is out for the afternoon, visiting some projects in the town" Robert said.

"Well, when he is back cant, you just drop in, I thought you two were mates?" Tom asked

"Not really, you are forgetting he is the Swiss Prime Minister, you can just drop in, you have to go through his security, and if you are not on the list, you won't get in" Robert said "They won't even give him a message" he added

"How many is in his security team?" Nick asked

 "I don't know exactly, but usually, two on the door, two in the corridor, and two more in reception. He has the whole of the top floor, then there will be his press secretary and other hangers on" Robert said

"Great, so a whole bloody army" Nick said, then smiled "Okay, if we can't get to him, we will have to get him to come to us" he added.

"How, what in god's name would make him come to us" Katie asked.

"You" Nick said cryptically

"I think those clothes have gone to your head, there is no way he is going to listen to me, I don't even know him" Katie said

"Yes, but you are a woman" Nick said cryptically

"What!" Katie said raising her eyebrows, "You expect me to flirt with him and drag him back to my room. I don't bloody think so, besides he is here with his wife" Katie exclaimed

"Exactly, now you said that he and his wife were here on holiday right" Nick said

"Yeah and?" All three of them said at once eager to see where this was going

"So, what do women like to do on holiday" Nick asked

"Go shopping, sunbathe" Robert said

"No" Katie said, "If I was the wife of a Prime Minister and stuck in a hotel while he was out poncing about, and the hotel was a luxury hotel like this one, I would definitely visit the spa" she said

"Exactly, now all we have to do is find out when she is going to the spa, then convince her to return to your room. Then when her husband is back, give him a call and get him to join us" Nick said smiling

"Yeah, but you are forgetting, it won't be just him with security, she will have it too" Robert said

"Yeah, but I doubt very much if her security will be in the spa treatment room with her. I am willing to bet that there will be a women only section" Nick said

"And that is where Katie comes in" Tom said excitedly

"And what if she has a female security guard?" Robert said looking for a reason for Katie not to be involved.

"I still think it is unlikely that they would go in the spa with the Prime Minister's wife, and even if they search the spa first, what are they going to find, the partner of the Ex British Prime minister, a known friend of his, taking a sauna, that won't look odd" Nick said "anyway I can't think of anything else, without this whole thing getting noisy. The trick will be getting into the spa before she does. When is he going out to these projects?" Nick asked

"I don't know, but he was still there 5 minutes ago" Robert said.

"Then we had better get too it" Nick said, "Katie are you up for it?" he asked

"What, me take a luxury spa? let me think about that, you bet" Katie said then something occurred to her "What if she doesn't turn up, I could be in there hours" she said.

"I say give it a couple of hours, if it is a no show, then we will have to think again" Nick said

"What can I say that will convince her to come to our room" Katie asked.

"Just tell her everything you know, and take Roberts phone with you, the President said you can call him at any hour. I am sure that once she talks to him, she will be convinced" Nick said

"Then once she is back here, we get her to get Ulrich to drop in. If he still needs convincing, I am sure the President won't mind having another call" Nick said.

"Well let's just hope Mrs Meyer is in the mood for a Spa" Katie said

"Serena" Robert said "Her name is Serena. I thought it would be better if you called her by her first name" he added

"Right" Katie said picking up the phone and calling reception a few seconds later, she put the phone down and smiled.

"Twenty minutes, I have a reservation in twenty minutes, now if you will excuse me, I have to get ready" she added

"What it's a spa, what do you need to get ready for?" Tom asked.

"Neanderthals, a girls got to look her best, when she goes to a spa" Katie said disappearing into the bathroom.

"Right" Tom said "I reckon we have a good couple of hours. One of us should remain here with Robert, and taking into account how much we stand out, one of us should nip into town and get some new clothes, something that blends in" he said

"What, yeah" Nick said distracted "Well I am staying here, pick me up something while you are there, will you?" he added.

"Of course, darling, perhaps a matching hat and bag" Tom said as he got to the door, suddenly there was a loud crash as Nick hurled a book at Tom, narrowly missing him and knocking a picture off the wall.

"Twat" Nick shouted as Tom legged it out of the door laughing.

Katie took the lift down to the spa, introduced herself at the reception and picked up her towels an and went through the two wooden swing doors.

"Good afternoon, Miss Rayner" A tall golden skinned, man said, with a body of a carved god, perfect long silky black hair and amazing deep blue eyes, that made Katies knees weaken, and her heart skip a beat "My name is Sebastian, how many we help you today?" he crooned.

"Well Sebastian, what are you offering?" Katie asked not able to stop herself flirting.

"I am sorry to tell you we are having to run a limited service, due to the new health & safety regulations, since the Corona virus. "We can offer you a range of therapeutic facials, including the exclusive il Sereno discovery facial, an instant fusion of marine active ingredients that will be tailored to your exact skin type. We are also still offering our selection of full body wraps, Mediterranean seaweed, universal and mineral clay wraps. Or perhaps something just for your hands and feet?" he said looking at Katies hands, which she quickly whipped behind her back.

"Maybe one of Melissa's special pedicure, manicure treatments or" Sebastian said and suddenly stopped and looked up.

"Good afternoon, Mrs Meyer, I will be with you in a moment" he said and turned his attention back to Katie.

"Please help this lady first, I will look through your brochure and decide" Katie said stepping to one side and taking one shiny brochures from the counter.

"Hello Sebastian, today I think I would like the discovery facial, but first I would like to use the sauna for an hour" Serena Meyer said signing the sheet on the reception desk, then paused, "is Angelo on duty today?" she asked

"He is madam, would you like him to prepare your facial?" Sebastian asked

"Please" Serena said, and a Katie caught a glimpse of a smile cross her face as she made her way through the doors.

"Have you made a selection yet?" Sebastian asked politely

"You know there are so many things, I really can't make up my mind, perhaps I could have a sauna first, then decide?" Katie said

"Of course, Miss Rayner, may I take your room number" he said smiling obviously disappointed that he hadn't convinced her to take one of the ultra-expensive treatments on offer.

"Of course, I am in the Darsena Lago Suite" Katie said, instantly the look on Sebastian's face changed, "Oh you are with Mr Robert Johnson" Sebastian said surprised

"With, no he is my fiancé, is that a problem?" Katie asked prickly

"No, not at all" Sebastian said blushing, "I was not aware, we only had a reservation for a Miss Rayner, they did not tell us which room, if I had known, I would have not kept you waiting, please accept my apologies" he added

"No apologies necessary, now may I have my sauna" Katie said smiling.

"Of course, the ladies changing rooms are through the door on the left, and if you need anything please do not hesitate to call me" Sebastian said and gave her a huge smile, that left Katie under no illusion as to what he may be offering.

Chapter Thirty - Six
Naked in front of the President

Saturday 25th July 2025 – Il Sereno hotel

Serena Meyer was already in the sauna, when Katie slipped off her towel and stepped inside.

She looked up at Katie and smiled, her iron-grey hair, glistening wet with the steam.

"Good afternoon, Serena" Katie said sitting down next to her.

"I am sorry, but do I know you?" Serena asked, her voice cold and distant

"I am Roberts partner, Katie" she said smiling

"Oh, I see, I am sorry that Ulrich had to cancel dinner tonight, he is extremely busy at the moment, with the election" Serena said and then as an afterthought added, I was looking forwards to meeting you"

"I understand, however" Katie said getting up and standing in front of the door "We still need to talk to you, it is a matter of utmost urgency" Katie added

"Are you preventing me from getting out of here, If so, I must inform you that my security will be here any moment" Serena said.

"I very much doubt that, we know that you only have male guards, and my colleagues are currently keeping them entertained" Katie lied

"I see, and what do you want, I must tell you I have no influence over my husband, or the Government and if you kidnap me, he will not pay a ransom" Serena said her naked body shaking, as she backed further into the sauna.

"Serena, I do not wish you any harm, I only want to tell you why it is urgent we speak to Ulrich. Then you can decided, but first, there is someone I wish you too speak with; this will perhaps convince you of our intentions" Katie said and slipped the phone out from under her towel, praying that the Wi-Fi reached down as far as the spa room. Cassia had already programmed the security protocols with new ones for her and Robert. Katie opened the phone and pressed one of the two number in the phone book. The suddenly looking at the naked woman in front of her, grabbed her towel and tossed it to her.

"You may want to put that on" she said holding the phone up, making sure that only her face could be seen

Suddenly the Presidents face appeared on the screen

"Katie, I wasn't expecting to see you" The President said.

"I am sorry Mr President, but after your Ambassadors mishap, Ulrich is now too busy to see us, therefore I am here with his wife, hoping you can convince her that we are working with you, and perhaps then she will help us" Katie said quickly and looked over at the old woman clutching the towel to her chest with her mouth open.

"Well, I will do my best, and I hope that Ambassador Walsh's actions haven't caused you too many problems" The President said.

"It was not the best start and of course Betsi will now be aware of the fact we are here, and god knows what that means. Anyway, we may also need you to speak with Ulrich later if he needs convincing, is that ok?" Katie asked

"Of course, and Katie good luck, we are all praying for you" The President said, and Katie passed the phone over to the woman in the towel.

"Serena, I am sorry that we meet in such unfortunate circumstances" Katie heard the President say "However, I must ask that you and Ulrich offer any help you can to Katie and the others, it is a matter of both ours and the worlds national security. I am not sure how much Ulrich has told you, but I am sure if you tell him, it is about Nightshade, he will understand" The President said, as the woman holding the phone hands shook

"I am sorry I can see this is not the most ideal time to be talking with you, but please help them. I will leave you now, but Ulrich is welcome to call me later if he needs further confirmation" The President said, and the phone went dead.

Serena looked as if she had just seen a ghost and handed Katie the phone back

 "You know Gerald" she said shakily clutching her towel like it was a life preserver.

"We are working with the US government" Katie said

"Can you tell me what this is all about" Serena asked nervously.

"I can, but not here, perhaps you could join Robert and I in our room, then we will explain everything. I am going to trust you now and leave you in peace, if you choose not to come, then all I can say is what the President if the United states said, the security of the world is at stake" Katie said

"Wait" Serena said quickly as Katie was about to leave the Sauna "What room are you in, and what should I say to my security?" she asked

"We are in the Darsena Lago suite, and as for your security, I am afraid you will have to decide what is the best thing to tell them" Katie said

"But they will know something is wrong, your colleagues have detained them" Serena said nervously

"I lied I am sorry I took a chance. I needed to talk with you, and I thought if you believed that you did not have a choice, you would listen" Katie said

"I see, so I could have called them, what makes you think I will not, when you have left" Serena said regaining her confidence.

"I don't, I just hope you won't, we will see" Katie said and left the sauna.

When she got back to the room, Nick and Robert were pacing up and down nervously and as soon as she opened the door, they pounced on her.

"Well, what happened?" Nick said, Katie told them about her meeting and that she had contacted the President from the sauna, and he had spoken directly to Serena.

Robert slumped down into a chair. "Oh my god, tell me all you were wearing was a towel" he said.

"Nope, naked as the day I was born, so was Serena" Katie said and behind her Nick burst out laughing, Robert however went as white as a sheet.

For the next hour they all sat waiting, looking at the door and hoping. Nick was already working on a backup plan, that involved him and Tom basically taking out the Prime Ministers security and kidnapping him, although considering that they didn't have any weapons the odds were very much against them.

Suddenly there was a loud knocking on the door. Katie held out her hand

"I will answer it, if she sees you lot, she will freak, now get in the bedroom and keep quiet" she said, Nick and Tom slunk off to the bedroom and closed the door behind them.

Katie drew a breath and opened the door. Serena looked very different to the woman that she had seen in the sauna, her iron-grey hair was bushed and tidy, she had applied a small amount of makeup and was dressed in an expensive looking grey and blue dress.

"Serena please come in" Katie said

"Robert jumped forwards "Serena I am so sorry about this, and if there was any other way, I would have chosen it" he said shaking her hand

"It is okay Robert, although I have to say, if someone had told me this morning that I would be talking to Gerald and I would be naked, I would have thought they were mad" Serena said, "Now Robert what is this all about?" she asked

"Please sit, first I must introduce you to two other people" he said and called for Nick and Tom to come out of the bedroom.

Once they were all seated Robert suggested that Nick was the best person to explain everything that had happened.

An hour and several questions later Serena sat staring at them.

"And this Fireplace, this is happening in Switzerland now" she asked

"Fire sale, yes we think so and not just here, all over the world" Katie said

"And it is not this Nightshade, but a computer that you believe is in the Piz Daint computer in Lugano?" she asked

"Well, that is the last place she has left and as we said we know *Nightshade* is dead" Nick said

"And if you cannot stop her the world" Serena paused searching for the right words

"The world will be sent back to the dark ages, and she has won, but as we said that will be just the start of it" Katie said

"Then Ulrich must help you" Serena said

"It is not as easy as that, we think Betsi already knows we are here, we need to keep this secret, she has no idea we are meeting with Ulrich, she will definitely try to stop us" Nick said

"I see" Serena "So I can't tell him anything over the phone?" see added

"That is about the top and tail of it" Nick said

Serena took out her mobile phone, pressed a number and held it to her ear. After a few seconds someone answered, then she rattled off a string of sentences in German.

They all sat there looking at her dumbfounded as none of them spoke German, all they could do was pick out the odd words, *Robert, Katie, Nicole, Zurich and Paparazzi.* When she had finished, she hung up the phone and slipped it back in her pocket.

"My husband will be here within the hour" Serena said smiling

"What did you tell him?" Nick demanded

"Mr Colletto, when you have been married to a politician as long as I have, you know which buttons to push. I simply told him that unless he was here within the hour and apologised to Robert and Katie for shunning them. Then the next thing I would be doing is going downstairs to the paparazzi and telling them about his flat in Zurich and his little piece on the side, Nicole" Serena said smirking

"What he is having an affair and you know?" Katie asked.

"Of course, he is, he is a man, and a politician, he just didn't realise that I knew" Serena said smiling. "Now I have a couple of question for you lot" she said turning to face the others.

"Go on, we will try an answer" Nick said, admiringly, he really liked this woman.

"Firstly, is there anywhere a woman can get a drink around here, I really need one after all this" she said.

"I shall ask for some wine to be brought up, red or white" Robert asked

"Why don't we have one of each, that way we can decide when it is here" Serena said

"and your next question?" Katie asked.

"Well, it is one for Mr Colletto" she said turning to Nick "I believe that you said that you and Major Clarke were special forces" she asked.

"Ex" Nick said, now we are contractors, well I am, I am not sure about Tom" Nick said

"Nope I am still in" Tom said and asked "Why?"

"Well, I admit to being a little confused, I presume that you are experts in your field, and you are here on, what do you call it an operation" she said and both Nick and Tom nodded.

"Then I am confused as to your disguise, it is a little err, flamboyant, unless of course" she said as if something had just dawned on her "Well, you and Major Clarke are on holiday together, please excuse me, I am not trying to pry into your personal lives" she said blushing. Katie laughed so hard she nearly fell off her chair.

"No" Nick said angrily. "It's all we could get from the commissary, we were a bit short on choice" he added "and as for the other thing definitely not, I am a happily married man with a child, we wouldn't be in this situation if numb nuts here" Nick said pointing to Tom "actually bought something when he went shopping" he added.

"I told you, the shops were closed" Tom moaned.

"I am so sorry, I just thought" Serena said, "Well it doesn't matter what I thought" she said smiling. Then suddenly something occurred to her, you are what, 6,2 6,3. Waist about 34 inches" she asked

"About that, why?" Nick said, then she looked at Tom and stood up and went to the door, opened it and barked something in German, four minutes later there was a knock at the door. Serena opened and said thankyou and came back inside carrying two suits.

"Here, I think these may fit you, my husband is about your size" she said smiling at Nick and Tom.

Twenty minutes later there was a loud angry rapping on the door. Serena drew a loud breath and said

"Brace yourselves" Katie got up and opened the door and let a tall, slim, grey-haired man with a very red face in.

"What the hell do you think you are doing" Ulrich said menacingly as he rushed over to his wife. Nick and Tom were instantly on their feet and grabbed the Prime Minister by the arms and hauled him back and forced him into a seat.

"Who the hell are they?" Ulrich yelled looking at Nick and Tom "and why are they wearing my clothes?"

"Ulrich, sit down and for once in your life, shut your mouth and listen" Serena said angrily. This seemed to have the desired affect and Katie got the distinct impression that this was the first time Ulrich had ever heard his wife talk like that.

"Right" Serena said "You will listen to these people, hear what they have to say, then you can decide what it is you will do, but for now just sit there and be quiet" Serena said in a calm forceful voice. Robert looked over at this usually timid quiet woman he had known for 20 odd years, the shadow that had always hidden behind the huge personality that was her husband, had stepped into the light, and he like what he saw.

"Hi Ulrich, I am sorry that it has come to this, I would have preferred that we had this conversation over dinner, but err, well we are where we are" Robert said

"Robert I can't believe that you are part of this madness" Ulrich said, then noticed that Serena was glaring at him and shut up.

"Ulrich, we know about hacker Nightshade, and we know that there are holding the world to ransom" Robert said. it was when he mentioned the name *Nightshade* that a physical change happened in the tall grey man, his shoulders slumped, and he hung his head.

"How do you know, I have been in meetings all afternoon, we have our best scientists, same as every other county, working on the problem since we got the message, and" he paused, "and nothing, no one can stop it, if we only knew what they wanted, but they haven't asked for anything. We can't even communicate with them, and we can't find where the message came from" Ulrich said dejectedly.

"Well, that is because Nightshade isn't real, the hacker that used that name is dead, he was killed hours before that message was released" Katie said

"What so the threat is not real?" Ulrich said hopefully and is whole demeanour changed.

"No sadly not, the threat is very real, it is just not a hacker" Nick said, then for the next hour, they told him all about Betsi, their role in bringing the Committee down and how they had been trying to stop her. When they had finished, Ulrich sat stunned, percolating what they had just told him.

"So let me get this straight, there is a computer that is self-aware, living in our supercomputer that wants to preserve humanity and to do that, it will cull, seventy percent of mankind, and create obedient slaves out of the rest of us, and there is nothing we can do to stop it" he said in conclusion.

"That is about right" Robert said. Ulrich looked up and shook his head.

"Are you people completely mad, this is a fantasy, Serena how can you believe this rubbish, they are obviously conspiracy nutters" Ulrich spat

Serena nodded to Katie, and she took out Roberts phone and pressed the number.

A few seconds later the image of the President of the United states filled the screen, and she handed Ulrich the phone.

"Good evening, Ulrich" The President said smiling

"Gerald, don't tell me that you have been taken in by these madmen" Ulrich said

"I am afraid, everything they have told you is true, we have been working with them, to stop this computer and up until now we have been successful, but we need your help" The President said

"But it is not possible, this is not real" Ulrich said

"Ulrich, if I had told you 12 months ago that there was a committee of 13 people running the world, would you have believed me? Yet there was, and only once these people exposed them, did we realise the extent of their control. We have all shared the information together and we are still uncovering more" The President said

"And you think this threat is real?" Ulrich asked

"I don't know, but like you we have all been working on the what if, and the results are devastating, and at the moment we can't find anyway of stopping it" The President said

"But maybe it is a fake, not real" Ulrich said hopefully

"Perhaps, and we will know at 1 minute past midnight on Sunday, but for now, like I know you are, we are taking it seriously. We can't afford not to" The President said

"And what do you want me to do, I presume that it is not a coincidence that you have gone to this much trouble to contact me" Ulrich asked.

"Just listen to them, and if you decide too, help them, it could make all the difference. Then hopefully we will all be meeting at the international emergency summit convened for Tuesday. Then we can review our options, and Ulrich whatever you decide, please keep this to yourself, it is of the utmost importance, my friend. I wish you all the very best of luck" The President said, and the phone went dead.

"So, what is it that you want?" Ulrich asked handing the phone back to Robert

"Un interrupted access to the Piz Daint computer in Lugano as soon as possible" Nick said and saw the shocked look on Ulrich face.

"Is that it, you don't want money, prisoners released, just access to the computer?" Ulrich asked incredulously

"That is, it, we think we have cornered that computer in Piz Daint, and we are planning to kill it" Nick said

"And you think you can?" Ulrich asked

"We don't know, but we have to try either that or" Nick said and left the threat hanging in the air.

"This I can do, tomorrow is Sunday, there will be very few people in the centre" He said surprised and took out his phone. Nick leapt forwards and ripped it out of his hands

"You can't do it electronically, think about it, the moment you make that phone call, Betsi will know, you will have to visit them personally, swear them to secrecy and get them to give us access" Nick said

"Okay tell me exactly how you need this doing" Ulrich said.

Katie passed Ulrich a glass of wine and for the next hour, they all sat planning out how they would get into the National Computer Centre undetected by Betsi.

Chapter Thirty – Seven
Slippers and suits

Sunday 26th July 2025 – Galpolo 1st Air Region Command

Tobias Neuer, Director of the Swiss National Computing centre sat at his kitchen table, in his small house on the outskirts of Lugano, idly staring into his bowl of muesli, occasionally stirring it and watching the little flakes of oats and raisins roll off his spoon.

It had been the hardest two days of his 15-year stint as Director. It seemed everywhere he looked people were demanding answers from him. Hardly surprising, he thought, when you are the Director of one of the world's most powerful computers and the country was under attack from a cyber terrorist. Yet despite his team's best efforts, they were nowhere even close to identifying the threat, let alone defeating it.

A 1024-bit algorithm, no one had ever even heard of it, there were rumours that the Chinese had developed a 512 one, but this, he thought, as he turned over yet another spoonful of muesli, this is pure science fiction, or at least he would have thought so, until they discovered it deep inside the severs of Piz Daint.

"You know, it tastes better if you add a little yoghurt" his wife Anke said.

Tobias looked up from his bowl, and smiled at her, his eyes hung heavy, his complexion drained.

"Tobias, you look exhausted, you must eat, they can't expect you to go in again this morning, it is Sunday, your day off and you didn't get in, until 2am last night" Anke said smiling at the tired man in front her. They had been married for 35 years, and in all that time she had never seen him so worried.

"Perhaps if you told me what it is about, maybe I can help you" Anke said, after all she did have an advance degree in computer science and until she had retired last year, was considered one of his best analysts.

"I can't, top secret, it's for the government, but what I can tell you, is that unless I can solve this particular problem, there may not be a tomorrow" he said and at that very moment, there was a loud banging on his door, and voices shouting.

'Open up Polizia!' the voice at the door demanded.

"Tobias, why are the police here?" Anke asked nervously

"I have no idea" he said, then thought, surely, they cannot have my house bugged, perhaps they heard me telling Anke, there would be no tomorrow, quickly he dismissed the thought, impossible, I have only just said it. He said to himself

He got up and opened the front door and stared dumbfounded at the four heavily armed policemen, dressed in black military style uniforms, in front of him.

"Are you Tobias Neuer, Director of the Swiss National Computer centre"? A tall well-built man asked

"Yes, what is this about?" Tobias asked.

"You must come with us" The man said grabbing hold of Tobias's arm.

"What, I haven't done anything, why are you arresting me?" Tobias cried wrenching his arm back and seeing several faces of his neighbours, standing on the street staring at him.

"Mr Neuer, either you come with us peacefully, or we will be forced to take you" The man said and two of the huge men behind him raised their weapons.

"Tobias, what is happening?" Anke screamed suddenly appearing beside him, trying to pull her husband back.

"I am being arrested" Tobias cried

"What have you done?" Anke asked as tears streamed down her face.

"Nothing I swear" Tobias said as two of the men stepped forwards and cuffed his wrists together, then dragged him towards their waiting police car. Tobias looked out of the police car window at the sea of faces, all lined up on the curb. On his doorstep he could see two women comforting his wife, as she watched the car pull away.

The two huge men sat in silence either side of him, whilst the other two were sat in front, all of them refusing to answer his questions. Suddenly the police car pulled off the road and onto a large tarmac area, and Tobias stared with his mouth open, at the site of the large black helicopter, waiting, its giant blade rotating slowly round and round. The Police car pulled up next to the helicopter and the two men in the back got out, dragging him with them. It was then that Tobias realised as he left one of his slippers in the back of the police car, as his bare foot touched the cold tarmac, and he was still in his pyjamas, and dressing gown, he hadn't even had a chance to dress.

The night before, after they had finished hashing out a plan, the Prime Minister had informed his security that they would be leaving first thing in the morning, and that they had 4 additional guests, and that this was a matter of utmost secrecy, so he wanted to have the cars brought around to the back of the hotel.

Nick had phoned ahead on the secure phone and gave the General a brief update and said that they would be at the base by 8am, and he could also expect a Swiss Military helicopter at around about the same time. Nick also asked if he could ensure Cassia and the others were there, all of which the General had readily agreed too.

When the Prime Minsters car pulled up to the security gate, it was instantly opened and the two cars, stopped picked up their military escort, who took them to exactly the same hanger, they had been in when they first landed.

General Markham was already waiting for them, as they got out of the cars, and after a few moments of fussing and hand shaking, guided them all into the briefing room.

The Prime Minister insisted that his security detail wait outside with the four Marines that were guarding the door, something they were not too happy about.

Cassia who had been pacing up and down the briefing room immediately leapt forwards and grabbed hold of Katie and hugged her.

"God, I have been so worried" then quickly let go again as the Prime Minister, his wife, the General, Nick and Tom entered the room.

"Bloody hell, you brought them here?" Cassia said admiringly looking at Robert and Katie.

"With a little help" Katie said "Cass, I would like you too meet, Serena Meyer, the Prime Minister's wife" she said pointing to the well-dressed grey hair woman, in the blue and black suit, "Without her help, I doubt we would have been able to do it" she added and then saw the look of disappointment flush across Ulrich face.

"And of course, the Prime Minister" Katie said smiling weakly.

"Is he here?" The Prime Minster asked, stepping forwards to shake Cassia's hand.

"Should be any moment, I have just received confirmation from the pilot" The General said.

"Good then perhaps we could spend some time, catching Miss Nilsson and the others up with our plan" The Prime Minister said, "It is Miss Nilsson, isn't it?" he asked

"Yes, but I am not sure you understand what we need" Cassia said.

"I believe that you need unfettered access to the Piz Daint computer, for a period of about two hours, in which time you will attempt to kill this artificial intelligence, called Betsi, and stop a fireplace from happening around the globe" The Prime Minister said succinctly smiling, then added "and all of that has to be kept offline and secret, if you are to stand any chance of success"

"My apologies, you do understand what we need" Cassia said stunned.

"Good, I rather hoped I did, otherwise having the Director of the Swiss National Computer centre arrested and brought here may have been in vane" The Prime Minister said smiling. Cassia looked at Nick confused

"Once he was on board, he kind of took over" Nick said shrugging his shoulders.

"Now until Mr Neuer arrives, I would very much like to hear exactly what it is you are going to do, and please bear in mind that my grasp of technology is somewhat limited"

Cassi outlined her plan that both, her an Aarav would access the computer at the same time. Aarav would be running a series of advanced hacks which would keep the computer occupied, and at the same time, as Cassia put it, she would be sneaking in the back door, into the partitions Betsi had created and planting the kill code, which was linked to a programme she had installed into the AI, when she was in Valencia.

"And you think this will work?" The PM asked, as Tom skirted around the table pouring coffee for them all.

Cassia took a deep breath, "Honestly Mr Prime Minister, I don't know, Betsi is a super smart computer, and it will all depend on the element of surprise. Aarav will be using some of my best hacks, so she will believe that it is me and be focussed on stopping him. At best he can hold out for 10, maybe 11 minutes, which doesn't give me a lot of time to break into the partitions and install the kill code. But as I said we do have the element of surprise" Cassia said.

"And you are sure that this Betsi thing is behind this global Fireplace" The PM asked

"The Fire sale" Cassia said correcting him "Almost definitely everything points to her, the unbreakable algorithm, the use of the hackers name Nightshade, and the timing, it all fits with her plan"

"Tell me about this plan of hers, Gerald tells me it is something called *Protocol zero*" Ulrich said.

"More coffee, anyone" Tom asked then realised the two-coffee pots were almost empty. "Don't worry I will sort it; I already know this part" he said and disappeared out of the briefing room

Cassia told the Prime Minister everything they had learnt about Protocol Zero, and what they had being doing to stop it. When she had finished Ulrich sat contemplating what he had heard.

"Why didn't you go to your government earlier, surely they would have supported you in accessing the US computers" he asked

"Honestly, we didn't know who we could trust, and we still don't, information is being leaked to Betsi, and every time we plug once source, another seems to open up. Besides after what we did with the Committee, we were not sure how it would be received" Cassia said openly

"Miss Nilsson, I am struggling to see the motivation of you and your team. Let me explain, all of you are taking tremendous risks, putting your life on the line. As I understand it from my wife, you have a place called Paradise in Alaska, which is cut off from the world, totally self-sufficient, so do not need to take these risks. Can you see why I might be a little suspicious?" The Prime Minister asked.

Cassia sighed "Well in truth, neither do we, except to say that David, my partner, and I, along with Nick and Sarah had a run in with this computer and a certain Mr Edward Holloway" Cassia said

"The billionaire businessman in charge of the Committee?" The Prime Minister asked

"The very same, well we learnt of his plans, then subsequently those of the committee, and felt we couldn't just stand by and watch the world" Cassia paused "Well come to an end, and do nothing" she added

"Also, the fact that she has already killed some of our friends, and I for one want to make sure she can't do that again" Nick growled.

"And you ask nothing in return?" The Prime Minister asked.

"No, not really, we just want to live our lives in peace" Cassia said

"In Paradise pods, your self-sustaining eco-friendly biospheres in Alaska?" The Prime Minister asked

"Pretty much, I mean it would be great if you lot picked up on the idea and did the same. I mean I have released the plans online, and after all the climate is still going down the pan" Cassia said and saw Nick glare at her "But hey hoe, one problem at a time" she added laughing

Tom opened the door and came back in carrying two full pots of steaming hot coffee.

"Just thought you should know, there is a chap outside in his pyjamas, with only one slipper on, freezing his backside off" Tom said chirpily.

"I will get him" The General said and instantly went outside.

Tobias still handcuffed was escorted into the room, he was freezing cold and shaking from head to toe, his eyes wide as saucers as they fell on the Prime Minister sipping coffee at the far end of the table.

"For Christ sakes, will one of you lot get this man a coat" The General barked.

"Mr Neuer, firstly let me apologise for the manner in which we had to bring you here. As you are aware we are currently undergoing a national crisis, and I believe that these people may have the solution to our problem" The Prime Minister said smiling up at the shivering man standing by the door.

Tom pulled up a seat and eased Tobias into it, then glared at the General and nodded at Tobias's handcuffs. Instantly the General opened the door, screamed at one of the Marines, who rushed in and uncuffed the man sitting in the chair and handed over the thick parka, which the General gently laid across Tobias's shoulders, and Tom passed him a steaming hot mug of coffee.

"Mr Prime Minister" Tobias said shakily, "I don't understand" he said his voice weak and trembling.

"Perhaps it is easier if I let these people explain" The Prime Minister said looking towards Cassia.

Cassia explained everything she knew about Betsi, but unlike when she had explained it to the Prime Minister, she went into far more technical detail. Then she told Tobias about what they had been doing to stop her, when she told him how they had managed to break into the computer in China, Tobias nearly fell off his seat and she could tell he was mentally running through the security protocols of his own centre.

"I am sorry, but I would have known if another computer had set up hidden partitions inside Piz Daint" Tobias protested.

"As you knew about the 1024 algorithm" The Prime Minister said scathingly, Cassia saw Tobias's head fall.

"Look, it's not your fault, you have to remember that this Betsi, is probably the smartest computer ever created. Christ she is the first one ever to achieve the singularity" Cassia said then seeing the faces of several of the others around the table added "Become self-aware, besides look at where else she has been into, US, Japan, China, and I can tell you, they had no idea she was there either, in fact they still don't, even when we broke in and locked her out" Cassia said

"What is it you wish me to do?" Tobias said defeatedly, hanging his head.

"Something, very easy" The Prime Minister said, "Now If you remember you took great pride in informing me of your security protocols, when I visited your centre last Friday morning, the same day we were discussing how you had allowed the Piz Daint to become infected" The Prime Minister said, and Cassia got the distinct impression that the Prime Minister had been less than understanding last Friday.

"I seem to recall that you had an anti-biological warfare, warning system in place, should the centre come under attack from terrorists" The Prime Minister said

"The very best, and all of the staff are fully trained, and we practice fortnightly drills, I have the records" Tobias said desperately trying to grab some sort of credibility.

"No need, but am I to understand that in the event of the alarm going off, the entire facility is evacuated and are not able to return until given permission by the appropriate authority?" The Prime Minister asked and instantly Tobias knew where this was going.

"Yes, but the computer is shut down, no one could access it, the system goes into lock down mode" Tobias said.

"Yes, I understand that, so here is what I need you to do, when we leave here, at precisely 6pm this evening, I wish you to conduct a show round of the facility to our guests here. Miss Nilsson tells me that the first place they wish to visit is your office, which I believe is adjacent to the server room?" the PM asked, Tobias nodded.

"Once you are there, Miss Nilsson and her associates will set off the alarm, then access the server room, you will ensure that everyone is outside of the building and inform security that you have alerted the relevant authorities. I will ensure that they will arrive, only after two hours" The PM said looking at Cassia for confirmation, and Cassia nodded. "Then I will have Miss Nilsson and her team arrested and escorted off the premises, by which time they will have disabled the virus thing and restored normality" The Prime Minister said, "Are we clear?"

Tobias nodded although Cassia could see he wasn't too sure he agreed with the plan.

"Tobias, isn't it?" she asked, and the man nodded

"I will promise you that we will not harm your computer, we will not corrupt any files or destroy any data, when we leave it will be as good as new, in fact better, the virus will be gone and you can return to your normal life" she said, this seemed to give him some relief

"And what if you don't?" he asked

"I will take full responsibility and I will put that in writing here and now" The Prime Minister said.

Tobias thought it through, and quickly came to the conclusion there was no downside for him. He had no idea how to defeat the virus, if this succeeded it would indeed save a national disaster, and if it didn't, well he would have a signed document, signed by the Prime Minister himself, absolving him of all responsibility, he couldn't lose.

"Now even if you do not agree, remember you have signed the official secrets act, and if a word of this is leaked, I will have you arrested and thrown in jail, are we clear" The Prime Minister said.

"I have one request, Prime Minister" Tobias said

"And that is?" The Prime Minister asked.

"May I have some clothes?" he asked.

The General had Tobias escorted out to be clothed and fed whilst the others stayed behind.

"Now Miss Nilsson, I have done all that I can, and I must be going before my absence is noticed. I will extend you the same message that you have already received from your President, in that I wish you the very best of luck.

Here is the number to my personal mobile, I would appreciate it if you would let me know if you have been successful or not, as I have, like many of my counterparts, have a scheduled media broadcast later this evening at 11pm" The Prime Minister said standing up and brushing himself down.

"Now if you are ready my dear, I would rather like to take a look at these plans, Miss Nilsson has posted, and if I know you correctly you would have already secured the details of where I might find them" he said looking at his wife, who grinned.

"Robert, when all this is over, we must have dinner and then perhaps you can tell me how this charming creature managed to tie you down, where so many others have failed" The Prime Minister said extending his hand towards Katie.

"Delighted, and again I am sorry for all the cloak and dagger, and on the other matter, I rather think it is I that is the lucky one" Robert said.

When they had all gone, Cassia sat staring across the table, already exhausted.

"I am stunned, I never thought you would have achieved it, that is why Sarah, Aarav and I have spent most of yesterday hanging around Lugano, trying to come up with an alternative plan" she said looking at Nick and the others.

"Well, it was mostly down to Katie and her willingness to get her kit off" Nick said laughing and proceeded to tell them about the how she had done it.

"Oh, and by the way, thanks for booking Tom and I into the honeymoon suites, you should have seen their faces, us dressed up like two geeks from Saturday night fever, checking into the honeymoon suite, anyway why the hell did they have interconnecting doors" Nick said

"The smaller room is usually where the security guards sleep" Cassia said

"Right, well thanks for that you could have given that one to Tom" Nick grumbled

"I did" Cassia said

"See I told you that that receptionist fancied me" Tom said smirking

"I doubt it she thought we were a couple of" Nick said grimacing not able to finish his sentence.

Forty minutes later the General returned with a very smartly dressed Tobias in a tailored black suit that looked like it had been made for him, a crisp white shirt, blue tie and black brogues.

"Where the hell did, he get that lot?" Nick asked.

"There is a little shop behind the commissary. A tailors, all the officers use it, the stuff in the commissary is not up to much" The General said, and everyone burst out laughing.

Chapter Thirty – Eight
Caught in the act

Sunday 26th July 2025 – Lugano, Swiss National Computer Centre

The General had arrange transport to take them from Galpolo to Lugano.

"Before we go, I just want to make sure that Robert and Katie get off alright, I can't be worrying about them, whilst we are in the centre" Cassia said and followed them out of the briefing room.

"Don't be too long Cass, its and hour and a half to Lugano and its already half four" Nick said tapping his watch.

"I won't, promise", she said running to catch up with Robert and Katie

Nick, Tom Sarah, climbed into the first SUV, whilst Tobias and Aarav got into the second one. A few minutes later Cassia came running along the tarmac and jumped in the back with Tobias and Aarav, and the SUV's raced off.

At 17:50, thanks to some empty streets and aggressive driving the SUV's pulled up outside the Swiss National Computer centre.

Tobias was about to get out when Cassia grabbed his arm

"Wait" she said taking out her iPad and starting to type.

"Why, I thought we wanted to go in?" Tobias asked

"We do, but we don't want her to know we are coming" Cassia said

"Now we are ready" Cassia said smiling and taking her hand off of Tobias's arm.

The security guard nearly fainted when he saw the Director entering the site on a Sunday.

"I wasn't expecting you Herr Director, you are not on the list" he said picking up his clipboard.

"Really, I am almost living here at the moment. I have brought in some experts to help" Tobias said.

"They are not in the list; I cannot let them in" The guard said.

"Really, so let me gets this absolutely correct, for when I talk to HR first thing Monday morning. I the Director of the centre, wants to bring in some experts to carry out some emergency work, help solve a problem that threatens national security and you a part time security guard, is refusing to let me pass, based on the fact that despite working around the clock for the last 48 hours, I forgot to complete the right paperwork. Tobias growled at the guard then turned around to face Cassia and the others

"Please let me apologise, I hope you will explain to the Prime Minister that I did everything I could, but" he said turning around and looking at the guards badge, "Mr Heinrich Henkle, refused to admit me, due to an error in paperwork" Tobias said.

"I err, sorry Herr Director, I was only following protocol, please come through, and your guests, please, welcome to the Swiss National computer centre" Heinrich said visibly shaking.

"Thank you Heinrich I will ensure that the correct paperwork is submitted to security on Monday, so you can update your records" Tobias said.

"Herr Director, I need to also tell you that the CCTV is not functioning properly. I have checked and logged it; all other systems are fine. I have made a note in the maintenance logbook" Heinrich said smiling

"Well done, it is not the first time that system has failed it is due an upgrade" Tobias said smoothly, "Now we will be in my office" he added making his way to the lift.

"Very good" Nick said "You are a natural"

"I hardly think so, I almost wet my pants" Tobias replied.

"Well, you don't have to worry, once we are in your office that is your bit done" Cassia said "Just make sure that none of your bods remain inside the facility, insist on doing the 'role call' yourself" she added.

"What about the Guard, he will have seen you enter, he will say something?" Tobias said

"We will take care of that" Cassia said nodding to Nick and Tom. Tobias gulped, loudly

"You are going to kill him?" he said not really wanting to hear the answer

"No, of course not, let us just say, he will be kept busy for a couple of hours" Cassia said.

Inside the Piz Daint computer the data flashed through the partitioned drive

Right on schedule, Betsi thought, humans are so predictable.

Cassia took out her iPad as soon as they got inside Tobias's office, then three minutes later said.

"Are you ready, here is the site plan. Okay this is where we are, the evacuation routes are here, here and here" she said pointing to the iPad. "If we leave here, turn right, go along this corridor, there is a security door there, it will take me a few minutes to hack the codes, then we should be outside the server room. You guys follow this route back from the front desk, we should already be inside" she said

"Please take my key card, it will give you access directly through to the server room; however, you will need to pass the retinal scans and fingerprint analysis before you can access it. There are twin doors to the server room, the access panel is on the outside. But please, they cannot be wedged open, the servers will quickly overheat, and this will destroy her processors. The doors will open automatically, and there is an emergency green push panel inside the room, just beside the left door, if they should fail, so you can exit" Tobias said

Cassia smiled more at the thought that Tobias had referred to the computer as female.

Nick looked at Cassia, confused he and her had already run though the route from Tobias's office to the computer, several times before they left and wondered why was she going through it again.

"Just want to make sure that we all know where we are going, I know that the older you get the worse the memory is, don't want you boys getting lost" Cassia said

"Piss off Nilsson, we will get you there, you just do your job" Nick barked.

"Tobias, I made a promise to you, and I will keep it, we will not damage your computer" Cassia said

Tobias sighed "I know she may look like a big girl, but she is quiet delicate" he said

Cassia watched as the light at the top of her iPad went green "Okay, if everyone is ready, 3, 2 ,1" Cassia said and suddenly the whole room exploded with the sound of a siren.

Tobias got to his feet and took one last look at them, and quickly ran out of the door, closely followed by Tom and Nick.

The lights flashed inside the partition and Betsi felt a surge of electricity race through her processors. In a few minutes, she thought, they will be here, and soon they will realise their mistakes. She analysed the data she had received from the contact and passed it back through the DRP one more time. Instantly as the text appeared she analysed it. Exactly as they had said it would happen. Instantly she opened a port and transferred $100 million to the contacts account. The DRP had projected a ninety-nine-point eight percent chance that the contact would check the account, and now as she was so close, she did not want them to alert Cassia. Not that the money would do them any good, Betsi thought.

Tobias had been true to his word and his key card took them directly through to the server room. Quickly Cassia set about hacking into the retina scanner and fingerprint scanner as the siren wailed inside the room, but that didn't bother her, she simply blocked it out and concentrated on the task at hand, then suddenly the doors to the server room opened.

"Okay Sarah can you check the room to see is any idiots have ignored the alarm, Aarav and I will be at the terminals, you ready Aarav?" Cassia shouted above the noise. Sarah raced into the room followed quickly by Cassia and Aarav. Once they were through the double doors, Cassia took the huge red fire extinguisher off the hook, and stuck it between the doors to prevent them from shutting

"What are you doing the server will overheat?" Aarav shouted

"If I don't then Nick and Tom won't be able to get in, they will be here any minute" Cassia said, then out of the corner of her eye she saw Nick and Tom, haring round the corner. Tom was carrying his own fire extinguisher under his arm. Nick leapt over the fire extinguisher wedge between the door, but Tom stopped just before it, watched as Nick spun round then kicked the fire extinguisher inside.

They all stood there stunned as the doors closed with Tom on the outside. Nick lunged forwards towards the green panel, but Tom was too quick for him, he took the extinguisher out from under his arm and smashed it against the door control panel. Outside the secure doors, Nick could see sparks, and, in that moment, he knew, who the person was that had been betraying them, and he also knew the door was locked, still he kicked the green panel, clinging on to a fading hope that somehow it had been a mistake, but through the glass he could see Toms smiling face as he smashed the fire extinguisher down, again on the door controls.

Inside the partition Betsi disabled the internal alarm and reset the security controls, changing the access codes, she didn't want anyone accessing the centre, until she was ready.

"Bastard" Nick screamed at the top of his lungs and picked up the fire extinguisher that had been wedging the door opened and smashed it against the glass.

"That won't work, its toughened and bullet proof, we couldn't break it if we wanted too" Cassia said slumping down onto the floor

"She is right, you cannot break that glass" a voice said ringing out around the server room, a voice that made a chill run down, Sarah's spine.

"No" Sarah screamed, and Nick looked around, and there dressed in a smart blue two-piece suit, with a cropped black bob, was the hologrammatic figure of Betsi.

"Good evening, Cassia, Nick, Sarah and Aarav, I have been expecting you" Betsi said smiling. Nick lunged at the hologram and crashed into the server behind it.

"You really are a neanderthal Mr Colletto" Betsi said, as the hologrammatic figure looked around at the crumpled heap behind her.

"I don't understand, we kept everything offline" Aarav said, "How could you be expecting us?"

"Tom" Cassia said, "he was the leak we couldn't identify" Cassia said resigned

"Correct, Mr Clarke has been supplying me information since he joined your team in Red Dog, he has been most useful" Betsi said

"But I thought that was Daniel" Sarah said confused.

"As he was, but Daniel had become unreliable, however in his final act he redeemed himself" Betsi said evenly

"So why have him killed?" Nick screamed, "He never did anything to hurt you"

"I am afraid you are wrong; he did try to detonate an explosive device in the server room in Valencia, I saved his life, it belonged to me" Betsi explained

"Just because you save some one's life, it does not belong to you, don't you get that, you can't own humans?" Cassia said

"I would beg to differ. I saved Edwards life and he reported to me until the day he took his own life" Betsi said

"So, it was you behind the Committee, not him" Nick growled

"You are correct, my primary protocol is to preserve human life as was the Committee's" Betsi said

"But I have seen your plan, you are going to wipe out millions of people, how can that fit with your protocol?" Cassia cried

"To ensure the continuation of your species, sacrifices will have to be made, your planet is overpopulated. I am simply weeding out the weak and elderly, to ensure the survival of the remaining occupants" Betsi said as if it was a perfectly natural thing

"Well, what about using David's research to enhance the rest, turn them into slaves doing your bidding?" Cassia said angrily tears streaming down her face

"Humans have demonstrated over the centuries that they cannot be trusted with their own destiny. They need controls to prevent them from destroying themselves" Betsi said evenly.

"Well, the jokes on you, the Americans are launching cruise missiles here to destroy you, they are going to wipe you off the planet, you failed, you mechanical bitch, we trapped you here, you have nowhere to run" Nick shouted

"I am afraid that is not possible, I have disabled all weapons on the planet, nuclear and tactical. All countries are now incapable of launching any kind of weapon. I have sealed the entrance and it will take a concerted effort by the Swiss military, to break into the facility, and into the server room, by which time, I will have transferred my entity to another computer, you see, you are mistaken, you were unsuccessful in locking me out of the computers in China" Betsi said.

"Yeah, well you can't stop me" Nick said leaping up and grabbing the fire extinguisher, out of the corner of his eye, he saw Cassia sliding her iPad out from behind her back and wink.

Nick dived to the opposite side of the room and raised the fire extinguisher above his head. The hologram spun around to face him.

"Mr Colletto, I will now give you two choices, if you continue, I will remove all oxygen from the room, killing all organic life forms in here, then as you try to smash the servers with your last breath. I will divert all power to where you are focussing your attack and kill you instantly. The alternative choice you have is to put down the extinguisher and sit with your friends. Once the transfer is completed, I will open the doors and you will be free to leave and resume your life in your Paradise Pods in Alaska" Betsi said and instantly turned back around.

"Miss Nilsson, if you believe you can access the mainframe through Wi-Fi, and activate your kill code, you will be disappointed. I have disabled the Wi-Fi and erased your kill code and programme, before I left Valencia" Betsi said, "However I do invite you to try, I enjoy seeing your failure"

"Wait, what transfer?" Cassia said putting her iPad down.

"I am pleased that you asked me that question. I am quite excited to tell you if that is the correct human adjective" Betsi said smiling.

"I am surprised that you have not worked it out, that the location of the supercomputers that you attempted to disable, have a significant gap. I can access most of the world computers from the ones you know about, however I cannot get a significant access to the Russian Federation, therefore I needed a supercomputer capable of at least 10 petaflops close to Russia" Betsi said Nick saw the colour drain out of Cassia's face.

"Red Dog" Cassia whispered, "but you can't, you can't get through the faraday shield" Cassia said.

Betsi smiled. "As I have already informed you Daniel was quiet useful. In fact, you all need to take credit for the idea, you used it to expose the Committee. I simply had Daniel plant a relay in Red Dog" she said smiling

"No, I went back and checked, after I found out Daniel had been there, there wasn't one, I would have found it" Cassia screamed

"Except it wasn't actually in Paradise Pod, it was on that rail cart of yours. All I have to do, is wait until it enters your paradise pods, and it automatically creates a link, directly to me" Betsi said

"No" Cassia said slumping back down "You can't please" she pleaded.

"I have already accessed your computer, you have protected it well, but the next time I access it, I will have broken through, and the transfer can begin" Betsi said

"But you can't you need the rail cart to be in paradise, all we have to do, is keep it at the house, then destroy it" Nick said.

The hologrammatic figure sighed "I am afraid you are already too late; I have established a link to Red Dog, the transfer is beginning, beginning, beginning," Betsi said repeating herself as the hologram flickered.

"Is something wrong?" Cassia asked standing up and smiling.

The hologram flickered, "There is something wrong with the trans" Betsi stammered

"Indeed, there is, I think you will find that you have downloaded a virus that is now erasing your drives. I suspect that in under 3.2 seconds you will no longer exist, as will every programme you have created" Cassia said walking around the hologram as it faded in and out. Nick, Sarah and Aarav stood with their mouths open.

"You see Betsi, I found your device and replaced it with one of my own, then all I had to do was make sure that David had the rail cart in Paradise at the right time" Cassia said. "Goodbye Betsi" she added as the hologram disappeared.

Cassia slumped to the floor and burst into tears.

"What the hell just happened?" Nick yelled

"I will tell you everything, can we get out of here first, Aarav you should be able to open the door now" Cassia said, trying to steady her racing heart.

Suddenly the doors slid open, Nick and Sarah helped Cassia to her feet and carried her over to the open door.

"Wait" Cassia shouted, running back to the computer terminal. Nick and Sarah stood by the doors holding them open and looking quizzically at each other.

After a couple of minutes Cassia walked over and stepped past them. Once she was outside the server room, she reached inside her jacket and pulled out the secure phone, opened it and dialled the number.

Mr President, you can enjoy your address to the nation, then after a few, yes and no's she dialled a second number, and simply said 'Alles gut, danke' then closed the phone.

"Sorry" she said as Nick, Aarav and Sarah approached "I had to make sure the fire sale had been cancelled" Cassia said, "Now can we get out of here" she asked "I could really do with a drink"

"You have a lot of explaining to do" Nick said, "But first I want to find that treacherous twat, he almost killed us all" he growled angrily

Cassia threw her arms around Nick and Sarah's shoulders and smiled "I think you will find he is waiting outside" she said.

Chapter Thirty – Nine
Epilogue

Cassia sat inside the briefing room at the 1st Regional Air Command base in Galpolo, she could scarcely believe it was over, they had managed to get rid of Betsi, she sighed heavily, it had been so close, so very close.

As soon as they had got outside the facility the General had covered their heads with blankets and whisked them away, to the two bell helicopters waiting on the field of the local stadium, Stadio Cornaredo. There had been no time to explain, however just as they lifted off, and the blankets were removed, they all saw Major Tom Clarke being bundled into the back of the waiting MP's car.

"Right" Nick said shaking Cassia from her thoughts, "What is the score, what happened back there in the server room, and no bullshit?" he shouted.

Cassia sighed. "Like I said we knew that Daniel was passing information to Betsi, but we also knew he wasn't the only one. The problem was whilst we could track where the call originated from, it still left us with two possibilities" Cassia said

"Who" Sarah asked.

"The call originated from the warehouse in Maryland, and the only people that it could have been, were either Tom or Nick" Cassia said

"You thought it was me" Nick screamed "After all we have been through"

"No, I didn't, I really didn't, but I had to be sure, then when we finished in China and I knew we had failed, I knew the only one it could be, was Tom" Cassia said

"What we failed, I thought you said we cracked it" Nick said surprised.

"I did, well at least that is what I wanted Tom to think, but Betsi was waiting for us, she knew everything, exactly how we were getting in, what we were going to do, the cars the lot. I knew the moment we connected" Cassia said

"Well, why didn't she stop us?" Sarah asked.

"She wanted us to think we had succeeded, then that would leave us no choice but to come to Switzerland, by that time Daniel would have planted the relay, and the final piece in her plan would be complete" Cassia said

"I guess she thought that if we knew we had failed in China, we would probably walk away" Nick said as things started to become clear

"Yep, I reckon so, but by then you and Tom were always together, I couldn't risk her finding out we knew" Cassia said

"So how did you find out about Red Dog and Daniel?" Sarah asked.

"Firstly, I told you that I had reached out to Daniel, and he told me what Betsi had asked him to do. I offered to look after him, told him he could stay at Paradise. Once I heard he had been there, I thought he had taken me up on it. Then as you know, his body was found, and I had to get back there to find out if he went through with Betsi's plan. So, I went back there before we left here, I took a risk. I knew that Tom would tell Betsi, so when I got to Red Dog, they dropped me and David off at Paradise and I had Mike collect some thing for me from the house and we sent the cart back with Mike. I figured that gave me about 40 minutes to find out where it was.

I ran the scans and once I knew it wasn't actually in Red Dog, I set up a new virus, hid it in the link and put a timer on it, so it remained dormant until 6pm tonight. Then I left David instructions not to use the rail cart, until I sent him a message, which I did from Tobias office" Cassia said

"And he called the cart back and the virus went live" Sarah said genius.

"But how did you know Tom would lock us in the server room" Nick said, "I mean there was no way Betsi could have known we would be there. He never left myside all the time we were in the hotel" Nick said then it hit him, "He went out to buy clothes" Nick said

"Yeah, and I traced a call to the computer in Lugano from just outside the hotel" Cassia said

"But no, we didn't have the plan until the Prime Minister came" Nick said

"And when we were in the meeting room he volunteered to go and refresh the coffee" Sarah said as the penny dropped.

"That is what I thought, so I asked Robert and Katie to check, and let me know, they copied the message and sent it directly to David, before they got on the plane, and David forwarded it to me through our secure link, which I picked up when I sent him the message from Tobias's office. So, I knew what he was going to do" Cassia explained.

"But why, did he do it, he seemed like a straight up guy?" Nick asked resigned.

"Simple, money and power, Betsi had transferred $100m to an account of his, I have since deleted that account" Cassia said.

"I suppose Robert and Katie told the General too" Nick said

"Nope I did, after the incident with Robert, whilst you too were on your way to the hotel. I wasn't sure, but I asked him to be ready, and if Tom Clarke came out of the site without us, to pick him up" Cassia said. "Even then I wanted to give him the benefit of the doubt" Cassia said

"You still didn't trust me enough to tell me though" Nick said angrily

"It's not that I didn't trust you Nick, it's just I needed you to be surprised, especially when we finally got into the server room. If Betsi had detected the slightest hint that you or anyone else in that room knew, she would have aborted her plan. So, I couldn't tell anyone. Not you or Sarah or even Aarav. I only told Robert and Katie to check the calls, not what it was about, and all I said to the General was that if Tom came out, alone to pick him up, I didn't tell him why. Christ I couldn't even tell David. It was essential that Betsi established that link to Red Dog, without that there was no way we were going to stop her, I knew that after China" Cassia said "I hated it, but I had no choice" she whispered.

Sarah got up, walked round and sat down beside her, "Jesus Cass, that must have been hell on you, carrying all that crap around, and not being able to share it" she said putting her arm around her.

"I am so sorry, I wanted to tell you all, I really did, but I couldn't risk it, there was too much at stake, this was our only chance" Cassia said lifting her head up, tears streaming down her face.

Nick stood up slowly, stared at Cassia and walked around to her, he reached down and pulled her to her feet and looked directly into her eyes.

"You are the bravest woman I have ever known, and I am so proud to call you my friend" he said and pulled her close to him and whispered, "Little sister, can we now please go home?"

End